CHARACTERS

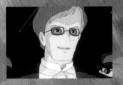

Muska

Assigned by the Special Agency to obtain the levitation stone. He plans on ruling Laputa.

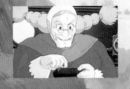

Dola

Captain of the pirate airship *Tiger Moth*. She helps Pazu and Sheeta.

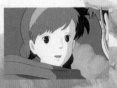

Sheeta

Although she is the rightful heir to the throne of Laputa, her levitation stone is now in the hands of Muska...

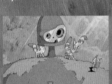

Robot Soldier

The giant robot guarding the deserted Laputa.

The Old Engineer

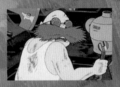

An old friend of Dola's, he's an experienced engineer on the airship *Tiger Moth*. He's stubborn.

The General

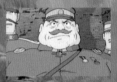

Commander assigned by the military to find the secret behind Laputa. Constantly at odds with Muska.

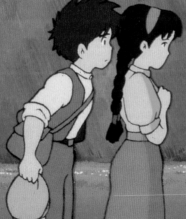

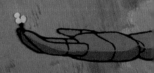

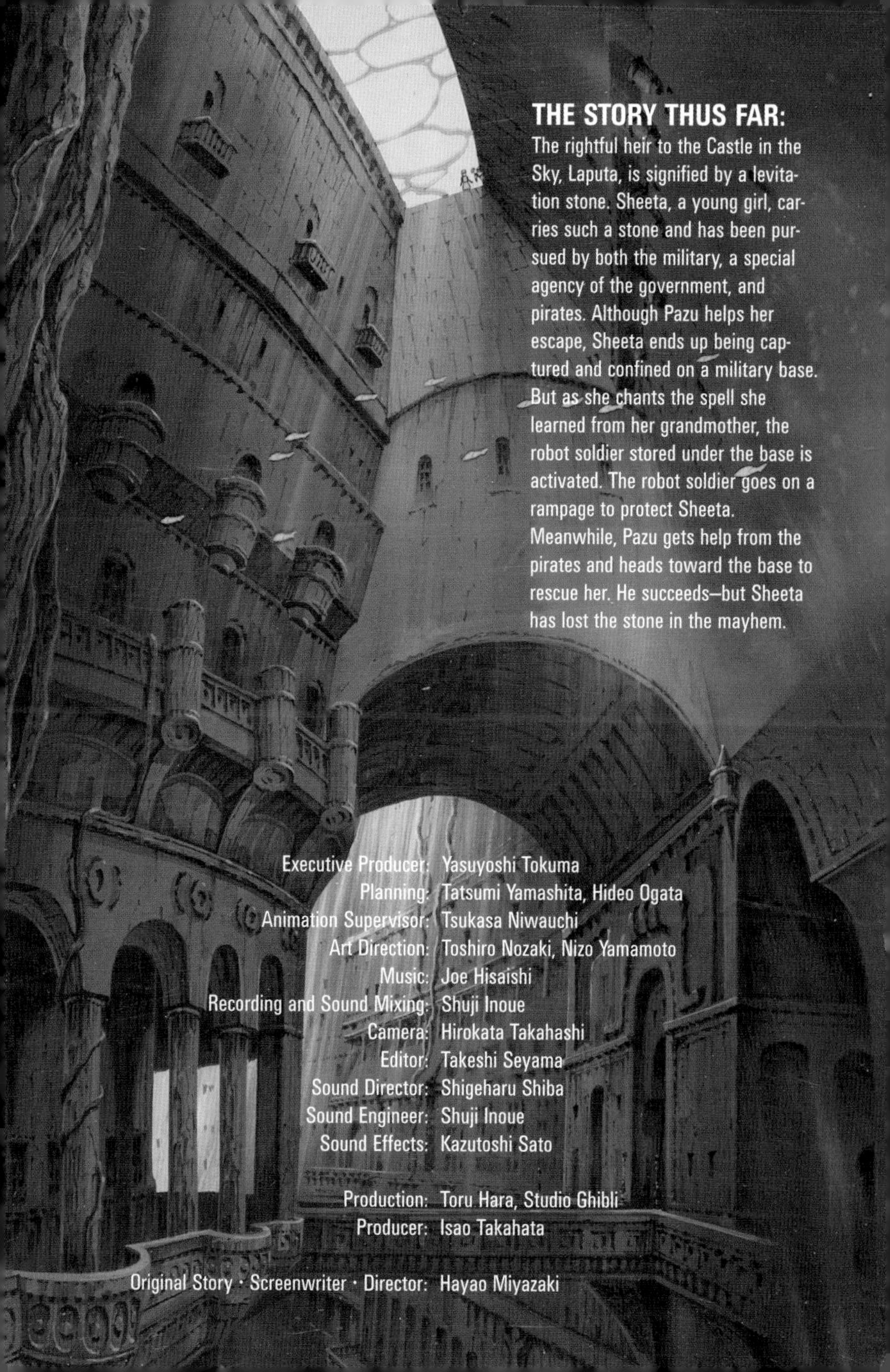

THE STORY THUS FAR:

The rightful heir to the Castle in the Sky, Laputa, is signified by a levitation stone. Sheeta, a young girl, carries such a stone and has been pursued by both the military, a special agency of the government, and pirates. Although Pazu helps her escape, Sheeta ends up being captured and confined on a military base. But as she chants the spell she learned from her grandmother, the robot soldier stored under the base is activated. The robot soldier goes on a rampage to protect Sheeta. Meanwhile, Pazu gets help from the pirates and heads toward the base to rescue her. He succeeds—but Sheeta has lost the stone in the mayhem.

Executive Producer: Yasuyoshi Tokuma
Planning: Tatsumi Yamashita, Hideo Ogata
Animation Supervisor: Tsukasa Niwauchi
Art Direction: Toshiro Nozaki, Nizo Yamamoto
Music: Joe Hisaishi
Recording and Sound Mixing: Shuji Inoue
Camera: Hirokata Takahashi
Editor: Takeshi Seyama
Sound Director: Shigeharu Shiba
Sound Engineer: Shuji Inoue
Sound Effects: Kazutoshi Sato

Production: Toru Hara, Studio Ghibli
Producer: Isao Takahata

Original Story · Screenwriter · Director: Hayao Miyazaki

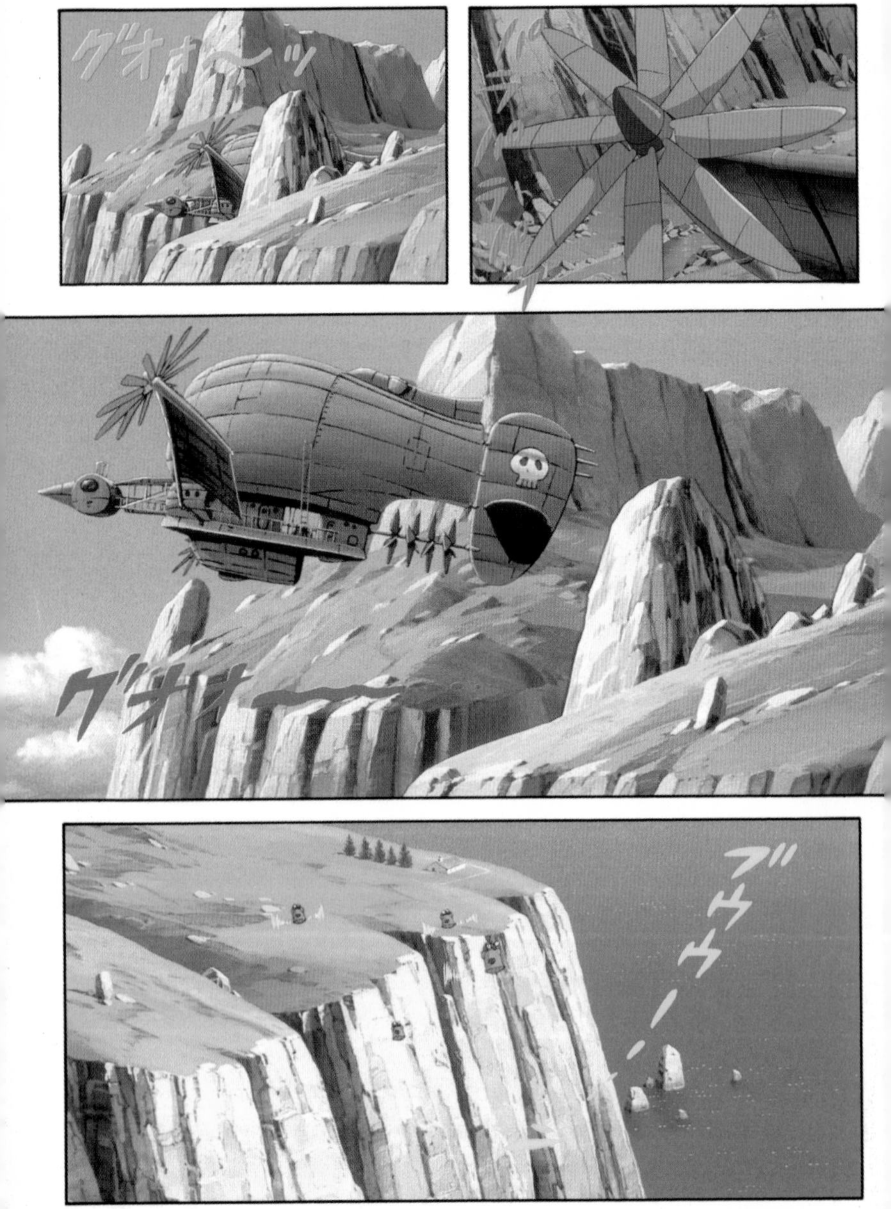
グオオ〜ッ
グオオーー
ブゥゥー

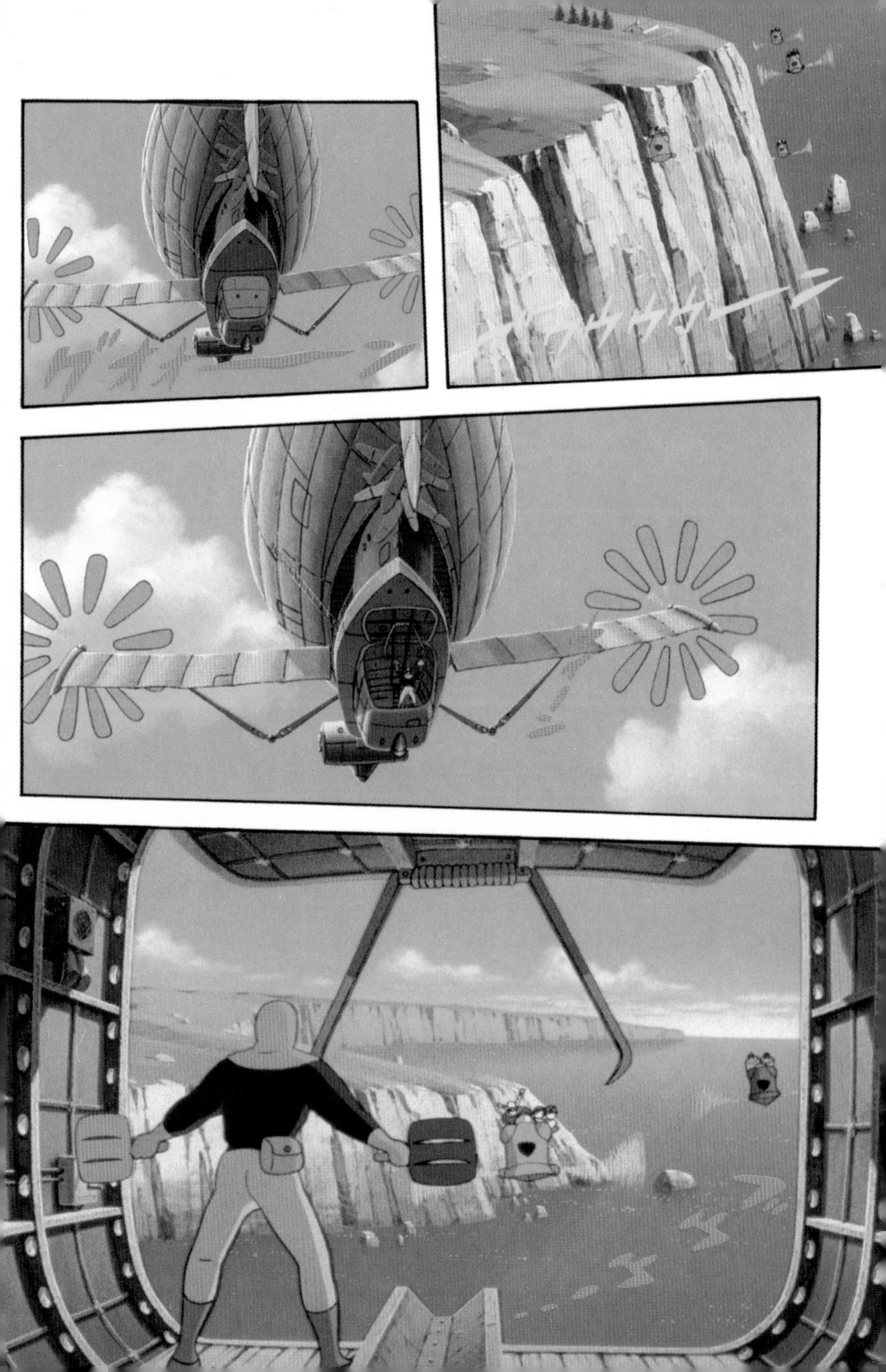

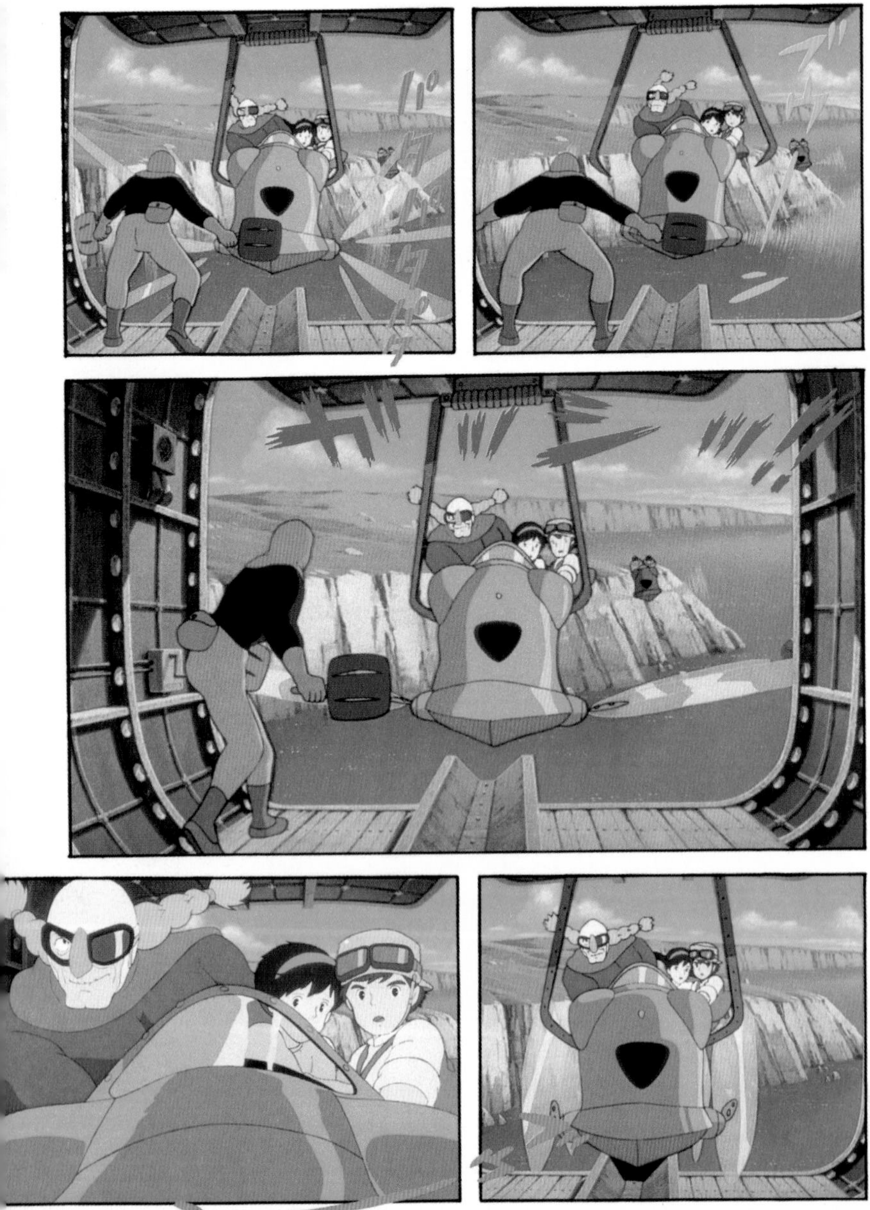

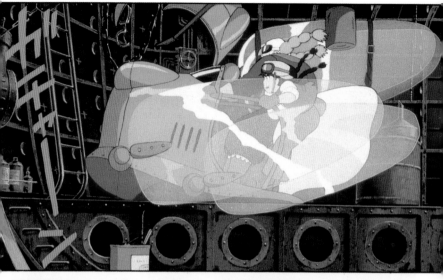

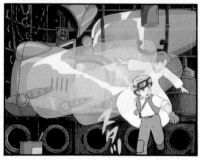

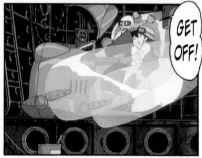

GET OFF!

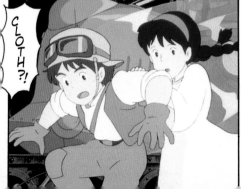

CLOTH?!

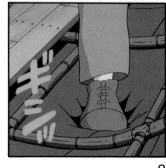

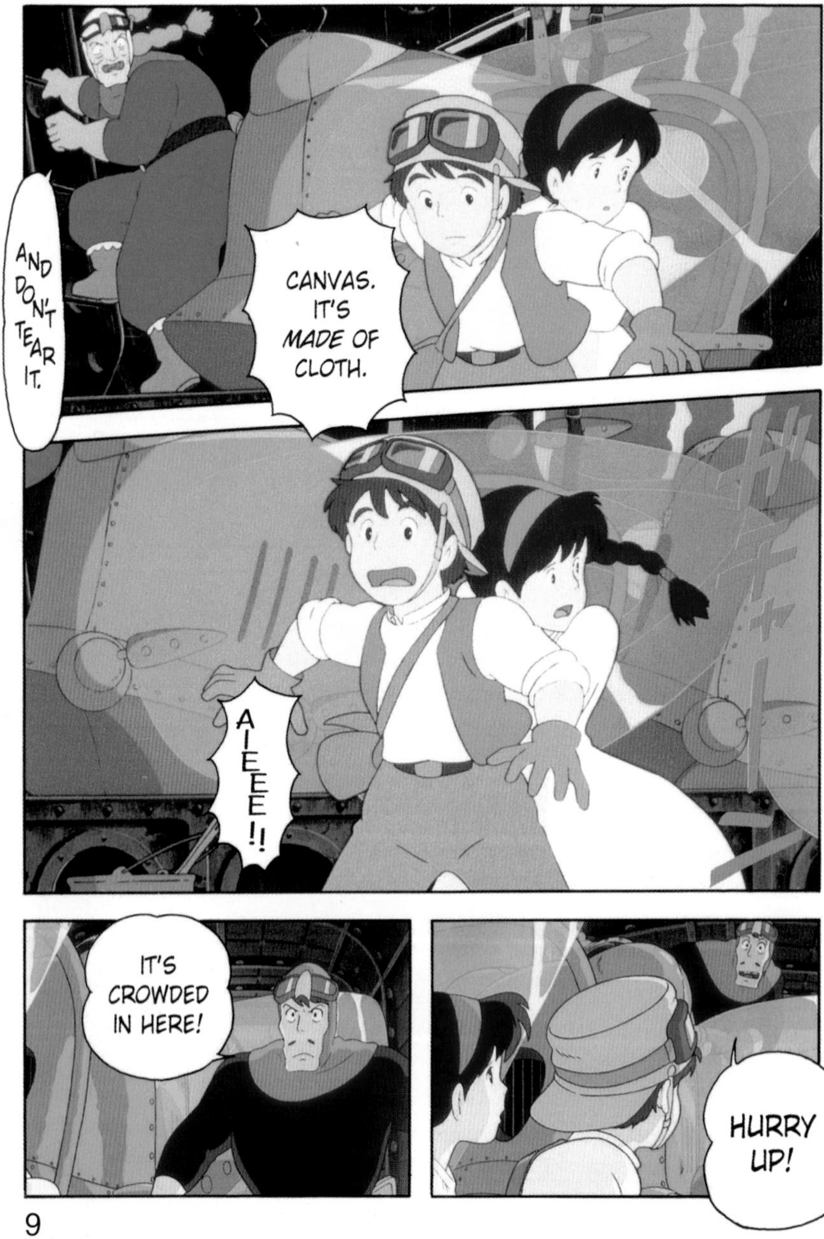
CANVAS. IT'S MADE OF CLOTH.
AND DON'T TEAR IT.
AIEEEE!!
HURRY UP!
IT'S CROWDED IN HERE!

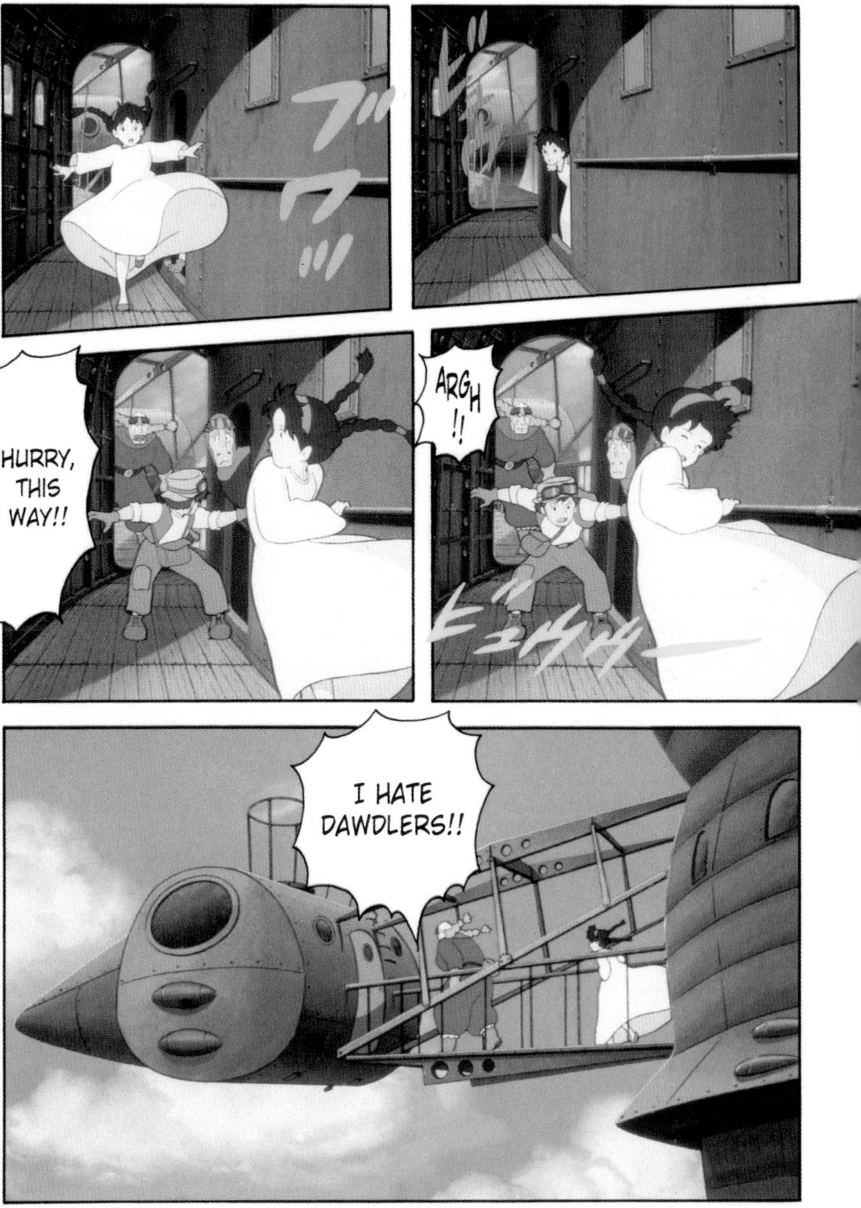
ARGH!!
HURRY, THIS WAY!!
I HATE DAWDLERS!!

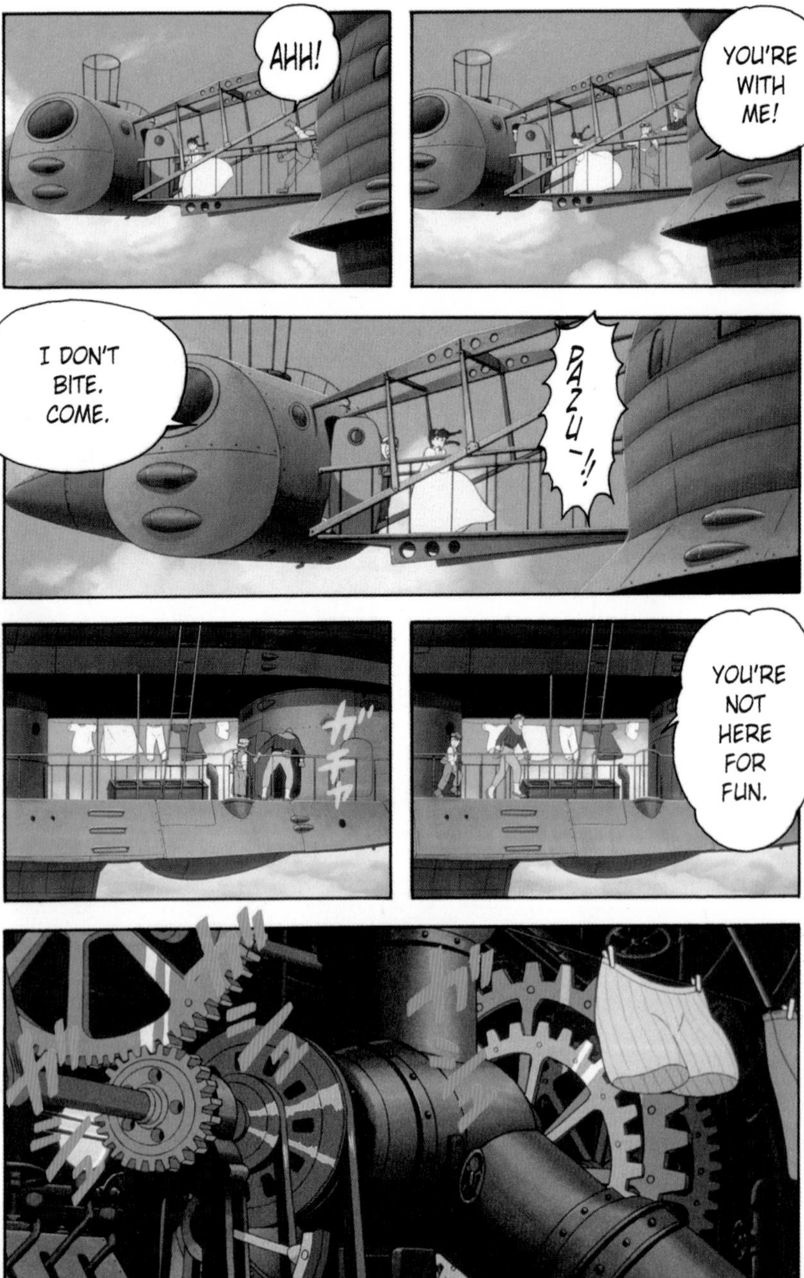
YOU'RE WITH ME!
AHH!
PAZU--!!
I DON'T BITE. COME.
YOU'RE NOT HERE FOR FUN.
ガチャ

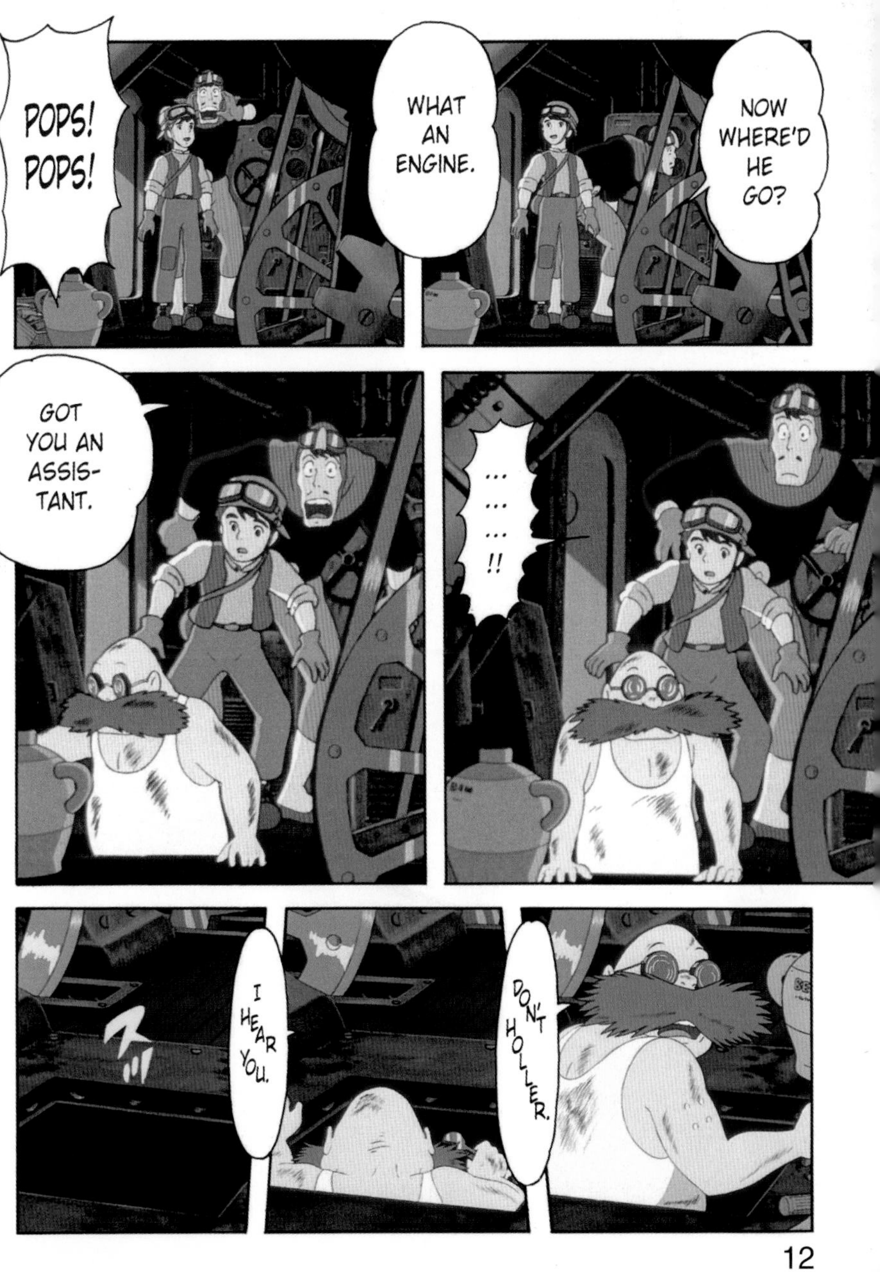
NOW WHERE'D HE GO?
WHAT AN ENGINE.
POPS! POPS!
... ... !!
GOT YOU AN ASSISTANT.
DON'T HOLLER.
I HEAR YOU.

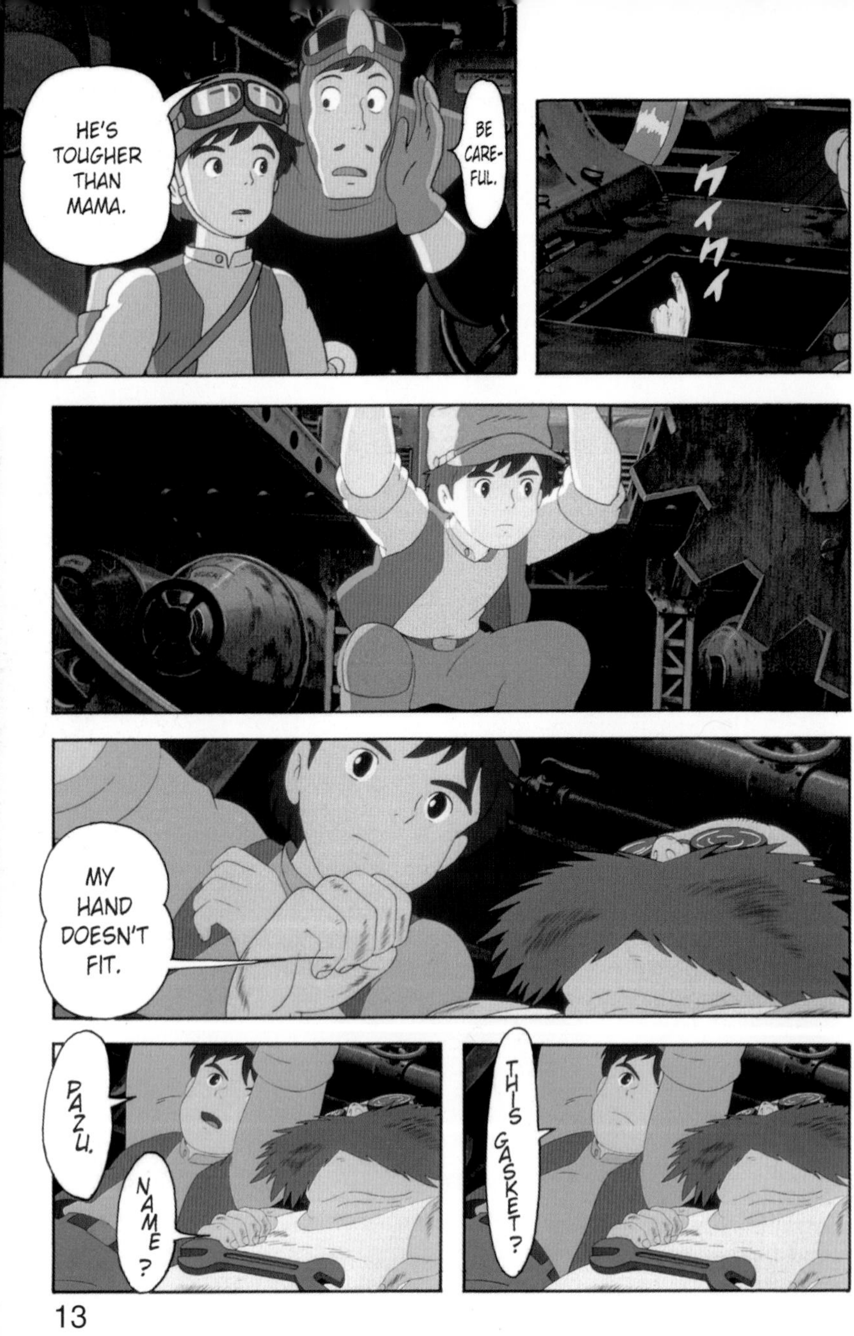
BE CARE-FUL.
HE'S TOUGHER THAN MAMA.
MY HAND DOESN'T FIT.
THIS GASKET?
PAZU.
NAME?

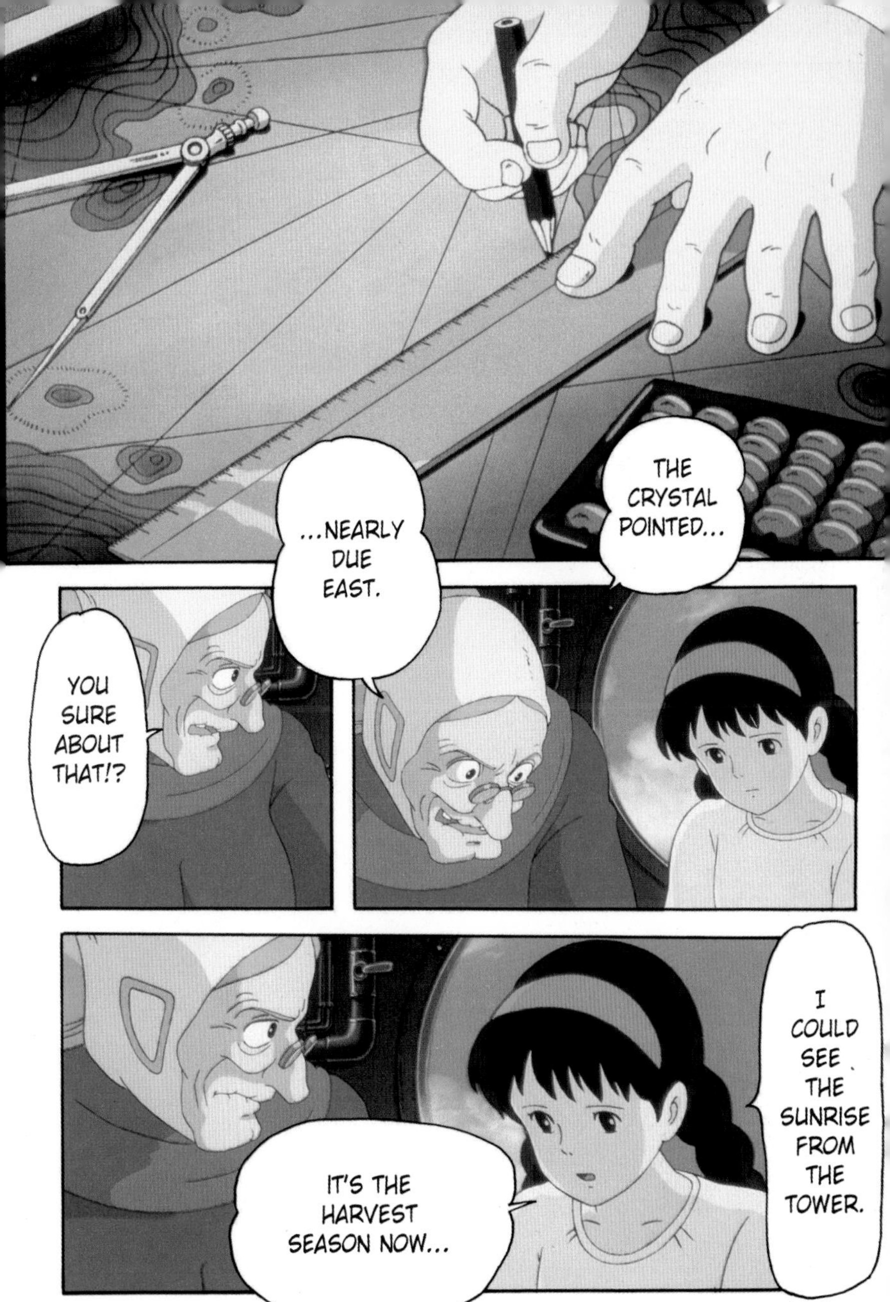
THE CRYSTAL POINTED...
...NEARLY DUE EAST.
YOU SURE ABOUT THAT!?
I COULD SEE THE SUNRISE FROM THE TOWER.
IT'S THE HARVEST SEASON NOW...

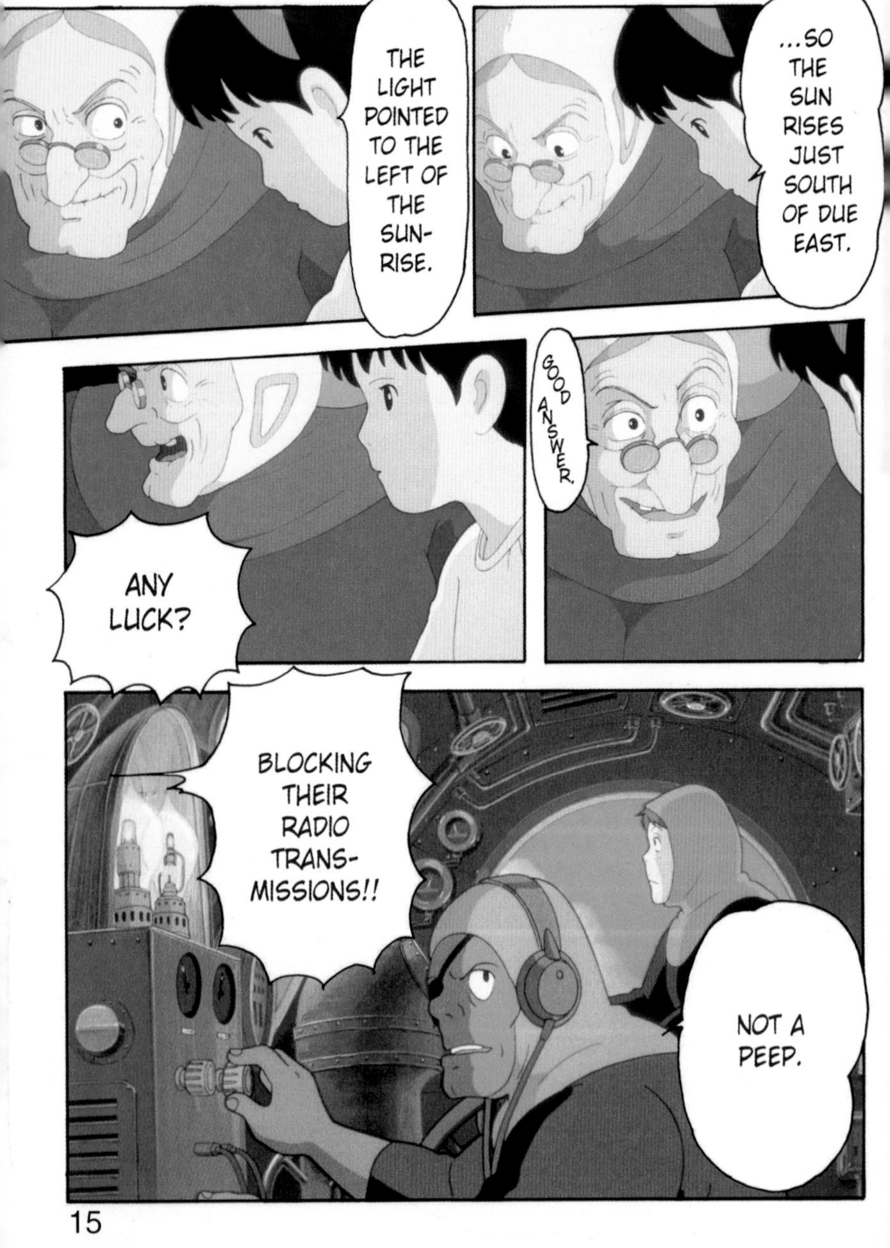
...SO THE SUN RISES JUST SOUTH OF DUE EAST.
THE LIGHT POINTED TO THE LEFT OF THE SUN-RISE.
GOOD ANSWER.
ANY LUCK?
BLOCKING THEIR RADIO TRANS-MISSIONS!!
NOT A PEEP.

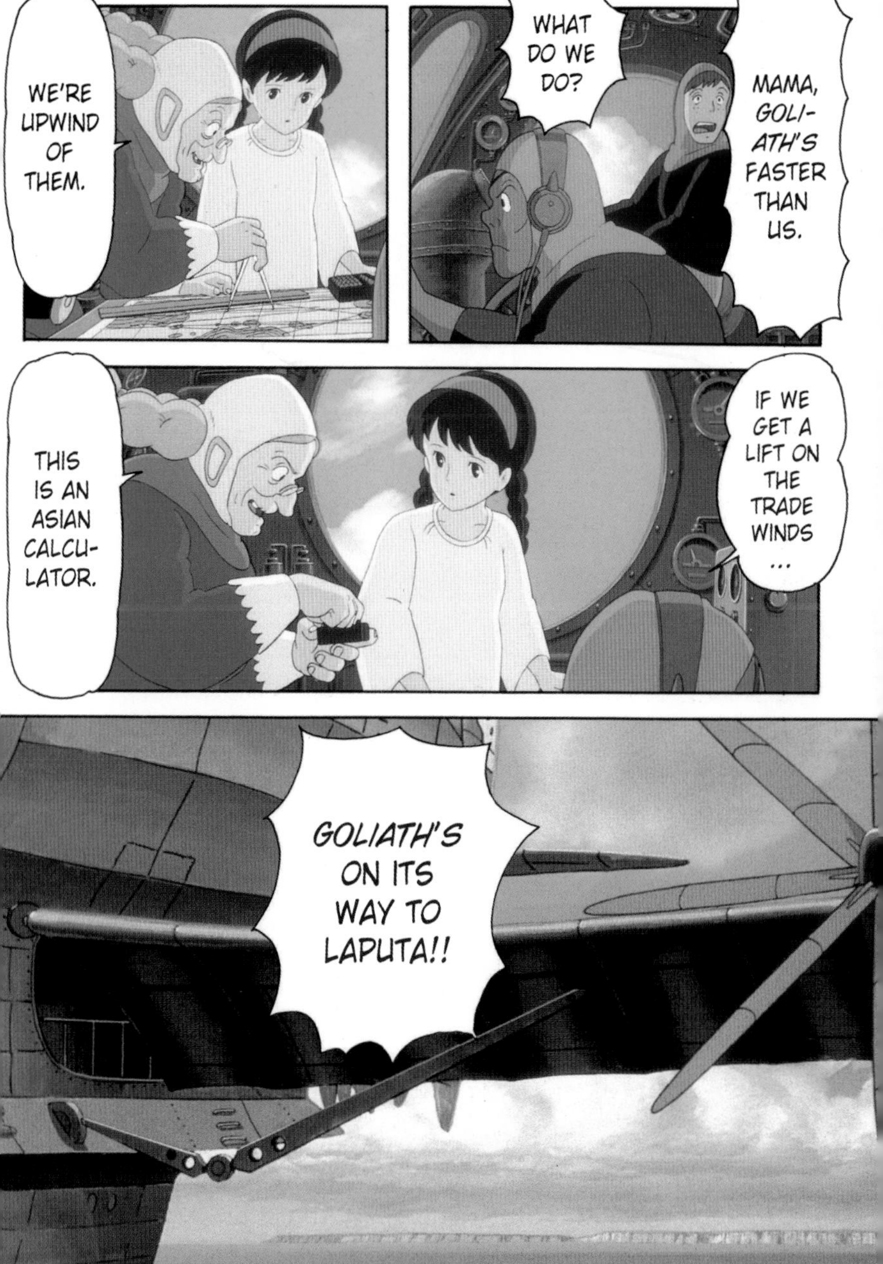
MAMA, GOLIATH'S FASTER THAN US.
WHAT DO WE DO?
WE'RE UPWIND OF THEM.
IF WE GET A LIFT ON THE TRADE WINDS ...
THIS IS AN ASIAN CALCULATOR.
GOLIATH'S ON ITS WAY TO LAPUTA!!

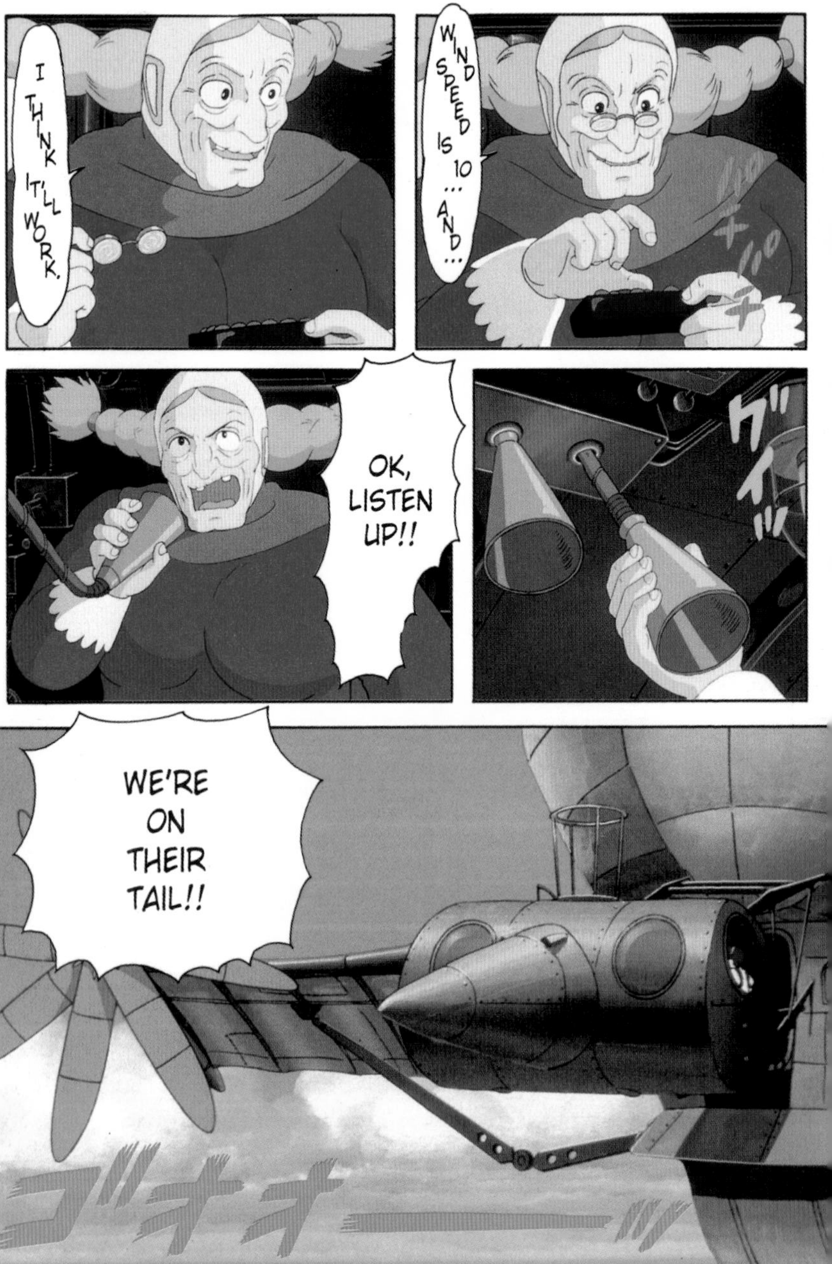
WIND SPEED IS 10... AND...
I THINK IT'LL WORK.
OK, LISTEN UP!!
WE'RE ON THEIR TAIL!!

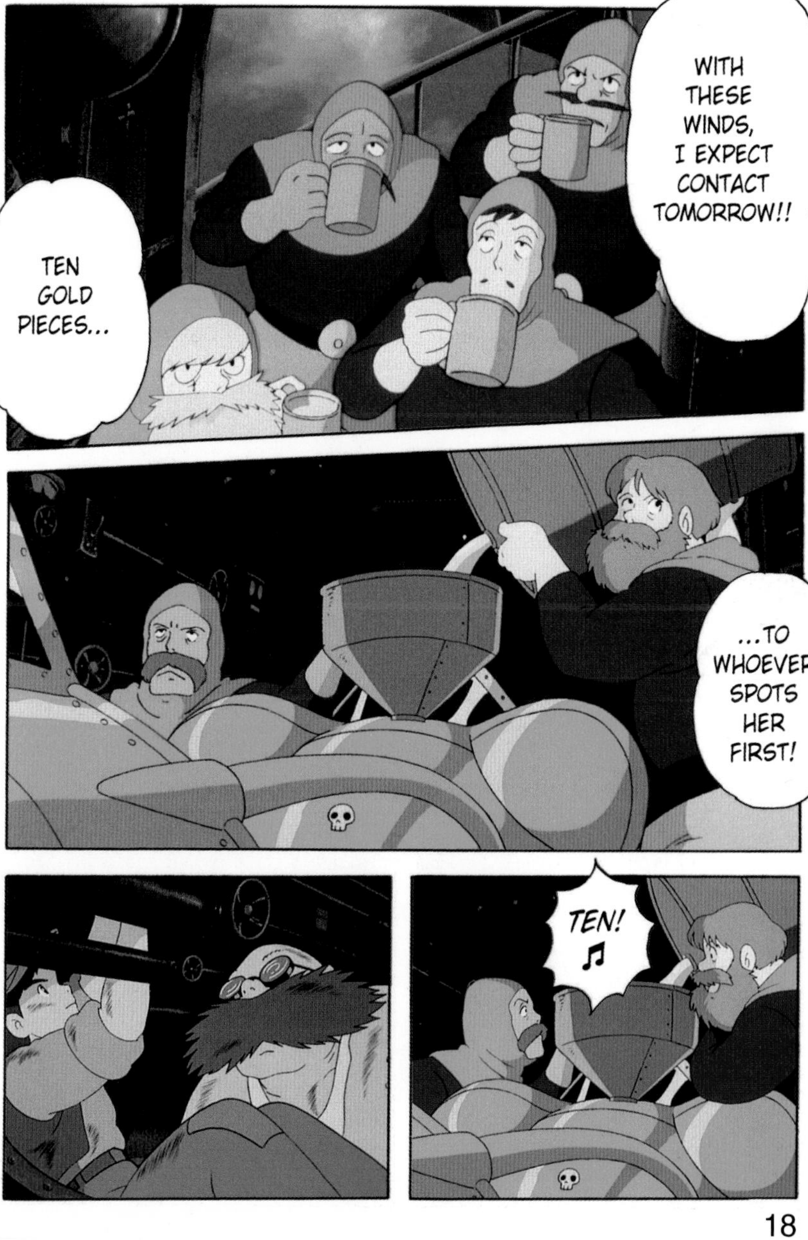
WITH THESE WINDS, I EXPECT CONTACT TOMORROW!!
TEN GOLD PIECES...
...TO WHOEVER SPOTS HER FIRST!
TEN! ♫

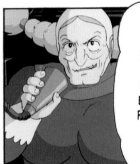

WHAT-EVER WE FIND...
...I'M SURE LAPUTA HAS RICHES ENOUGH FOR ANY PIRATE GANG!
EARN YOUR KEEP, BOYS!

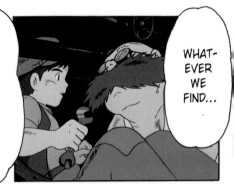

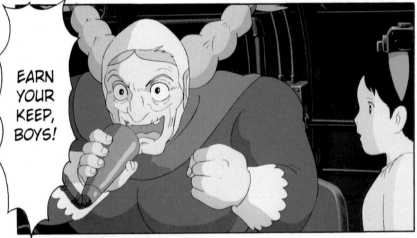

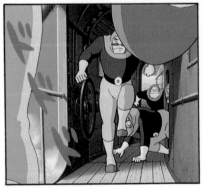

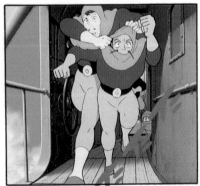

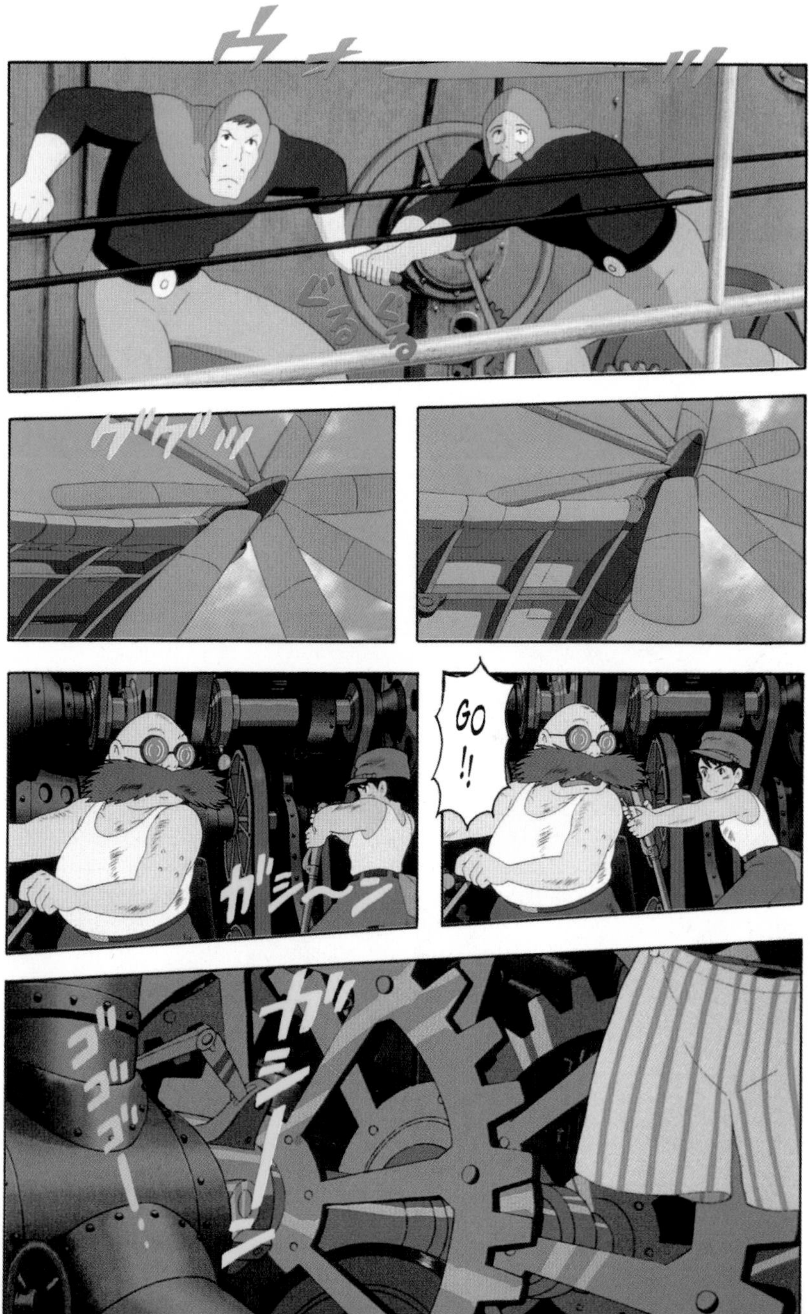
ぐるぐる
GO !!
ガシ〜ン
ガシーン
ゴゴゴー

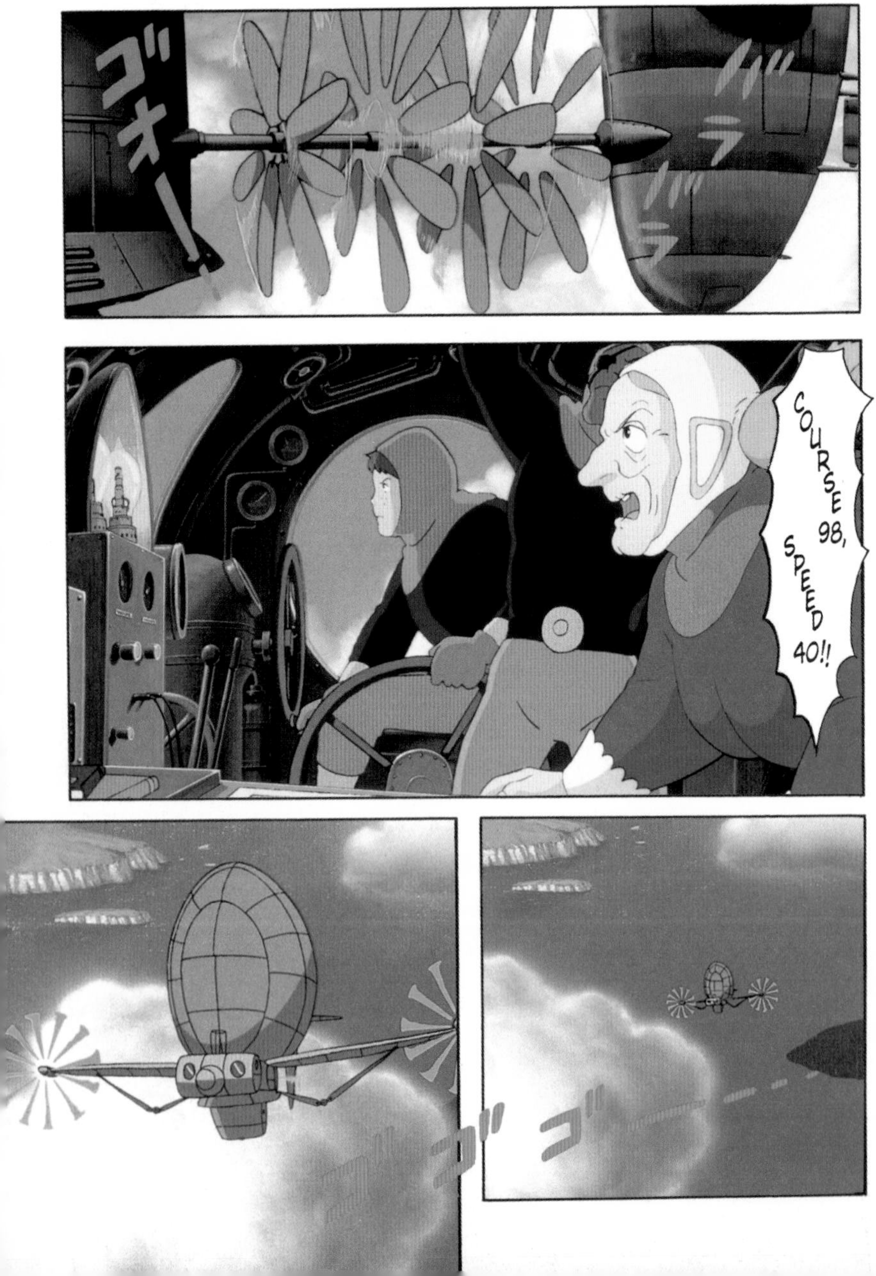
バラバラ
ゴオー!
COURSE 98, SPEED 40!!
ゴゴゴ

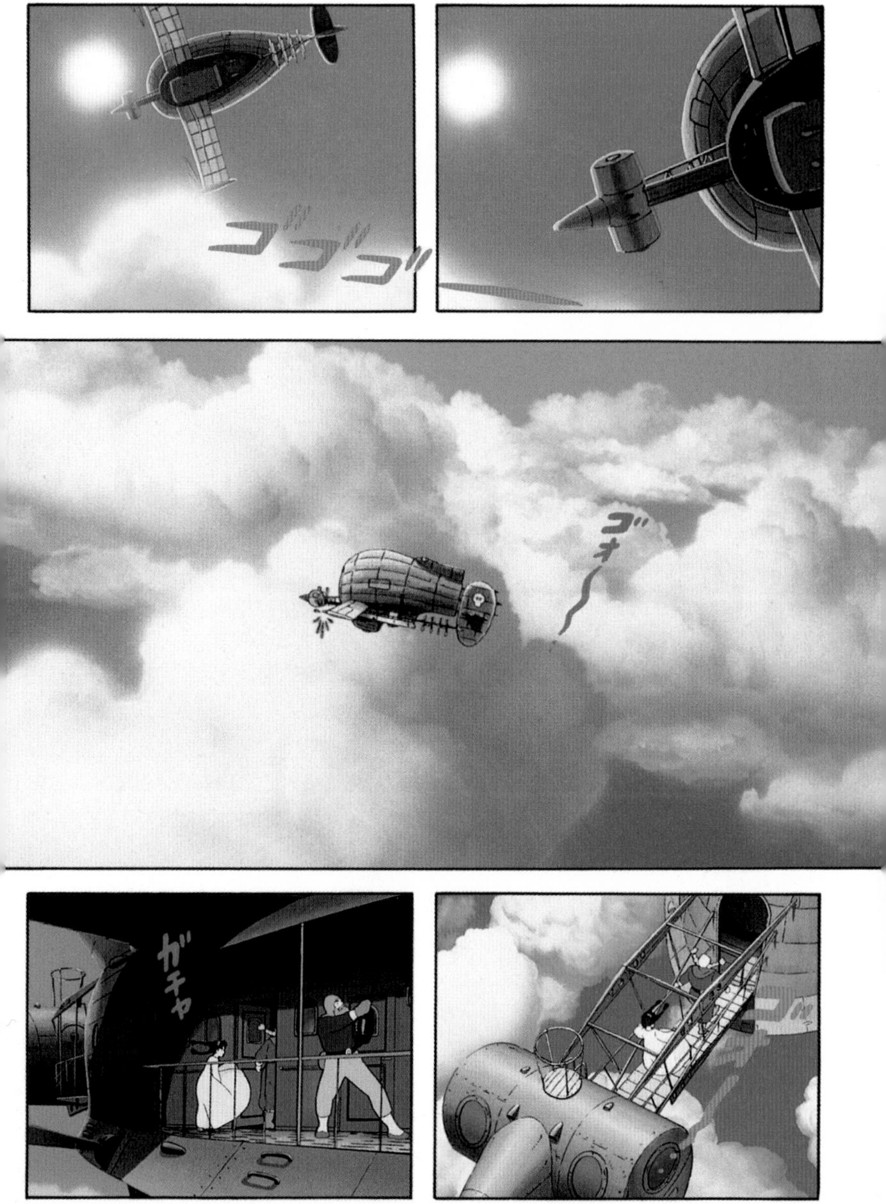
ゴゴゴ
ゴォ〜
ガチャ

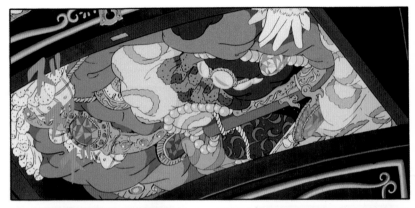

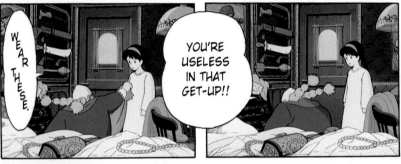

WEAR THESE.

YOU'RE USELESS IN THAT GET-UP!!

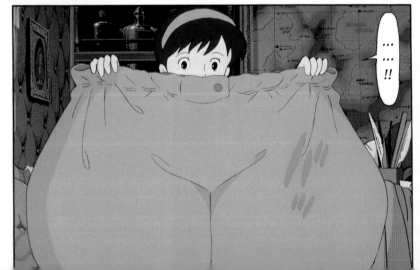

...
...
!!

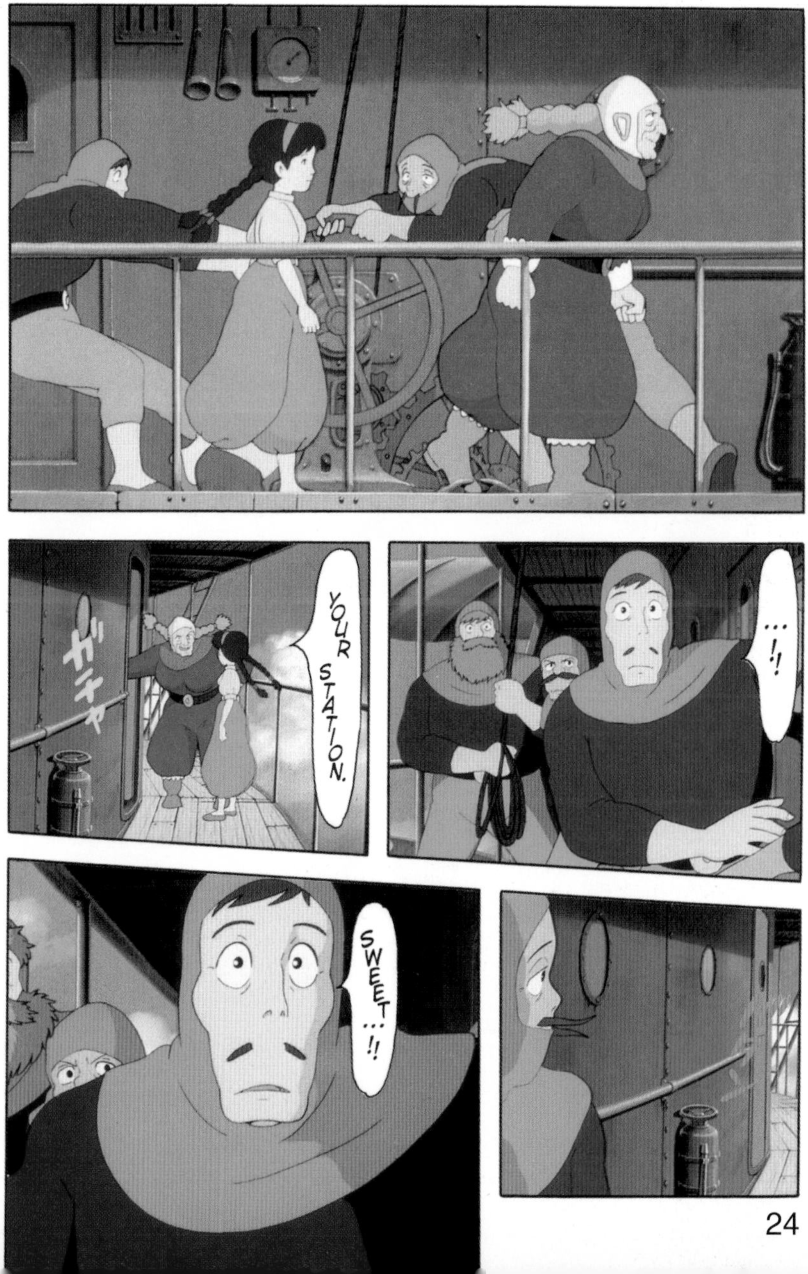
...!!
YOUR STATION.
ガチャ
SWEET...!!

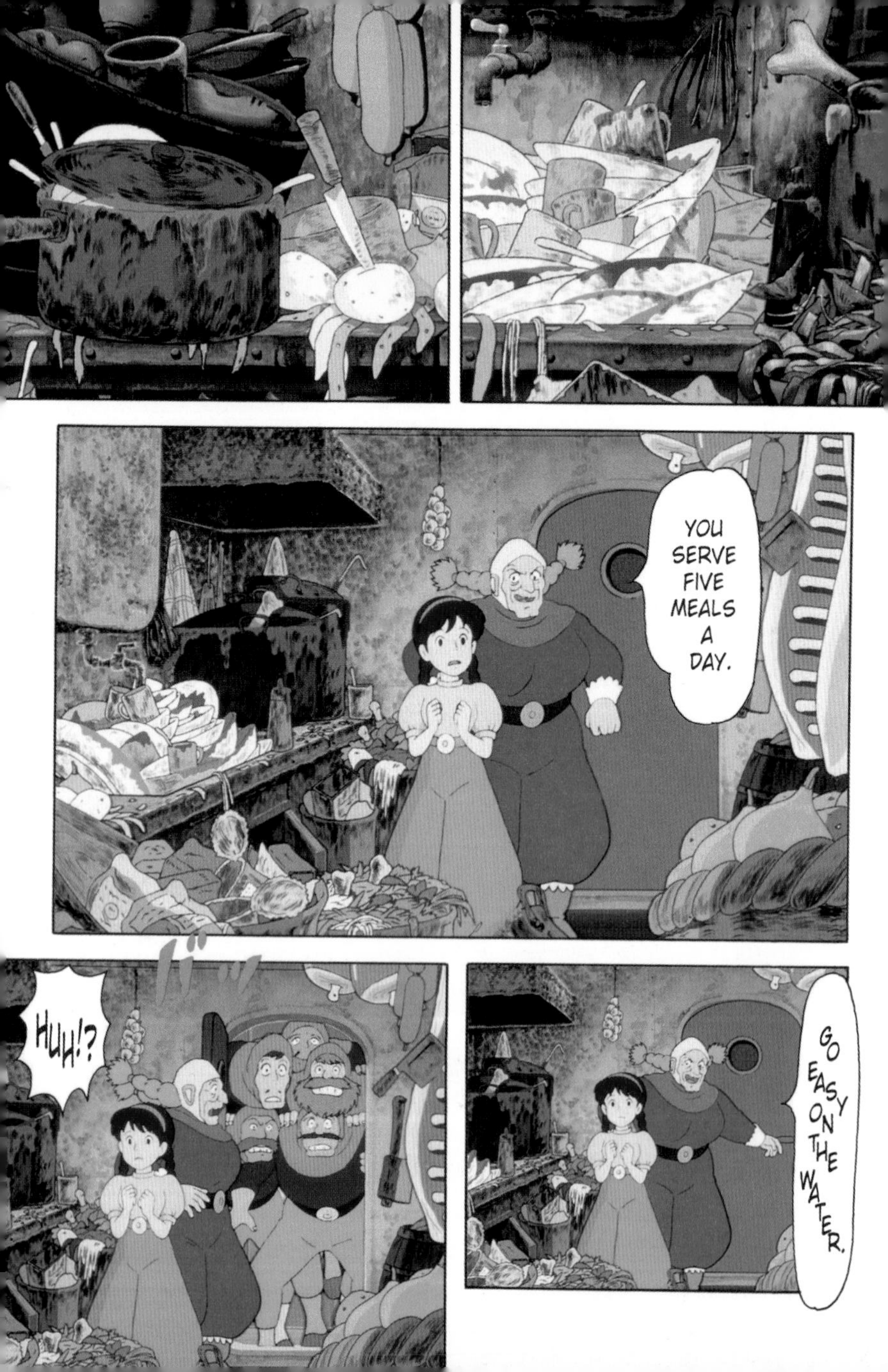
YOU SERVE FIVE MEALS A DAY.
GO EASY ON THE WATER.
HUH!?

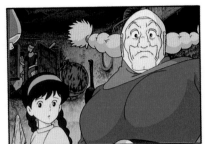

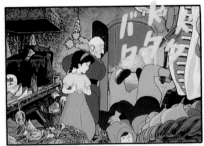

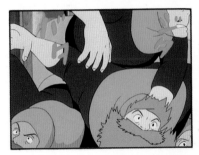

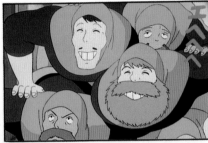

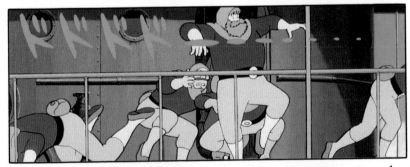

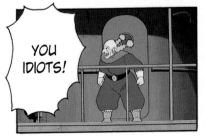

YOU IDIOTS!

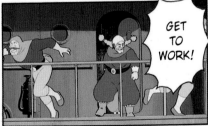

GET TO WORK!

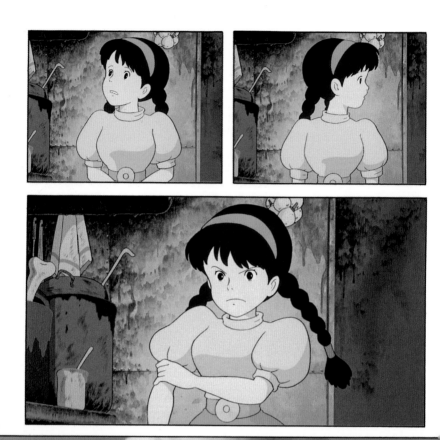

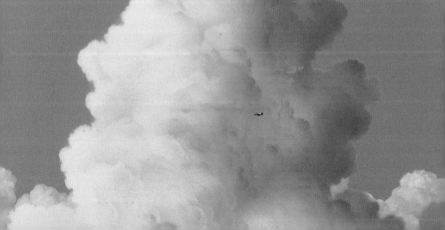

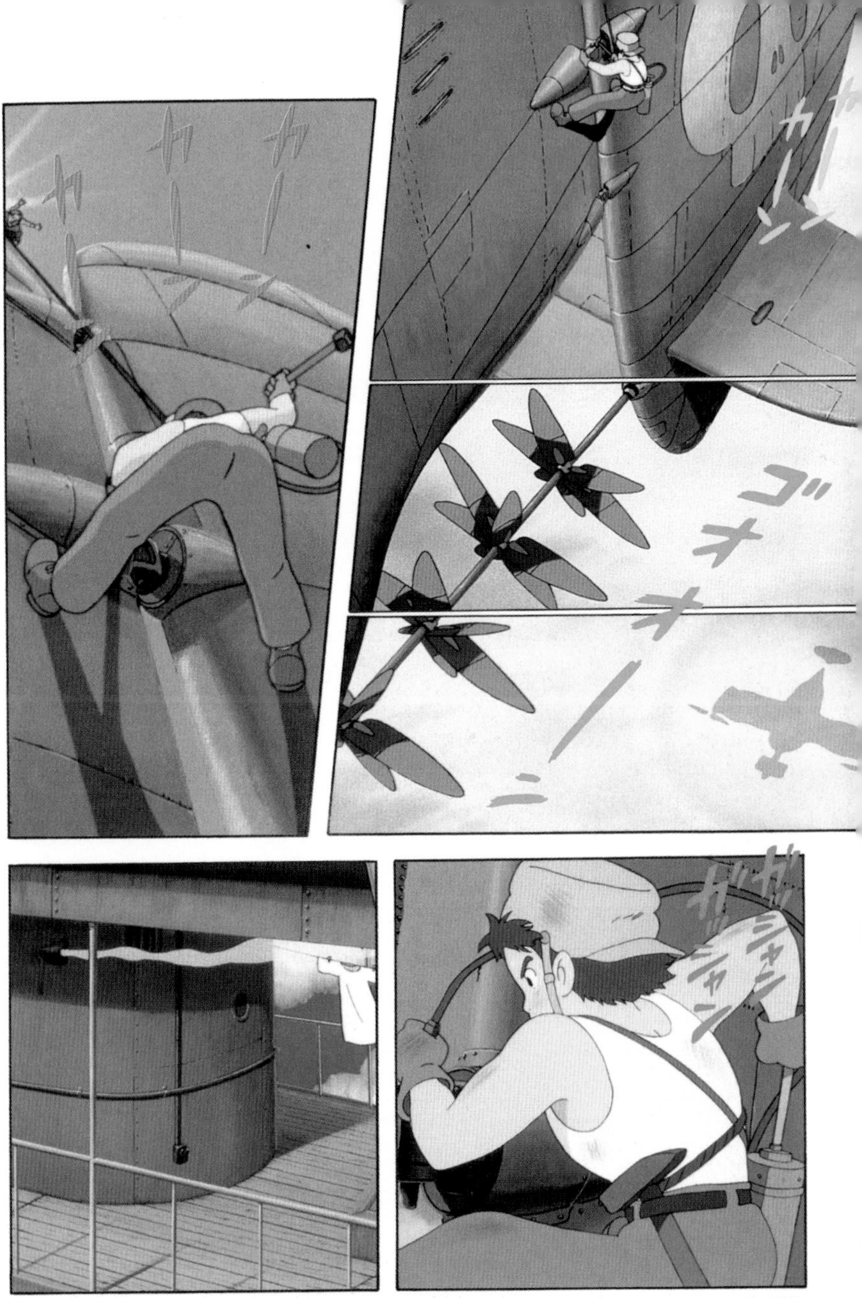
カーン
ゴオオー
ガシャン
ガシャン

カリカリ
ぐつぐつ
チロチロ!!
すすっ!!

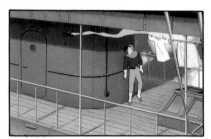

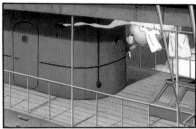

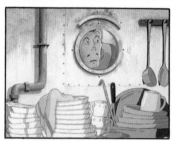

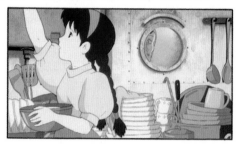

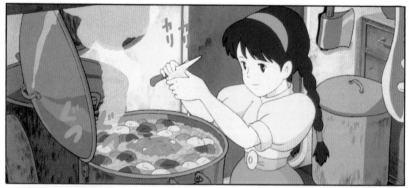

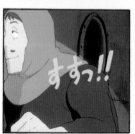

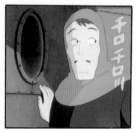

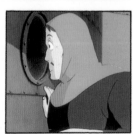

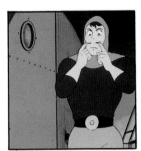

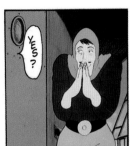

YES?

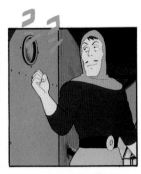

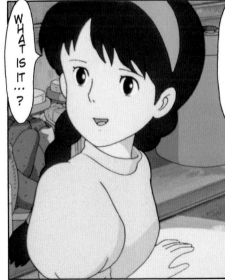

HEH-HEH...

I'M SORRY... DINNER ISN'T READY YET.

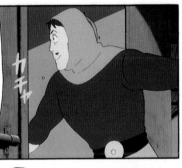

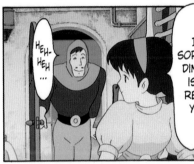

WHAT IS IT...?

I'VE NEVER COOKED ON AN AIRSHIP...

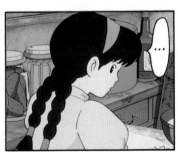

...

30

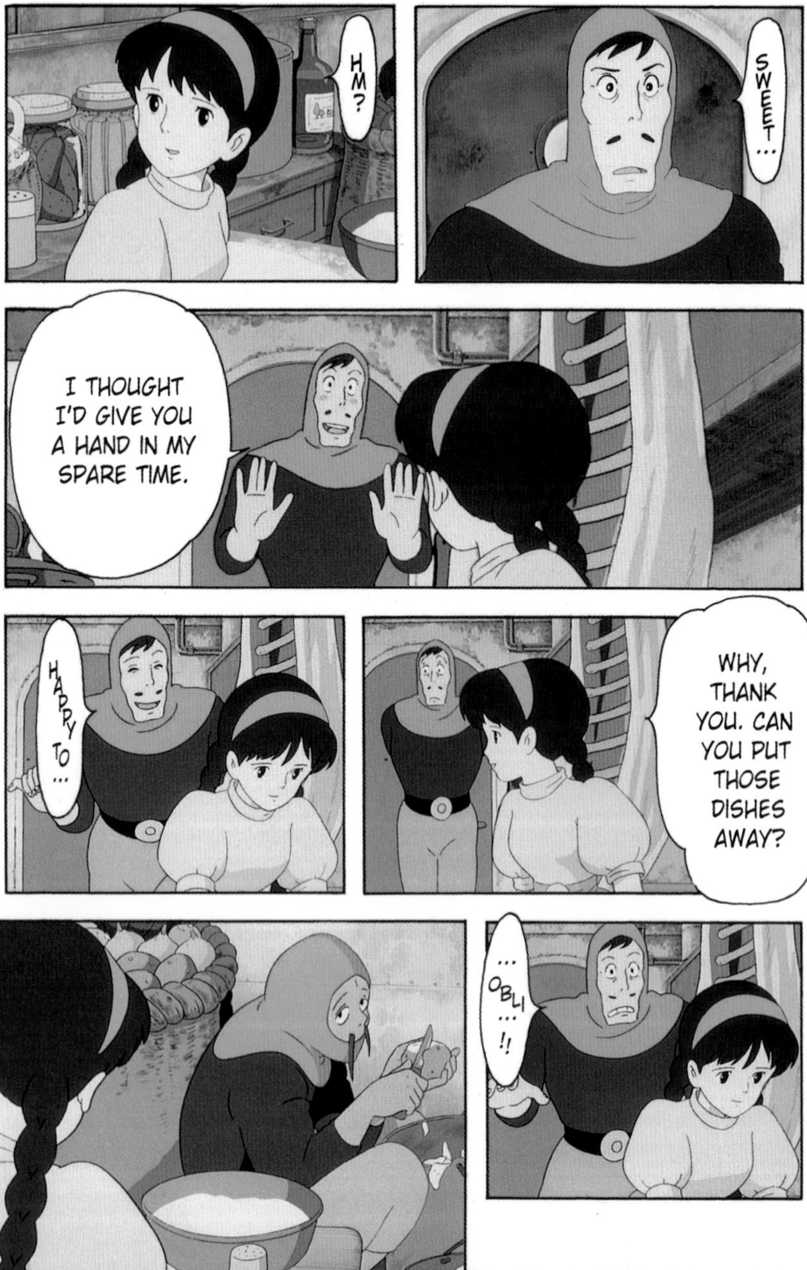
SWEET...
HM?
I THOUGHT I'D GIVE YOU A HAND IN MY SPARE TIME.
WHY, THANK YOU. CAN YOU PUT THOSE DISHES AWAY?
HAPPY TO...
...OBLI...!!

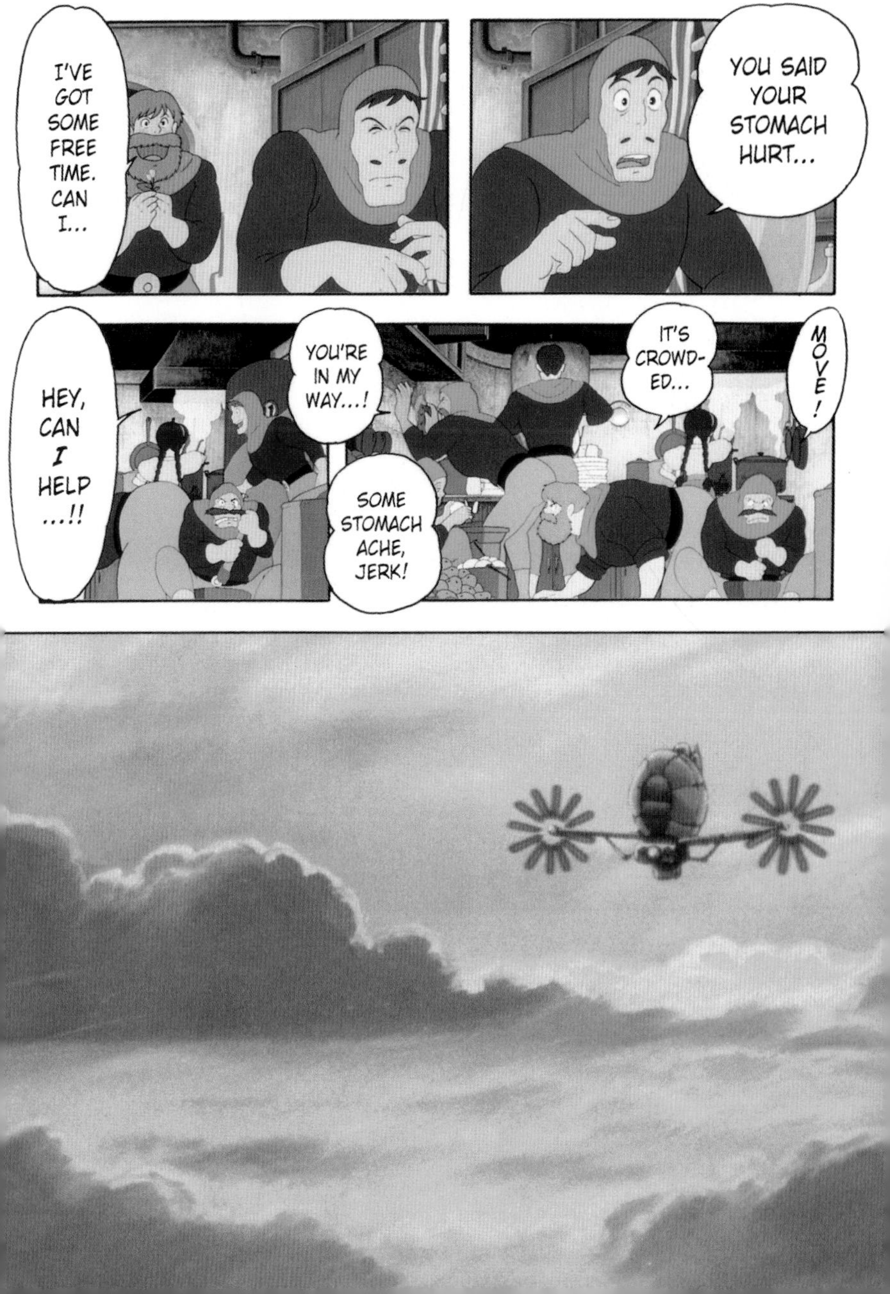
YOU SAID YOUR STOMACH HURT…
I'VE GOT SOME FREE TIME. CAN I…
MOVE!
IT'S CROWD-ED…
YOU'RE IN MY WAY…!
SOME STOMACH ACHE, JERK!
HEY, CAN I HELP …!!

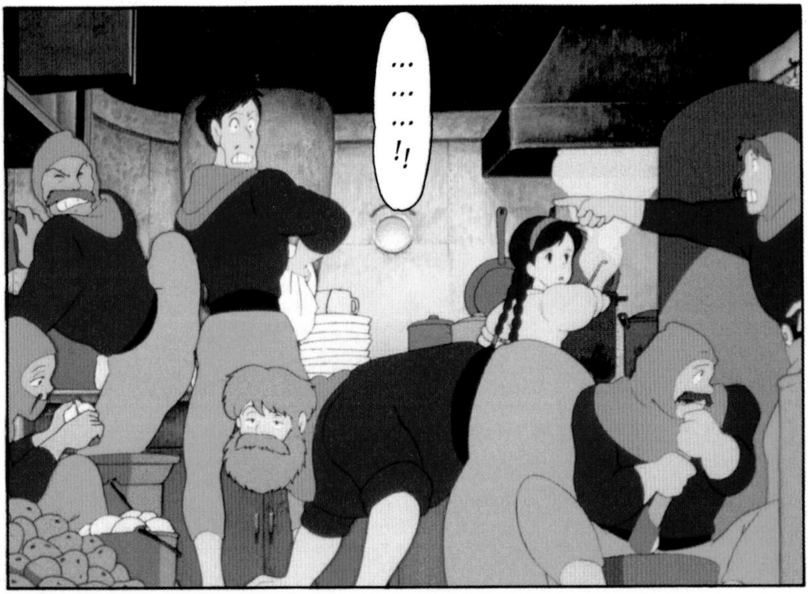
………!!

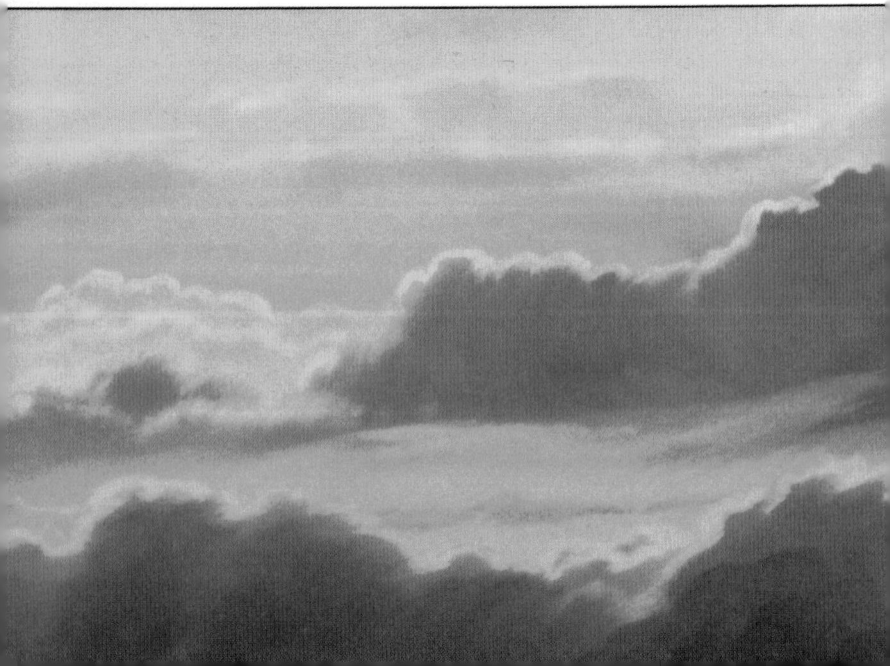

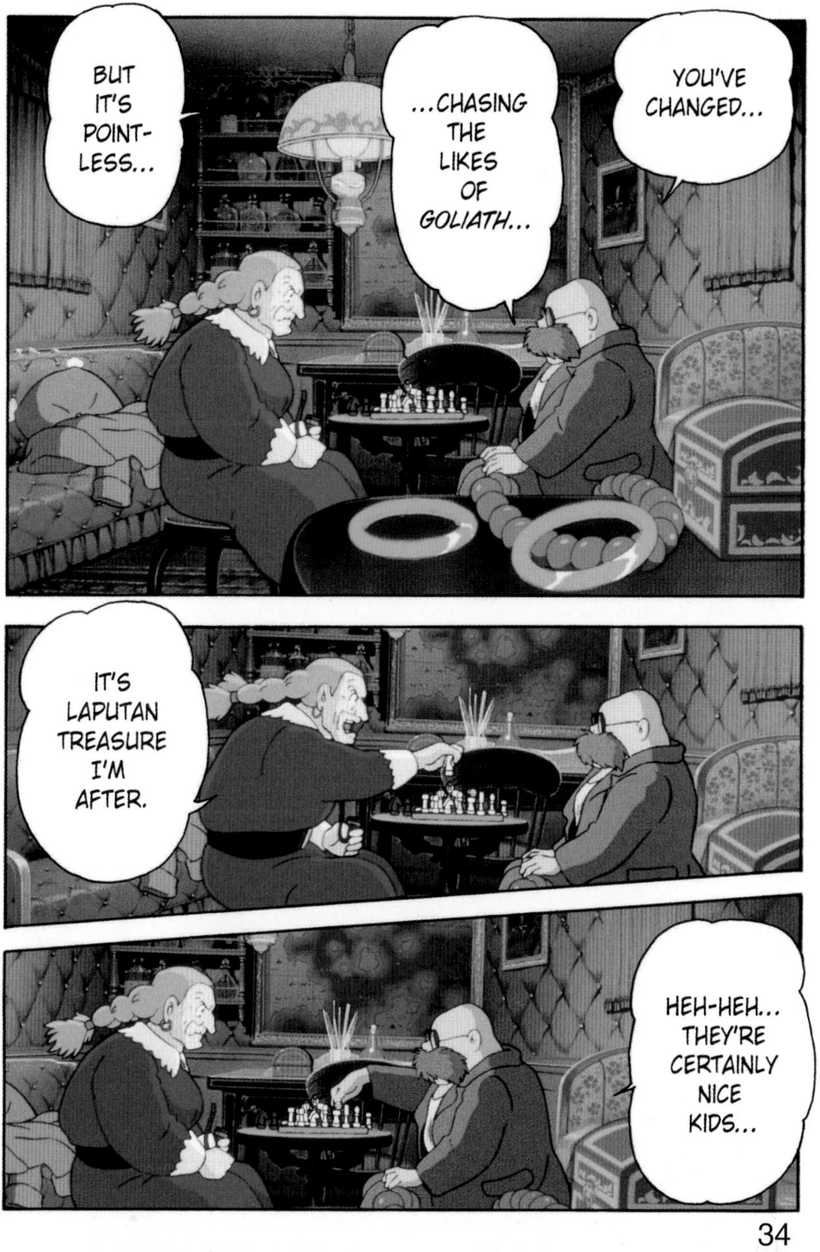
YOU'VE CHANGED...
...CHASING THE LIKES OF GOLIATH...
BUT IT'S POINT-LESS...
IT'S LAPUTAN TREASURE I'M AFTER.
HEH-HEH... THEY'RE CERTAINLY NICE KIDS...

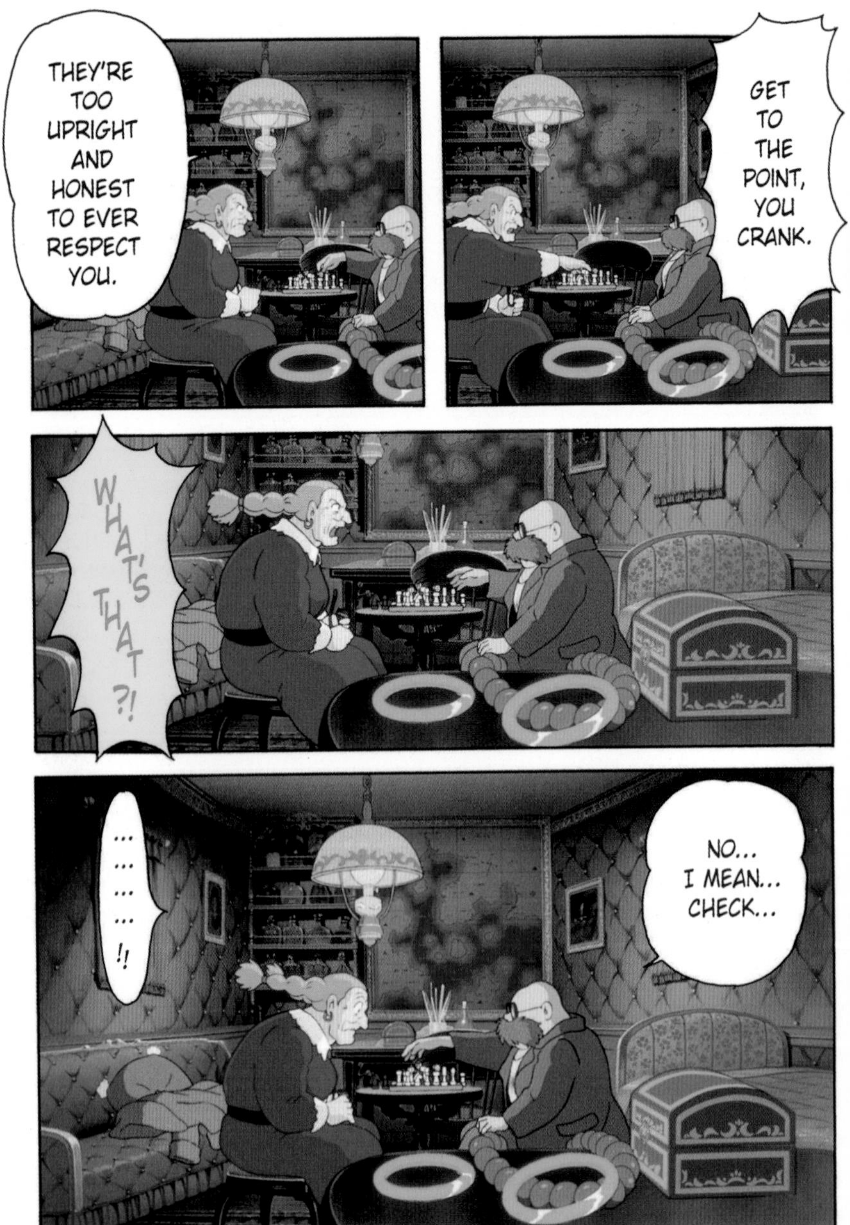
GET TO THE POINT, YOU CRANK.
THEY'RE TOO UPRIGHT AND HONEST TO EVER RESPECT YOU.
WHAT'S THAT?!
NO... I MEAN... CHECK...
... ... !!

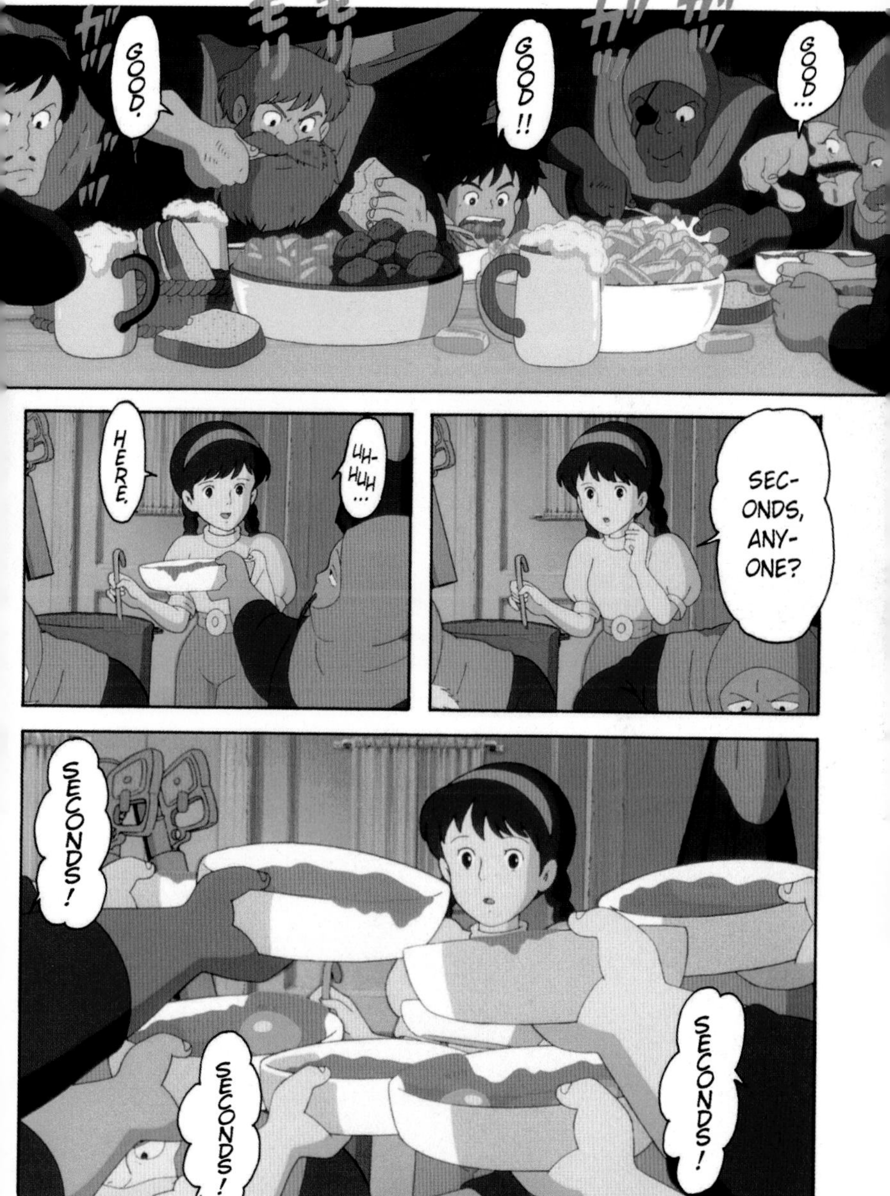
GOOD...
GOOD!!
GOOD.
SECONDS, ANYONE?
UH-HUH...
HERE.
SECONDS!
SECONDS!
SECONDS!

ゴン
ゴン
ゴン
ゴオオーン

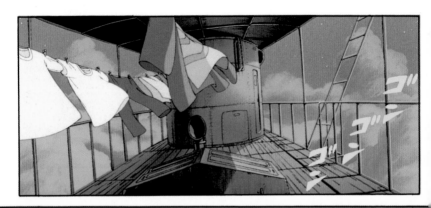

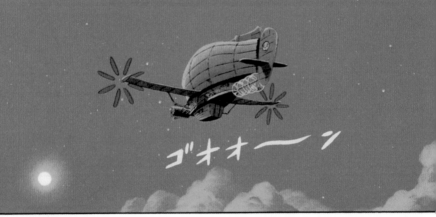

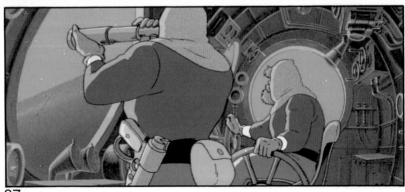

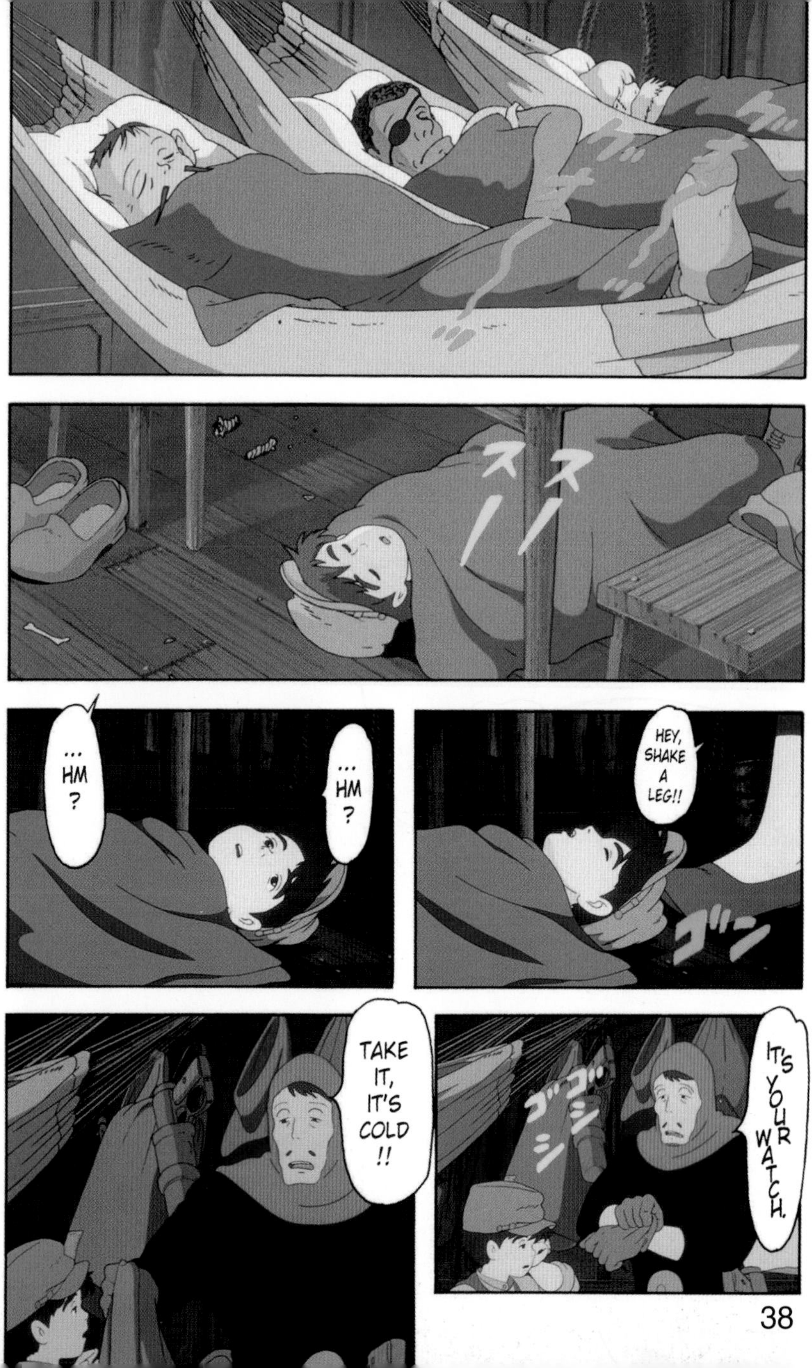
スースー
HEY, SHAKE A LEG!!
ゴン
...HM?
...HM?
IT'S YOUR WATCH.
ゴシゴシ
TAKE IT, IT'S COLD!!

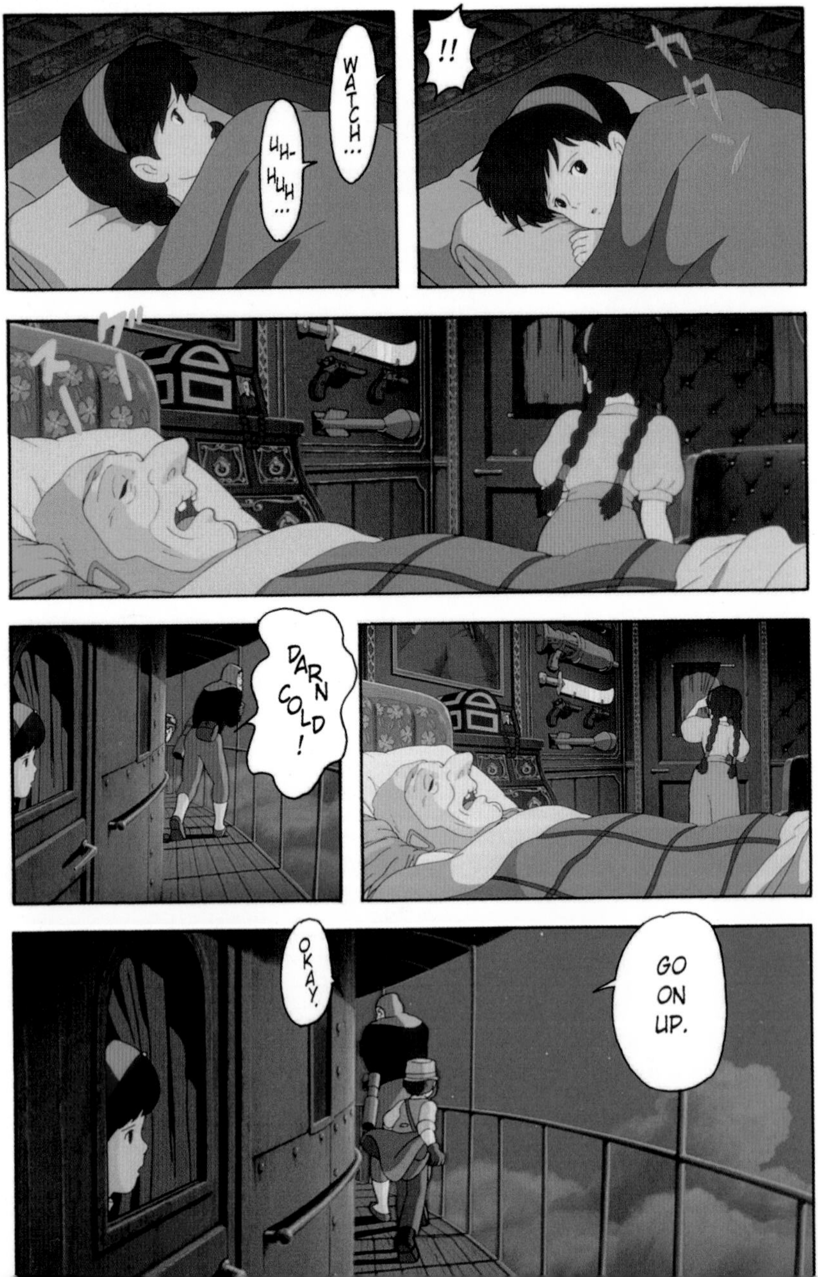
!!
WATCH...
UH-HUH...
DARN COLD!
GO ON UP.
OKAY.

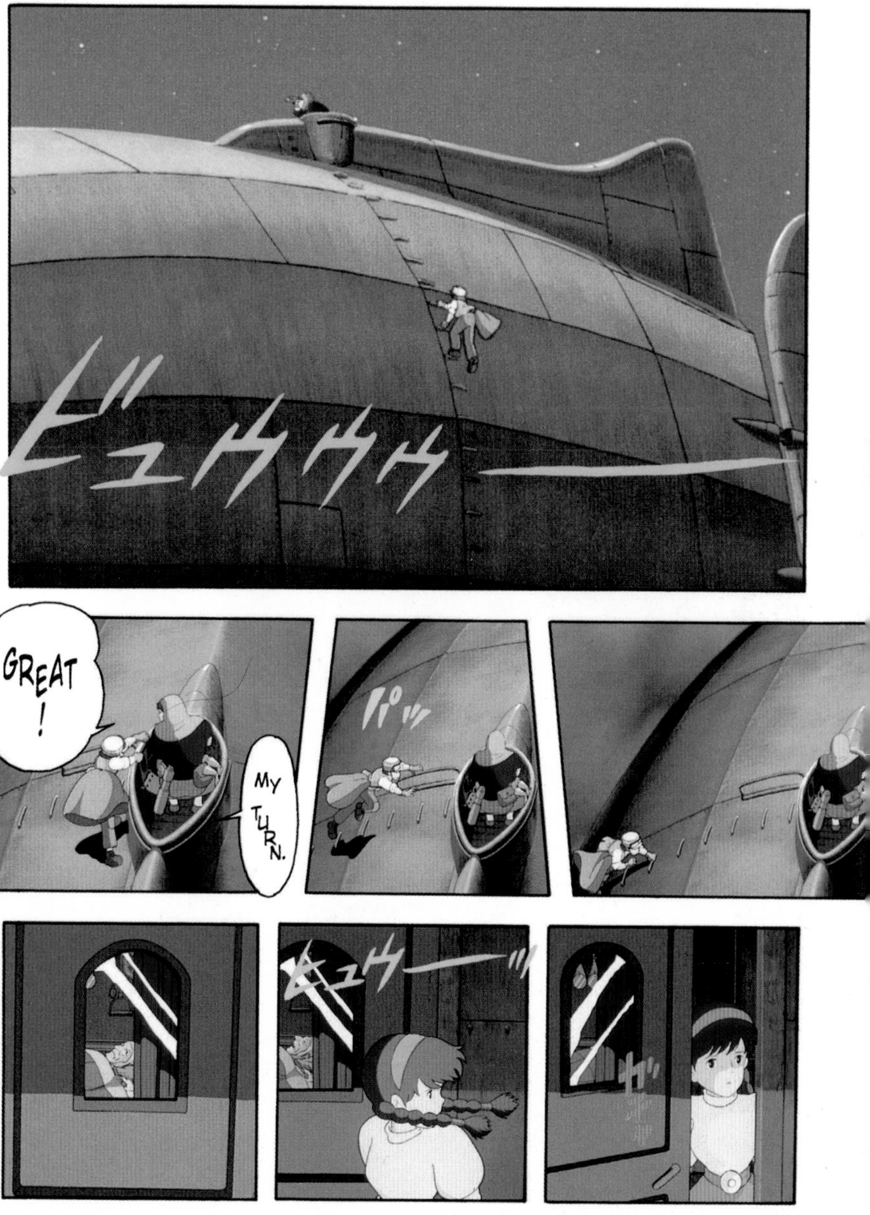
ビュウウウー
パッ
GREAT!
MY TURN.
ガッ
ヒュウーッ

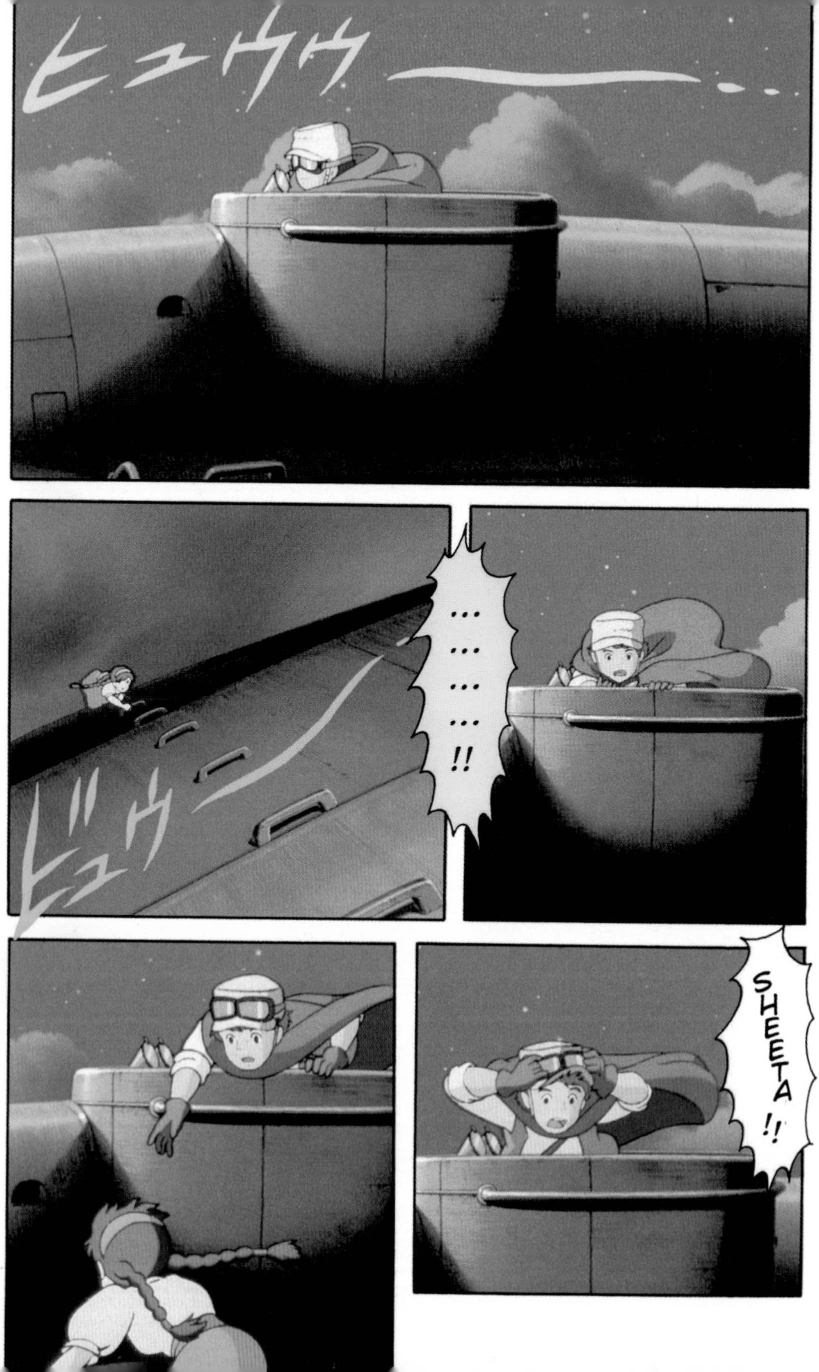
ヒュウウー
............!!
ビュウー
SHEETA!!

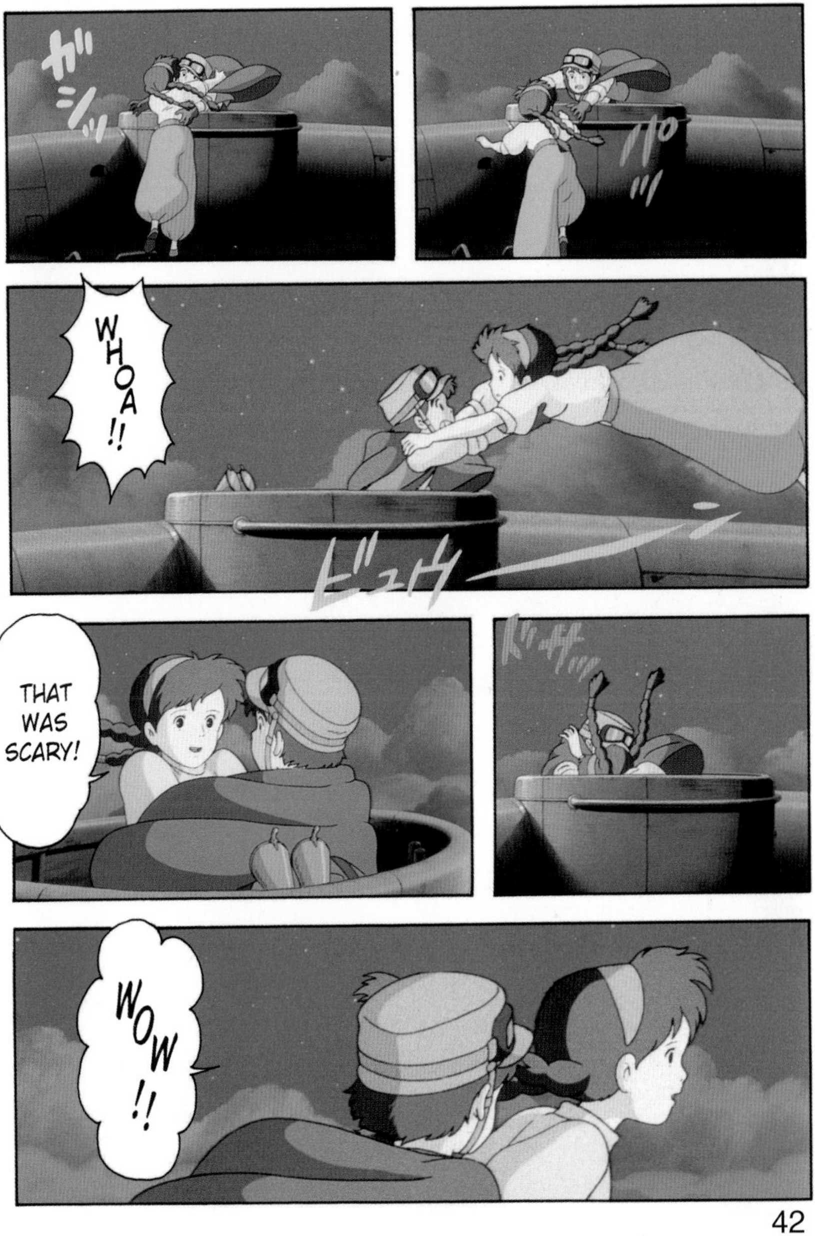
ガシッ
WHOA!!
ビュウ
THAT WAS SCARY!
WOW!!

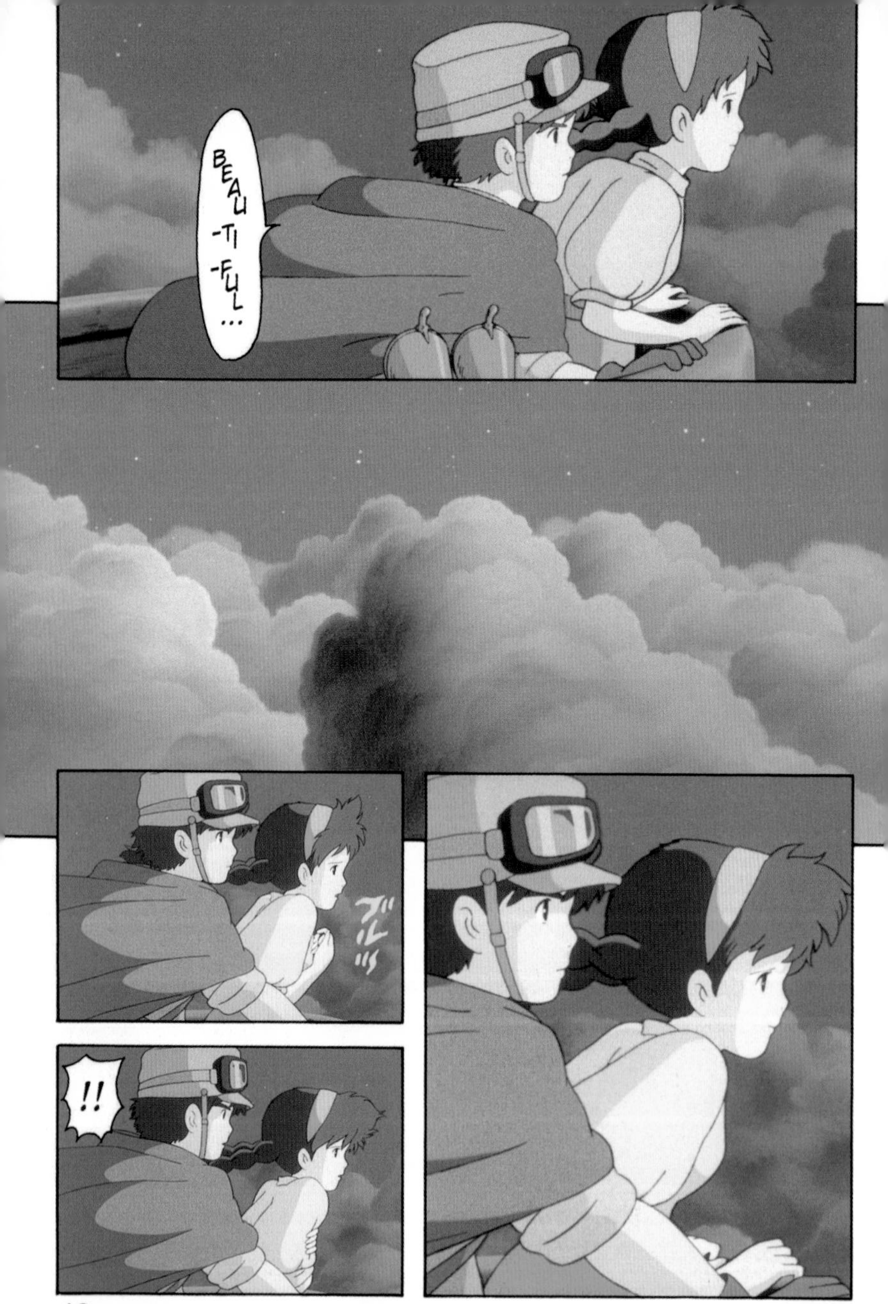
BEAU-TI-FUL...
ブルッ
!!

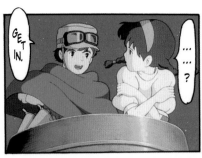

GET IN.

....
.....?

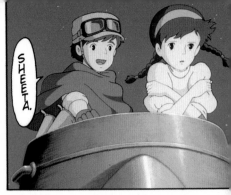

SHEETA.

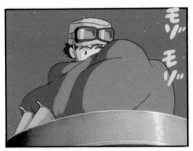

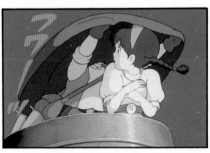

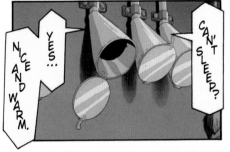

NICE AND WARM.

YES...

CAN'T SLEEP?

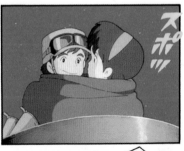

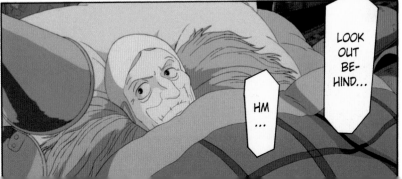

LOOK OUT BE- HIND...

HM...

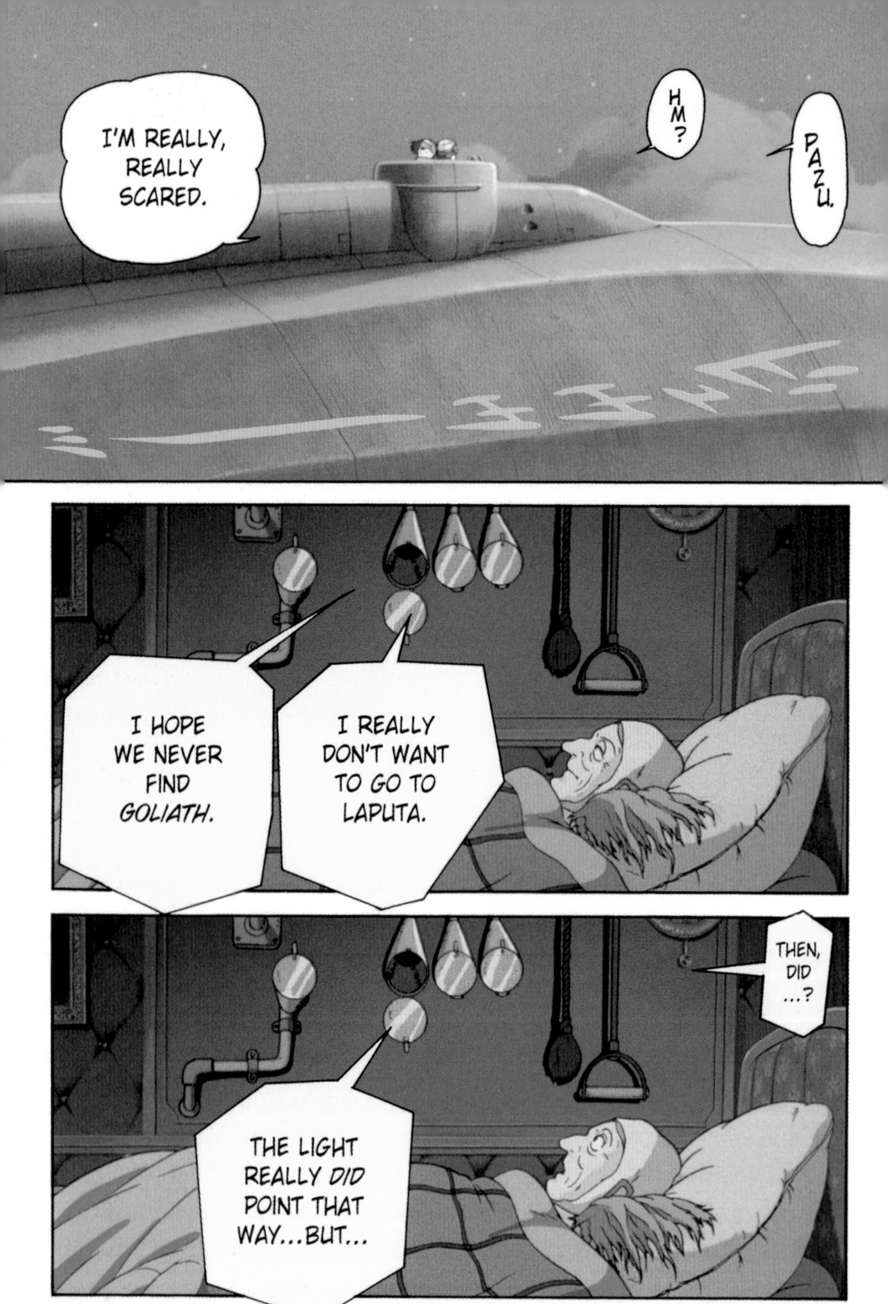
PAZU.
HM?
I'M REALLY, REALLY SCARED.
I REALLY DON'T WANT TO GO TO LAPUTA.
I HOPE WE NEVER FIND *GOLIATH*.
THEN, DID ...?
THE LIGHT REALLY *DID* POINT THAT WAY...BUT...

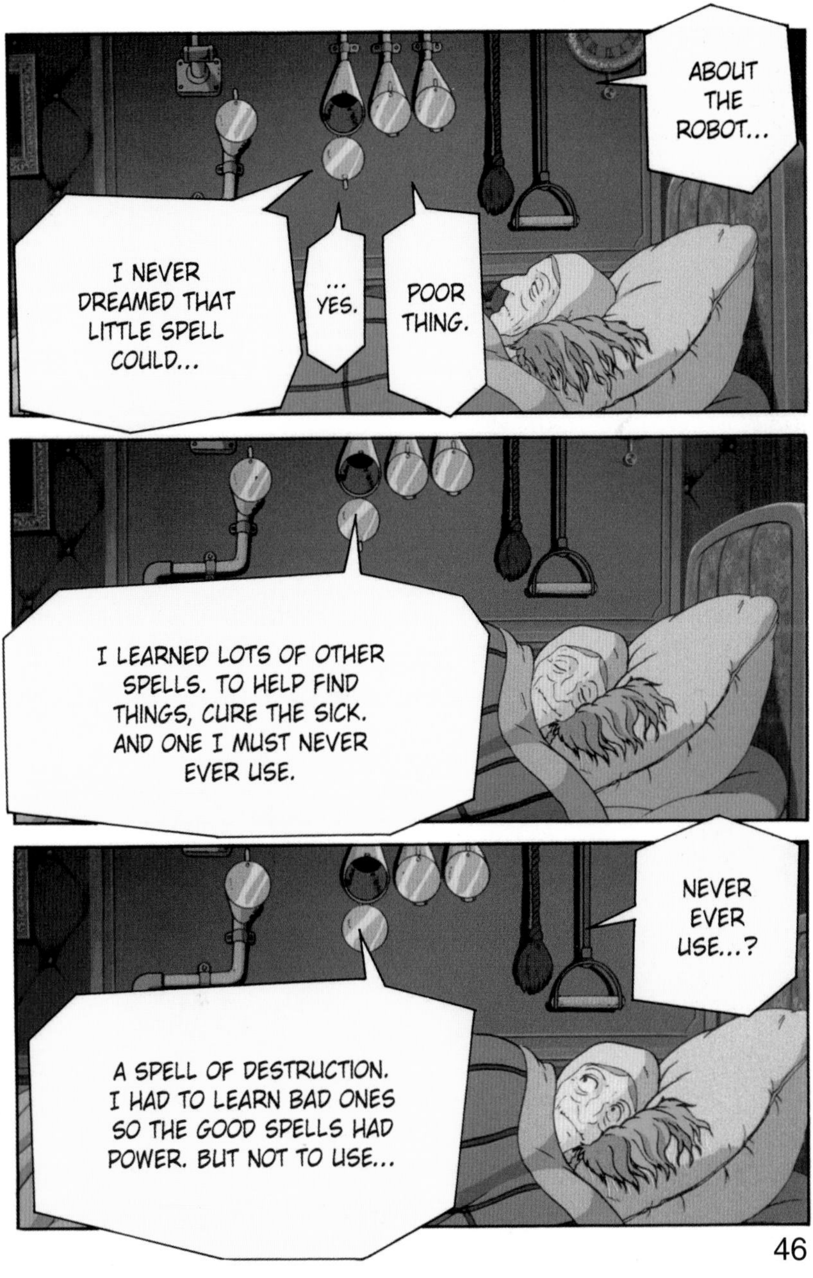
ABOUT THE ROBOT...
POOR THING.
... YES.
I NEVER DREAMED THAT LITTLE SPELL COULD...
I LEARNED LOTS OF OTHER SPELLS. TO HELP FIND THINGS, CURE THE SICK. AND ONE I MUST NEVER EVER USE.
NEVER EVER USE...?
A SPELL OF DESTRUCTION. I HAD TO LEARN BAD ONES SO THE GOOD SPELLS HAD POWER. BUT NOT TO USE...

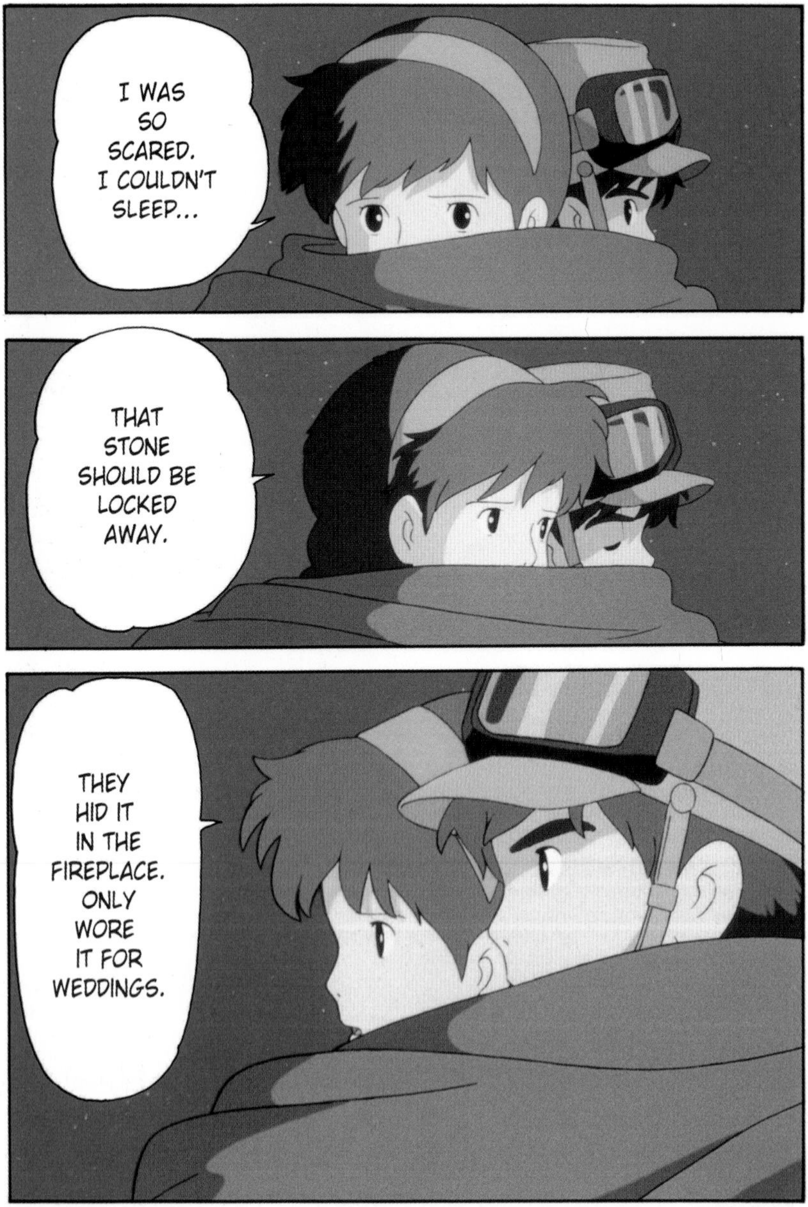
I WAS SO SCARED. I COULDN'T SLEEP...
THAT STONE SHOULD BE LOCKED AWAY.
THEY HID IT IN THE FIREPLACE. ONLY WORE IT FOR WEDDINGS.

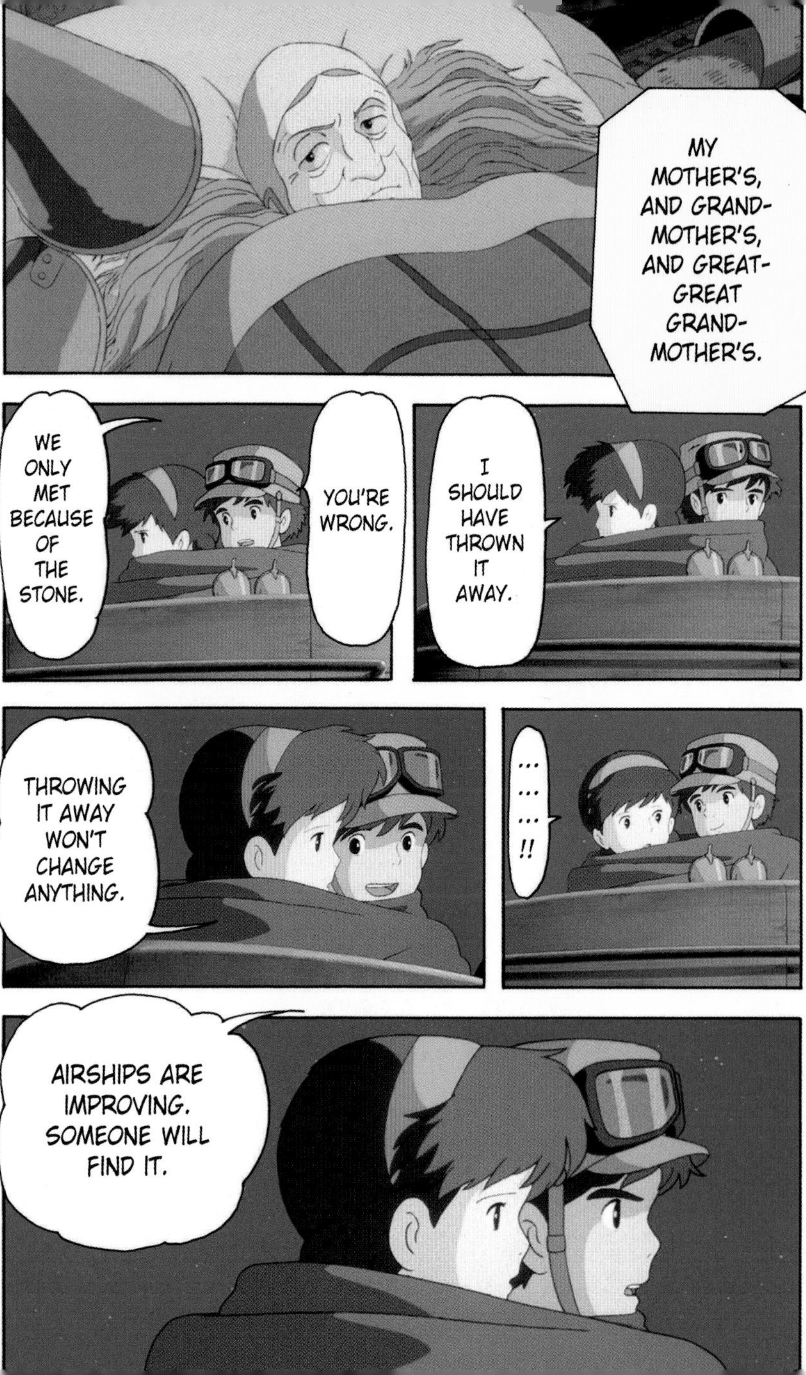
MY MOTHER'S, AND GRAND-MOTHER'S, AND GREAT-GREAT GRAND-MOTHER'S.
I SHOULD HAVE THROWN IT AWAY.
YOU'RE WRONG.
WE ONLY MET BECAUSE OF THE STONE.
.........!!
THROWING IT AWAY WON'T CHANGE ANYTHING.
AIRSHIPS ARE IMPROVING. SOMEONE WILL FIND IT.

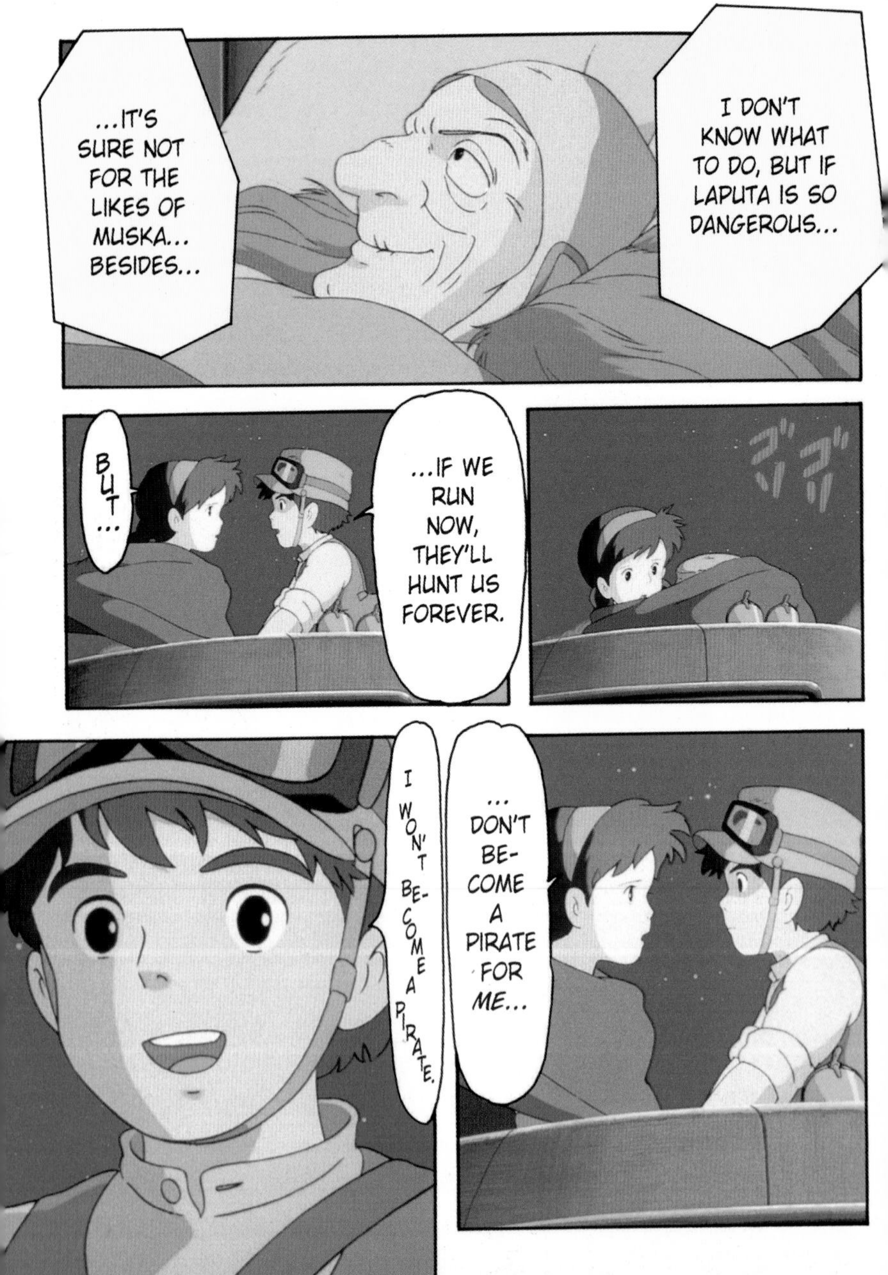
I DON'T KNOW WHAT TO DO, BUT IF LAPUTA IS SO DANGEROUS...
...IT'S SURE NOT FOR THE LIKES OF MUSKA... BESIDES...
...IF WE RUN NOW, THEY'LL HUNT US FOREVER.
BUT...
...DON'T BE-COME A PIRATE FOR ME...
I WON'T BE-COME A PIRATE.

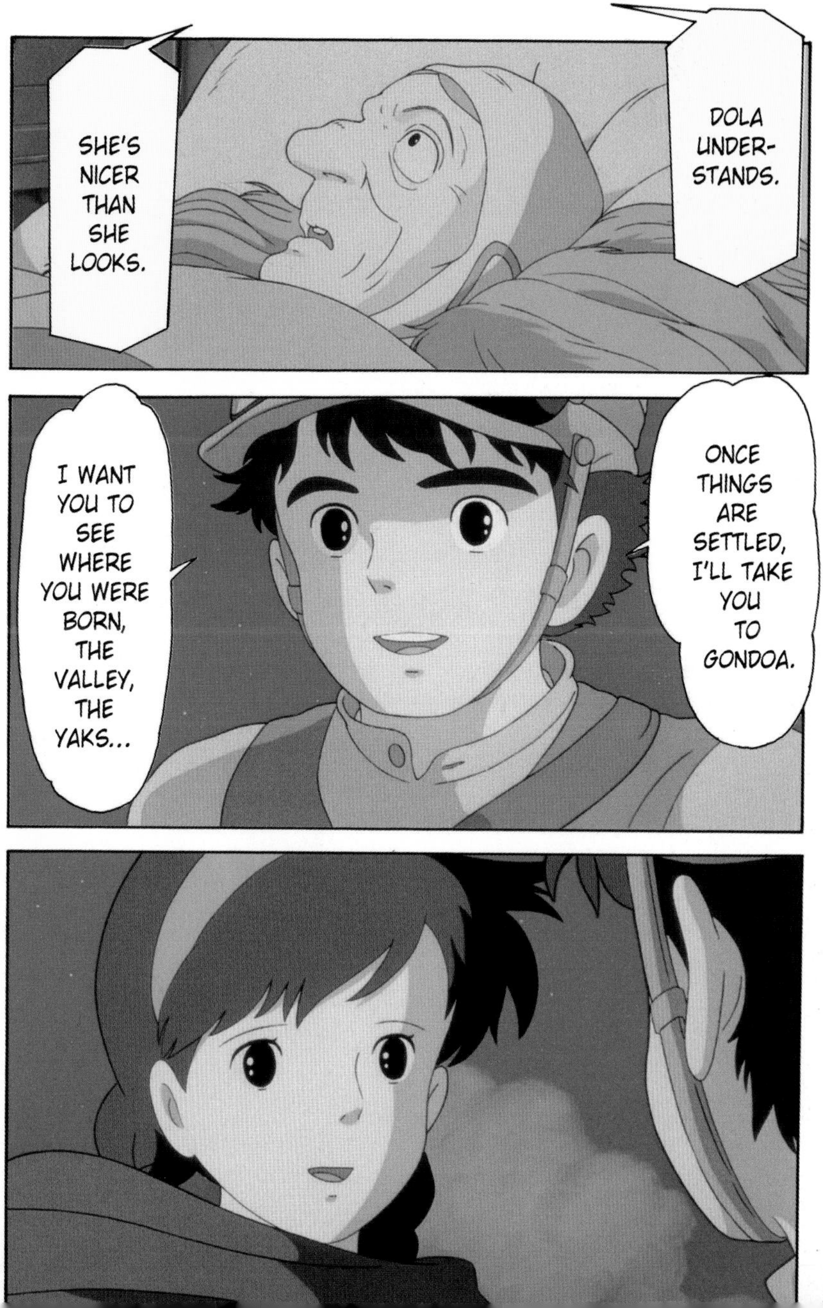
DOLA UNDER-STANDS.
SHE'S NICER THAN SHE LOOKS.
ONCE THINGS ARE SETTLED, I'LL TAKE YOU TO GONDOA.
I WANT YOU TO SEE WHERE YOU WERE BORN, THE VALLEY, THE YAKS...

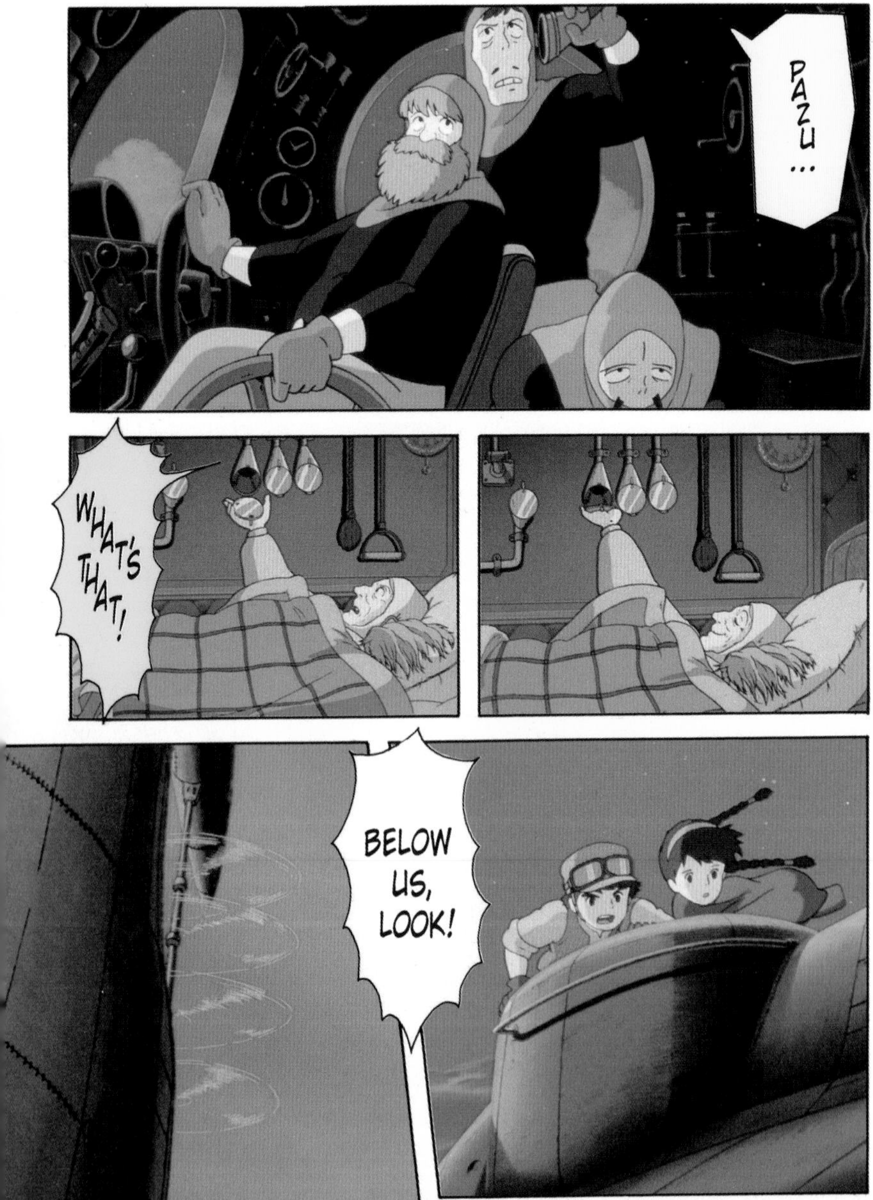
PAZU...
WHAT'S THAT!
BELOW US, LOOK!

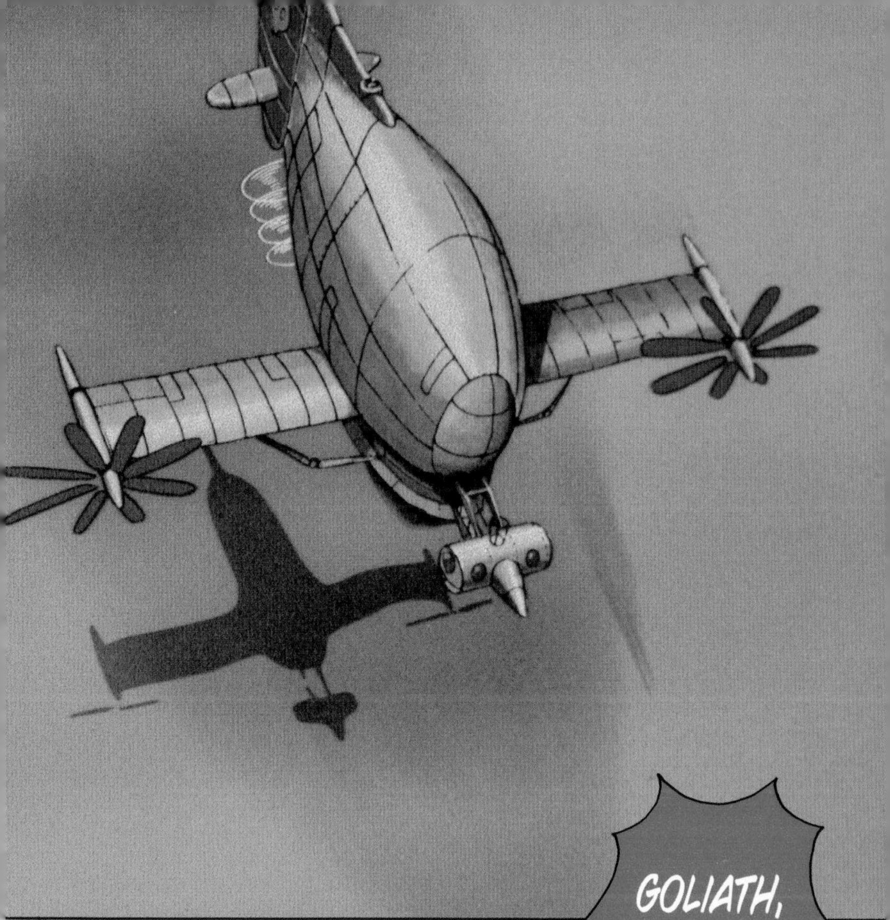

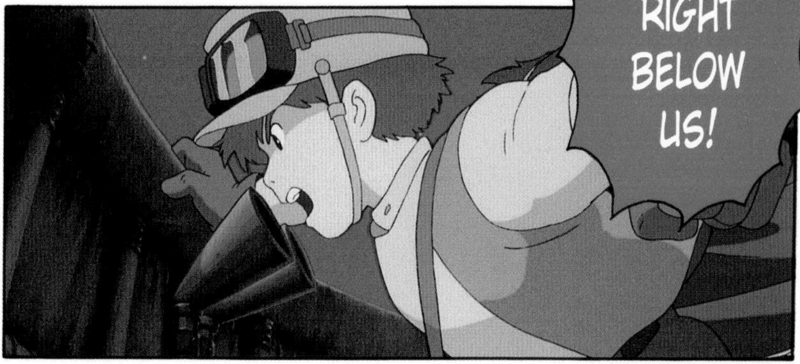
GOLIATH, RIGHT BELOW US!

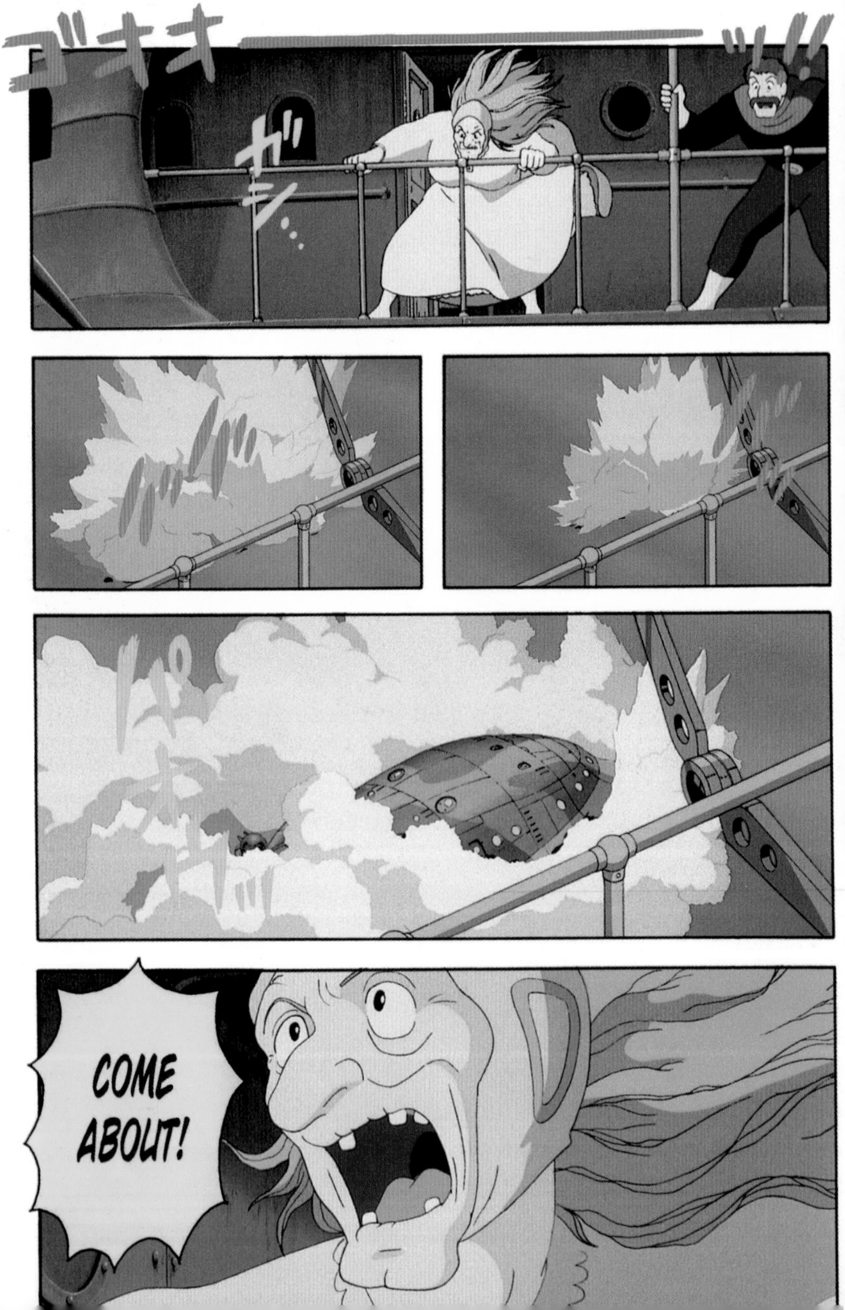
COME ABOUT!

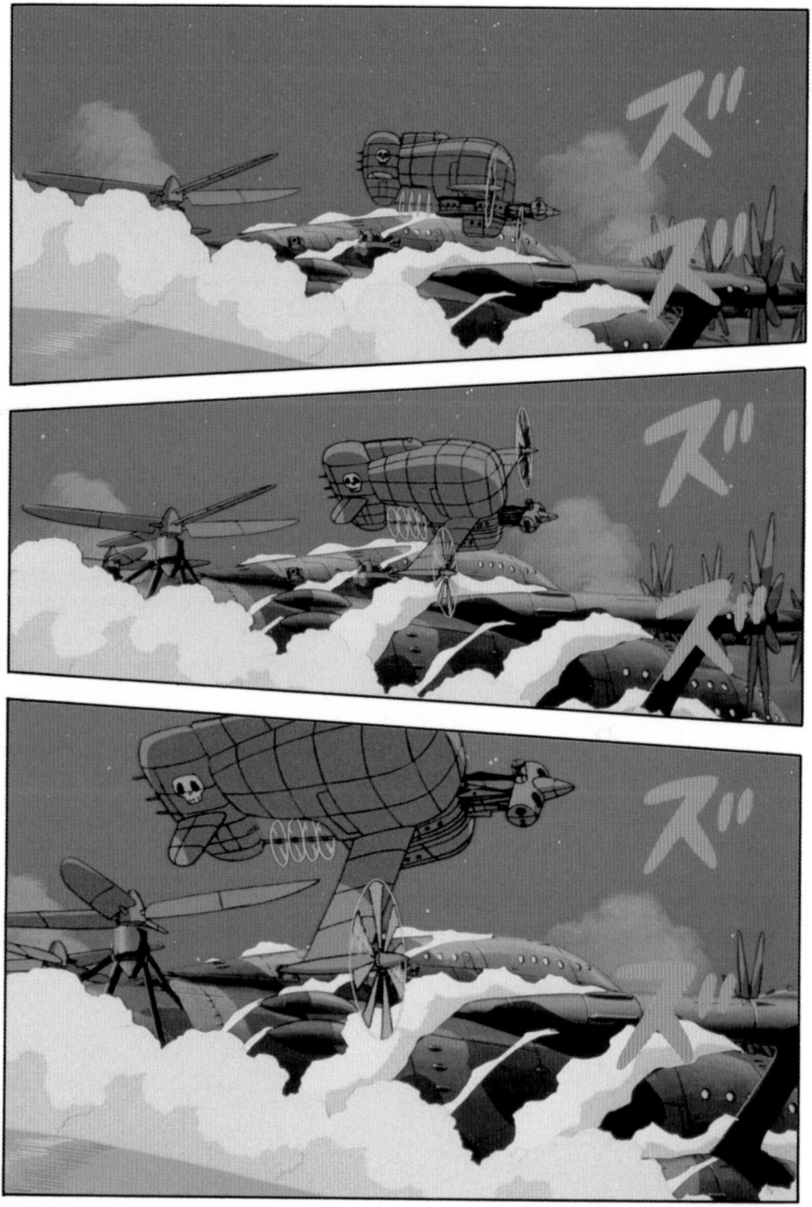
ズズ
ズズ
ズズ

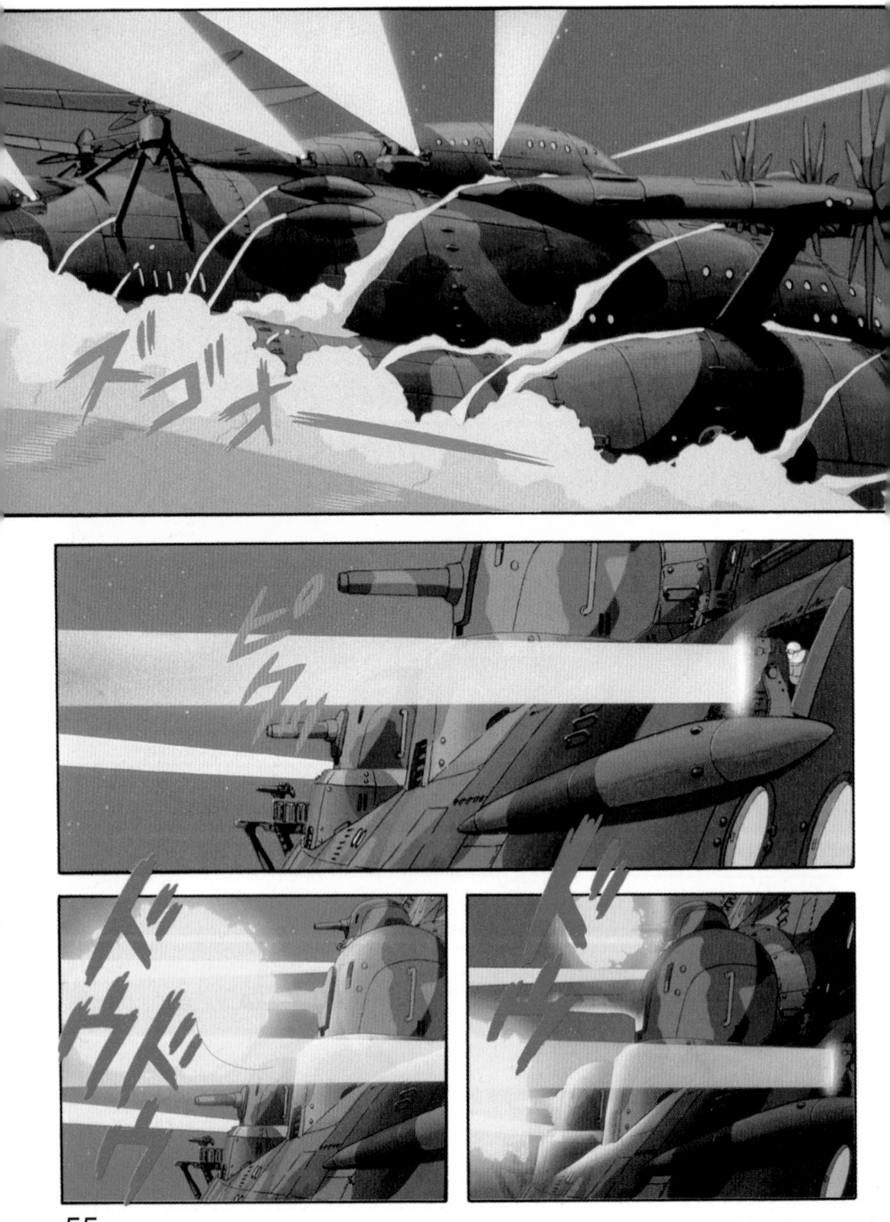
ズゴォ
ピシュッ
ドォ
ドウドウ

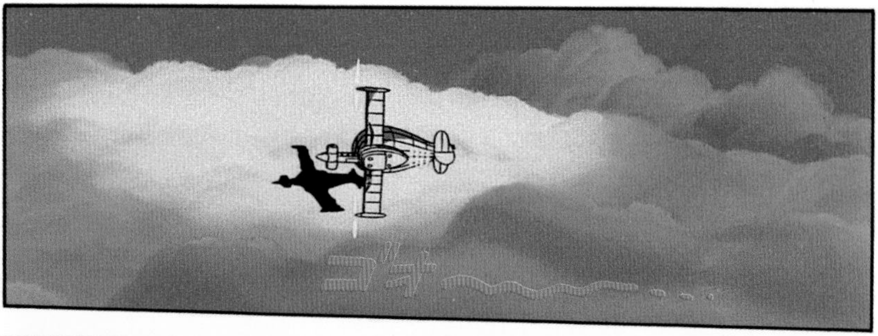
ゴヴ〜……
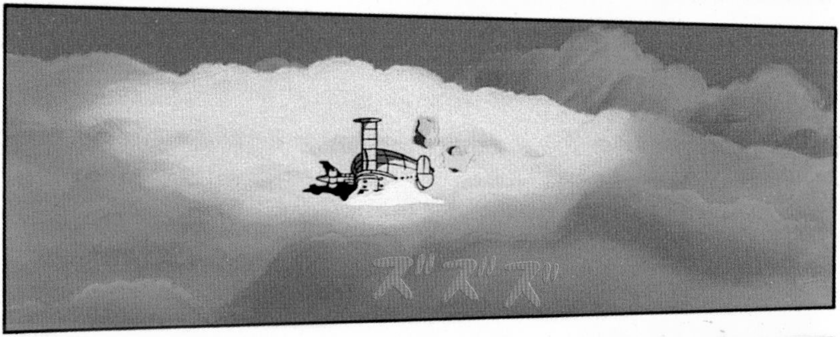
ズズズ
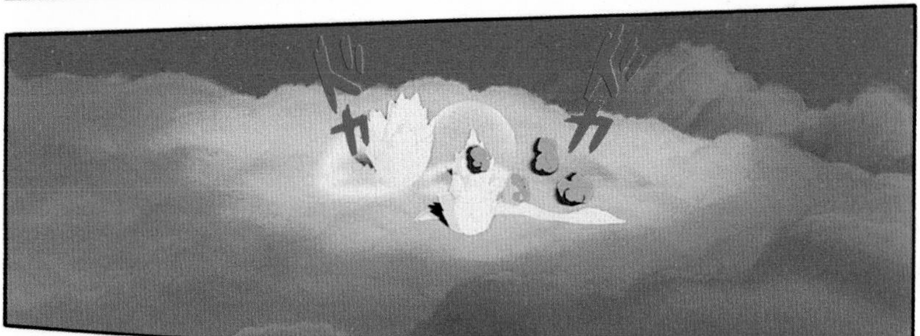
ドガ
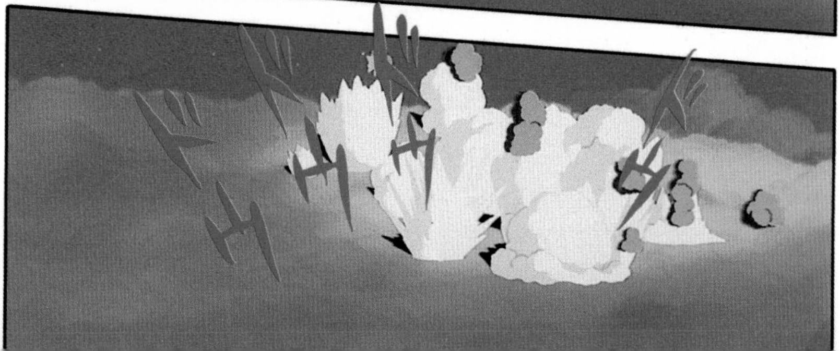
ドガ

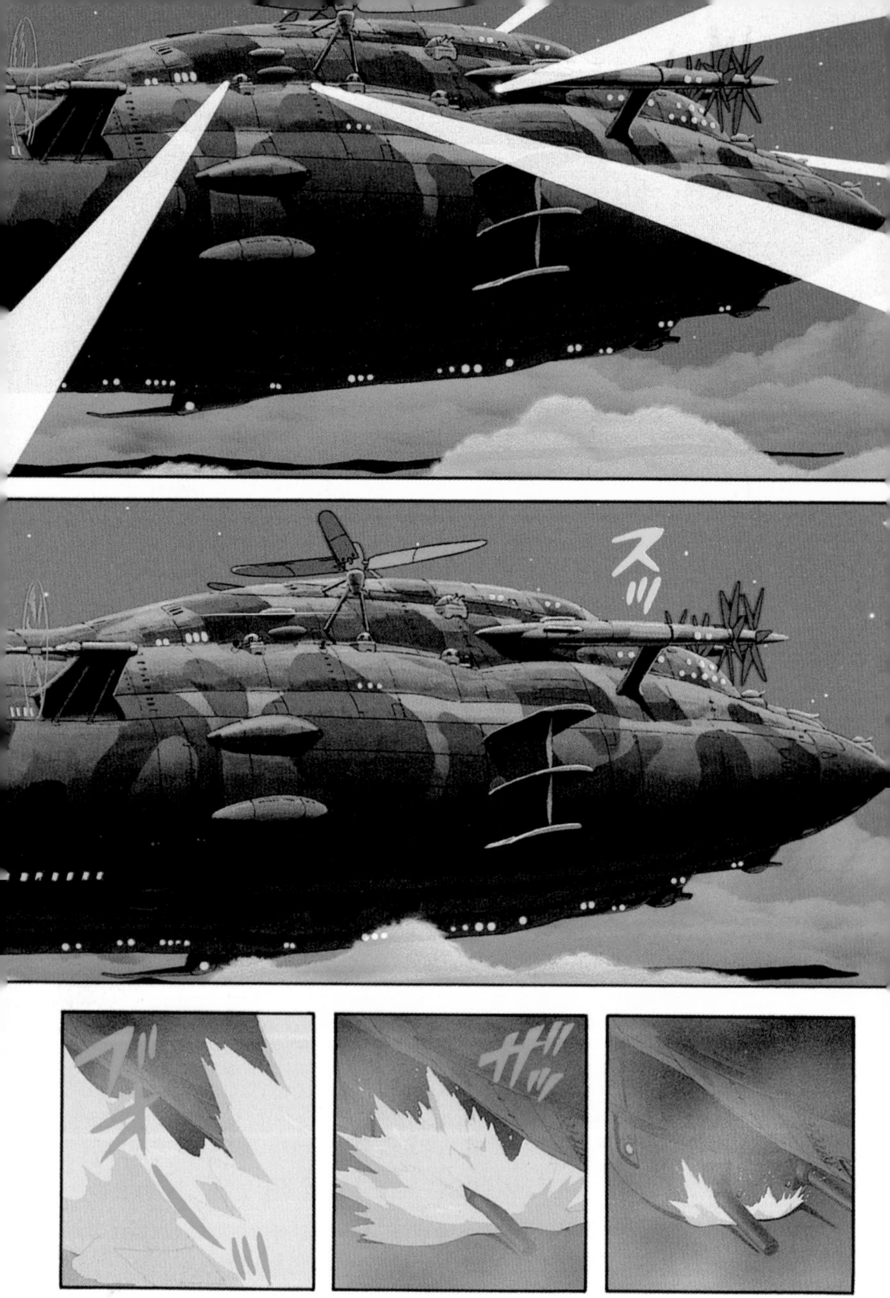
スッ
ザッ

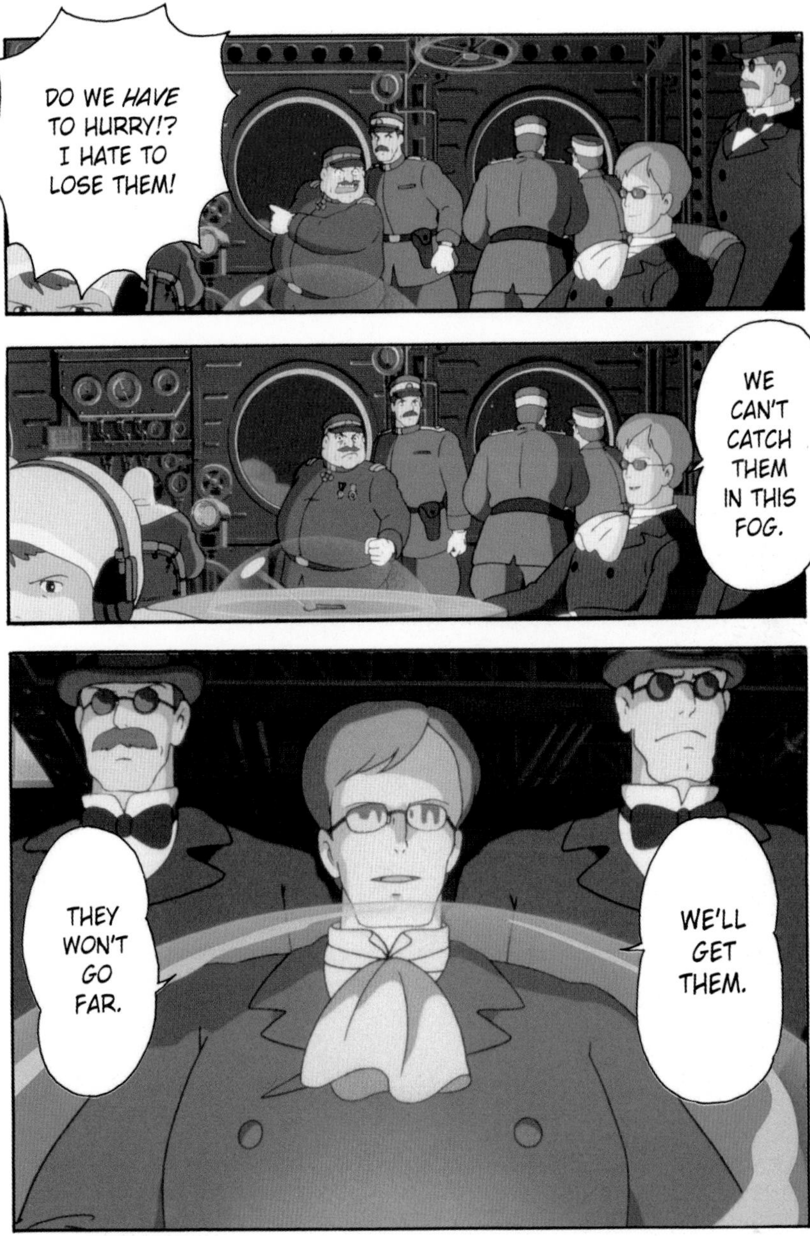
DO WE *HAVE* TO HURRY!? I HATE TO LOSE THEM!
WE CAN'T CATCH THEM IN THIS FOG.
WE'LL GET THEM.
THEY WON'T GO FAR.

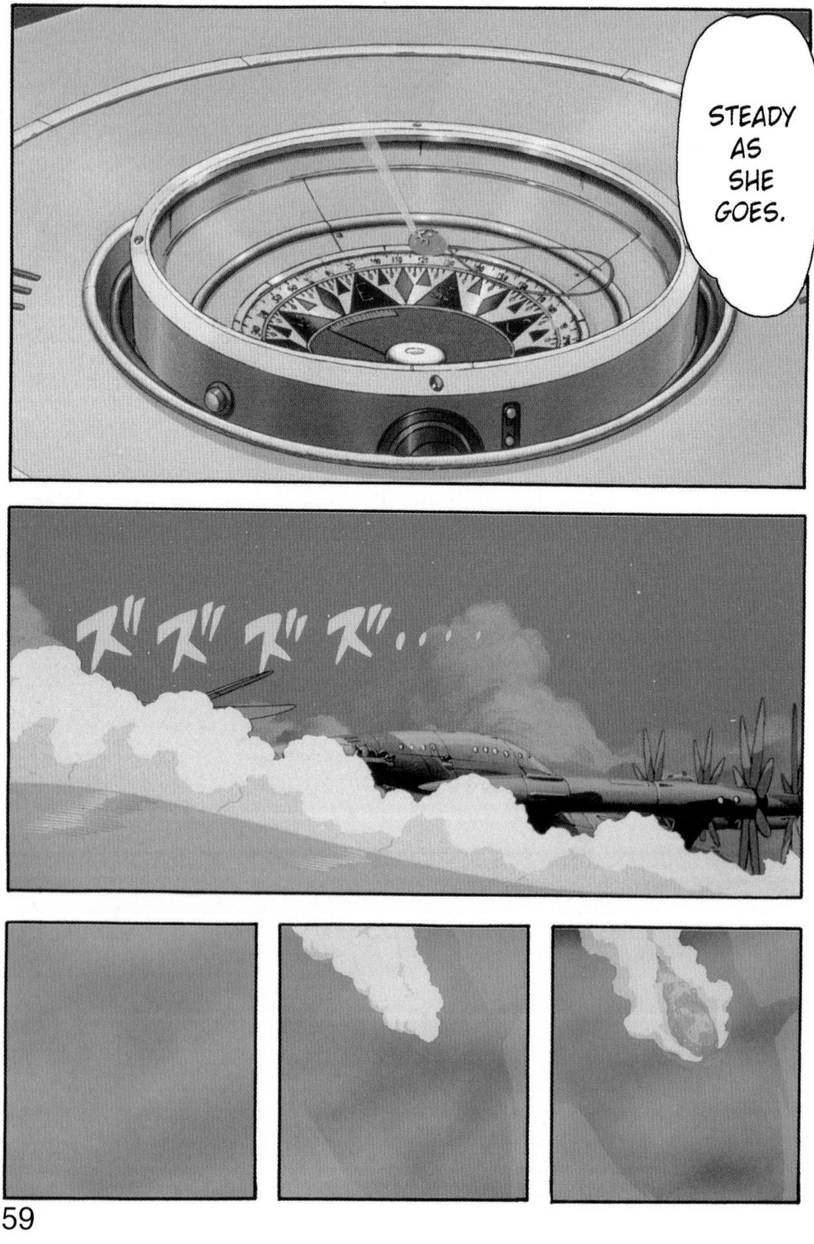
STEADY AS SHE GOES.
ズズズズ....

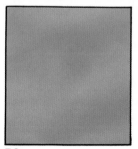

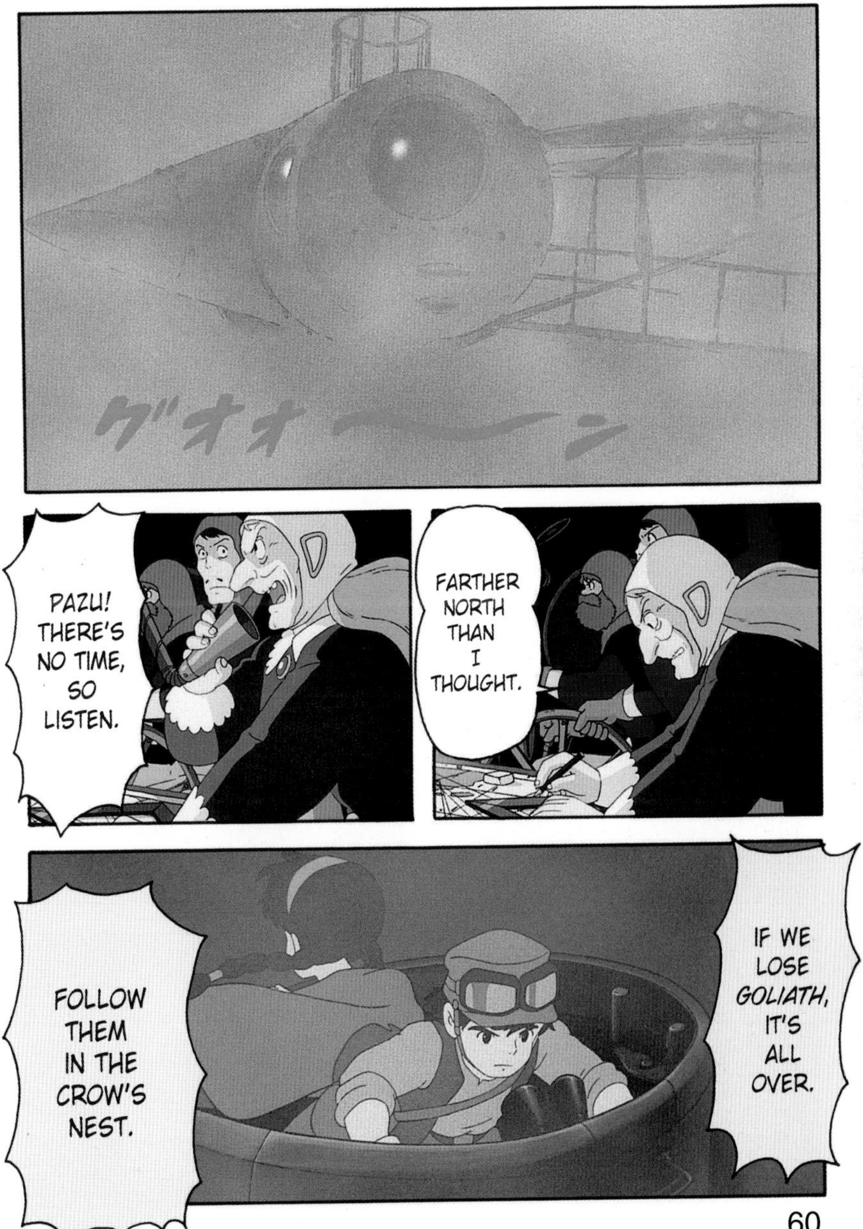
グオオ〜〜ン
FARTHER NORTH THAN I THOUGHT.
PAZU! THERE'S NO TIME, SO LISTEN.
IF WE LOSE GOLIATH, IT'S ALL OVER.
FOLLOW THEM IN THE CROW'S NEST.

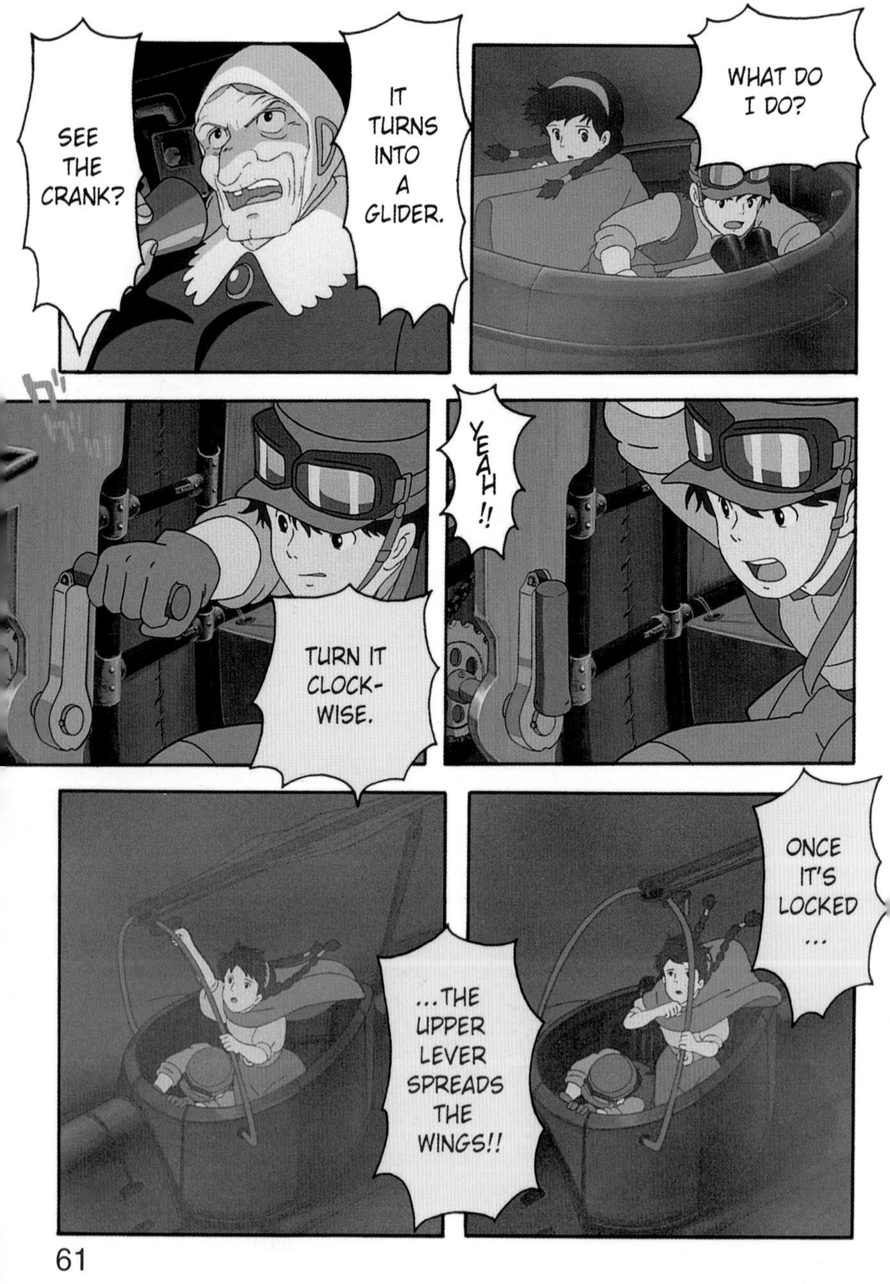
WHAT DO I DO?
IT TURNS INTO A GLIDER.
SEE THE CRANK?
YEAH!!
TURN IT CLOCK-WISE.
ONCE IT'S LOCKED ...
...THE UPPER LEVER SPREADS THE WINGS!!

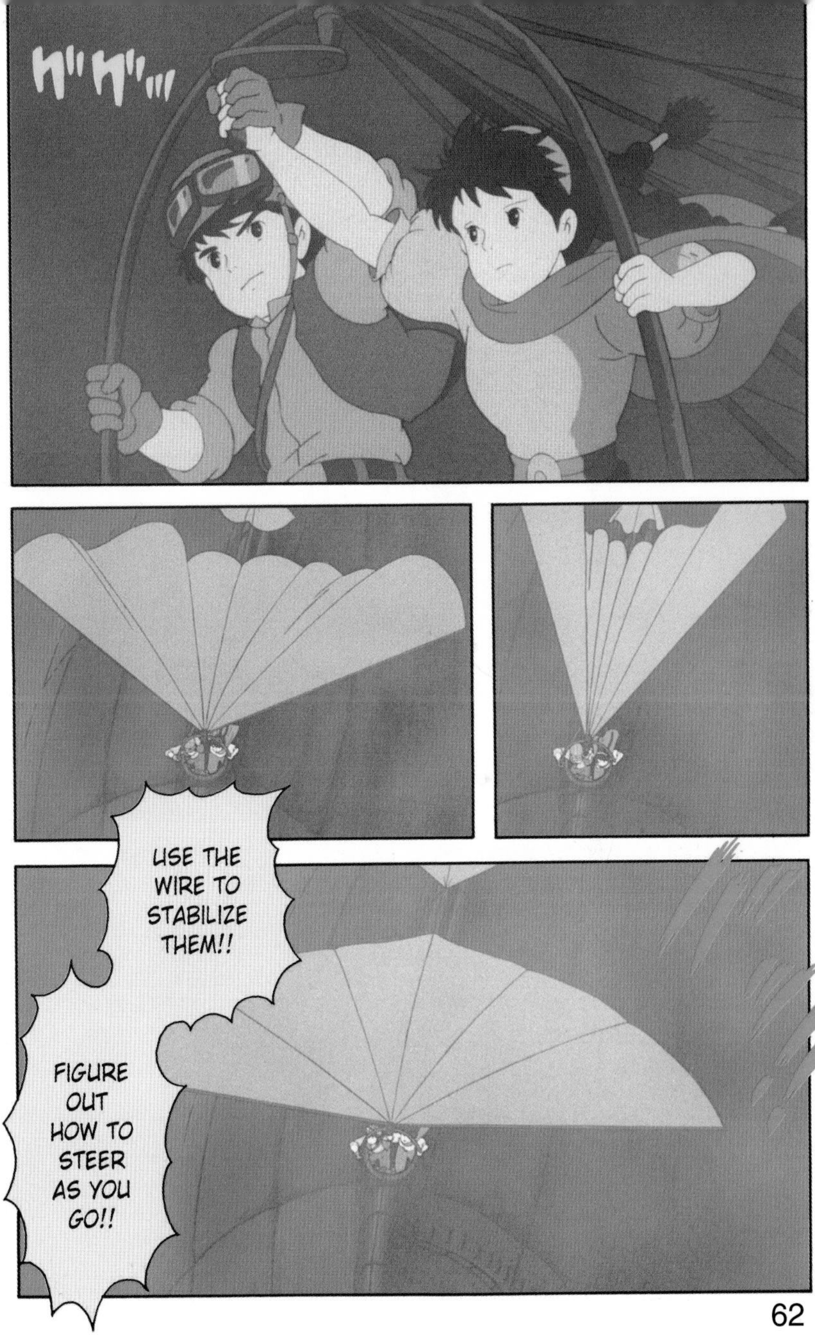
USE THE WIRE TO STABILIZE THEM!!
FIGURE OUT HOW TO STEER AS YOU GO!!

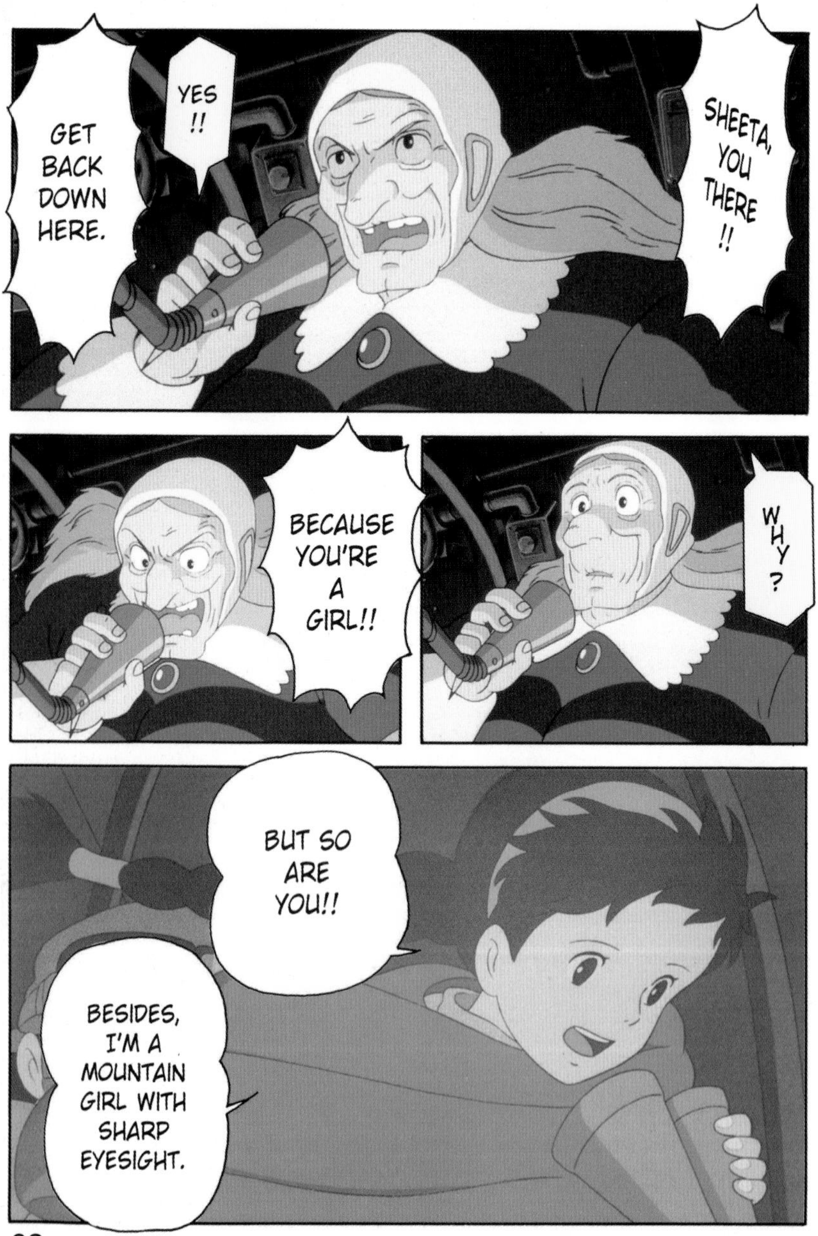
SHEETA, YOU THERE!!
YES!!
GET BACK DOWN HERE.
WHY?
BECAUSE YOU'RE A GIRL!!
BUT SO ARE YOU!!
BESIDES, I'M A MOUNTAIN GIRL WITH SHARP EYESIGHT.

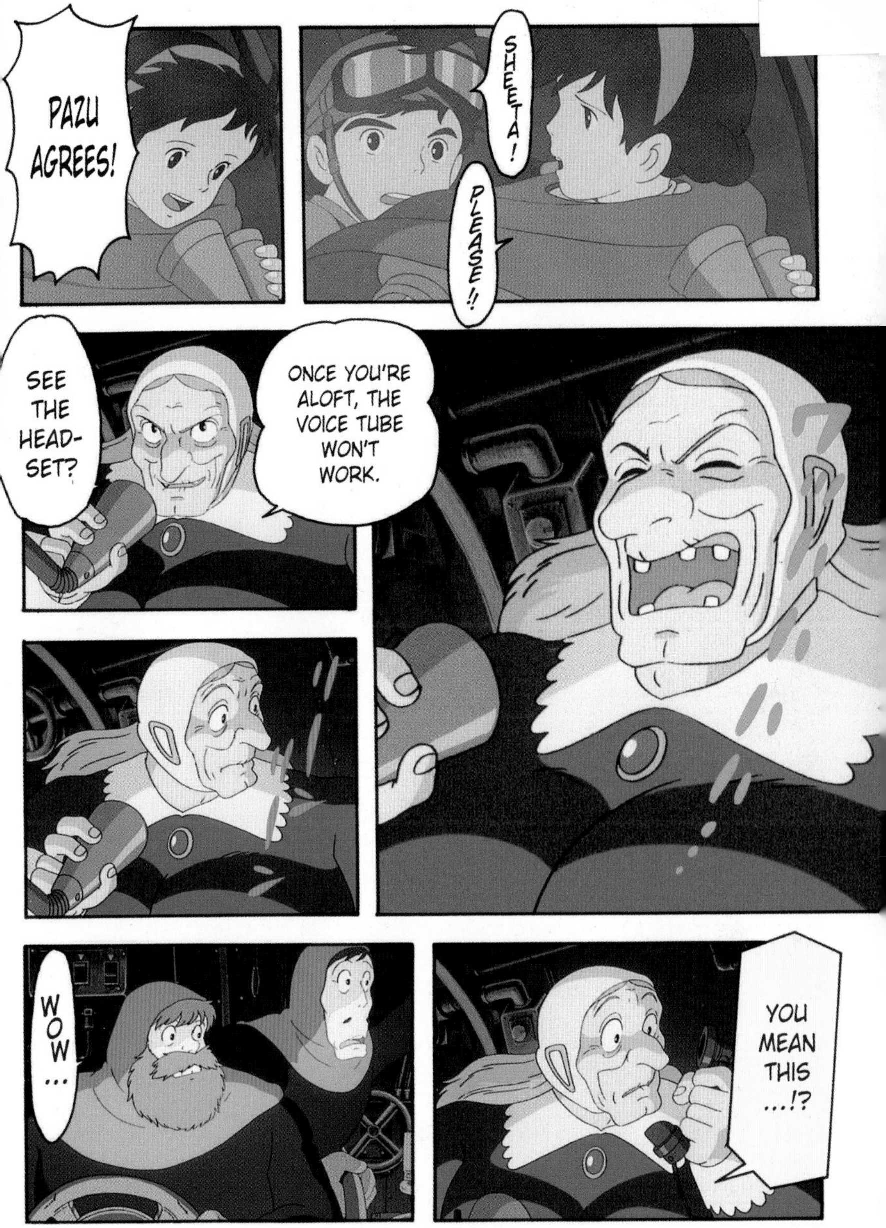
SHEETA!
PLEASE!!
PAZU AGREES!
ONCE YOU'RE ALOFT, THE VOICE TUBE WON'T WORK.
SEE THE HEAD-SET?
YOU MEAN THIS ...!?
WOW...

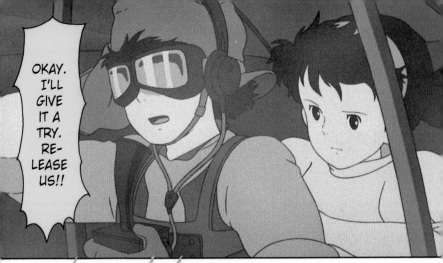

OKAY.
I'LL
GIVE
IT A
TRY.
RE-
LEASE
US!!

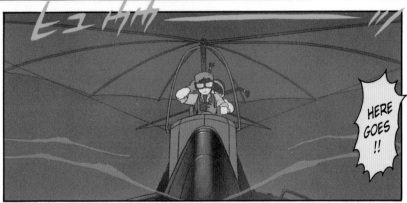

HERE
GOES
!!

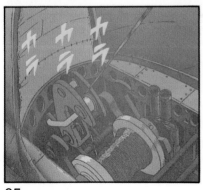

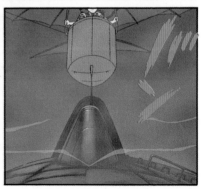

65

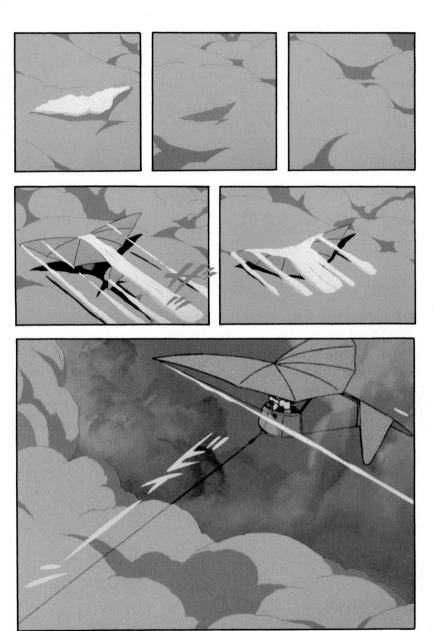

66

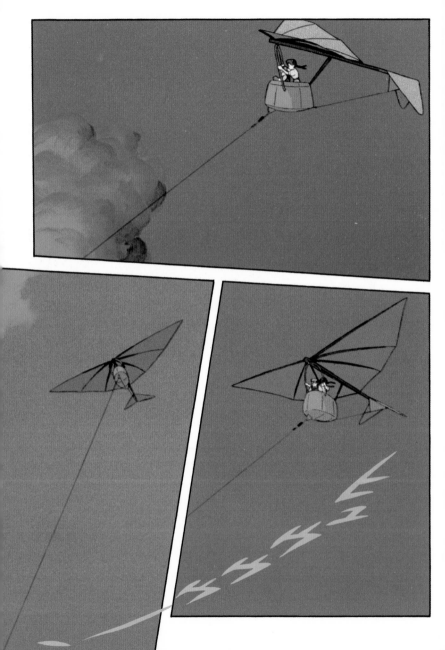

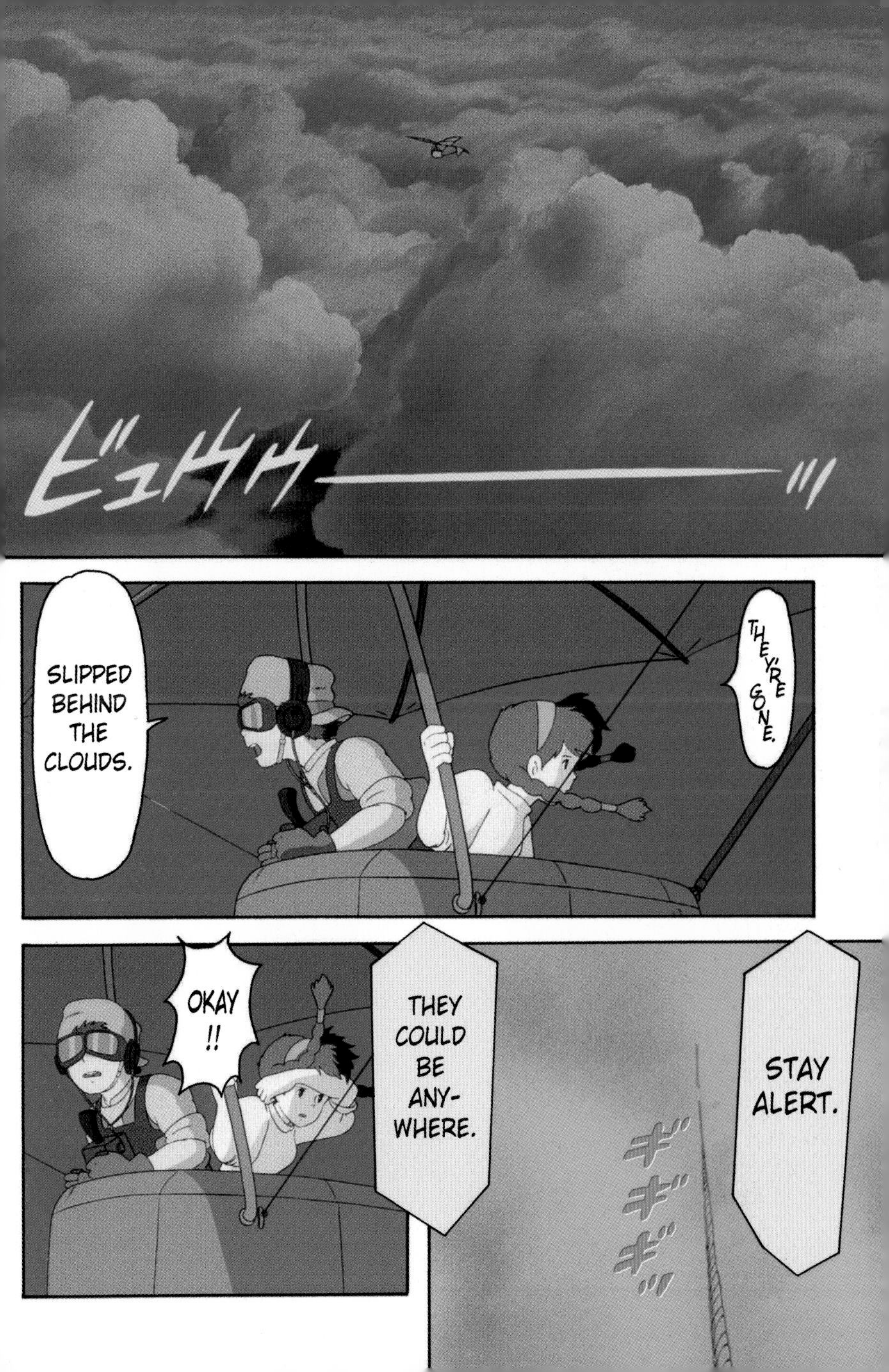
ビュウウーッ
THEY'RE GONE.
SLIPPED BEHIND THE CLOUDS.
STAY ALERT.
ギギギッ
THEY COULD BE ANY-WHERE.
OKAY !!

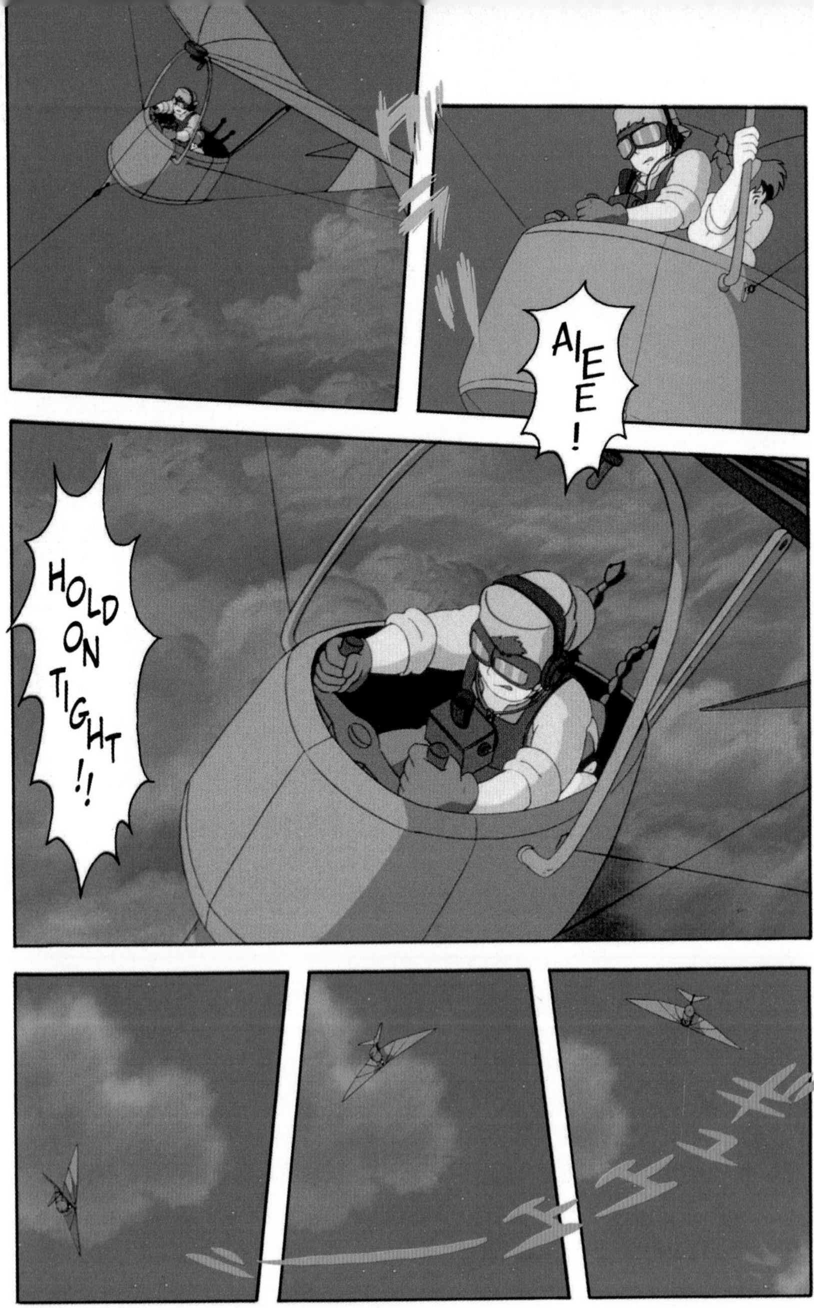
AIEEE!
HOLD ON TIGHT!!

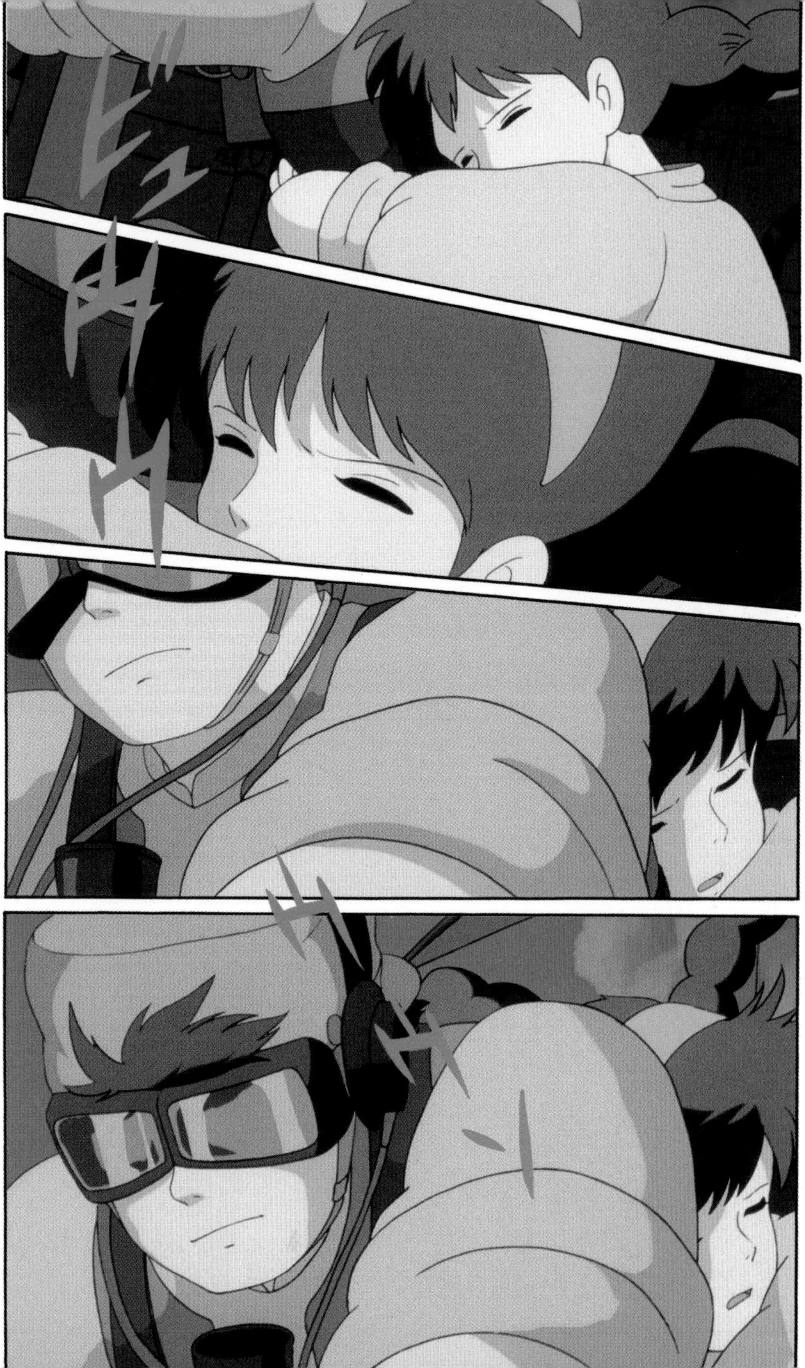
ビュ

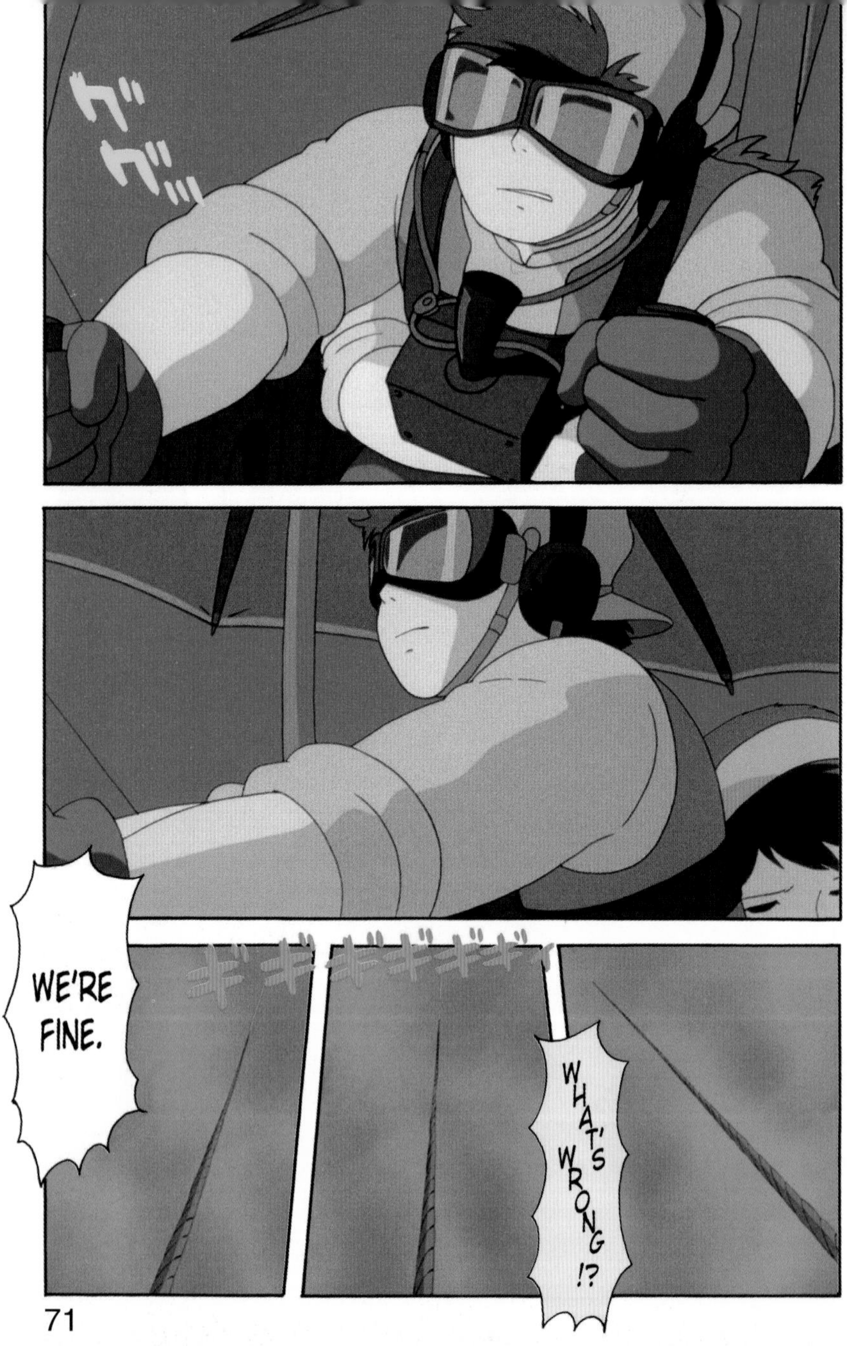
WHAT'S WRONG!?
WE'RE FINE.

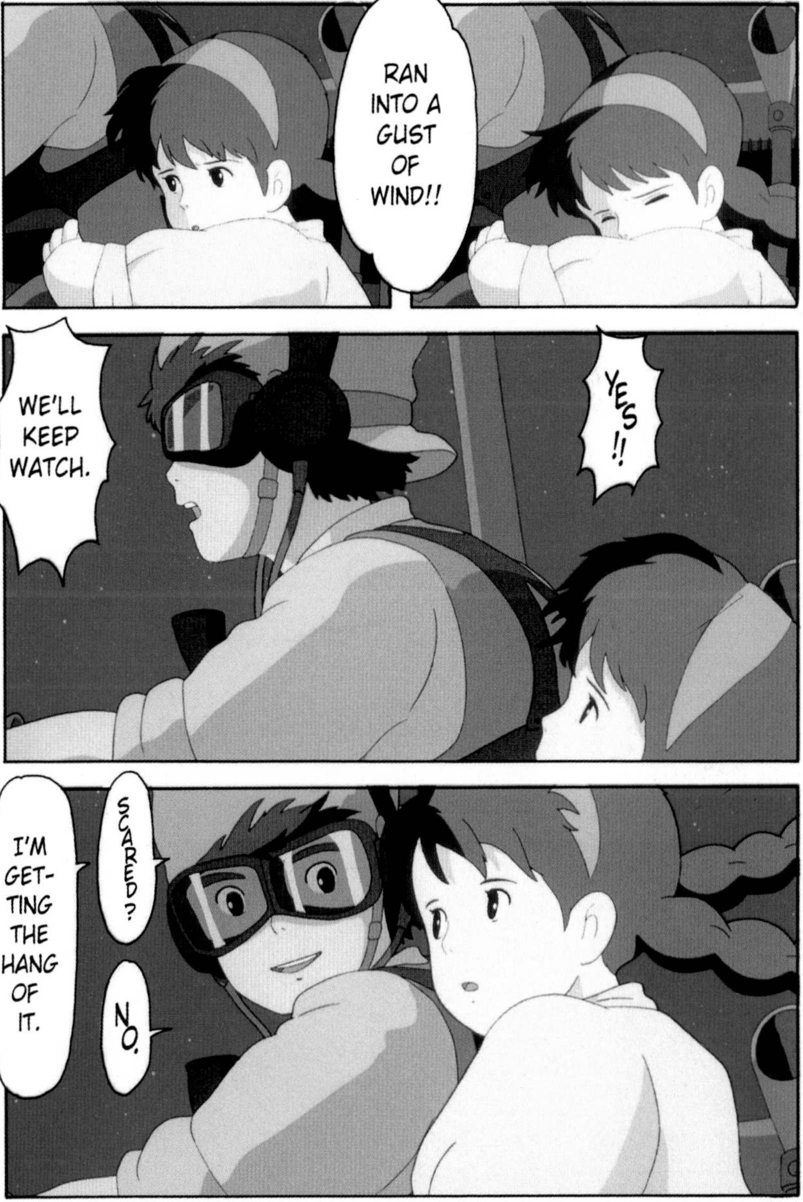
RAN INTO A GUST OF WIND!!
YES!!
WE'LL KEEP WATCH.
SCARED?
NO.
I'M GETTING THE HANG OF IT.

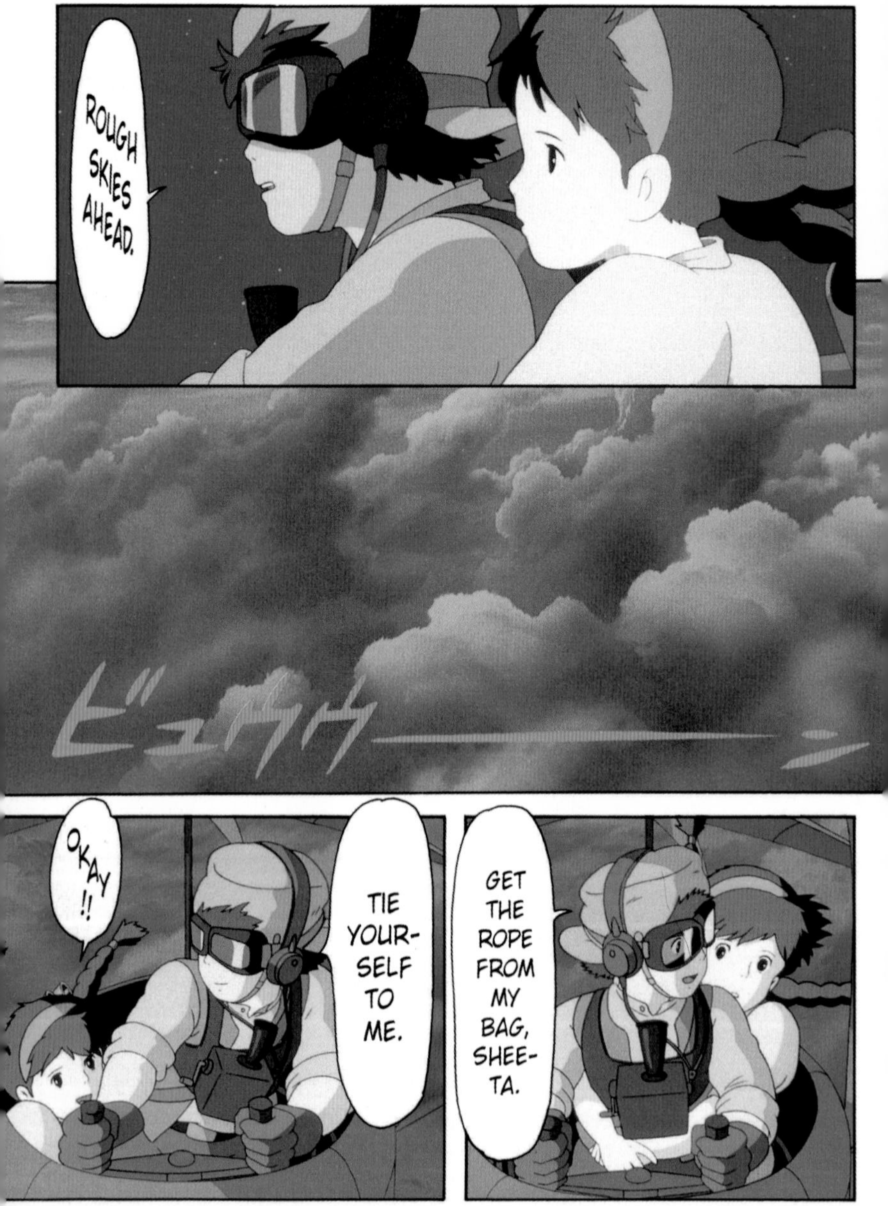
ROUGH SKIES AHEAD.
ビュウウ
GET THE ROPE FROM MY BAG, SHEETA.
TIE YOURSELF TO ME.
OKAY!!

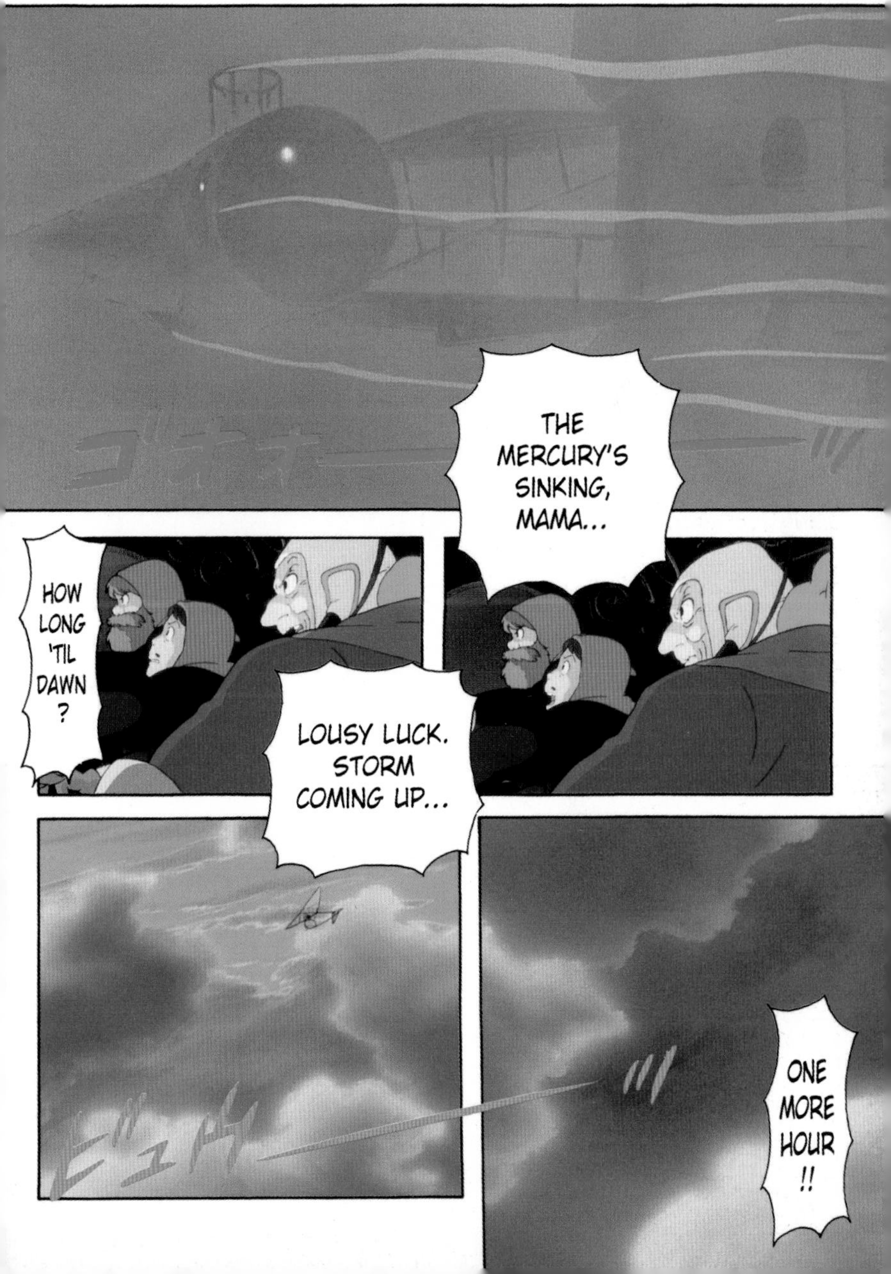
THE MERCURY'S SINKING, MAMA...
LOUSY LUCK. STORM COMING UP...
HOW LONG 'TIL DAWN?
ONE MORE HOUR!!

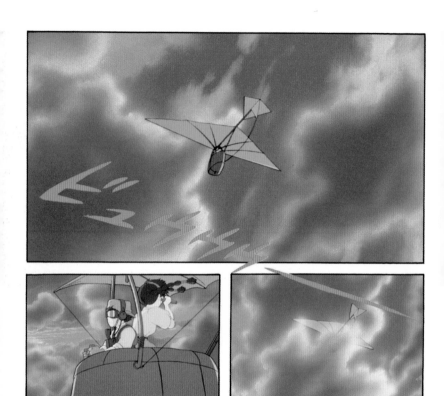

IT'S DAWN!!

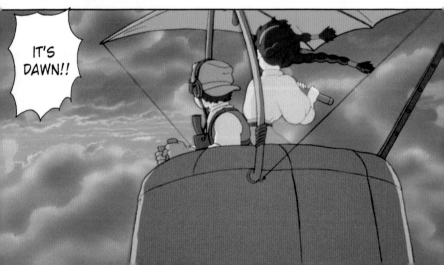

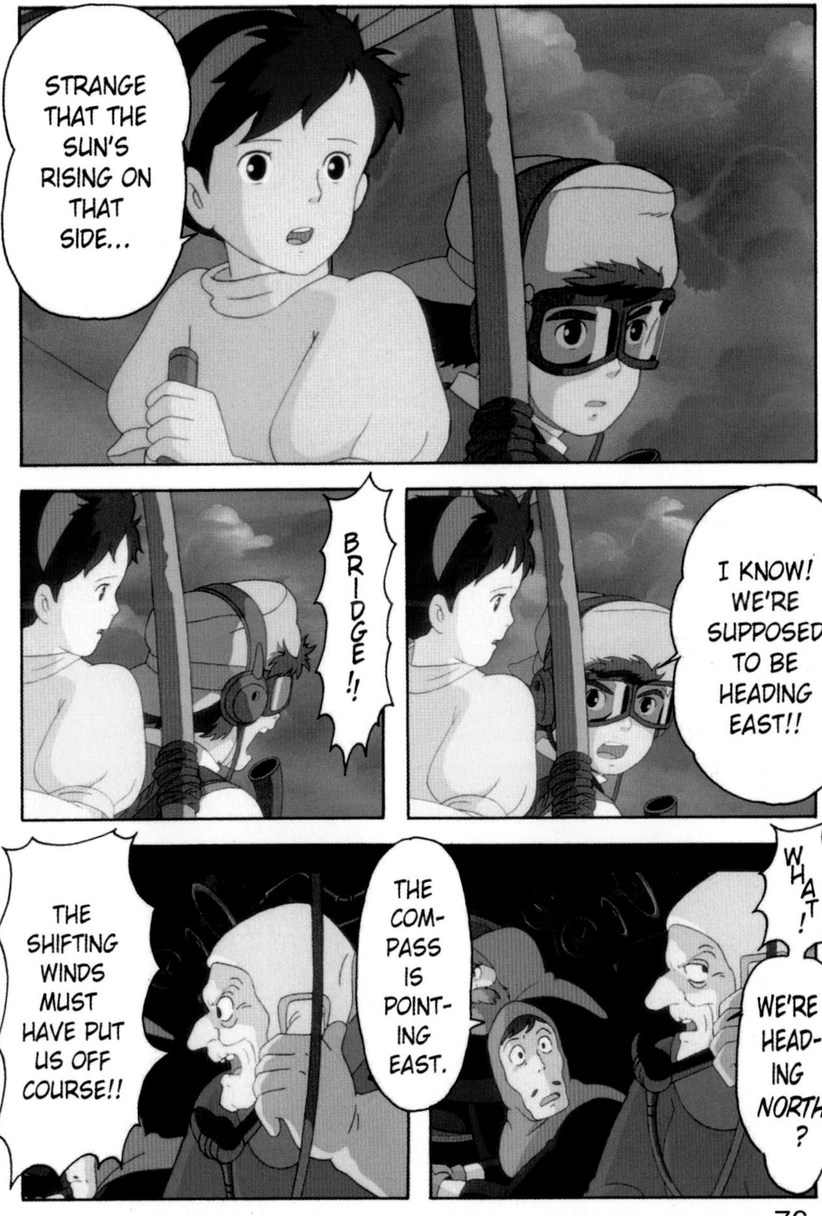
STRANGE THAT THE SUN'S RISING ON THAT SIDE...
I KNOW! WE'RE SUPPOSED TO BE HEADING EAST!!
BRIDGE!!
WHAT!
WE'RE HEADING NORTH?
THE COMPASS IS POINTING EAST.
THE SHIFTING WINDS MUST HAVE PUT US OFF COURSE!!

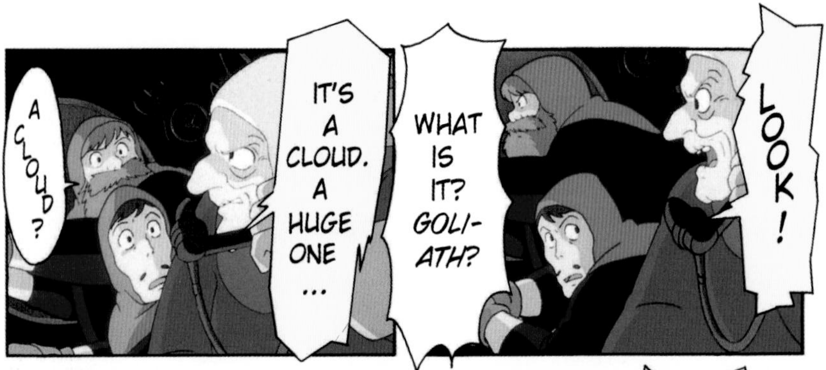
LOOK!
WHAT IS IT? GOLI-ATH?
IT'S A CLOUD. A HUGE ONE...
A CLOUD?
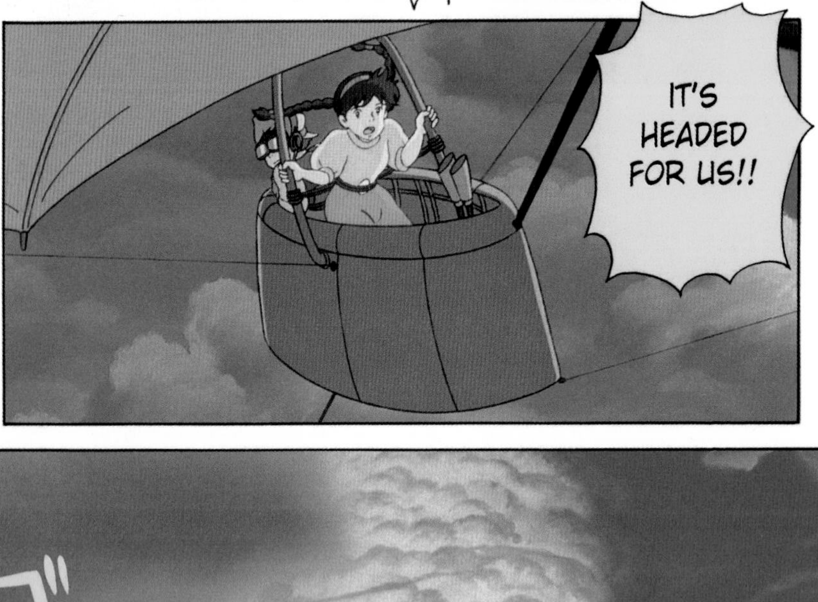
IT'S HEADED FOR US!!
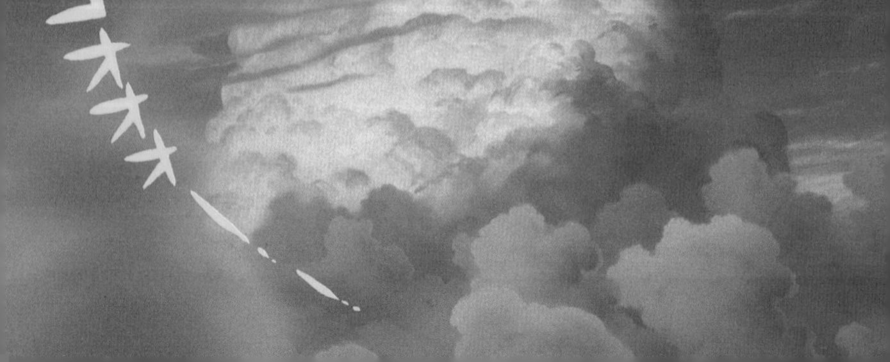
ゴオオオー

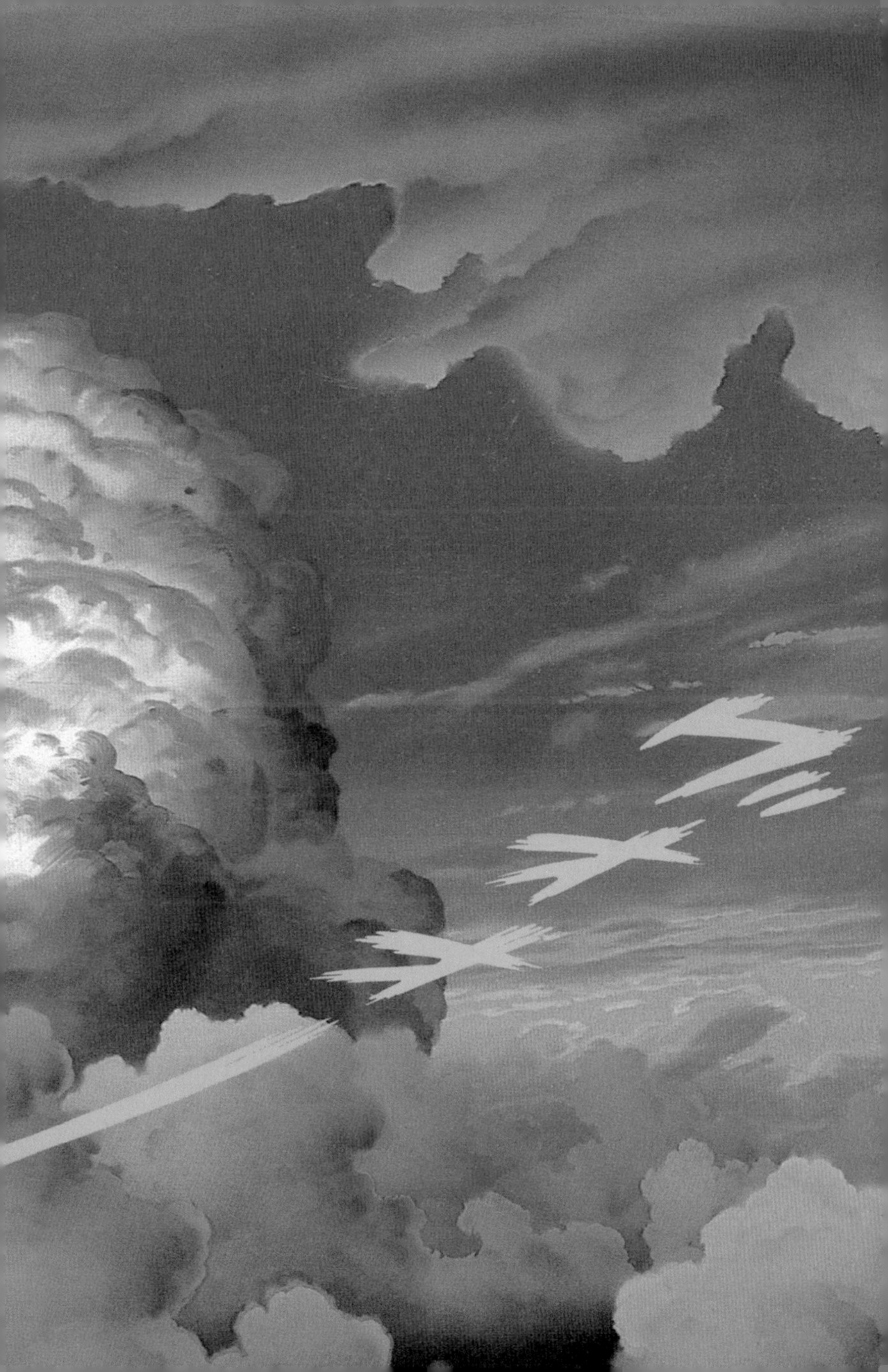

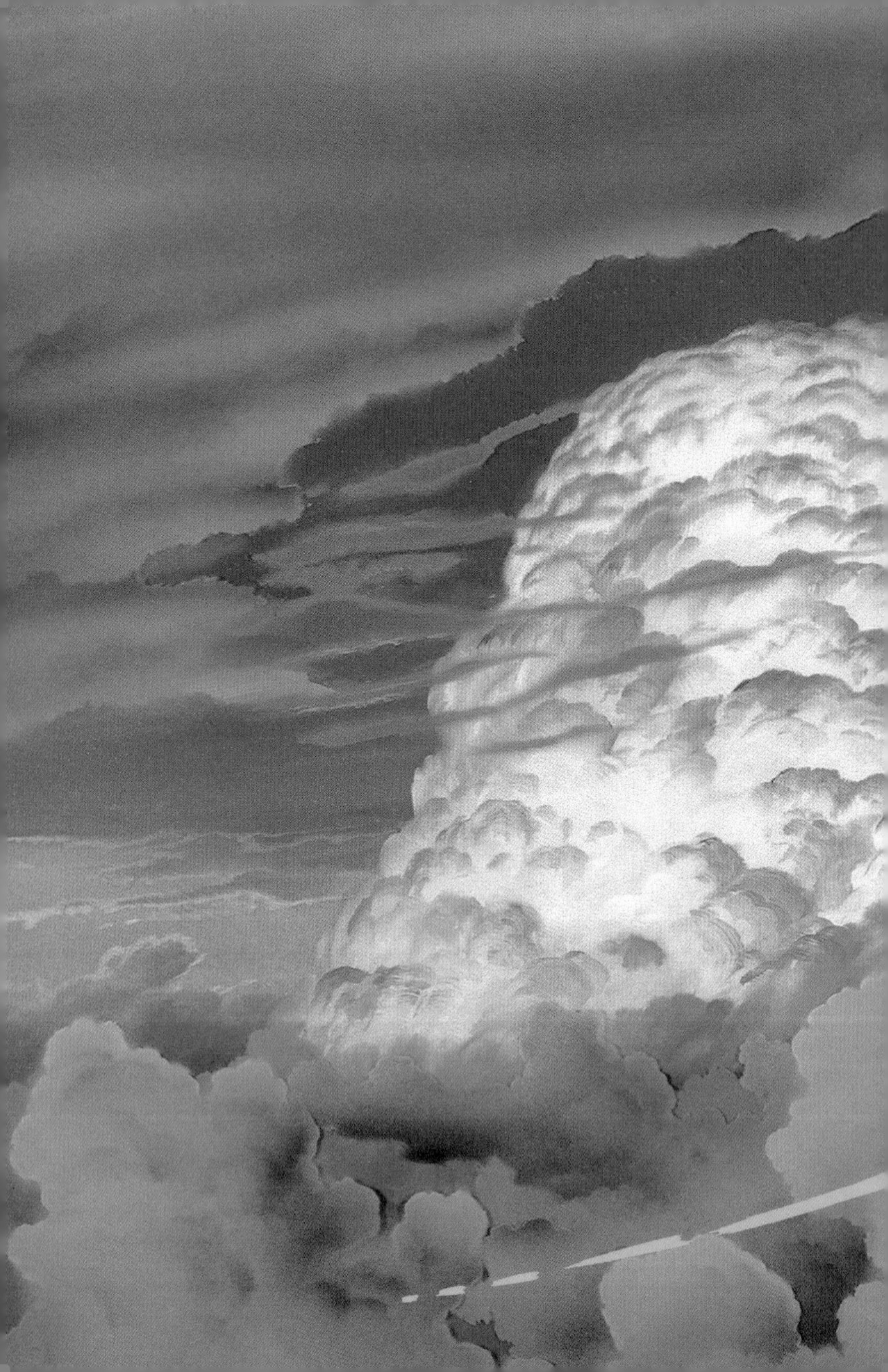

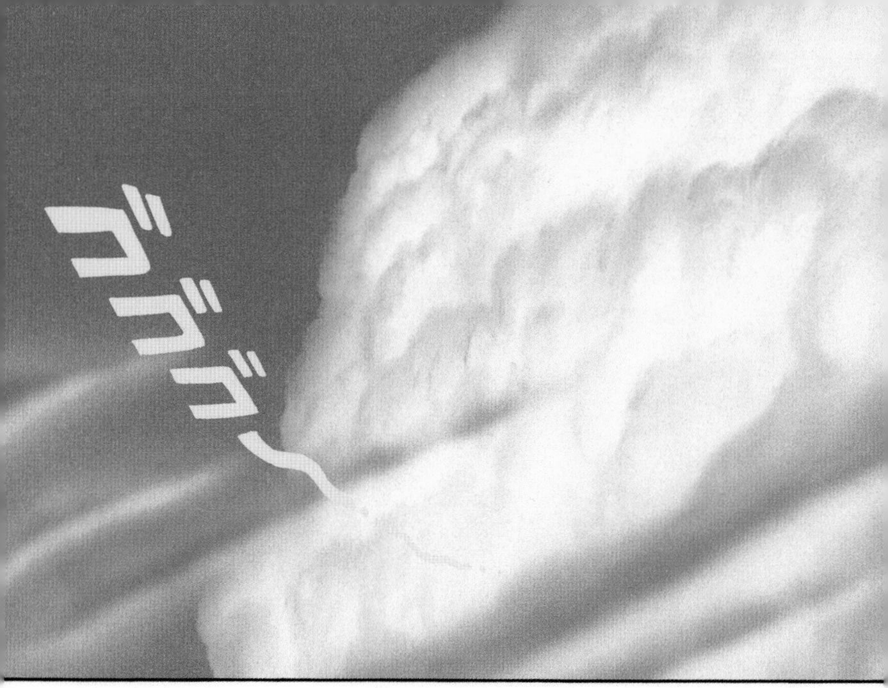
ゴゴゴ〜

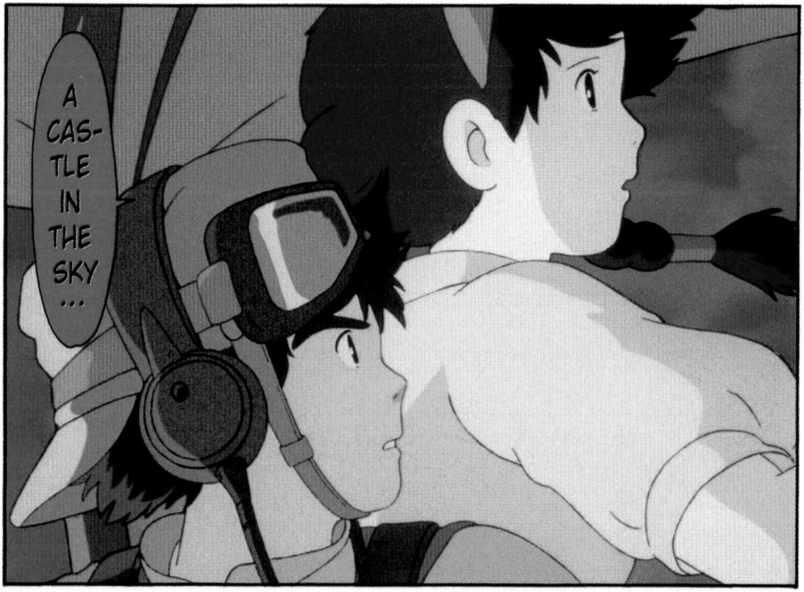
A CASTLE IN THE SKY...

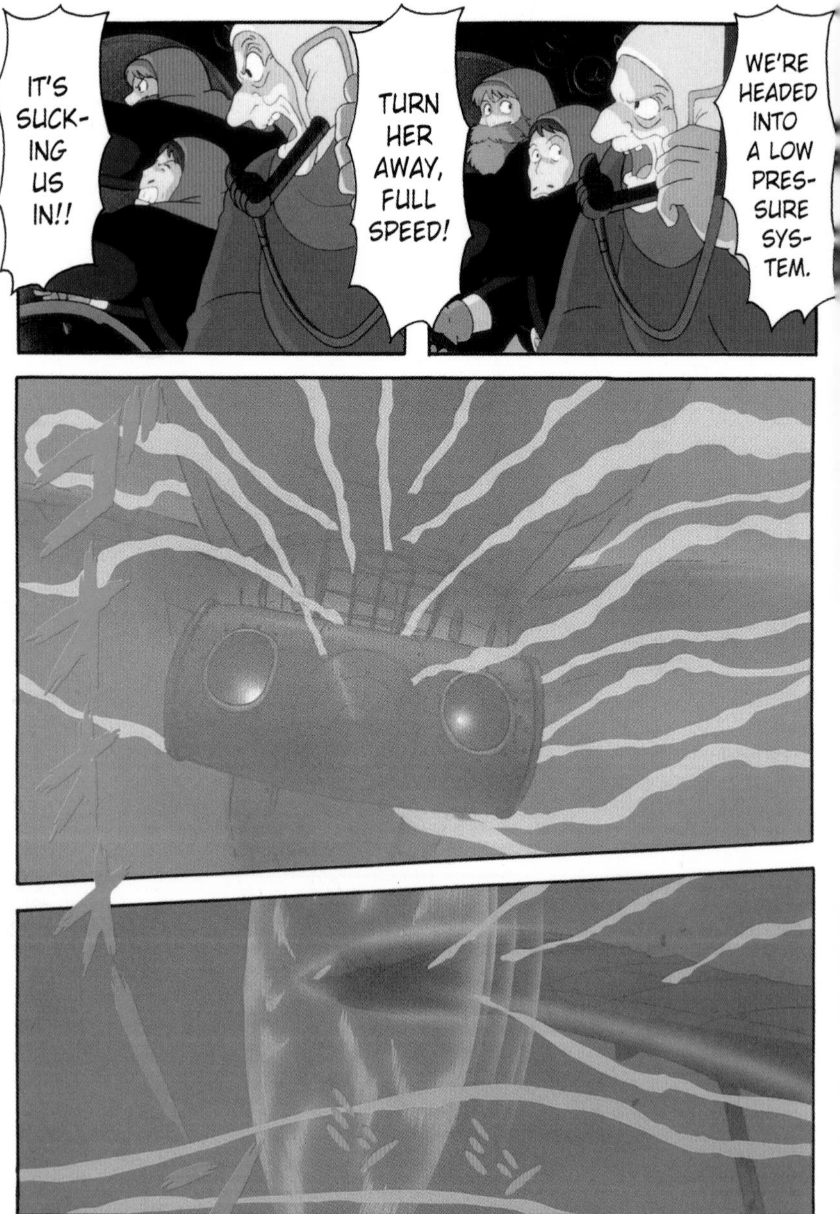
WE'RE HEADED INTO A LOW PRES-SURE SYS-TEM.
TURN HER AWAY, FULL SPEED!
IT'S SUCK-ING US IN!!

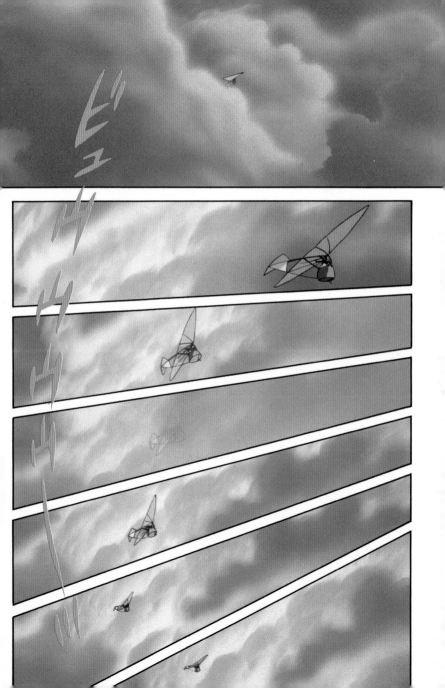

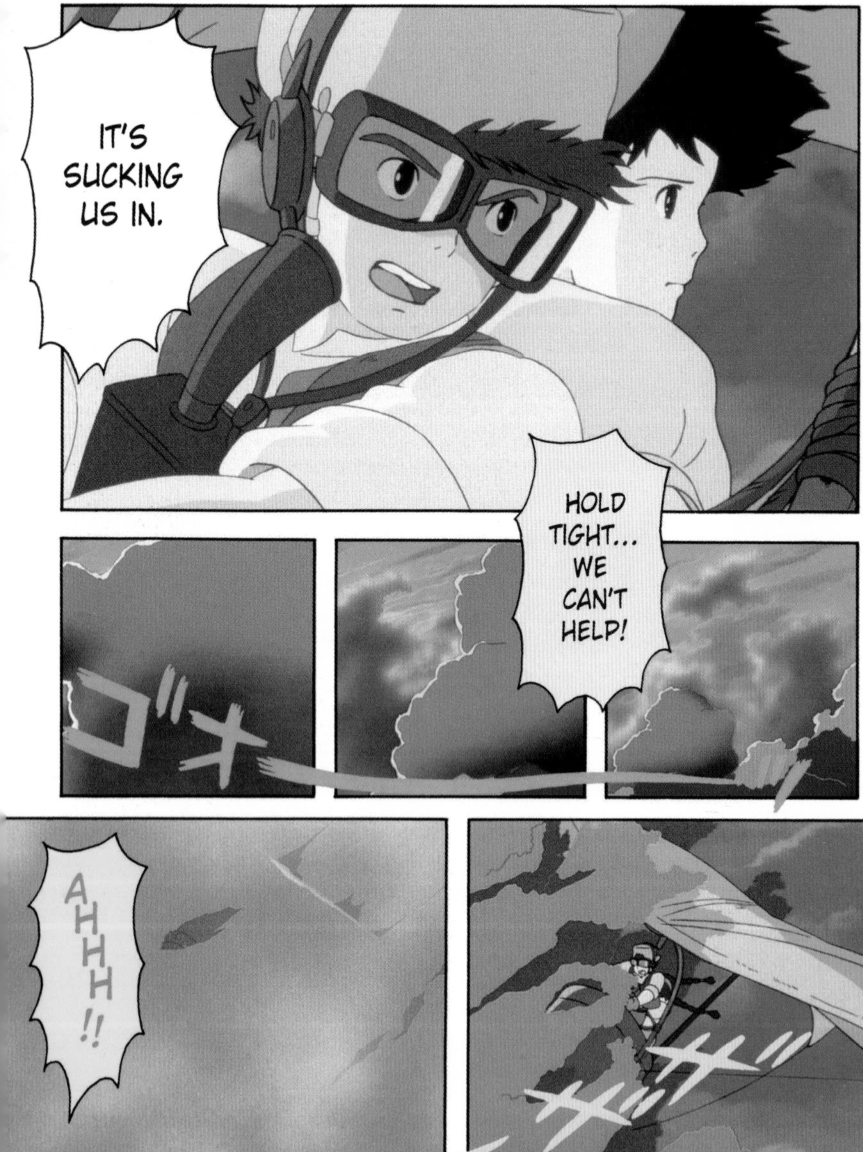
IT'S SUCKING US IN.
HOLD TIGHT... WE CAN'T HELP!
ゴオ
AHHH!!

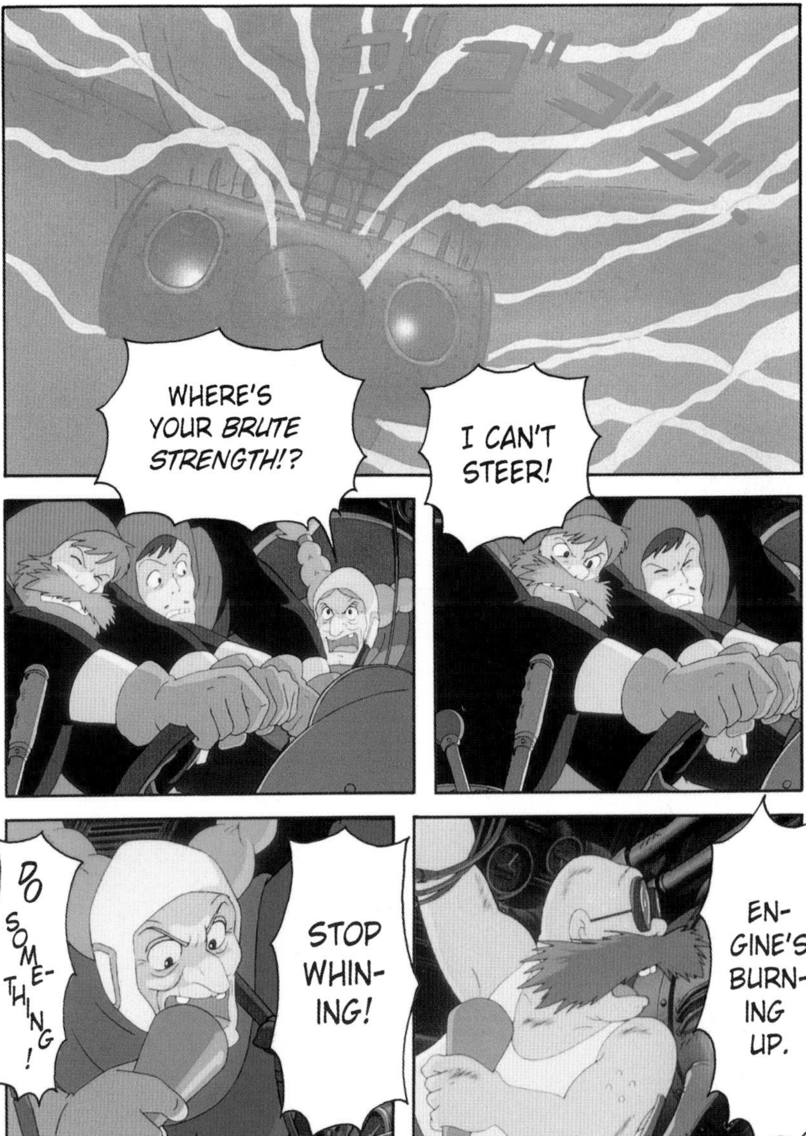
ゴゴゴゴ…
I CAN'T STEER!
WHERE'S YOUR BRUTE STRENGTH!?
ENGINE'S BURNING UP.
STOP WHINING!
DO SOMETHING!

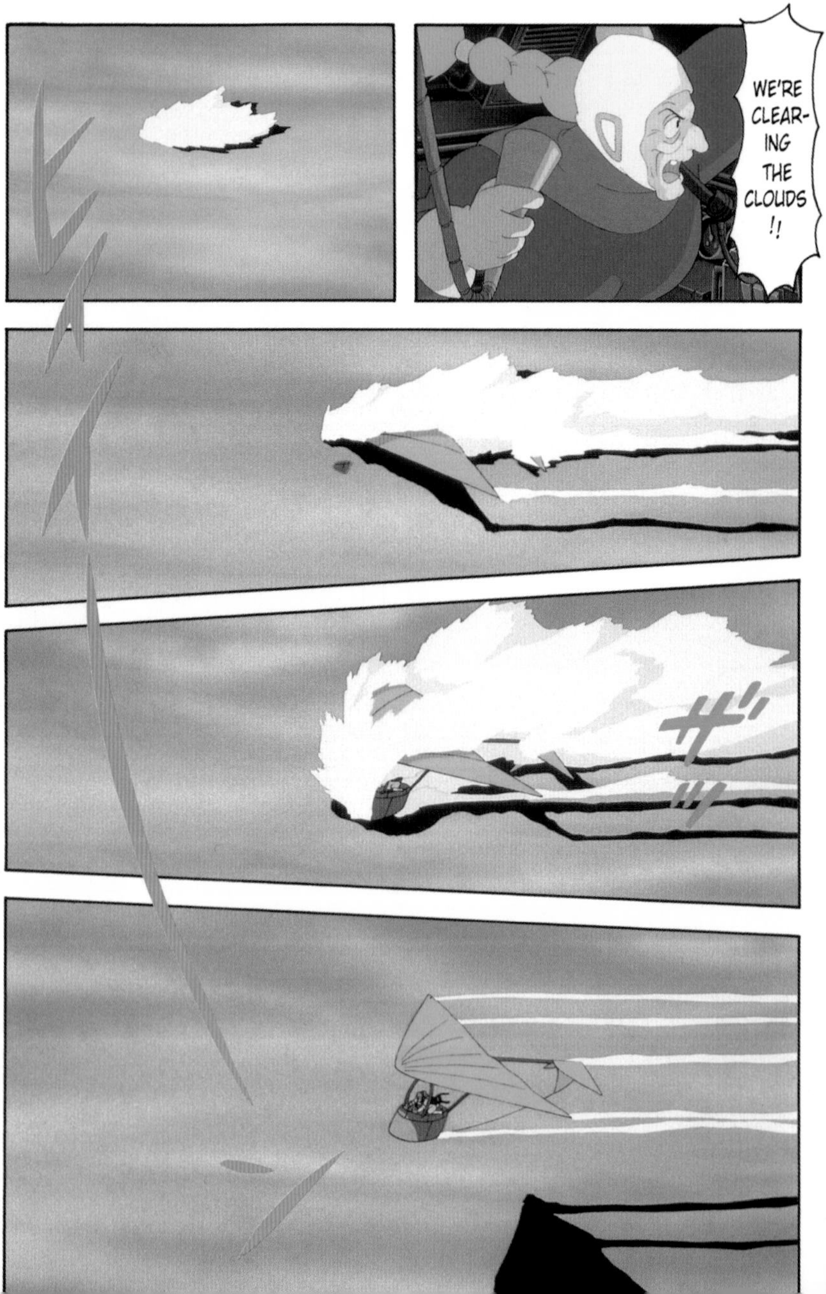
WE'RE CLEARING THE CLOUDS!!

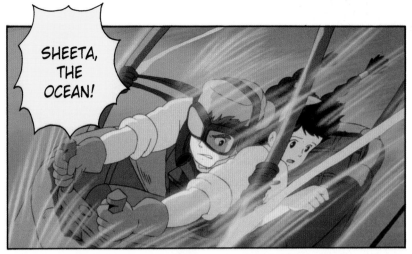

SHEETA, THE OCEAN!

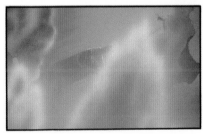

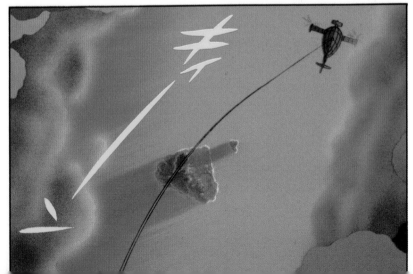

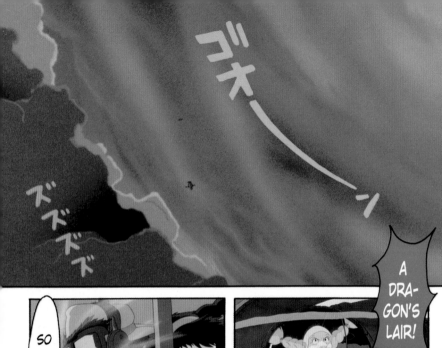

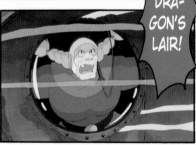

A DRA-GON'S LAIR!

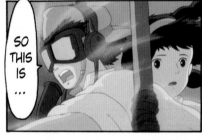

SO THIS IS ...

...A DRA-GON'S LAIR ...!?

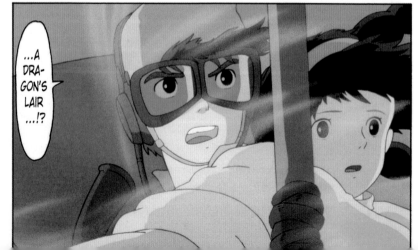

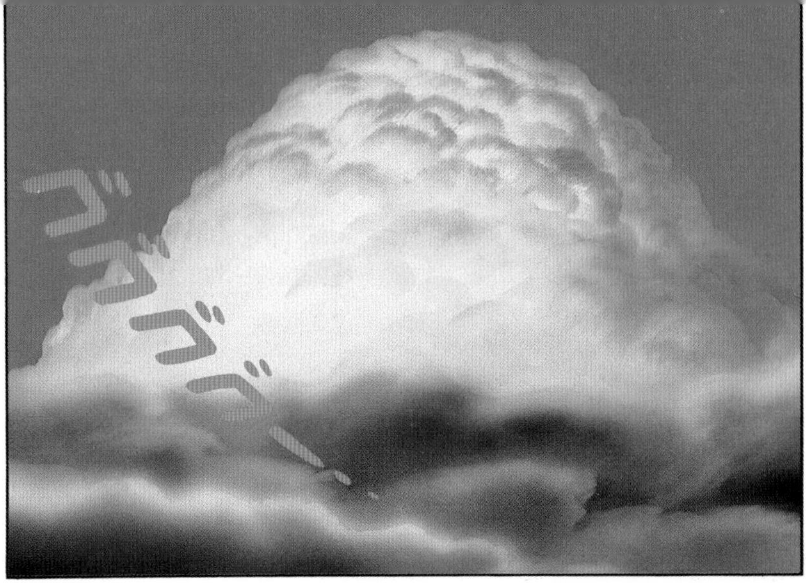
ゴゴゴゴー
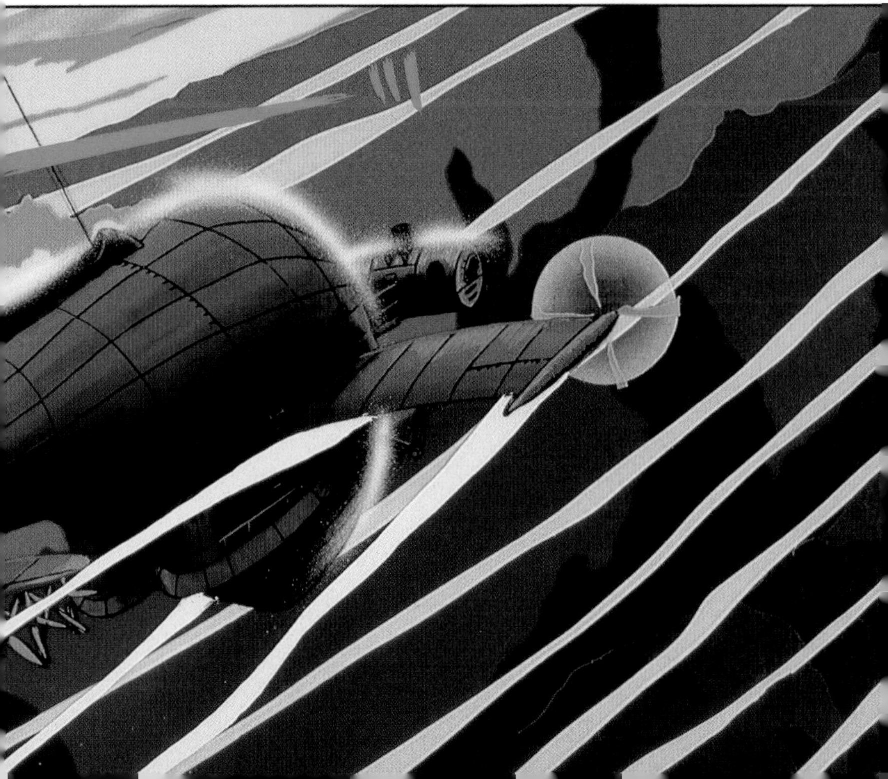

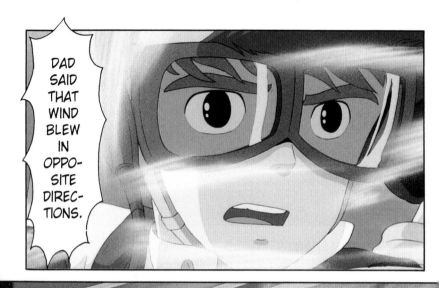

DAD SAID THAT WIND BLEW IN OPPOSITE DIRECTIONS.

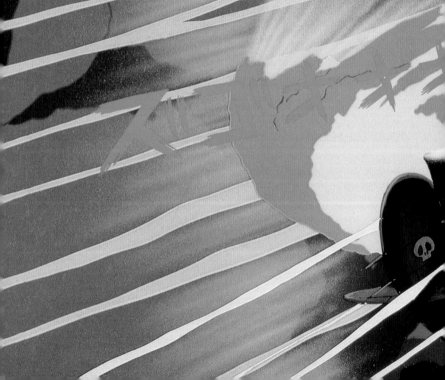

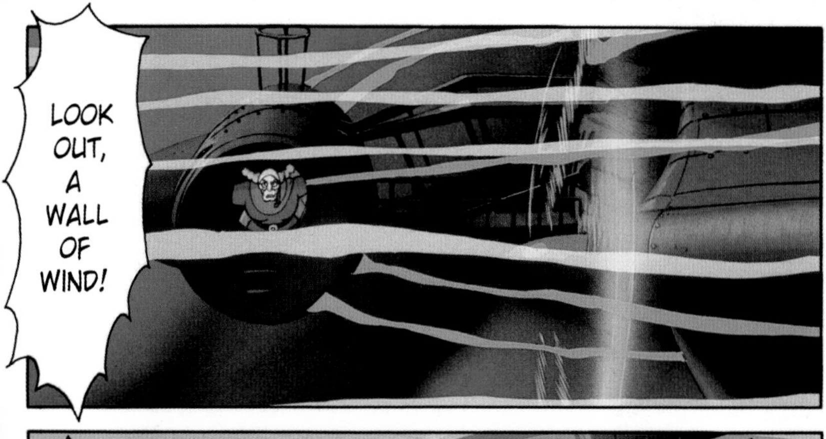
LOOK OUT, A WALL OF WIND!

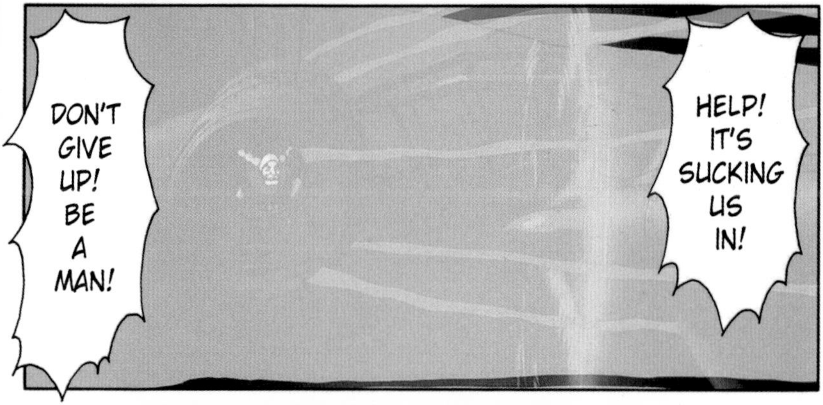
HELP! IT'S SUCKING US IN!
DON'T GIVE UP! BE A MAN!

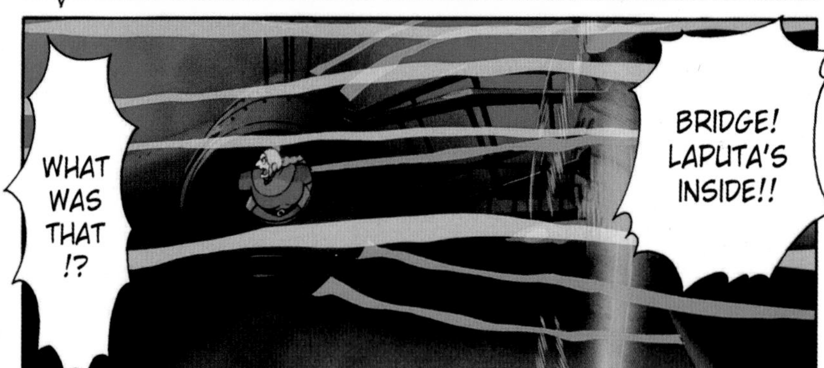
BRIDGE! LAPUTA'S INSIDE!!
WHAT WAS THAT!?

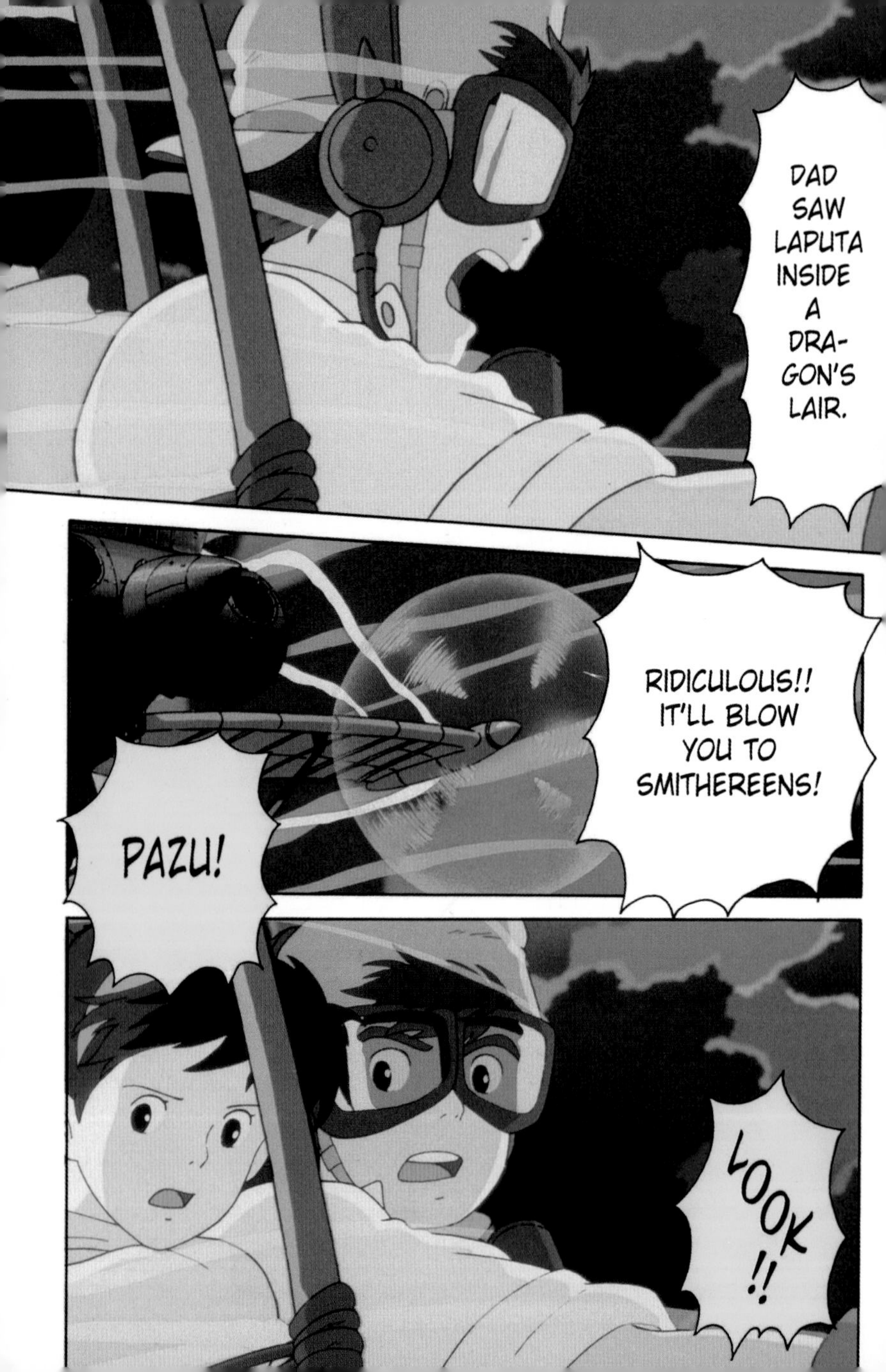
DAD SAW LAPUTA INSIDE A DRA-GON'S LAIR.
RIDICULOUS!! IT'LL BLOW YOU TO SMITHEREENS!
PAZU!
LOOK!!

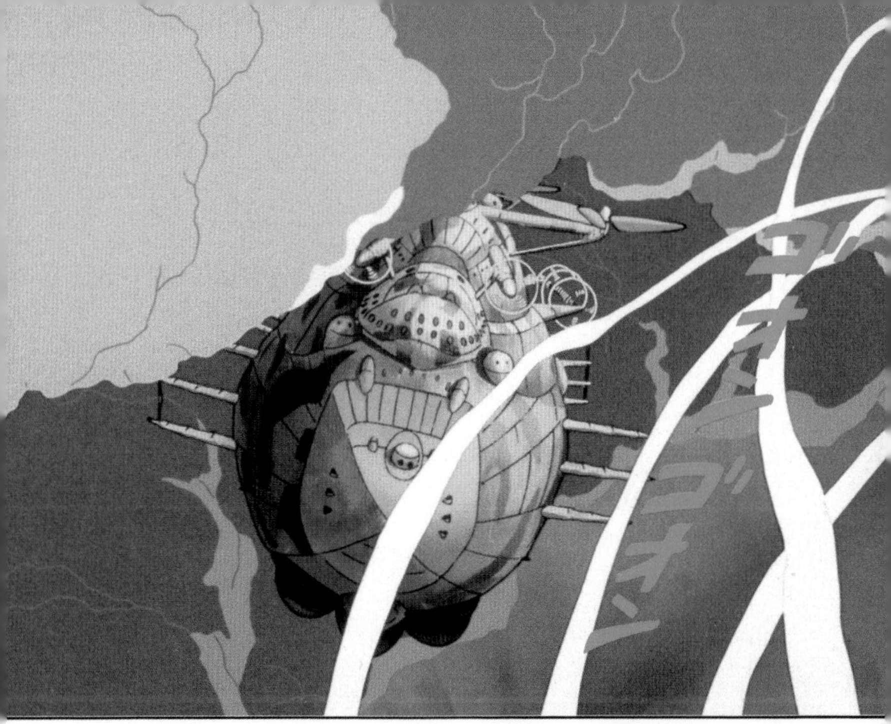

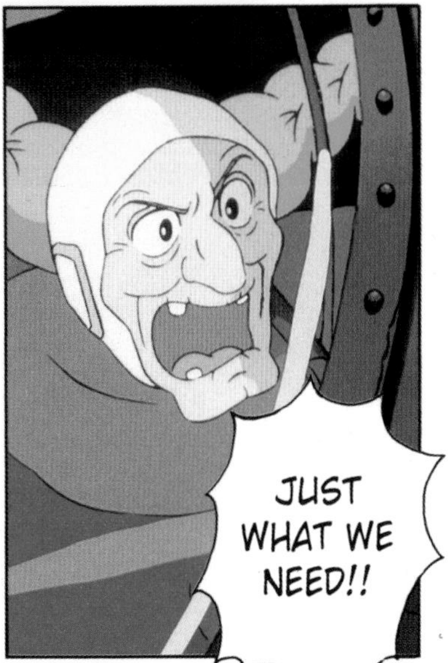
JUST WHAT WE NEED!!

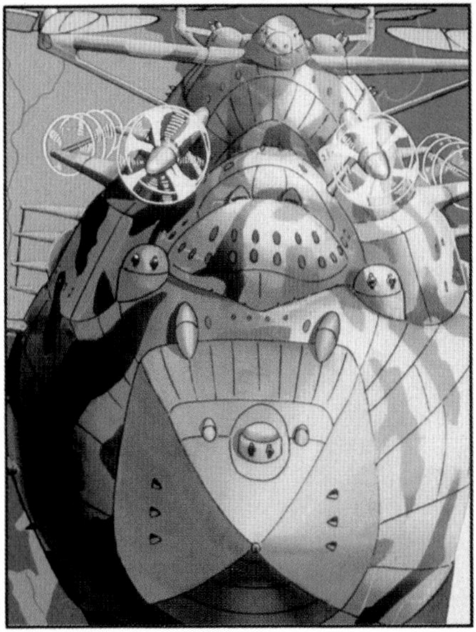

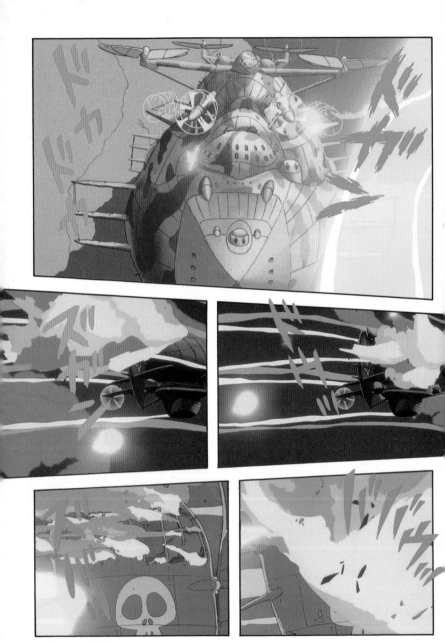

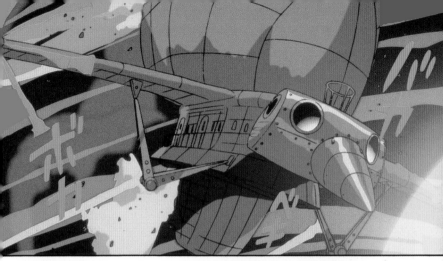

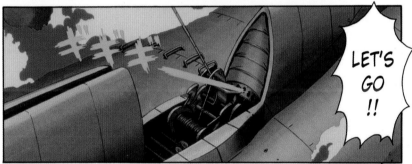

LET'S
GO
!!

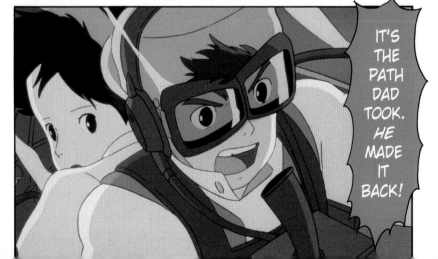

IT'S
THE
PATH
DAD
TOOK.
HE
MADE
IT
BACK!

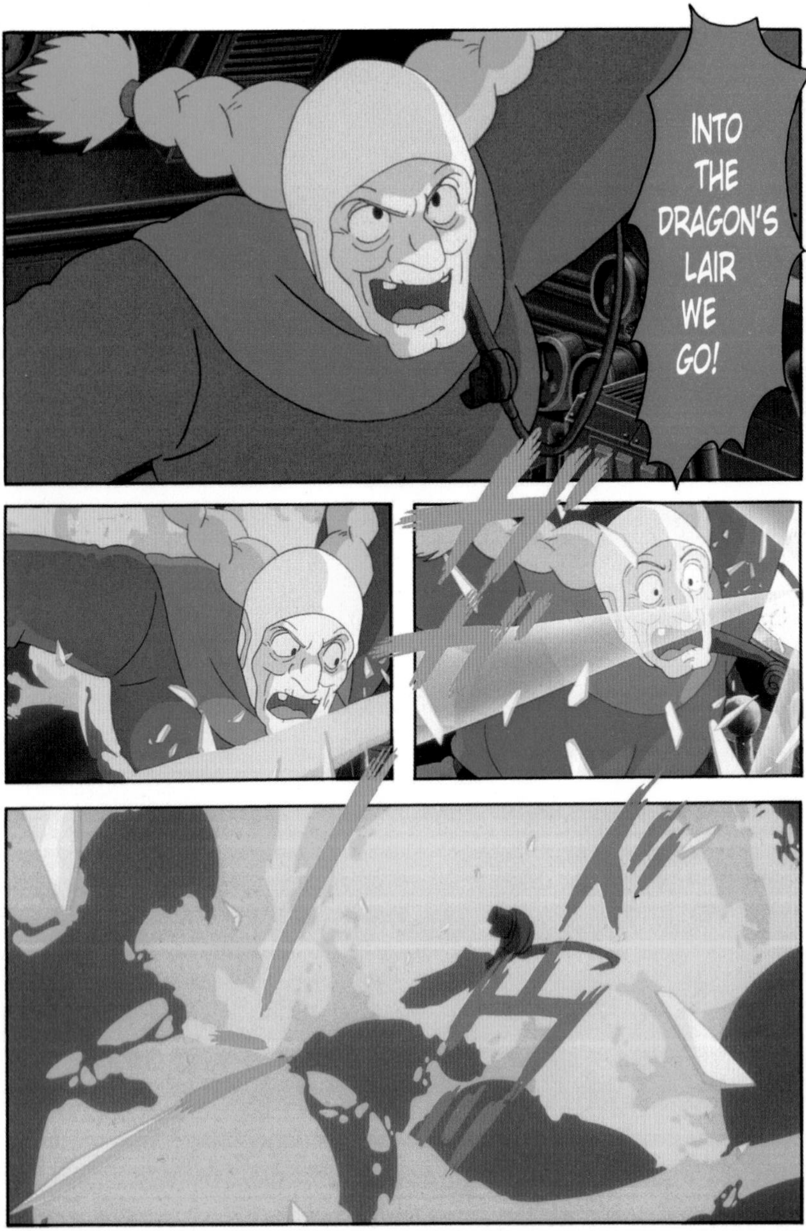
INTO THE DRAGON'S LAIR WE GO!

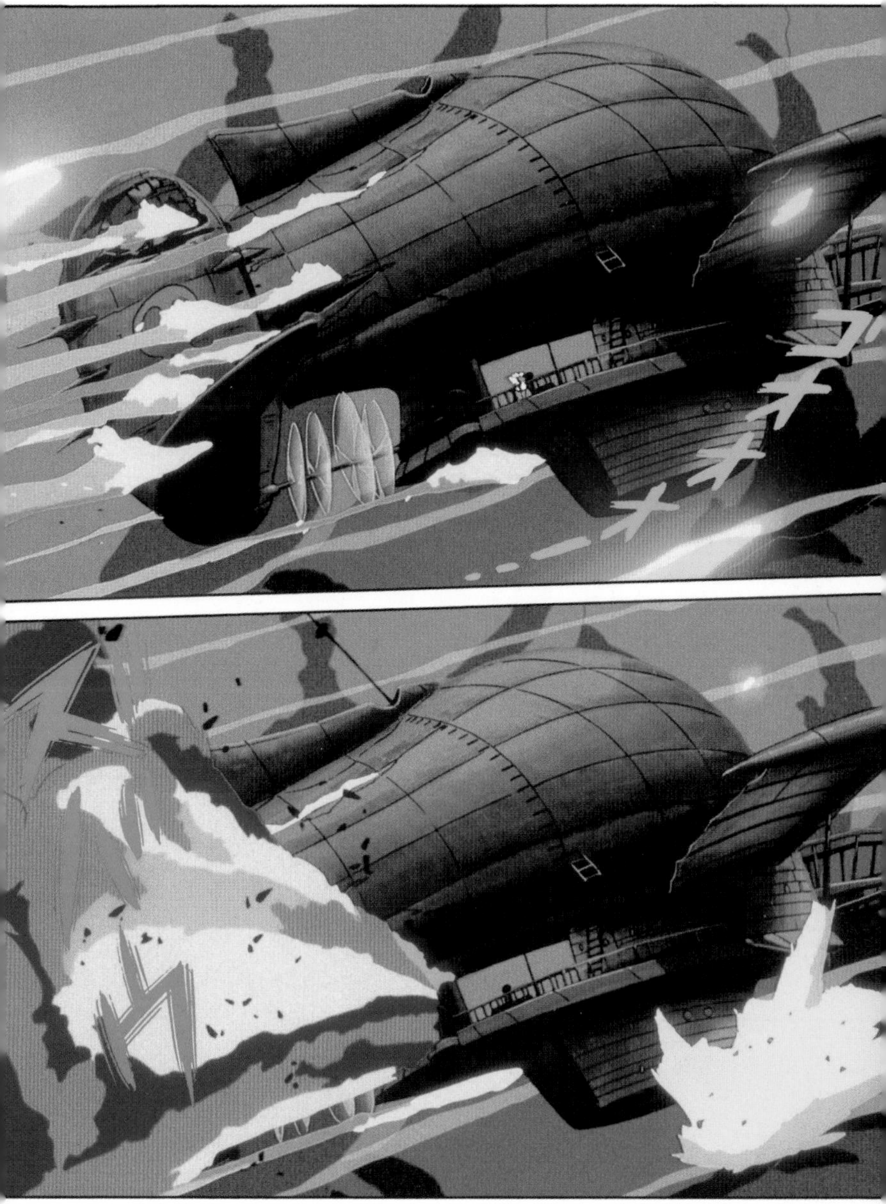
ゴオオオオ

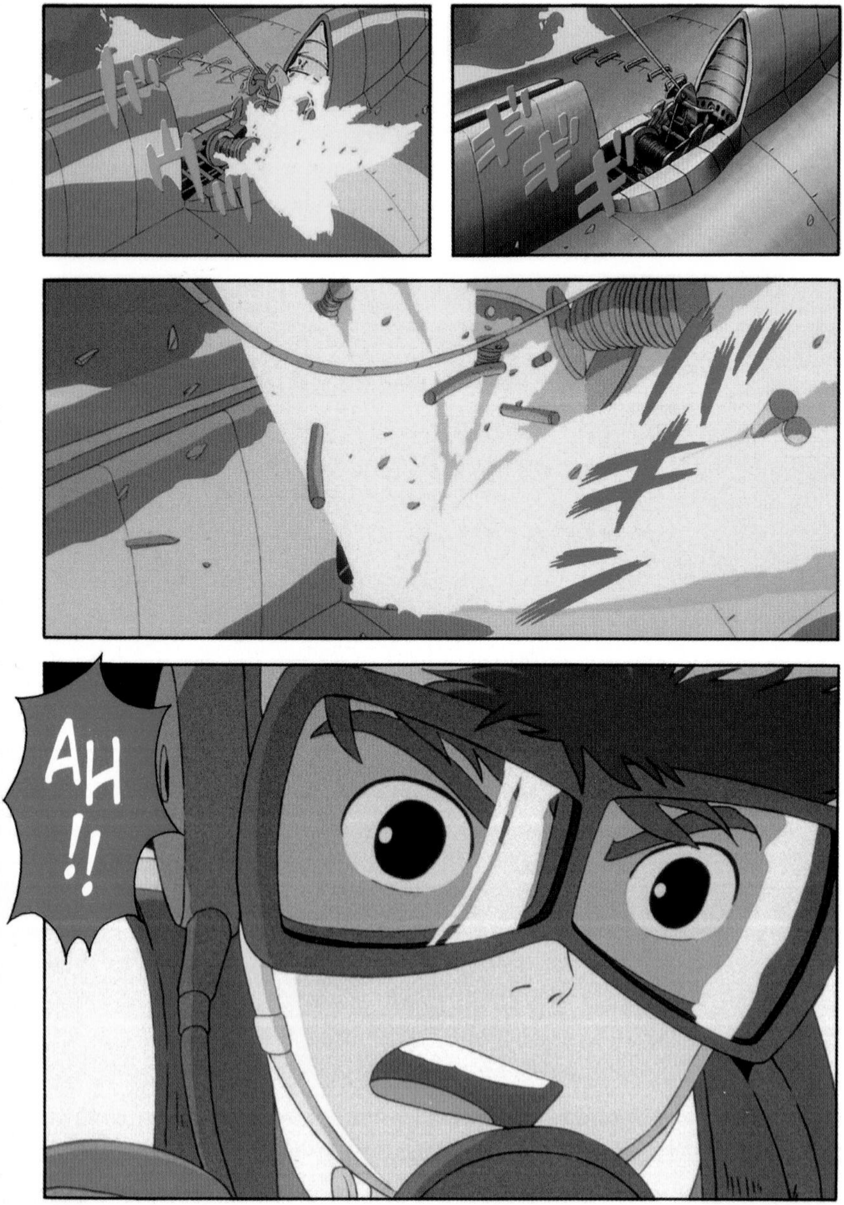
AH !!

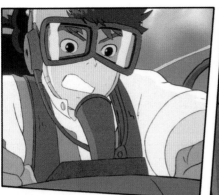
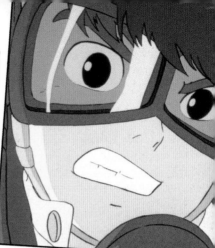
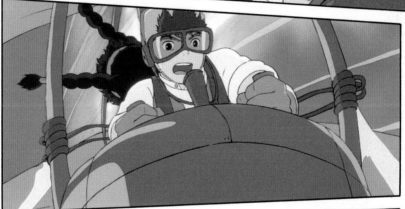
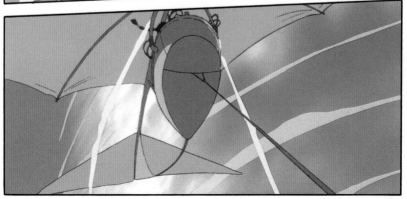

98

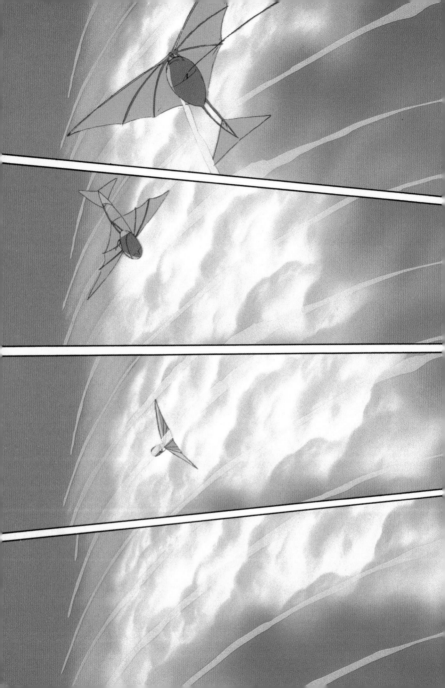

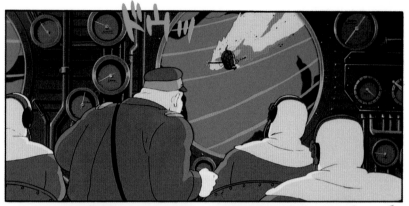

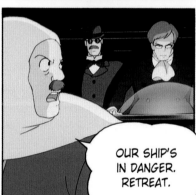

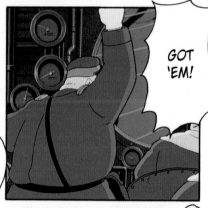

GOT 'EM!

OUR SHIP'S IN DANGER. RETREAT.

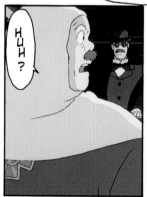

HUH?

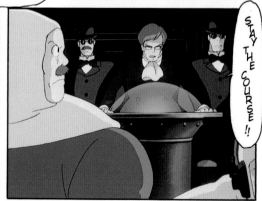

STAY THE COURSE!!

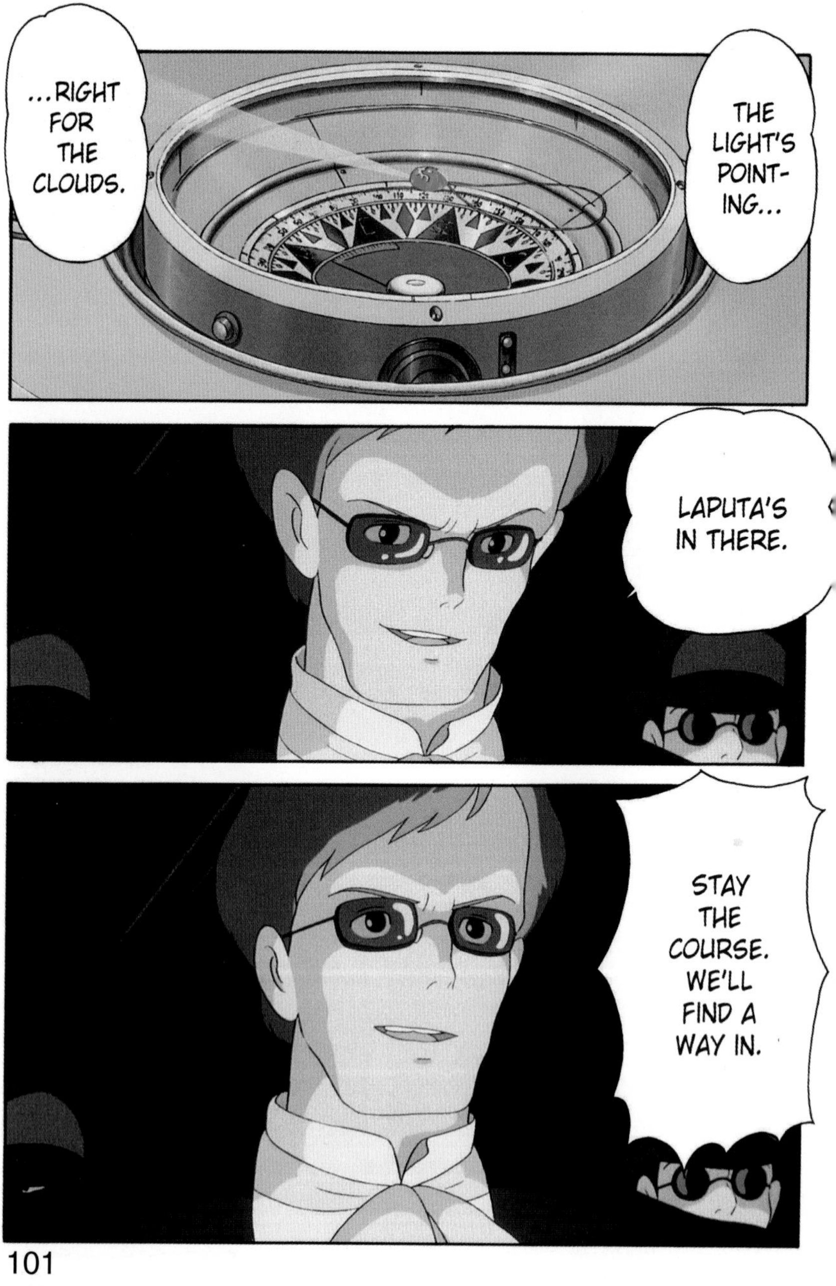
THE LIGHT'S POINTING...
...RIGHT FOR THE CLOUDS.
LAPUTA'S IN THERE.
STAY THE COURSE. WE'LL FIND A WAY IN.

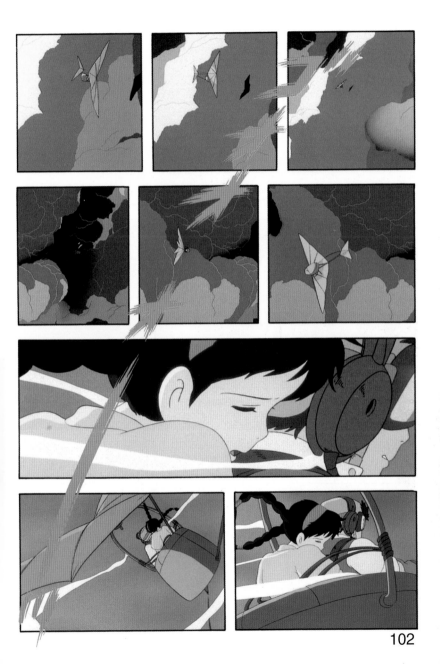

102

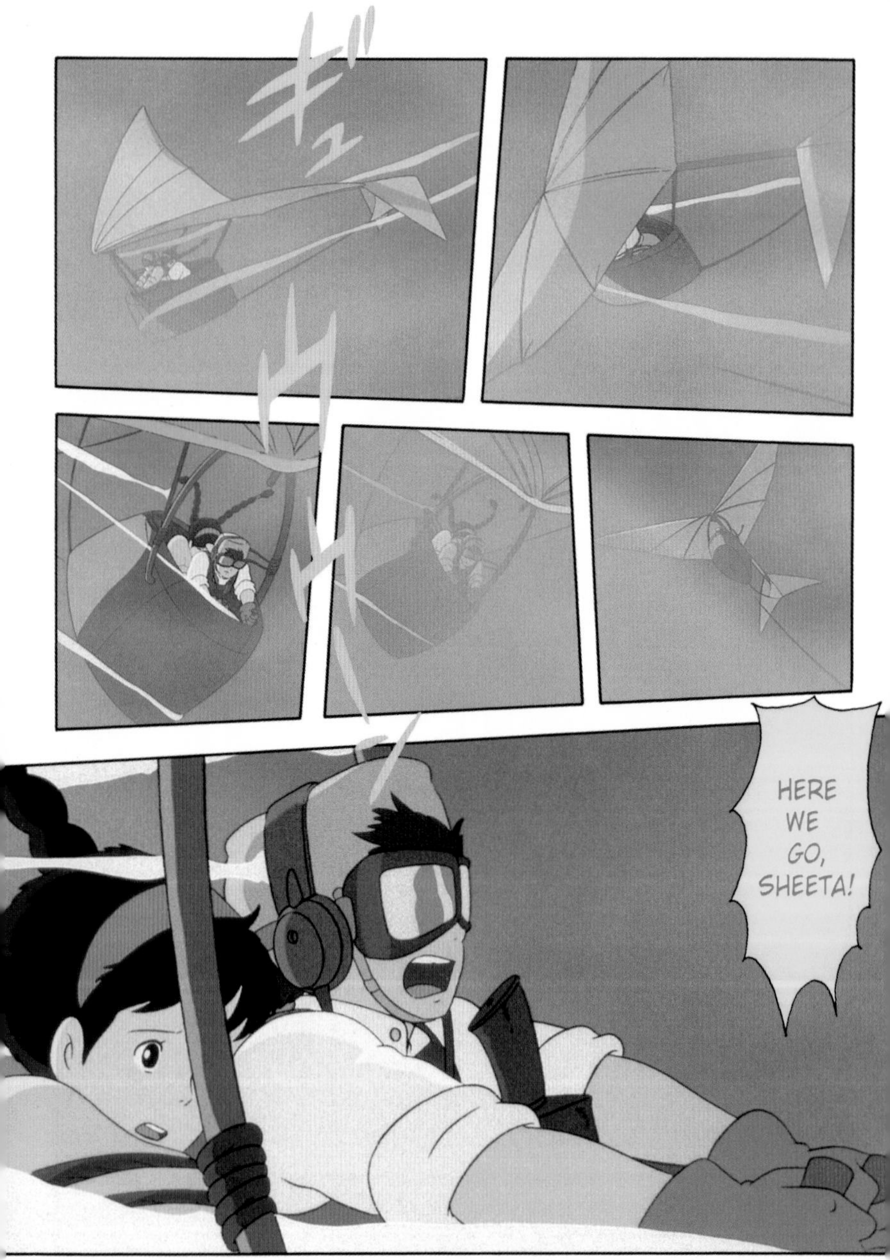
HERE WE GO, SHEETA!

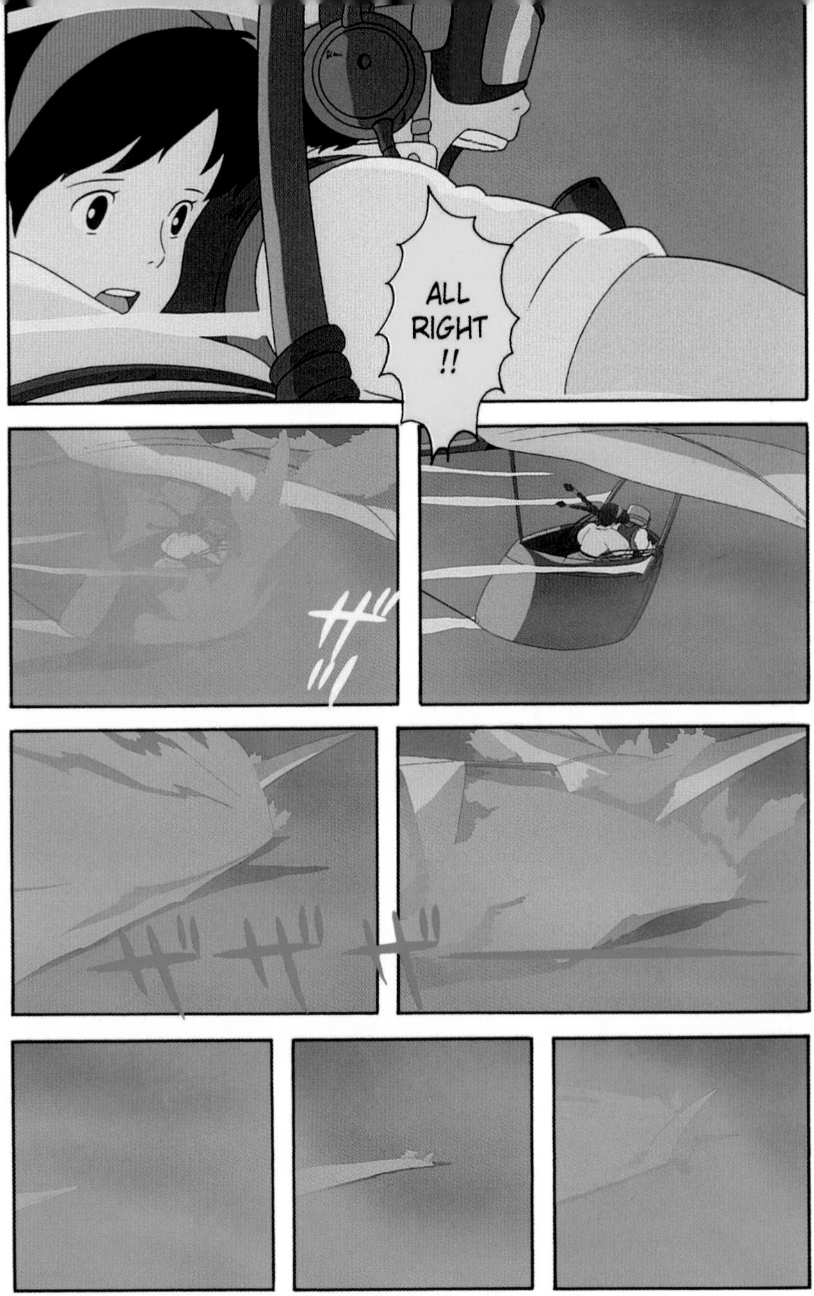
ALL RIGHT !!

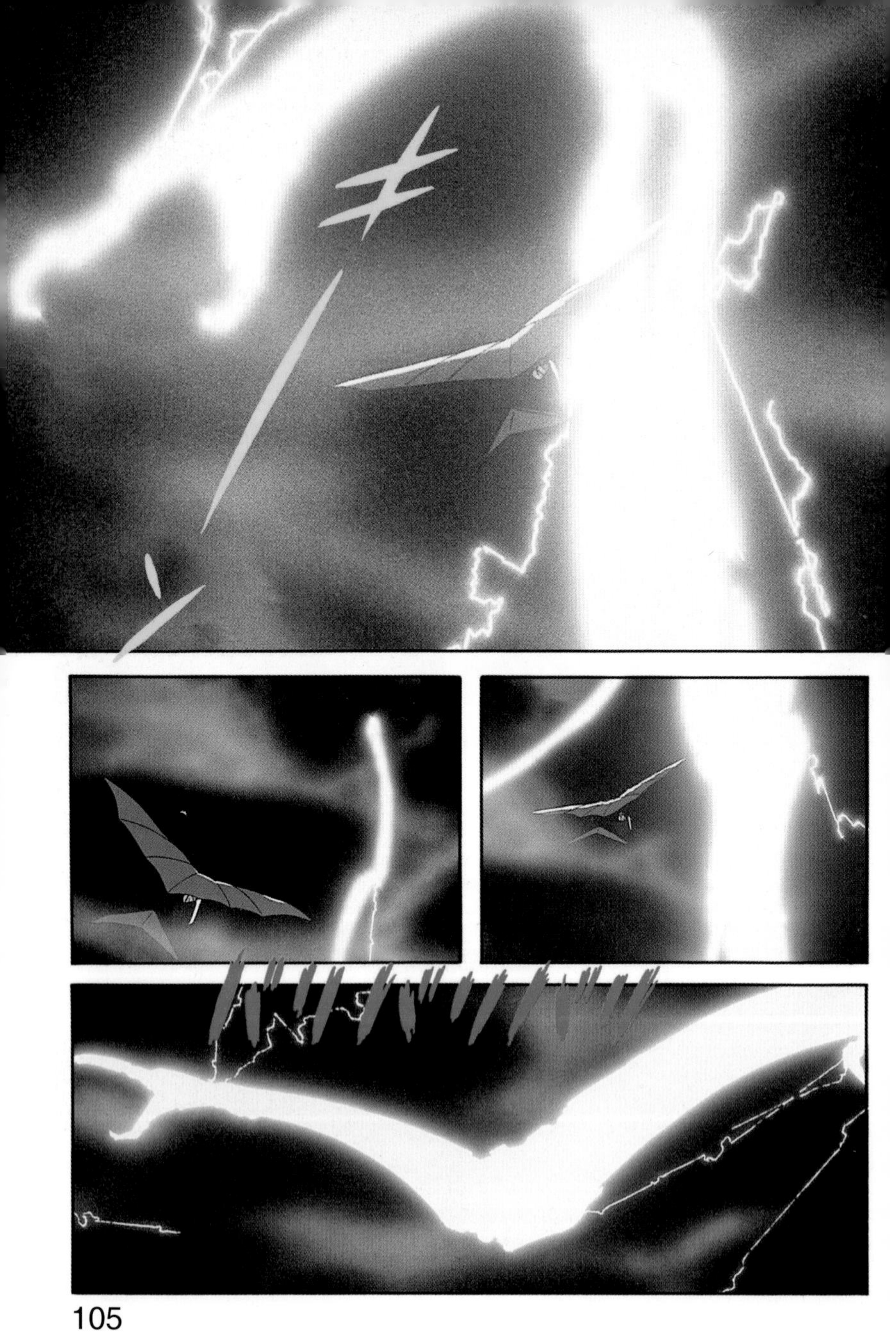
キ
バリバリバリバリ

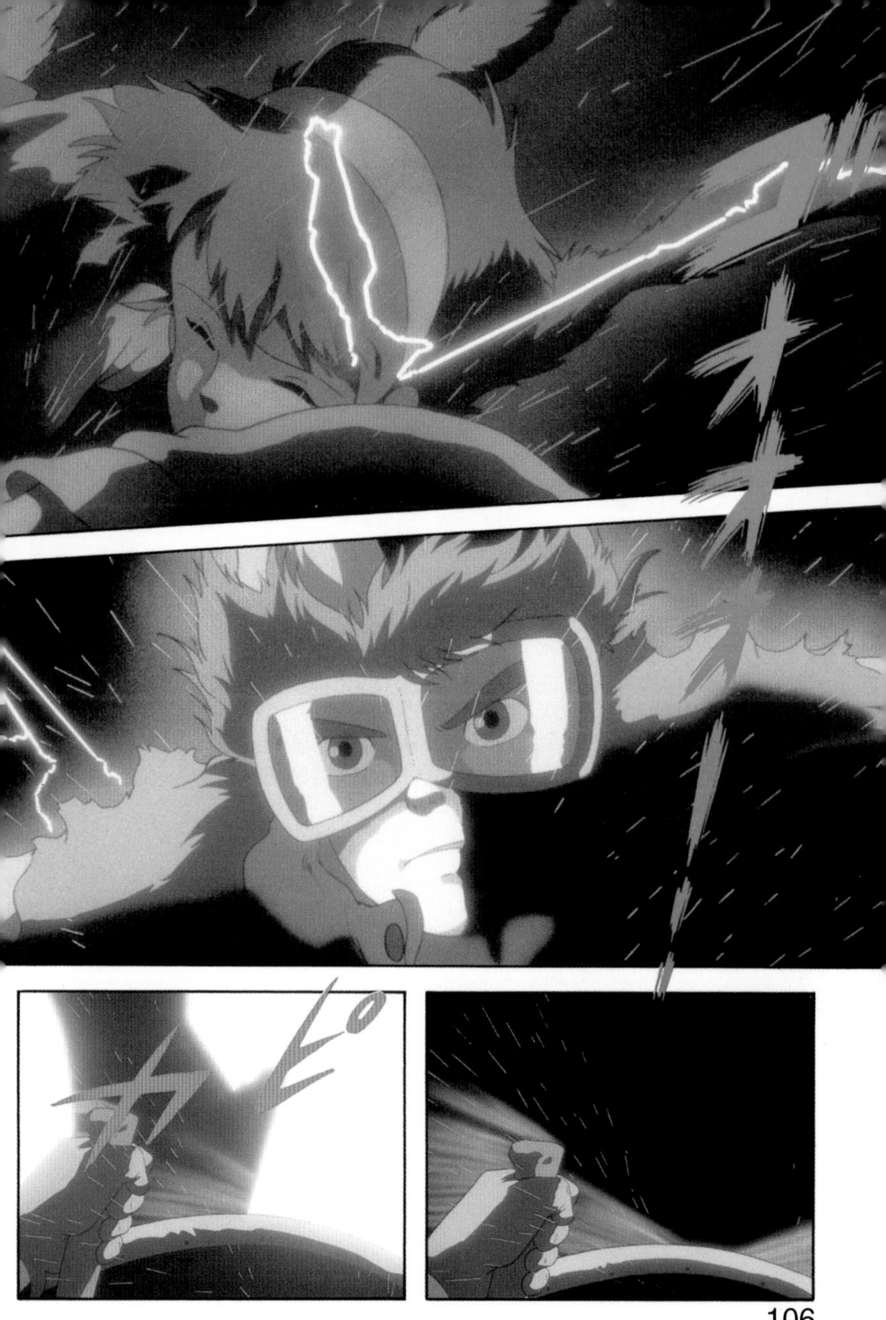

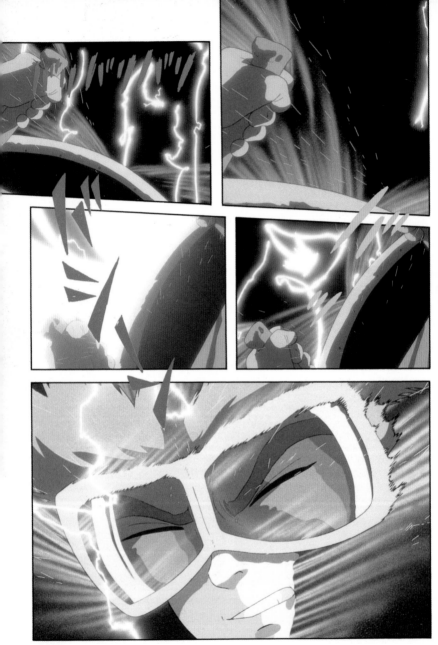

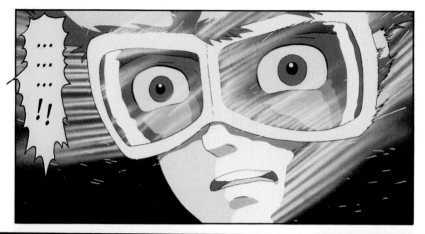

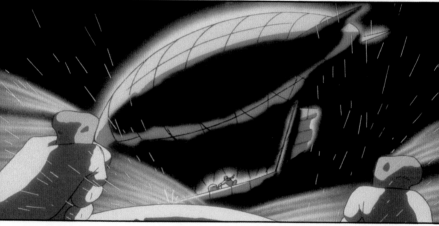

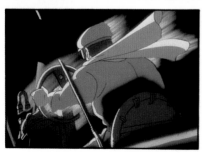

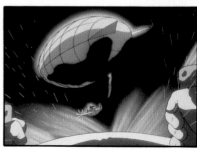

108

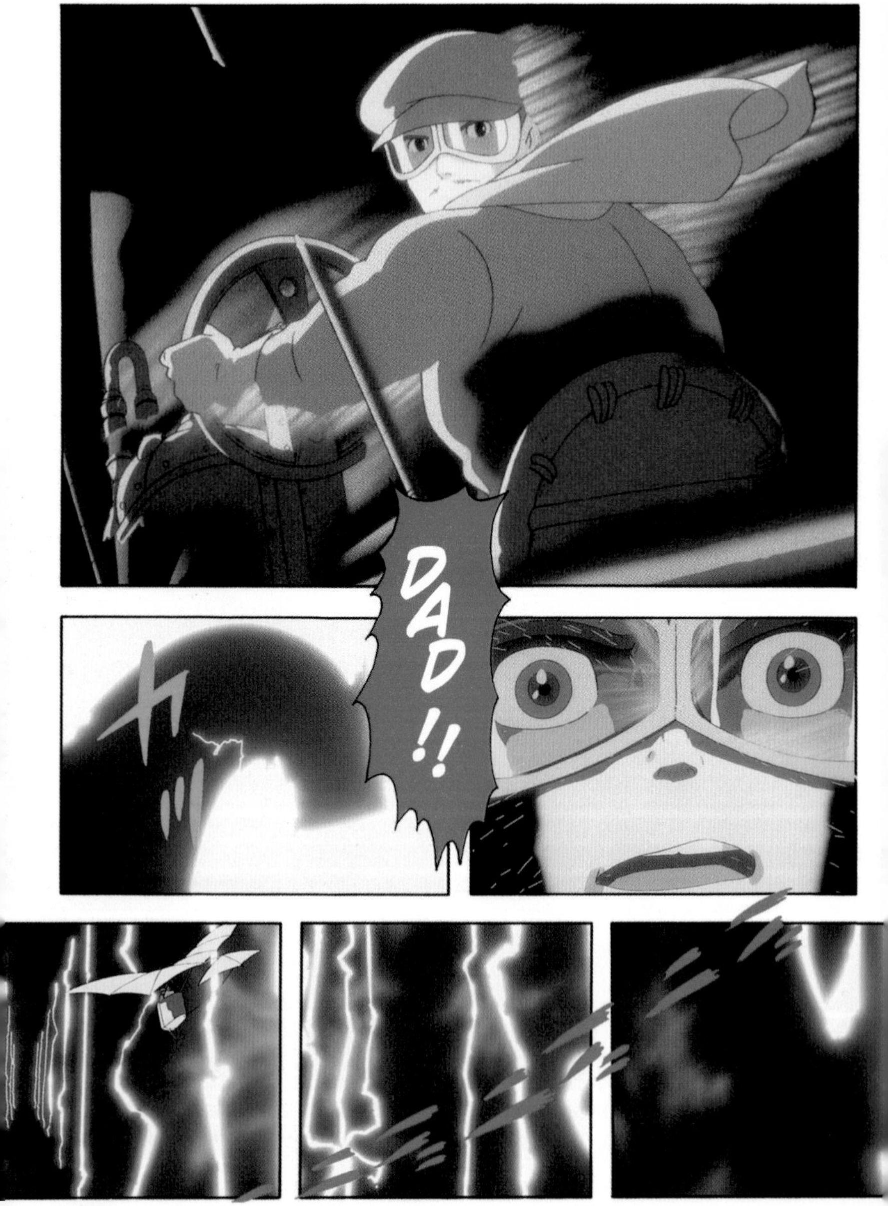
DAD!!

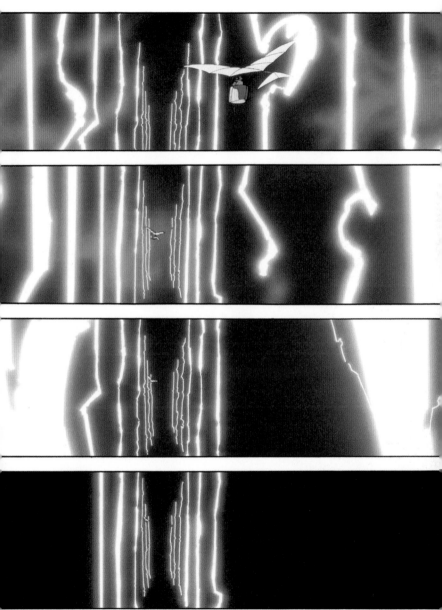

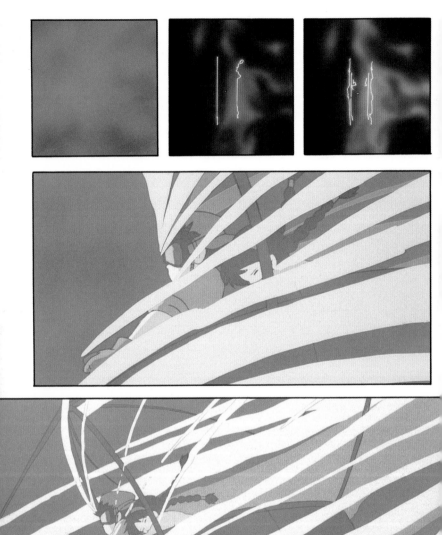

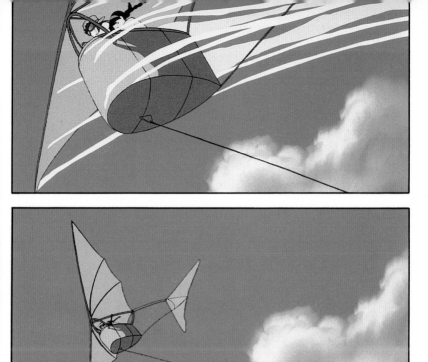

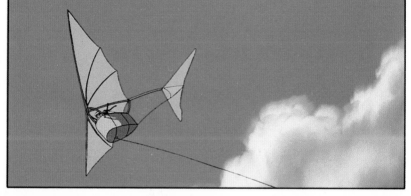

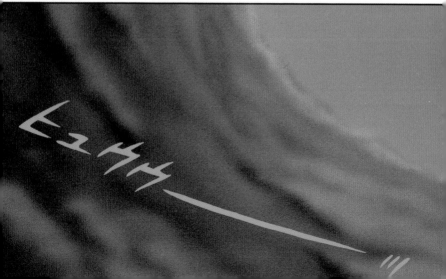

ヒュルルル

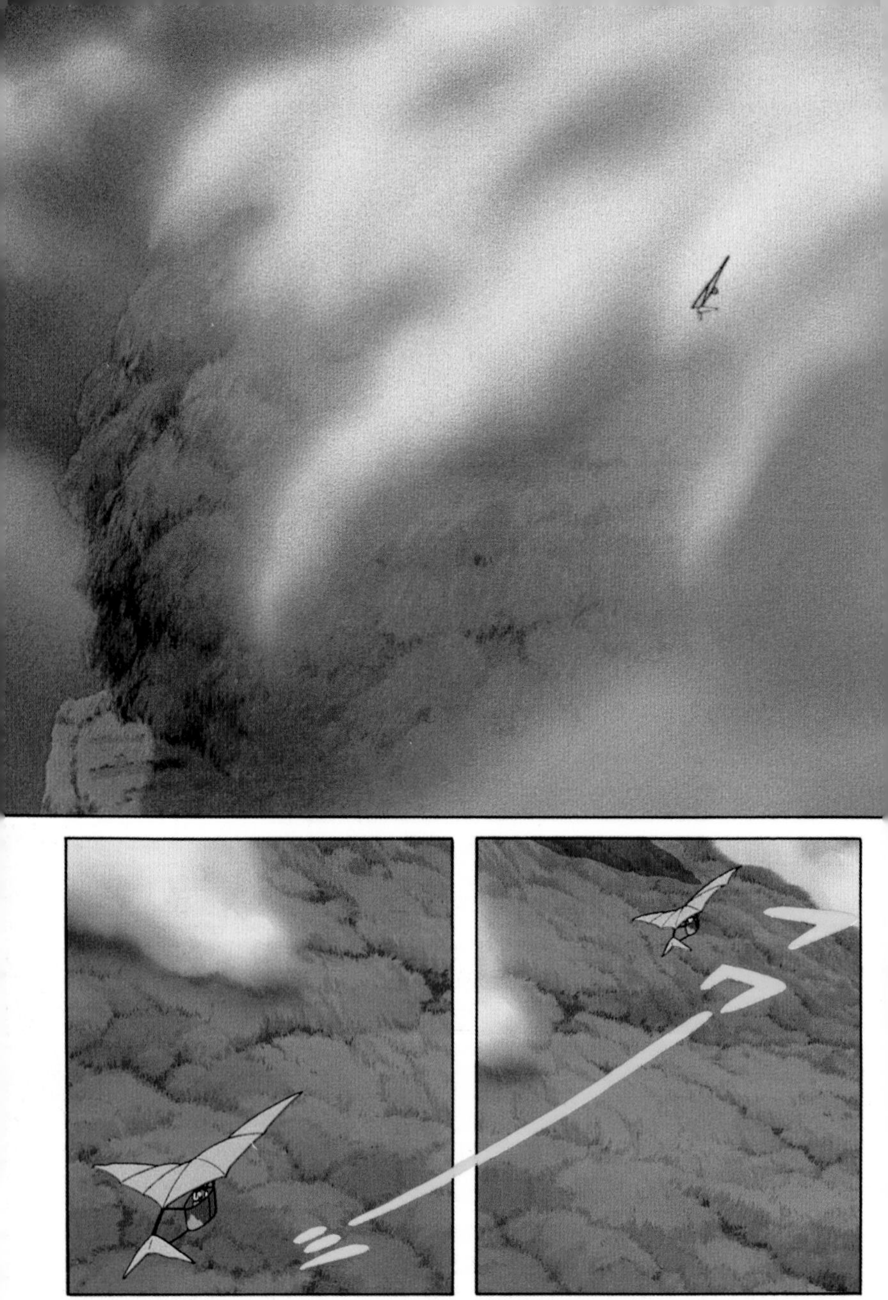

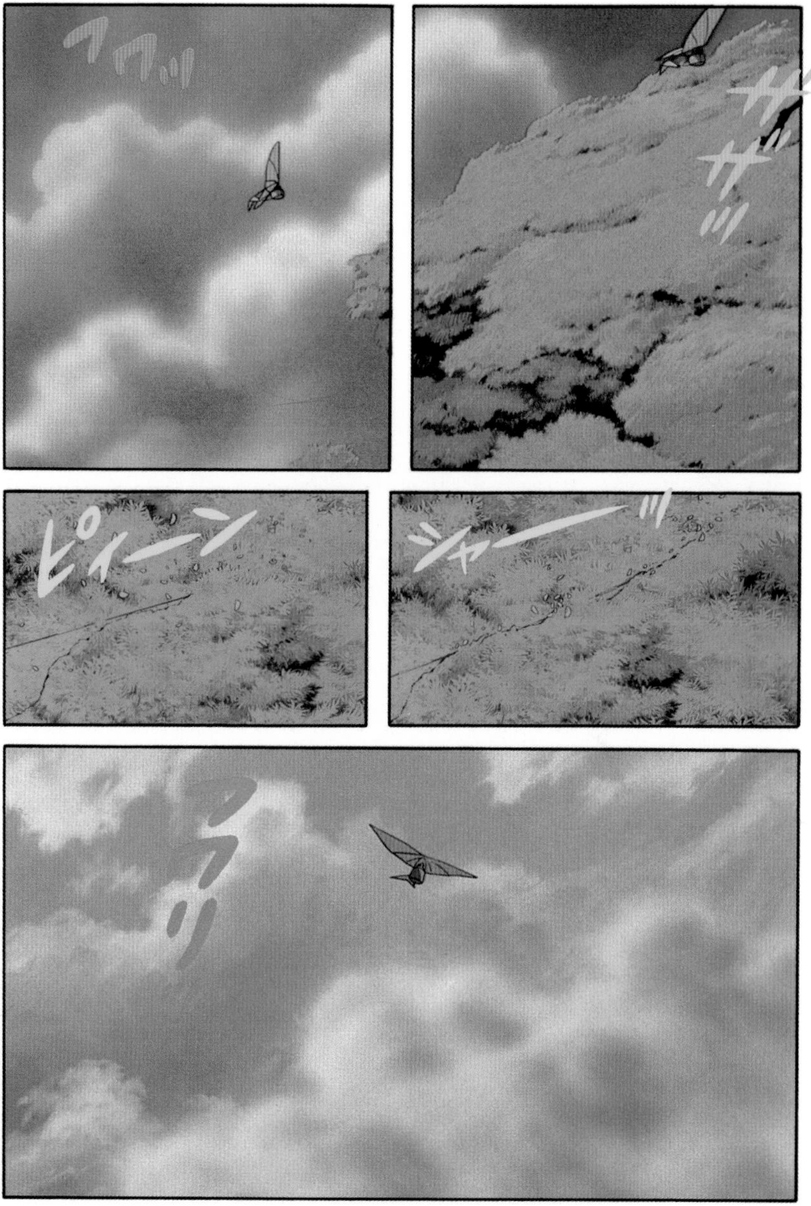
ザザッ
フワッ
シャーッ
ピィーン
フワリ

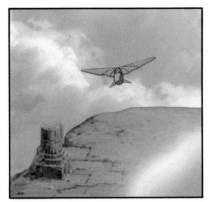

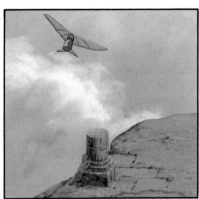

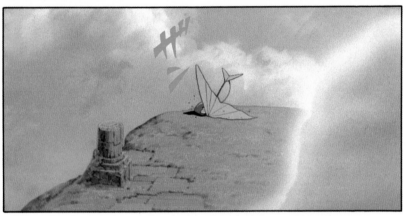

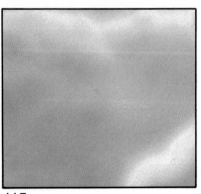

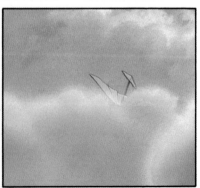

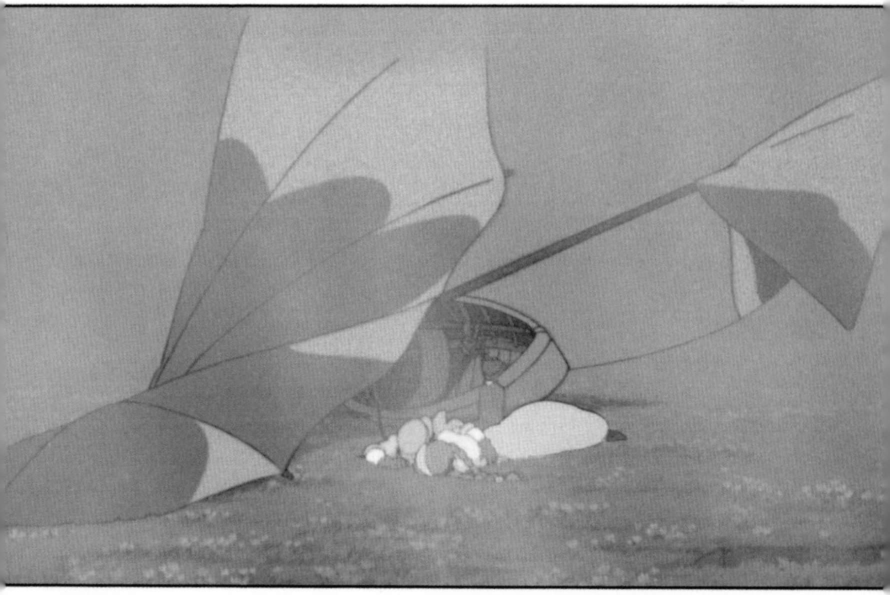
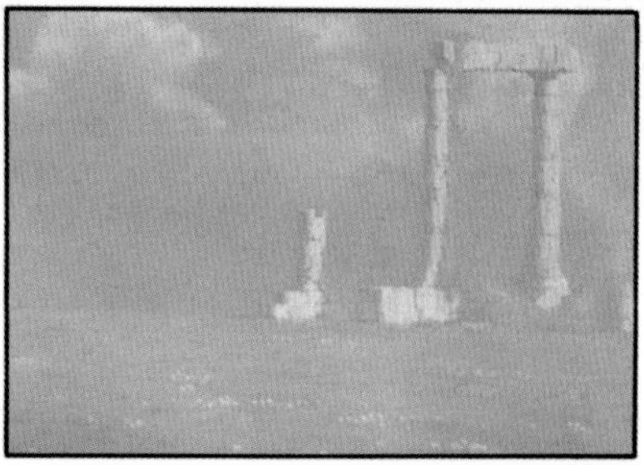
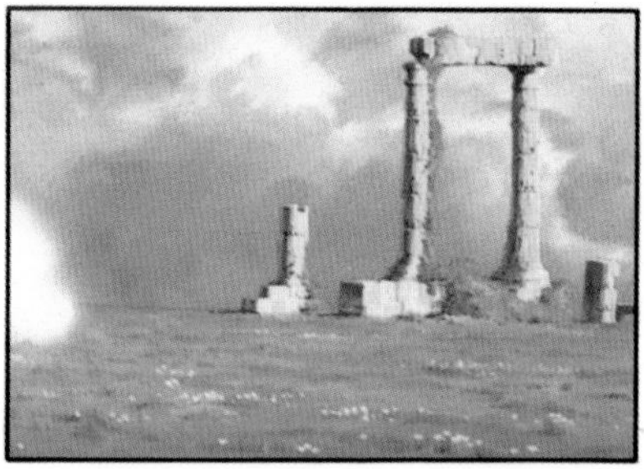
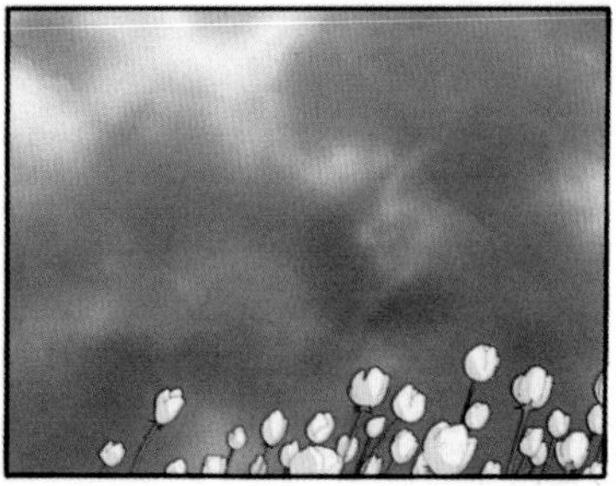
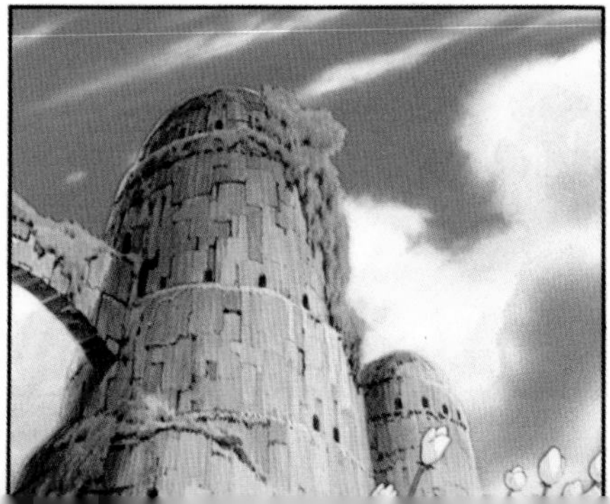

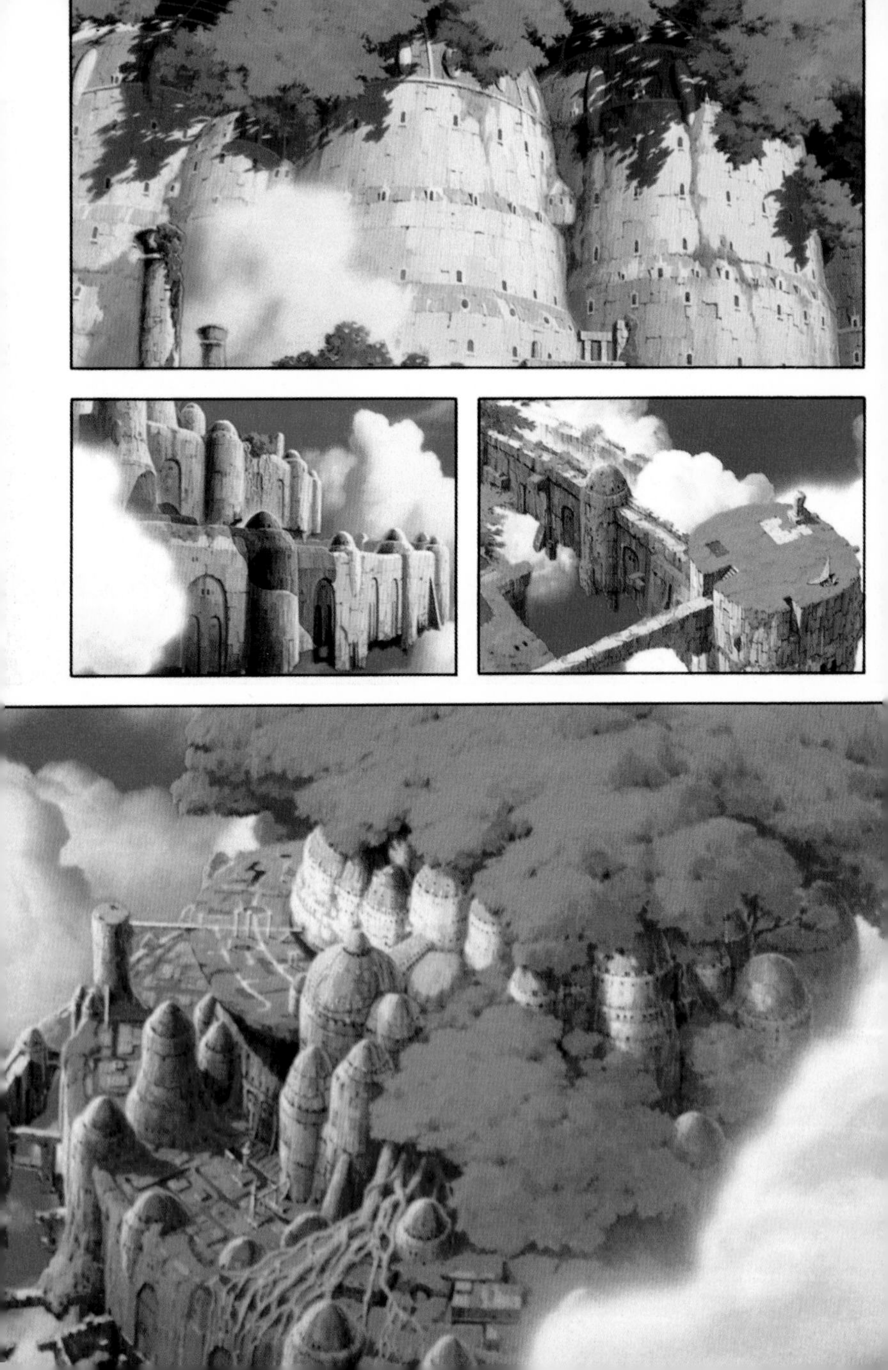

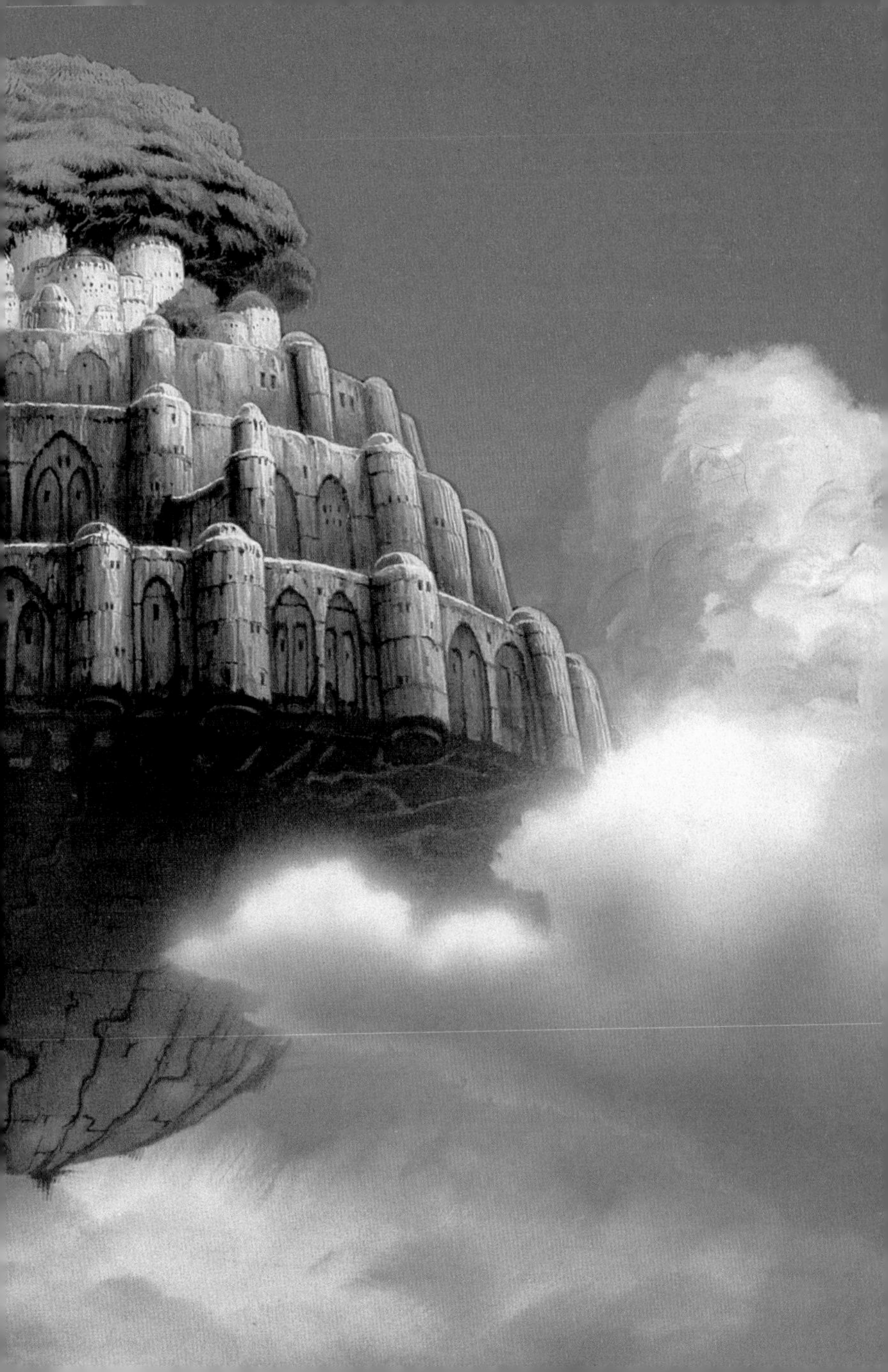

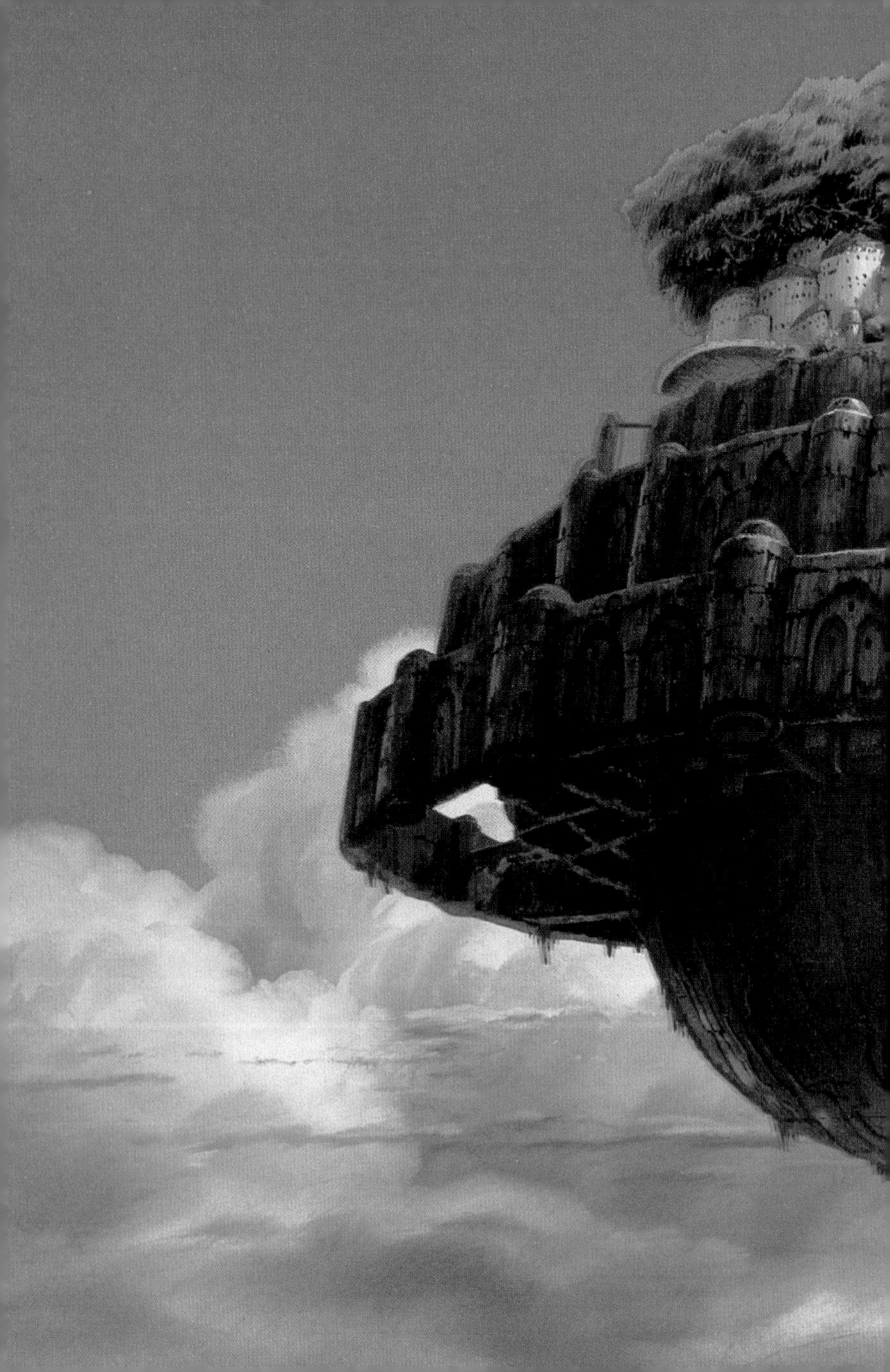

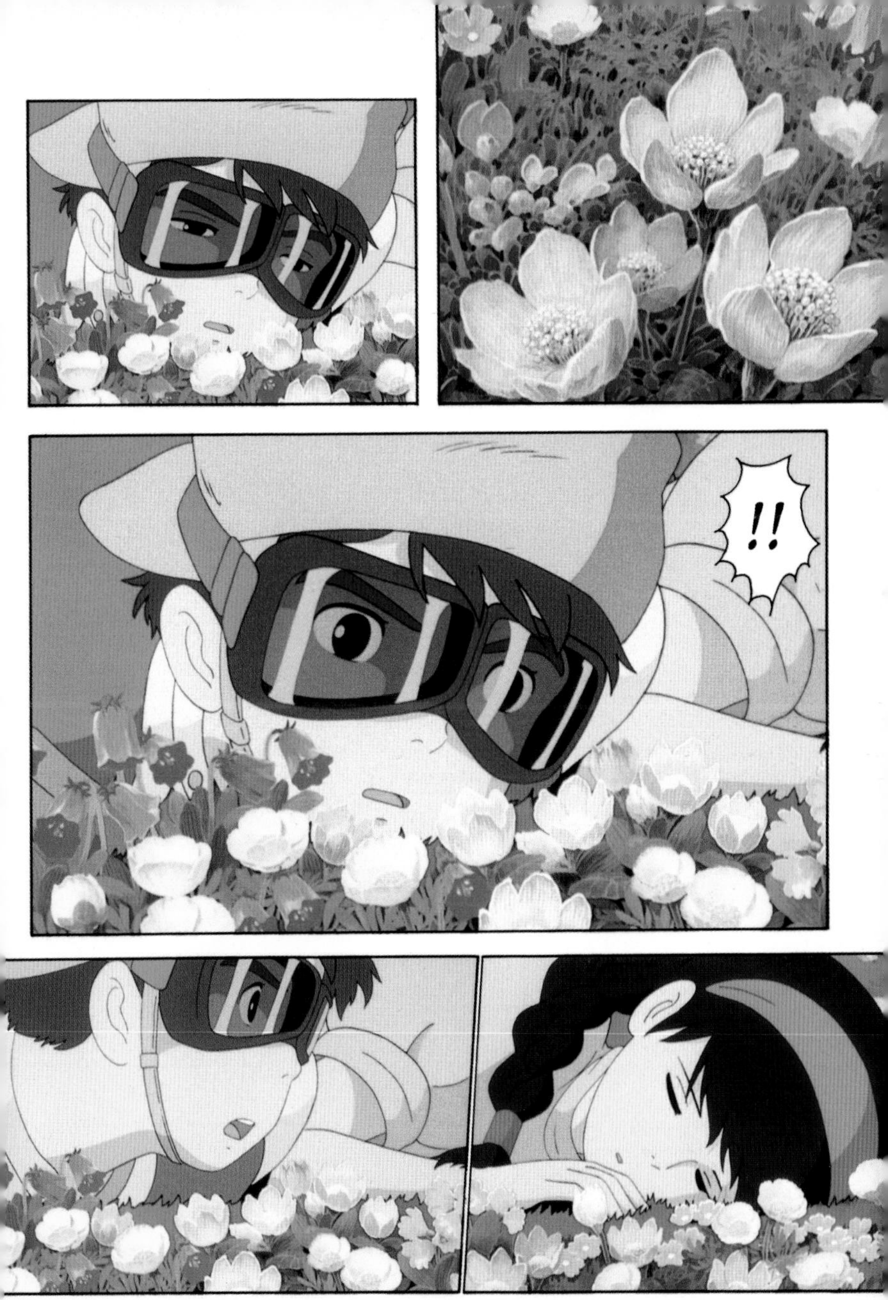
!!

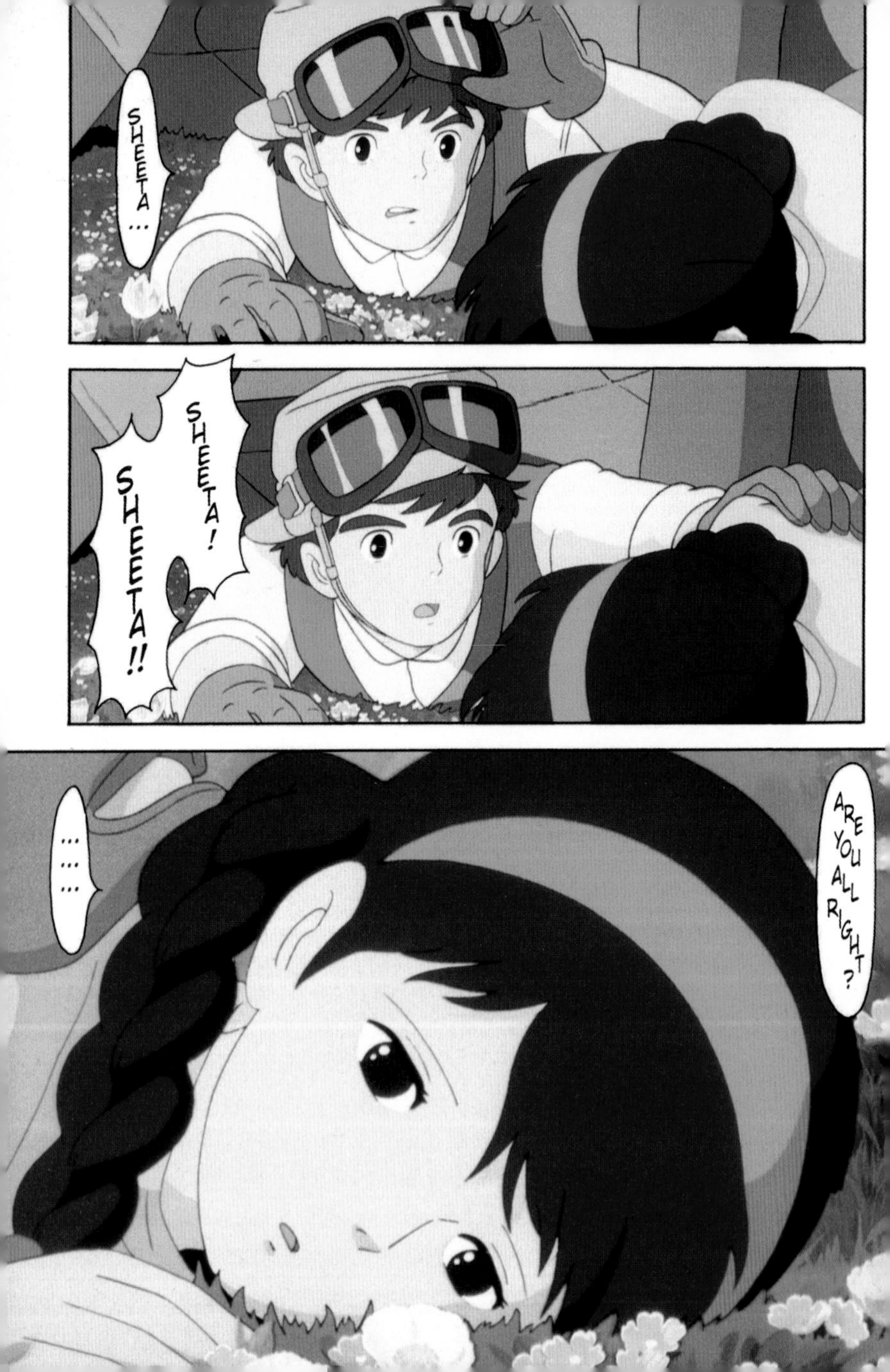
SHEETA...
SHEETA! SHEETA!!
ARE YOU ALL RIGHT?
....

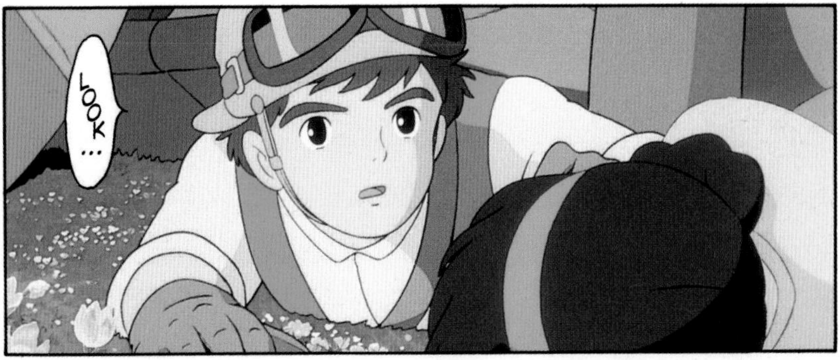
LOOK...
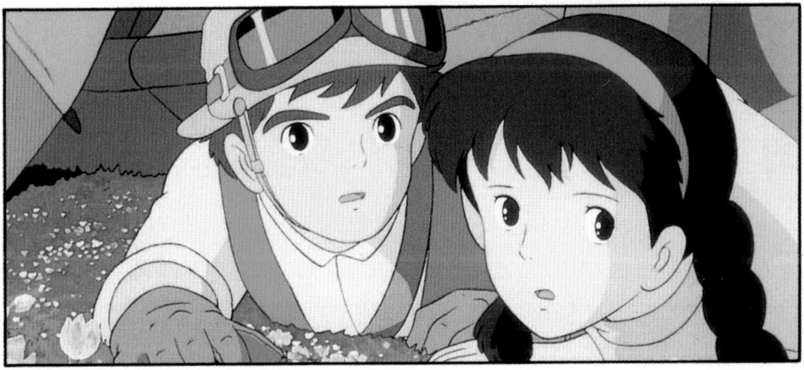
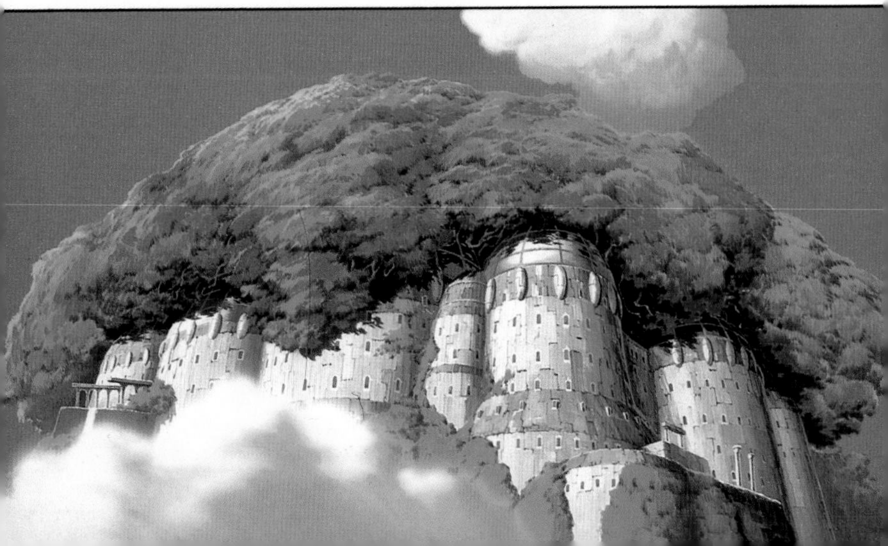

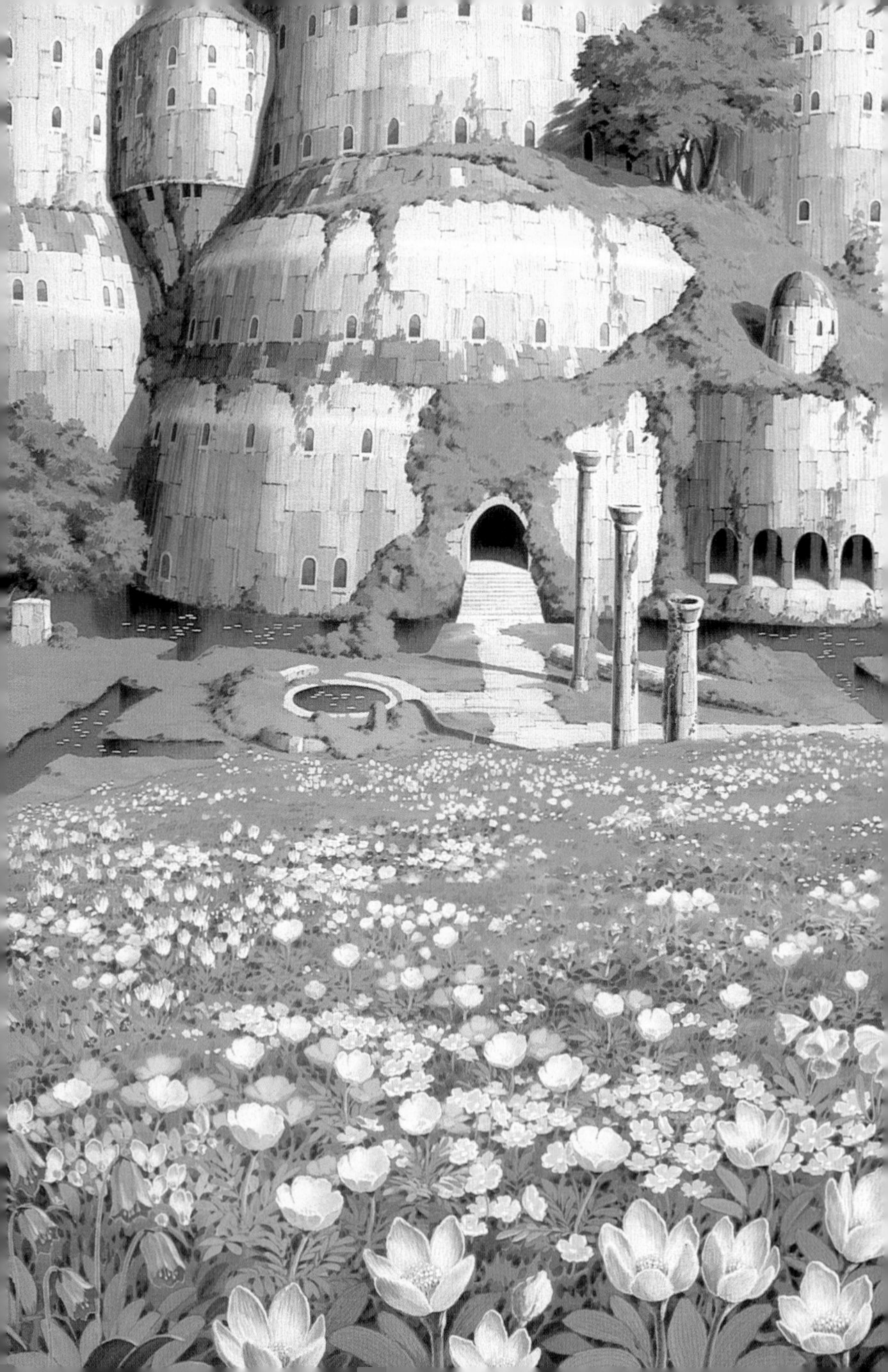

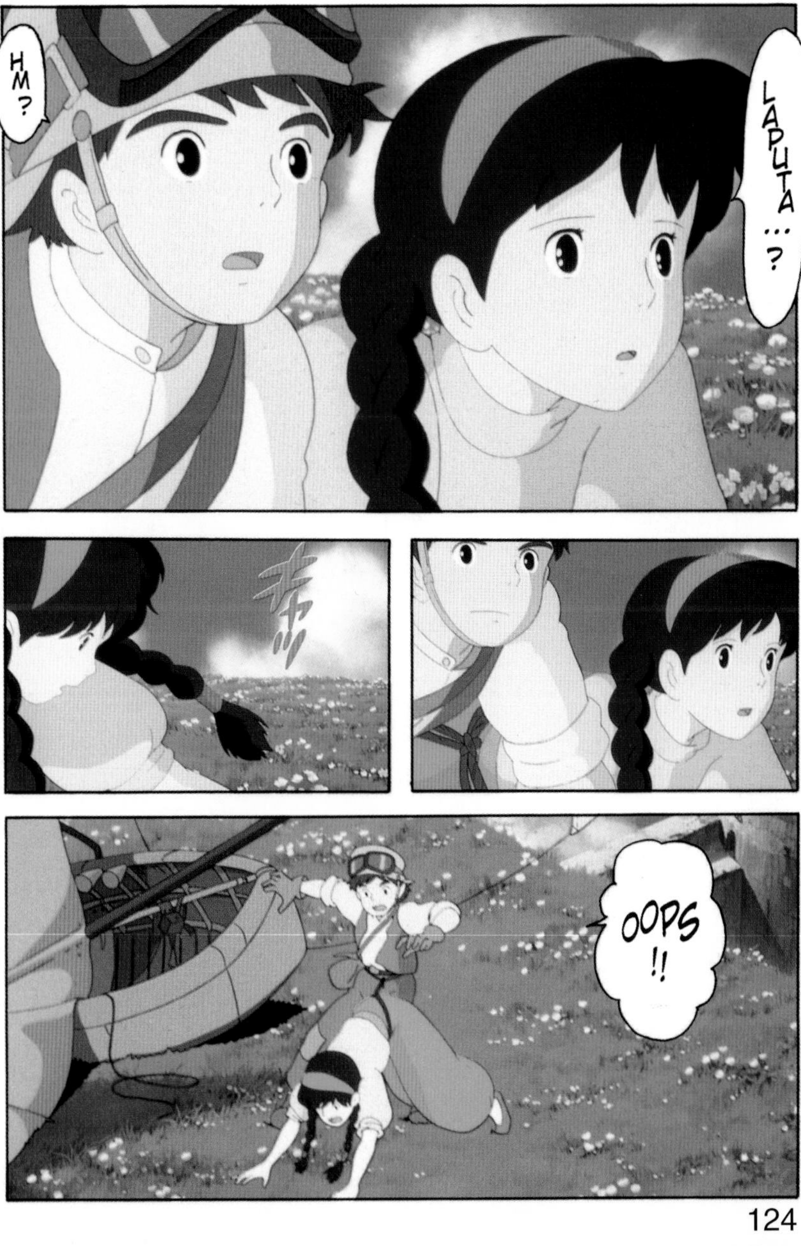
LAPUTA...?
HM?
OOPS!!

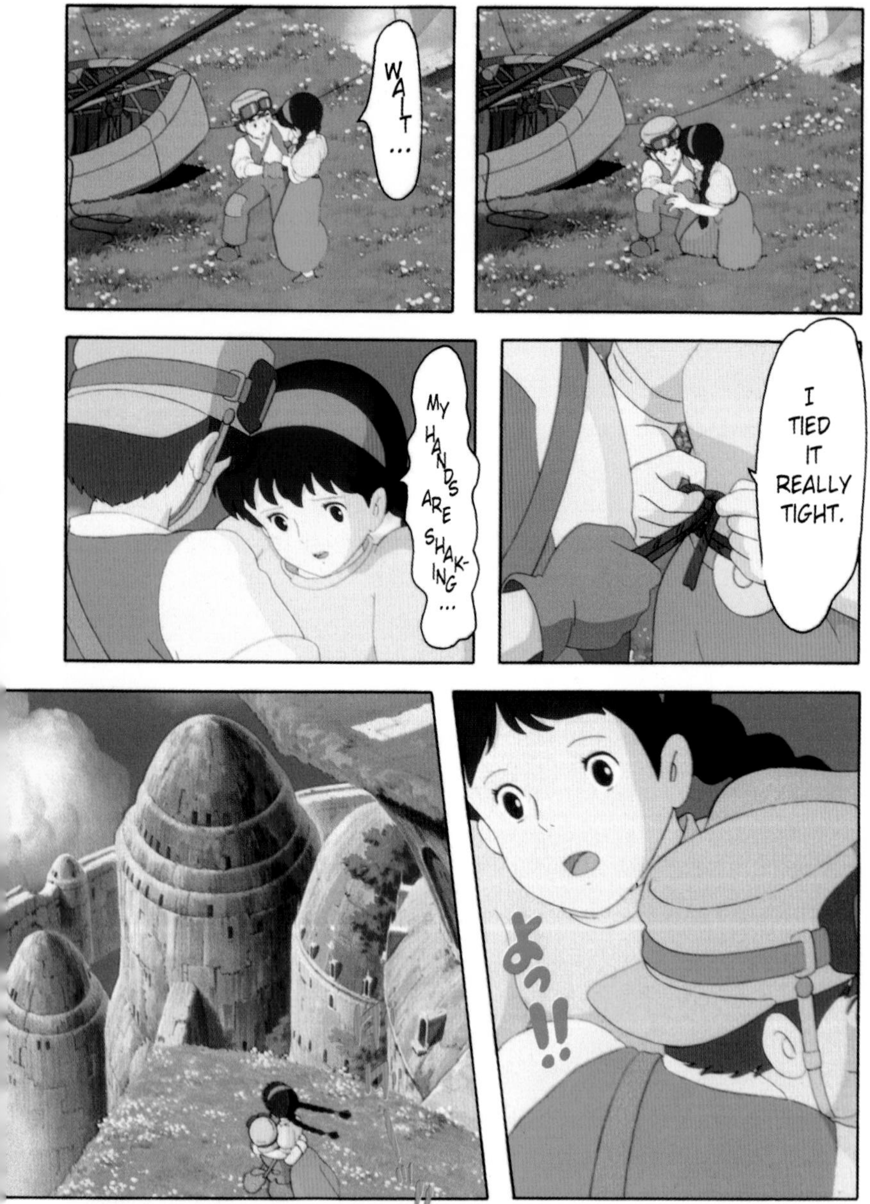
WAIT...
I TIED IT REALLY TIGHT.
MY HANDS ARE SHAKING...
よっ!!
!!

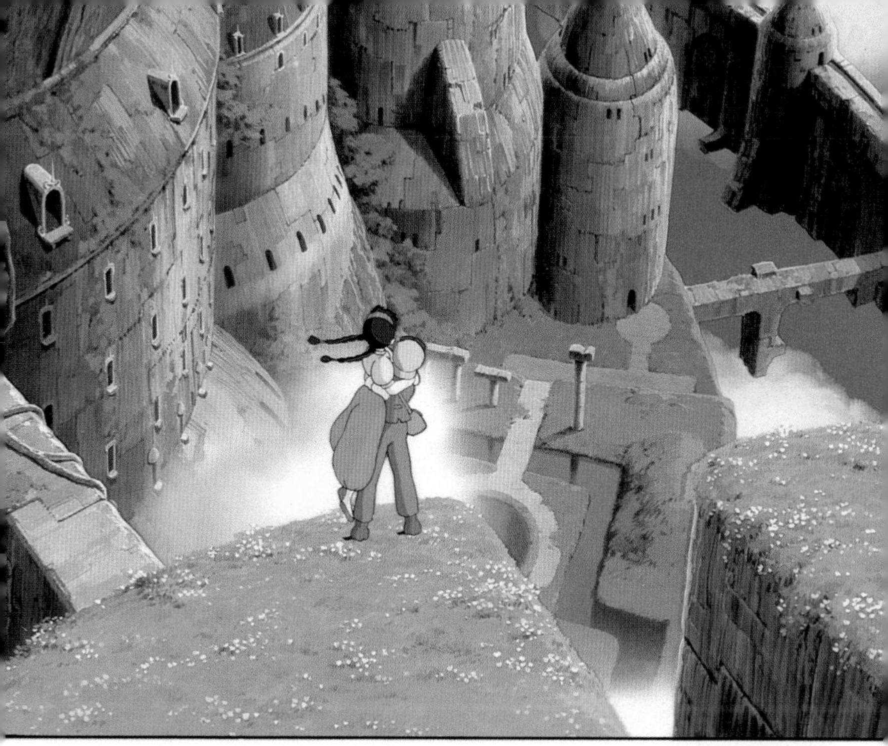
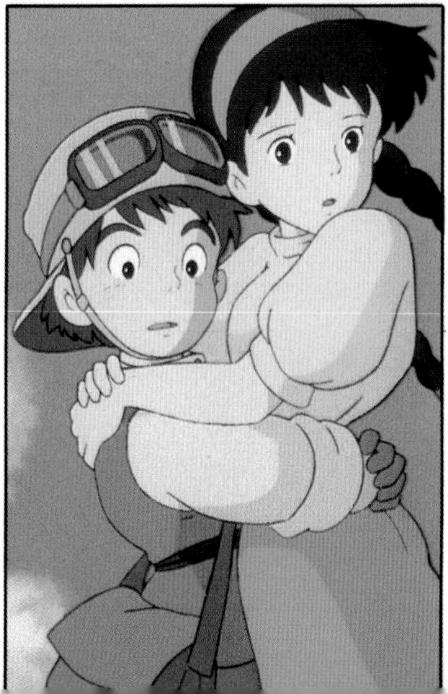
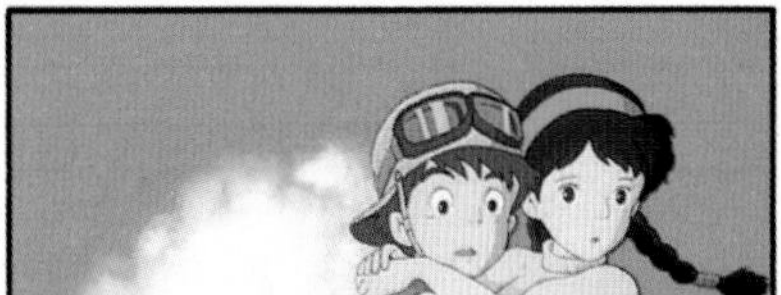
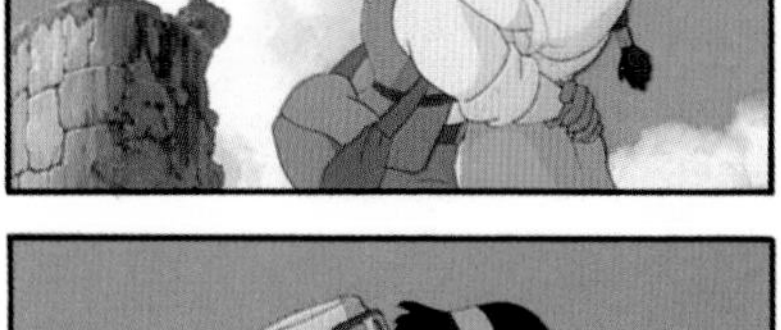

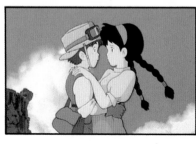

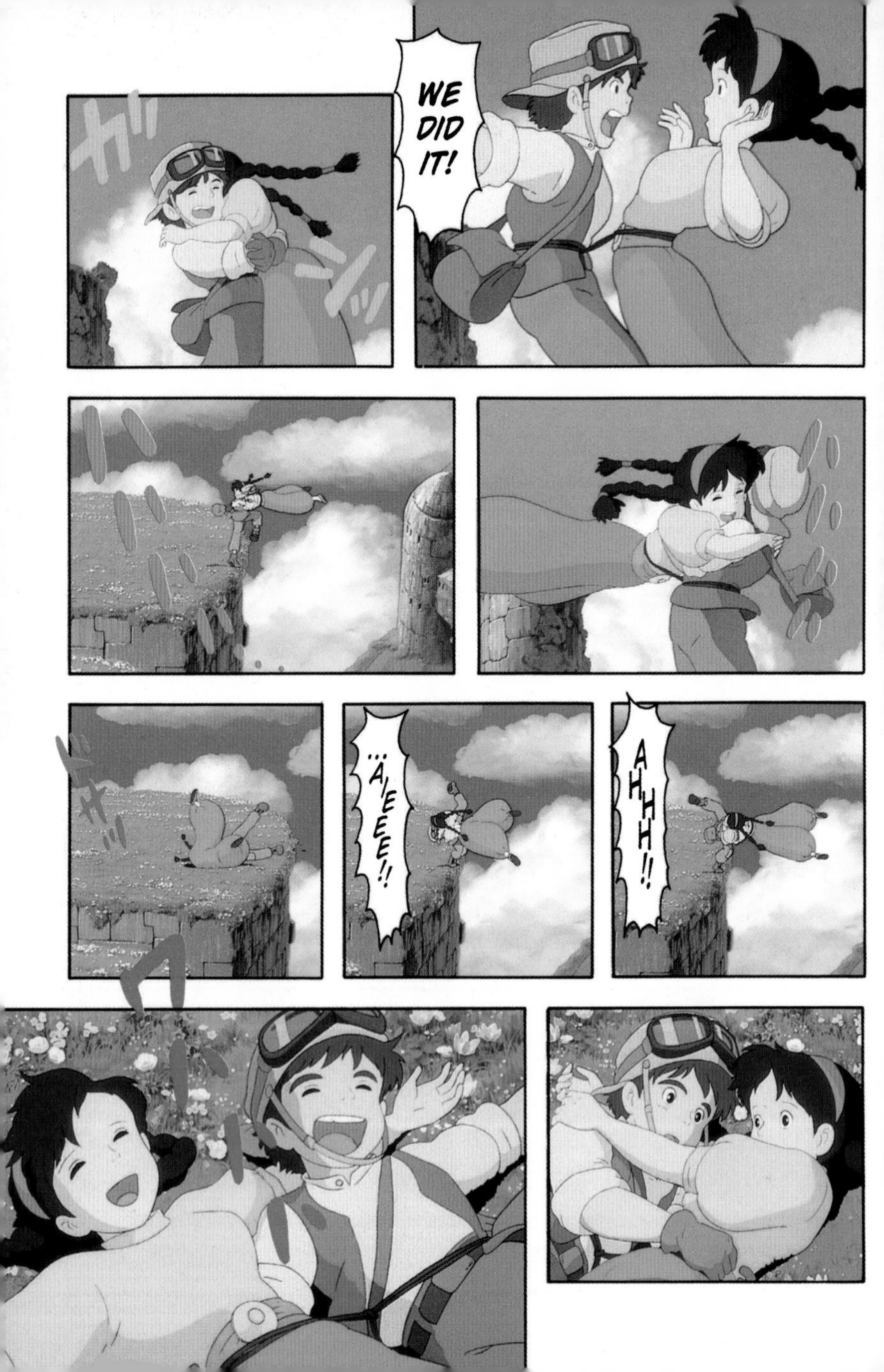
WE DID IT!
AHHH!!
..AIEEE!!

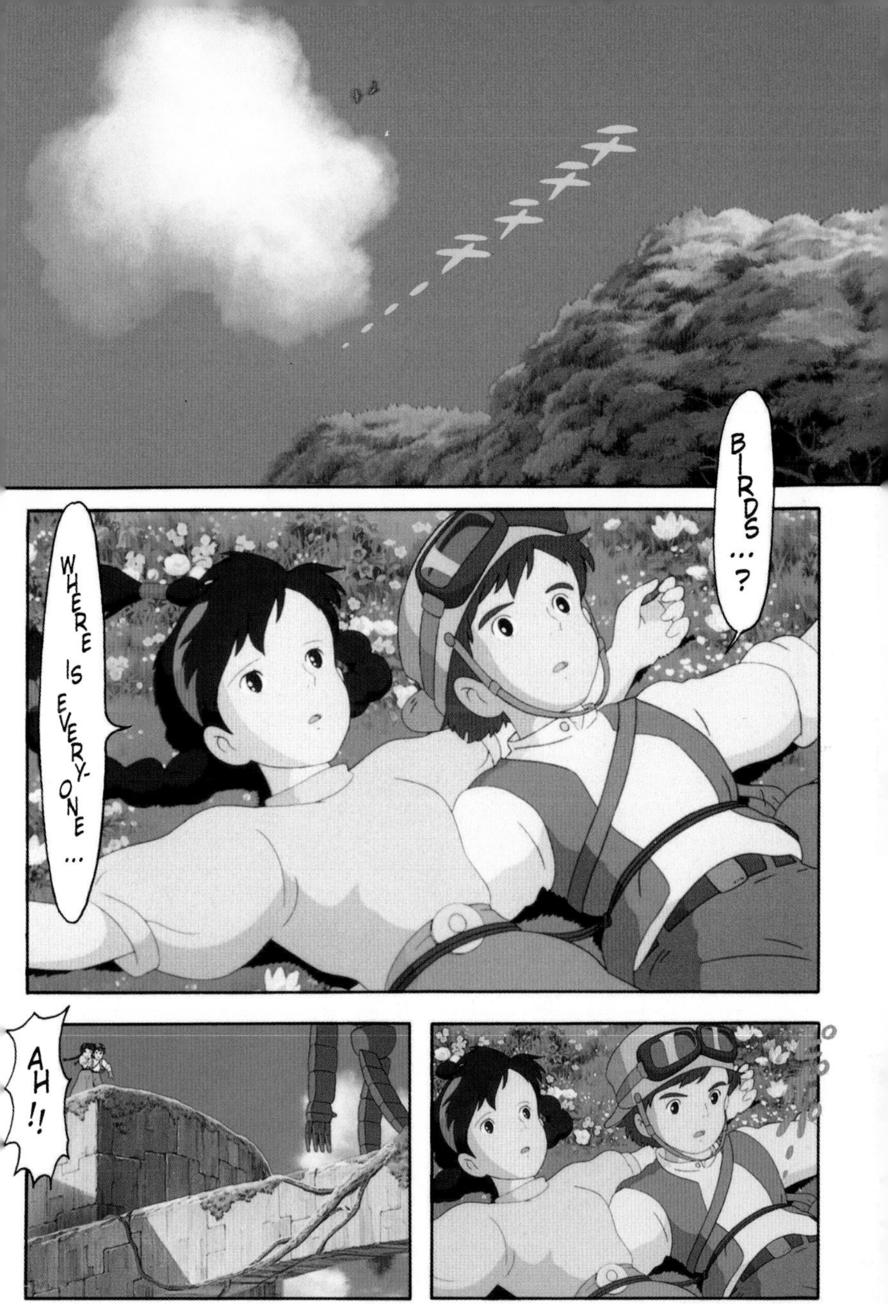
BIRDS...?
WHERE IS EVERYONE...
AH!!

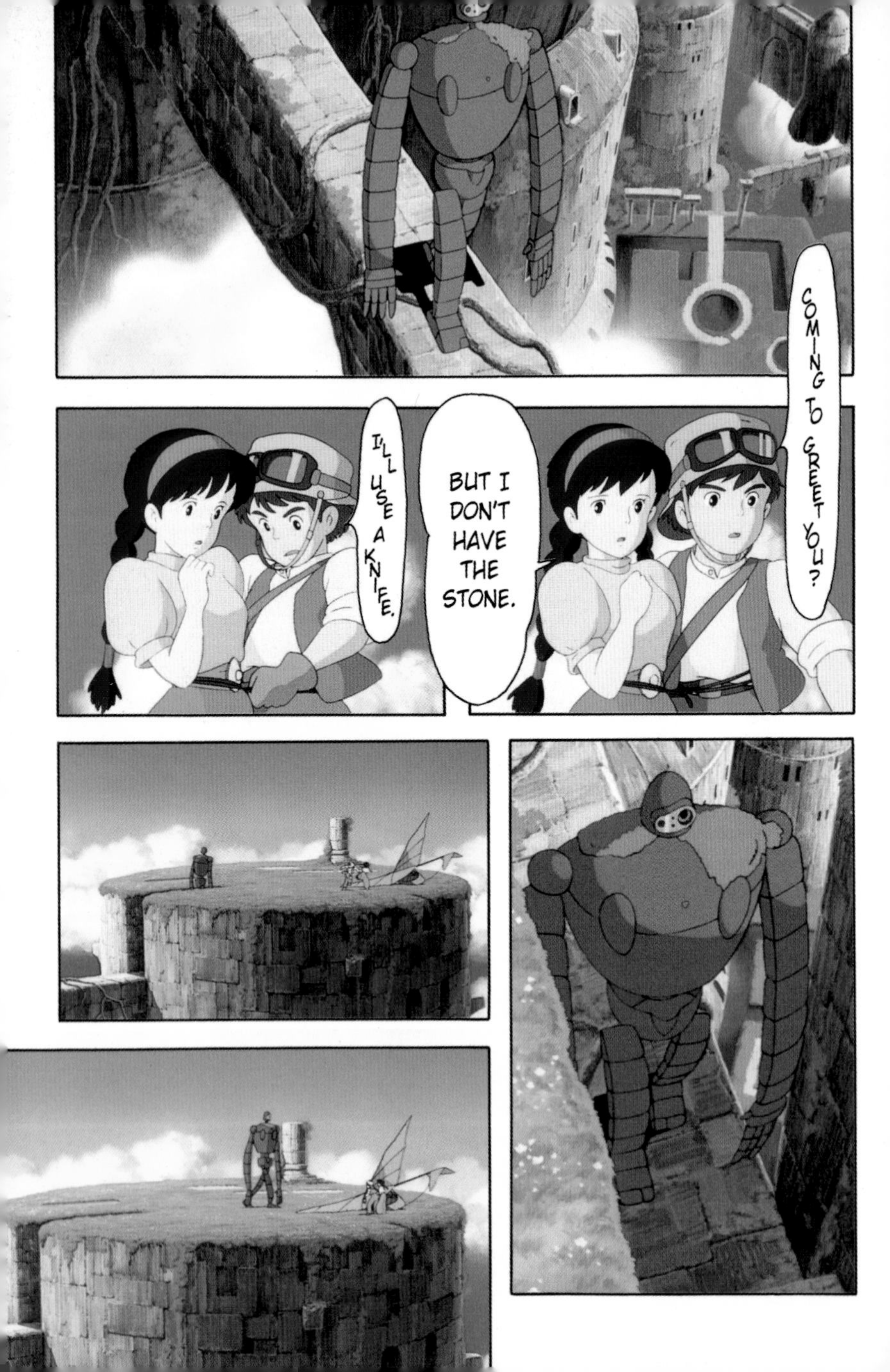
COMING TO GREET YOU?
BUT I DON'T HAVE THE STONE.
I'LL USE A KNIFE.

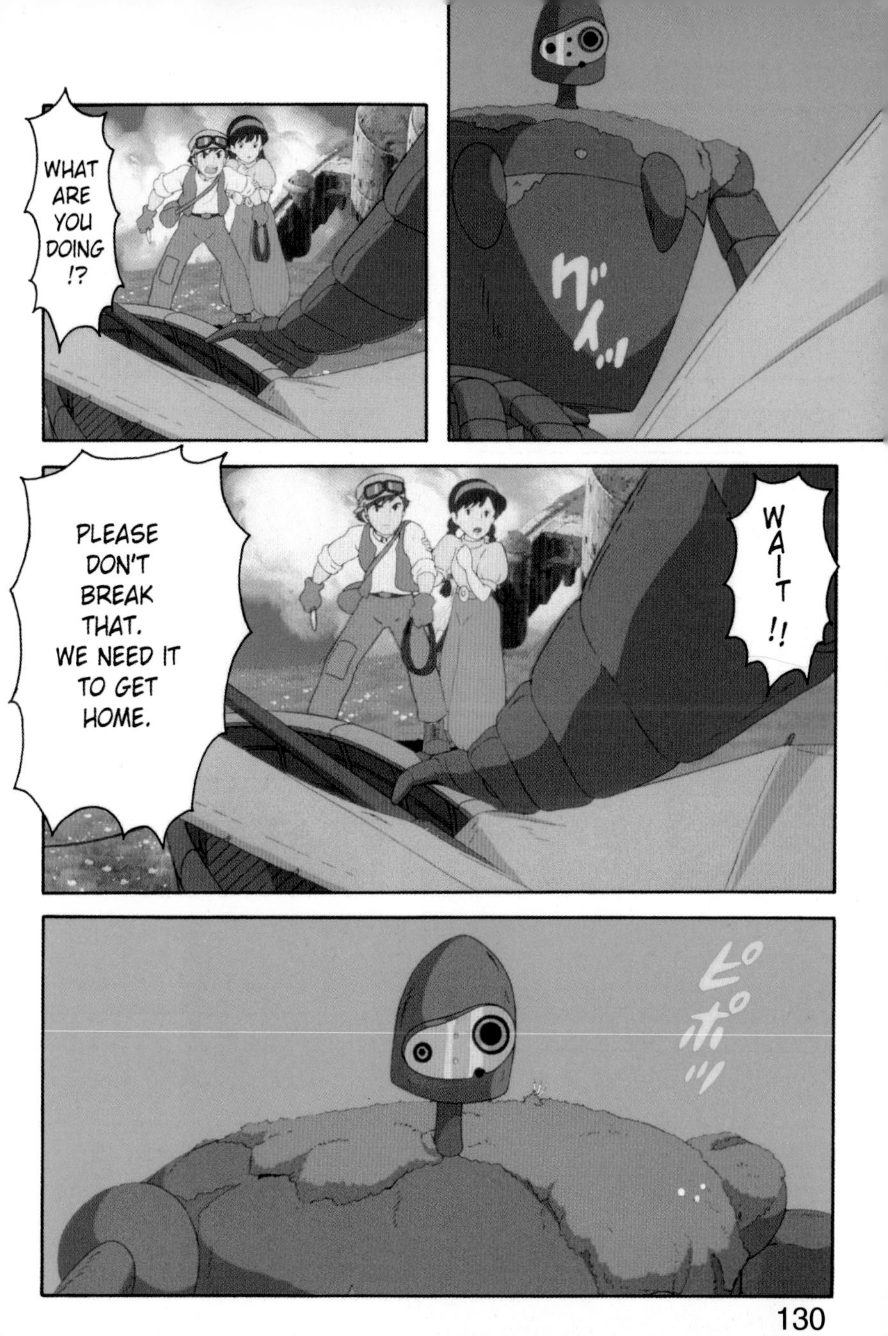
ヴィッ
WHAT ARE YOU DOING !?
WAIT !!
PLEASE DON'T BREAK THAT. WE NEED IT TO GET HOME.
ピポポッ

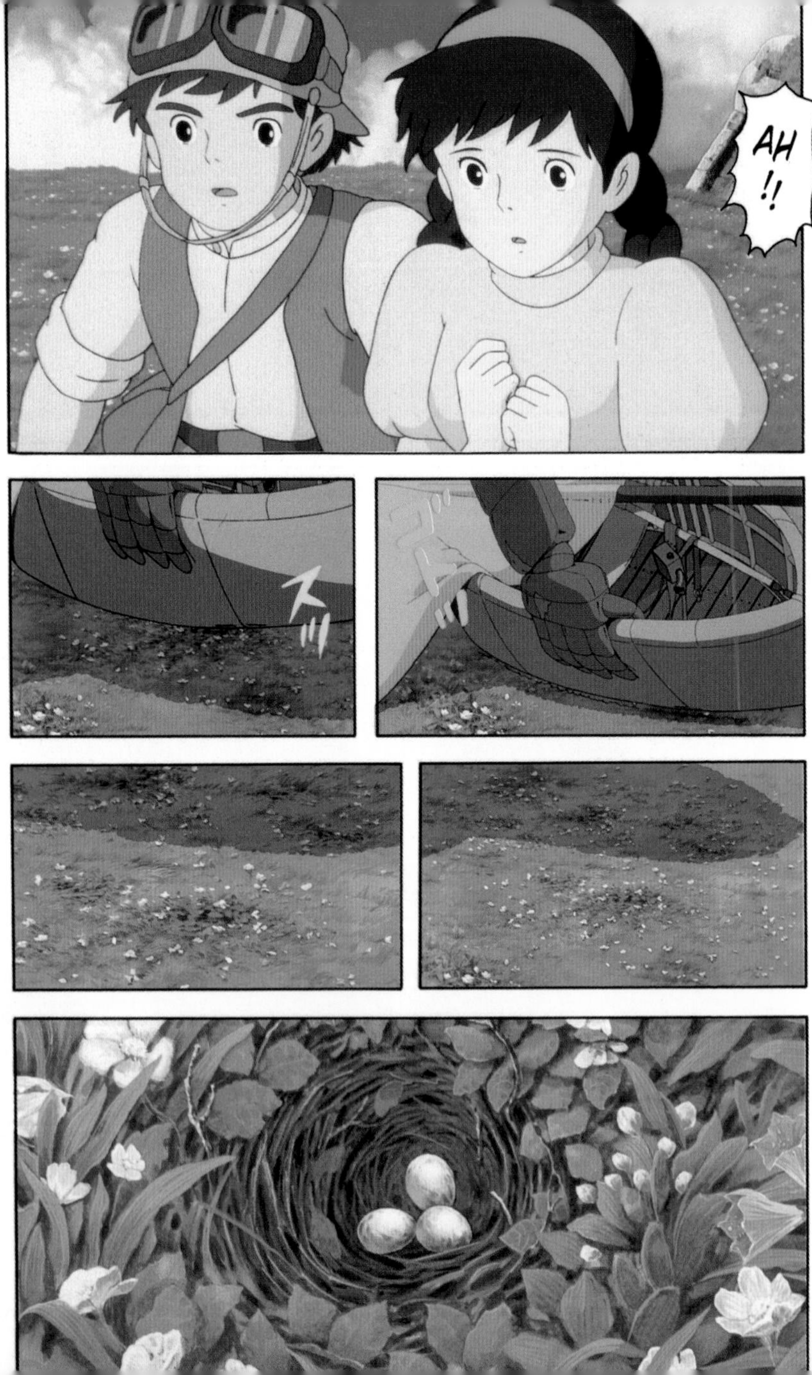
AH !!
スッ

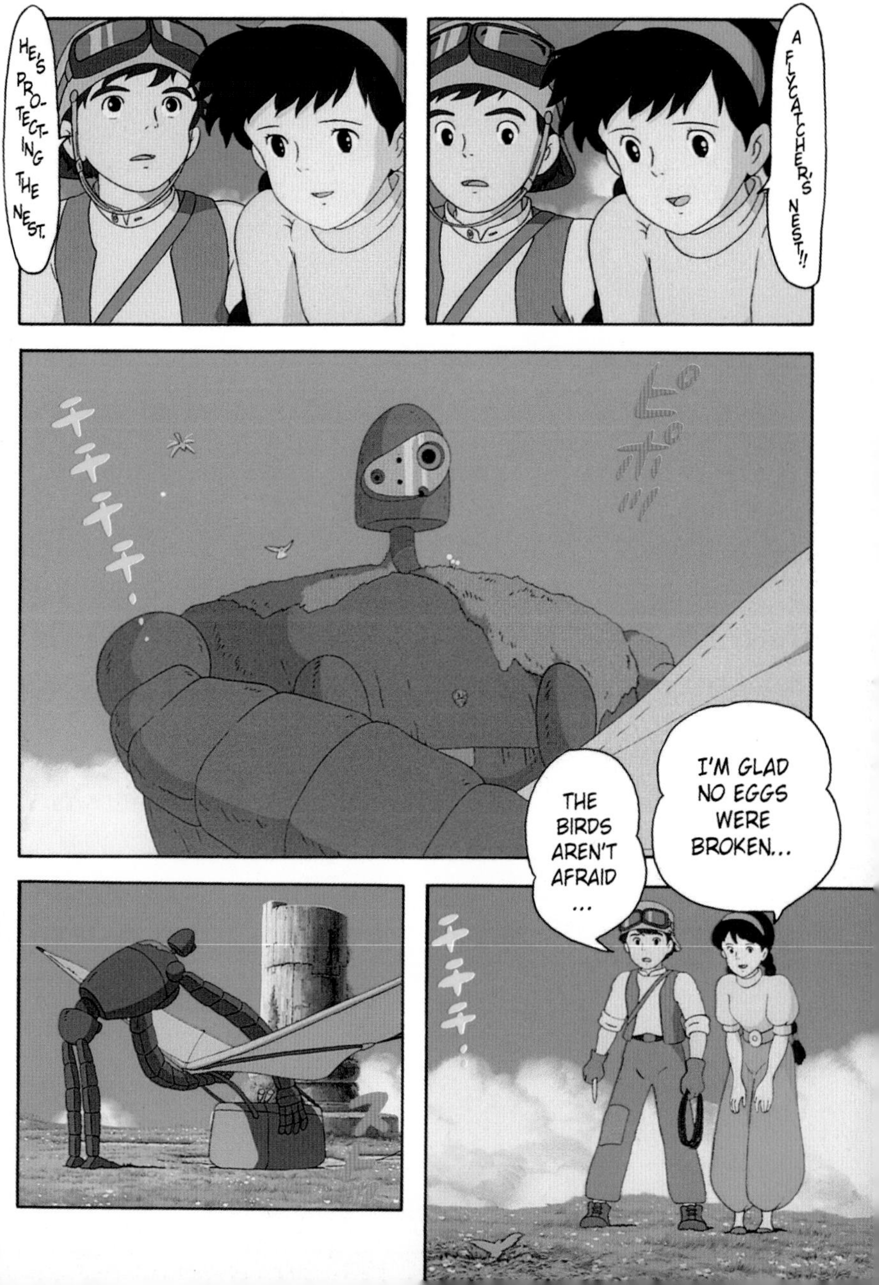
A FLYCATCHER'S NEST!!
HE'S PROTECTING THE NEST.
チチチチ。
I'M GLAD NO EGGS WERE BROKEN...
THE BIRDS AREN'T AFRAID...
チチチ。

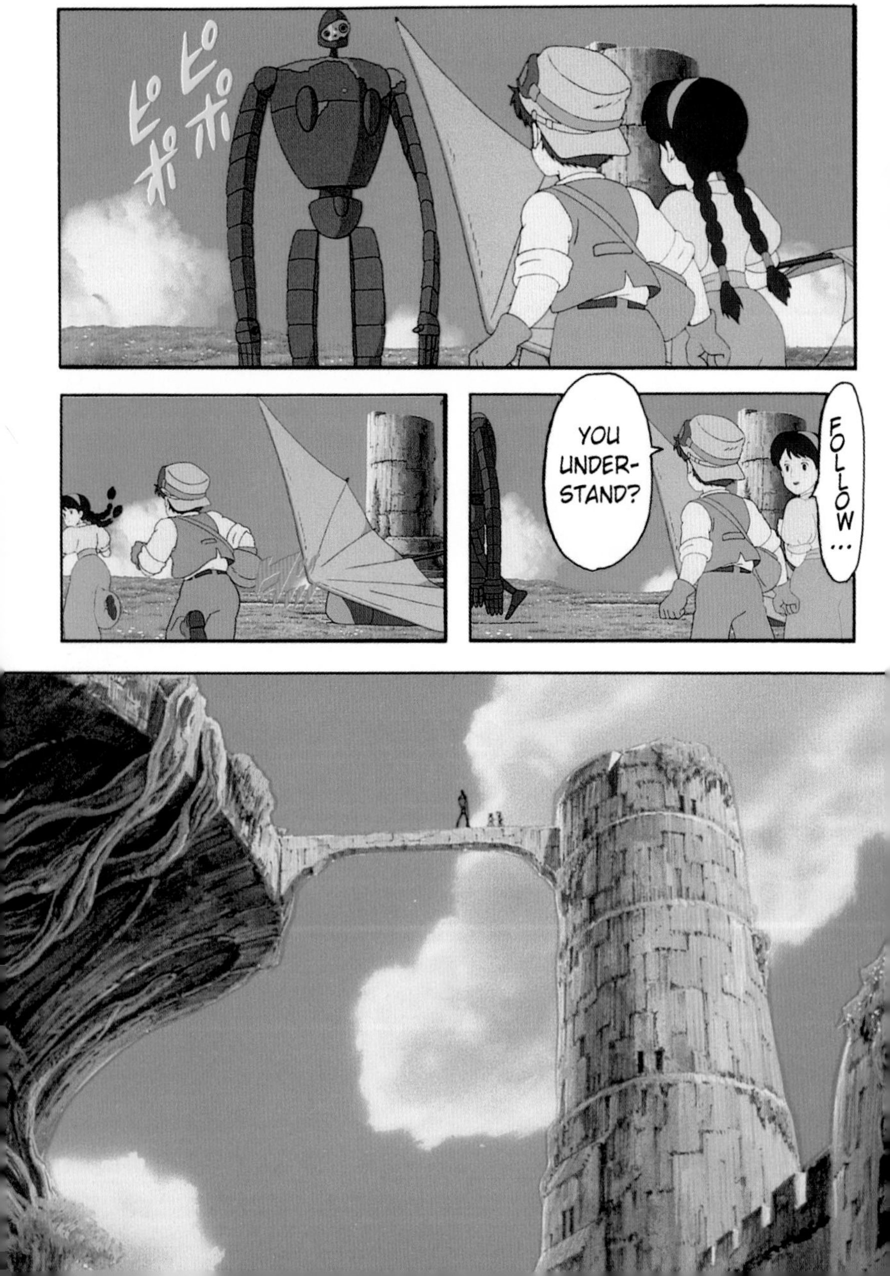
ピポ ピポ
FOLLOW...
YOU UNDERSTAND?

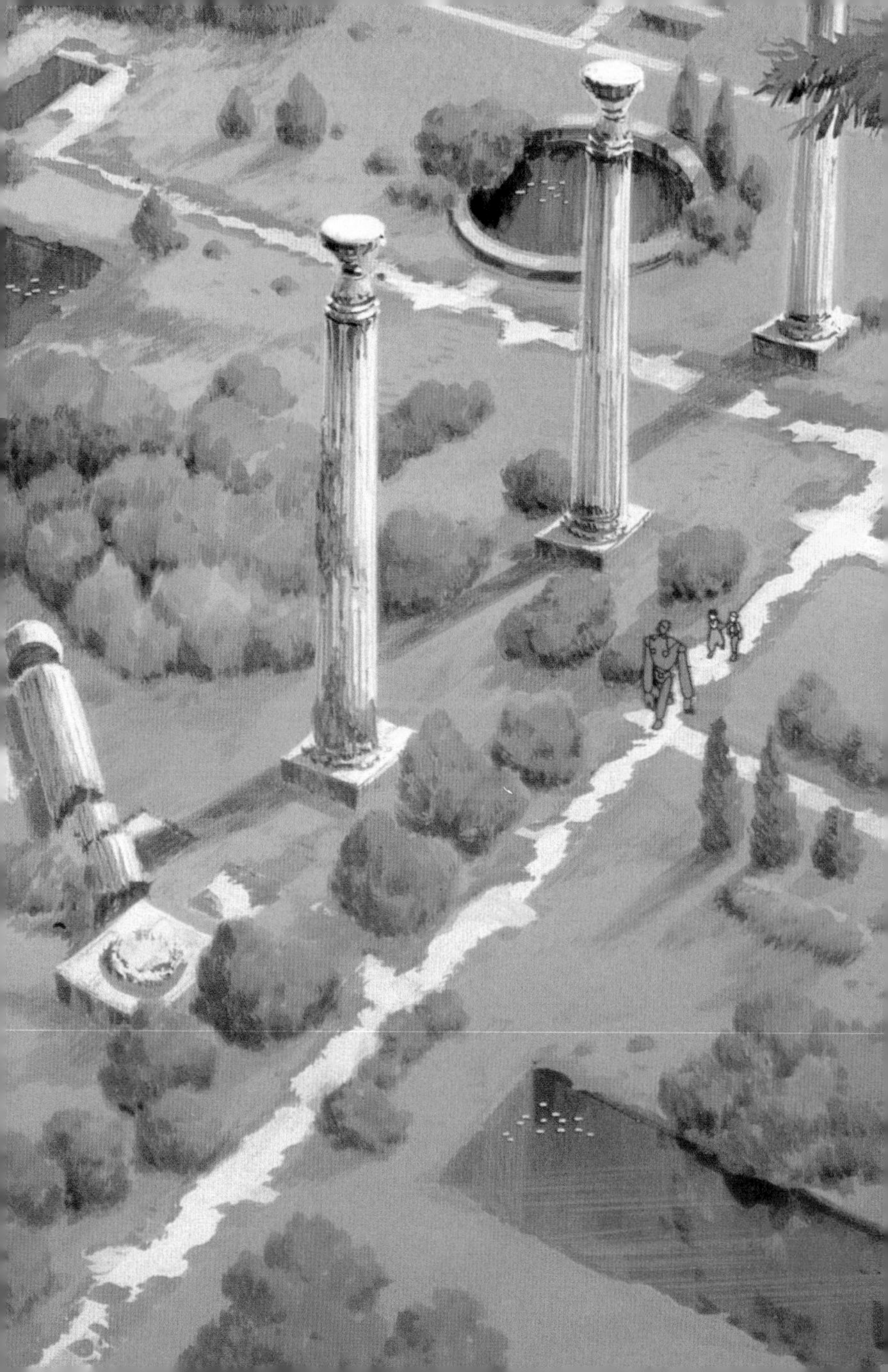

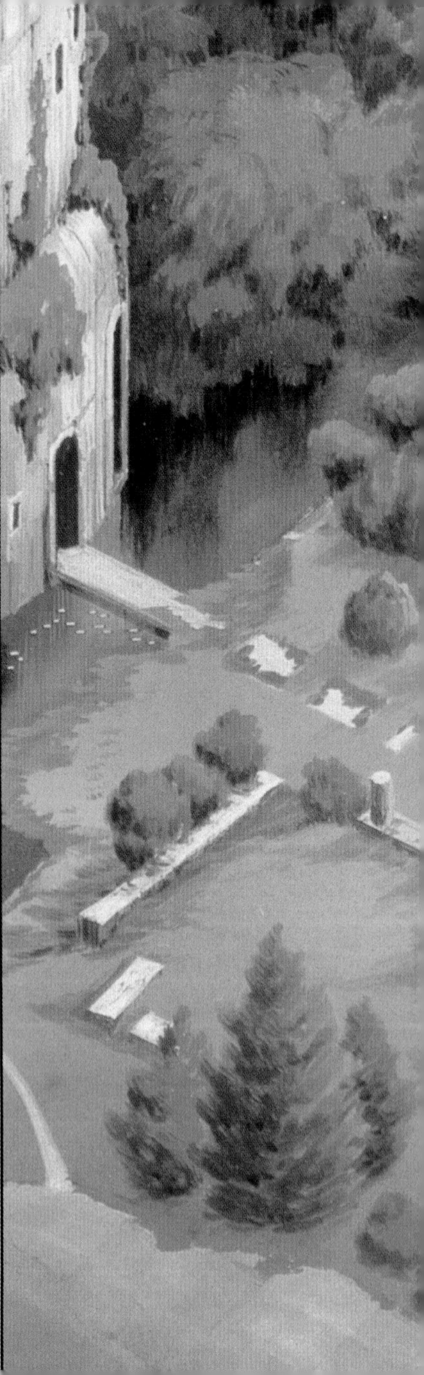

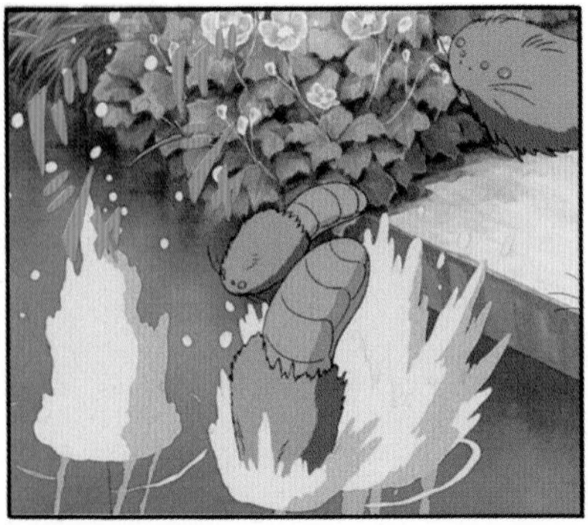

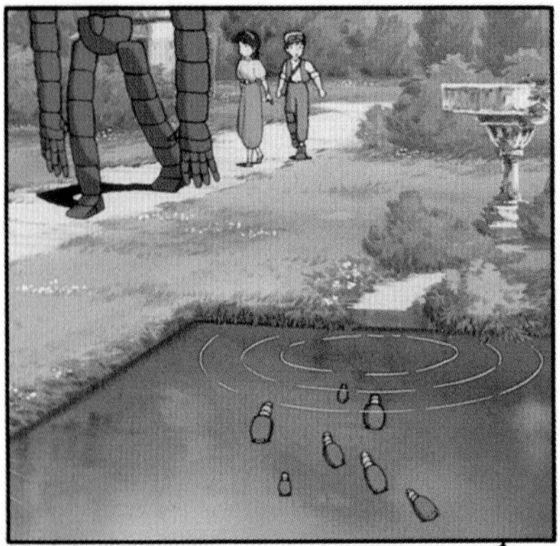

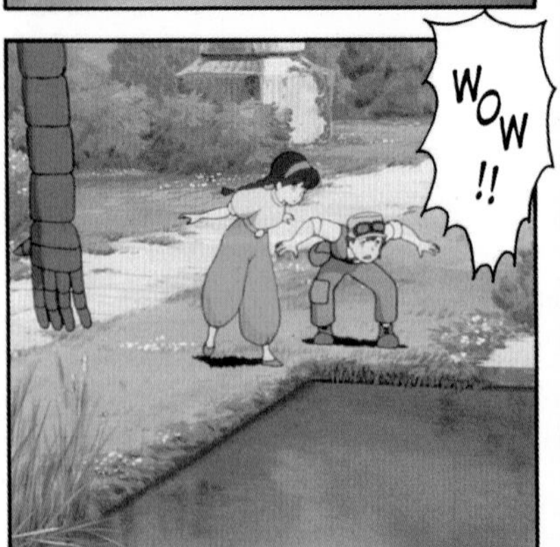
WOW !!

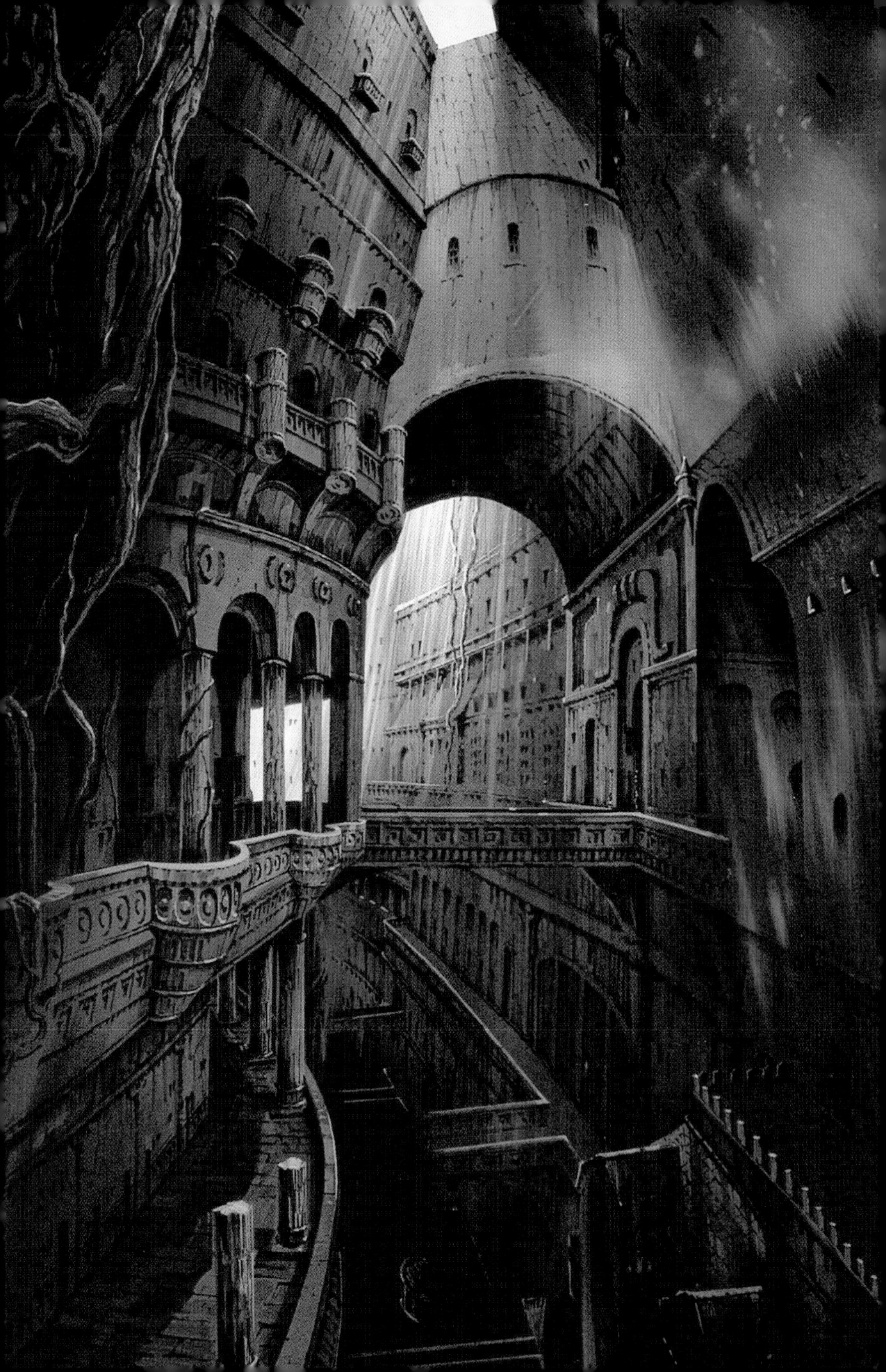

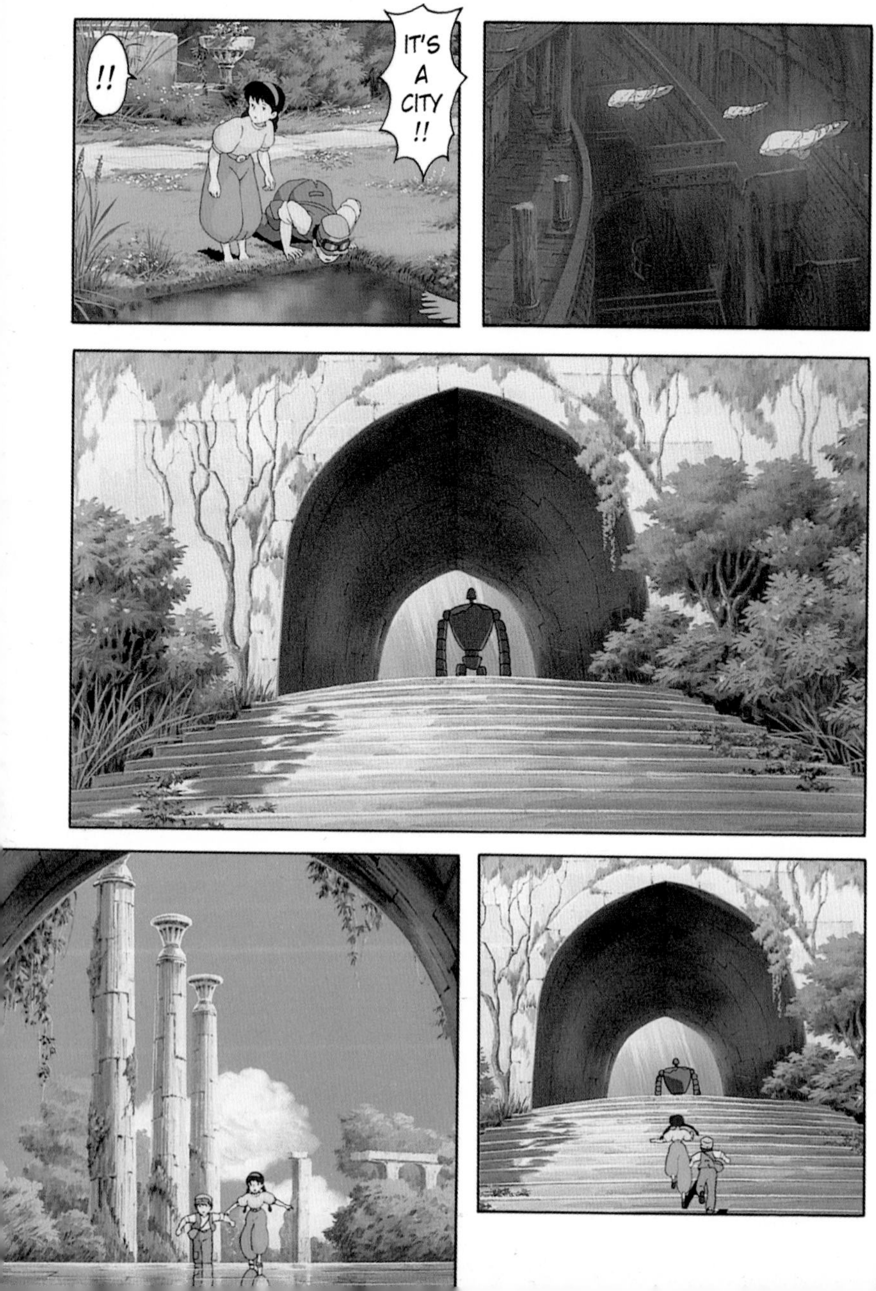
IT'S A CITY !!
!!

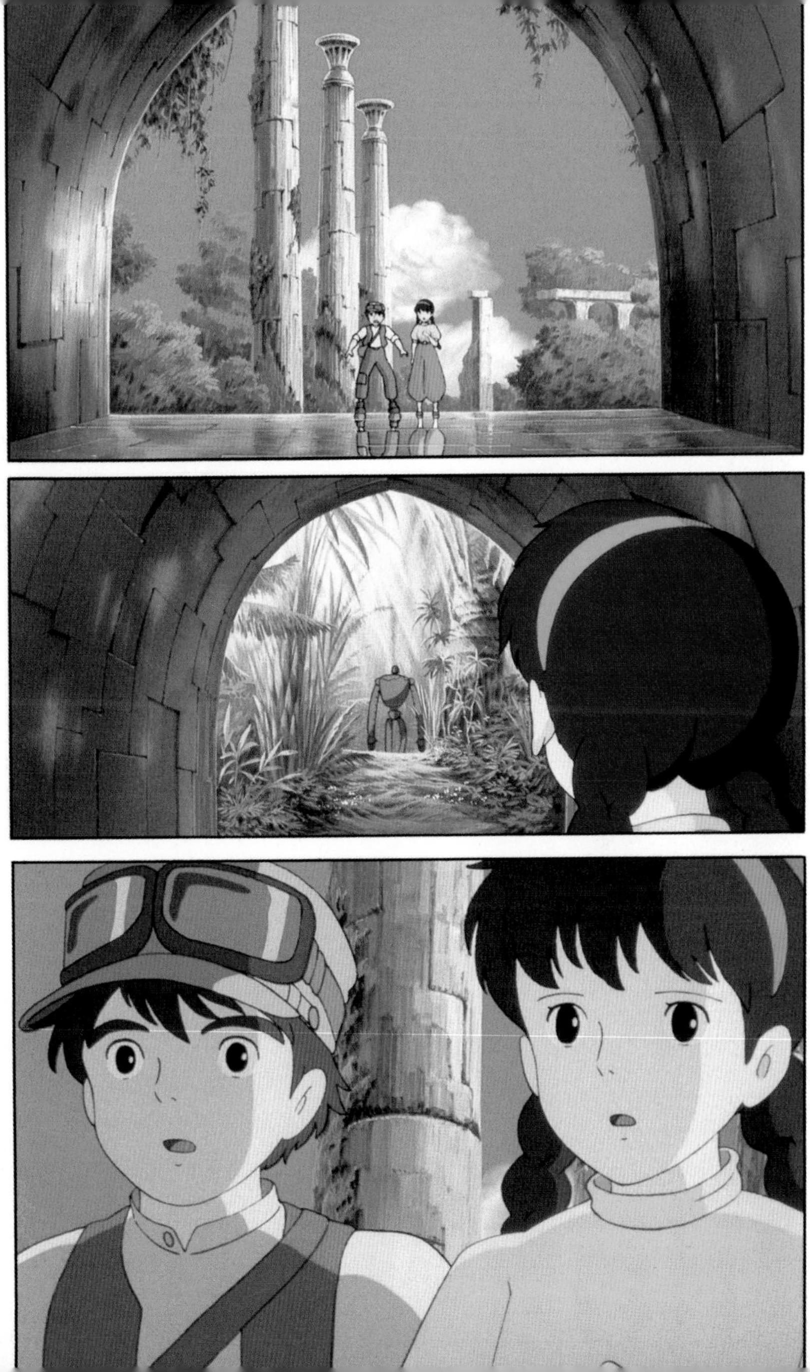

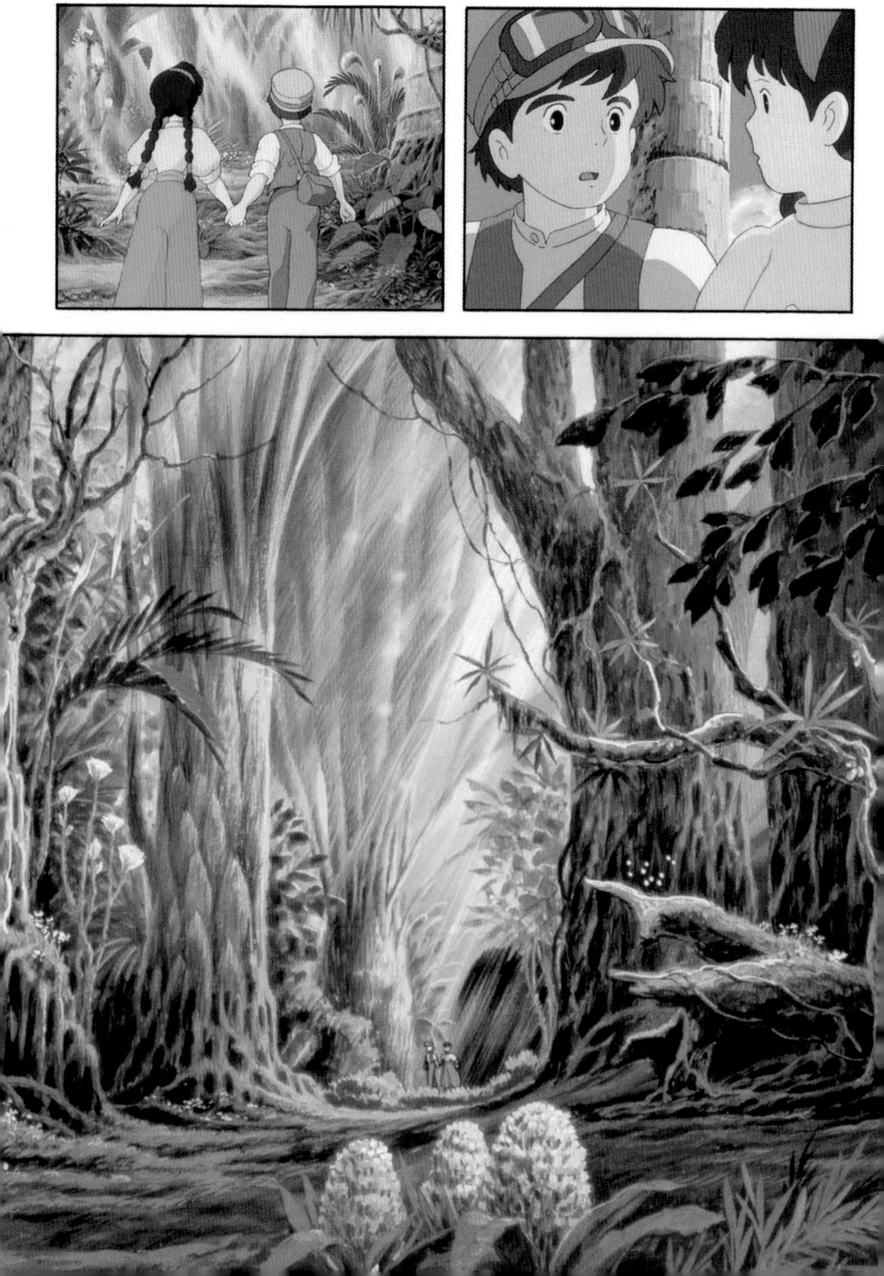

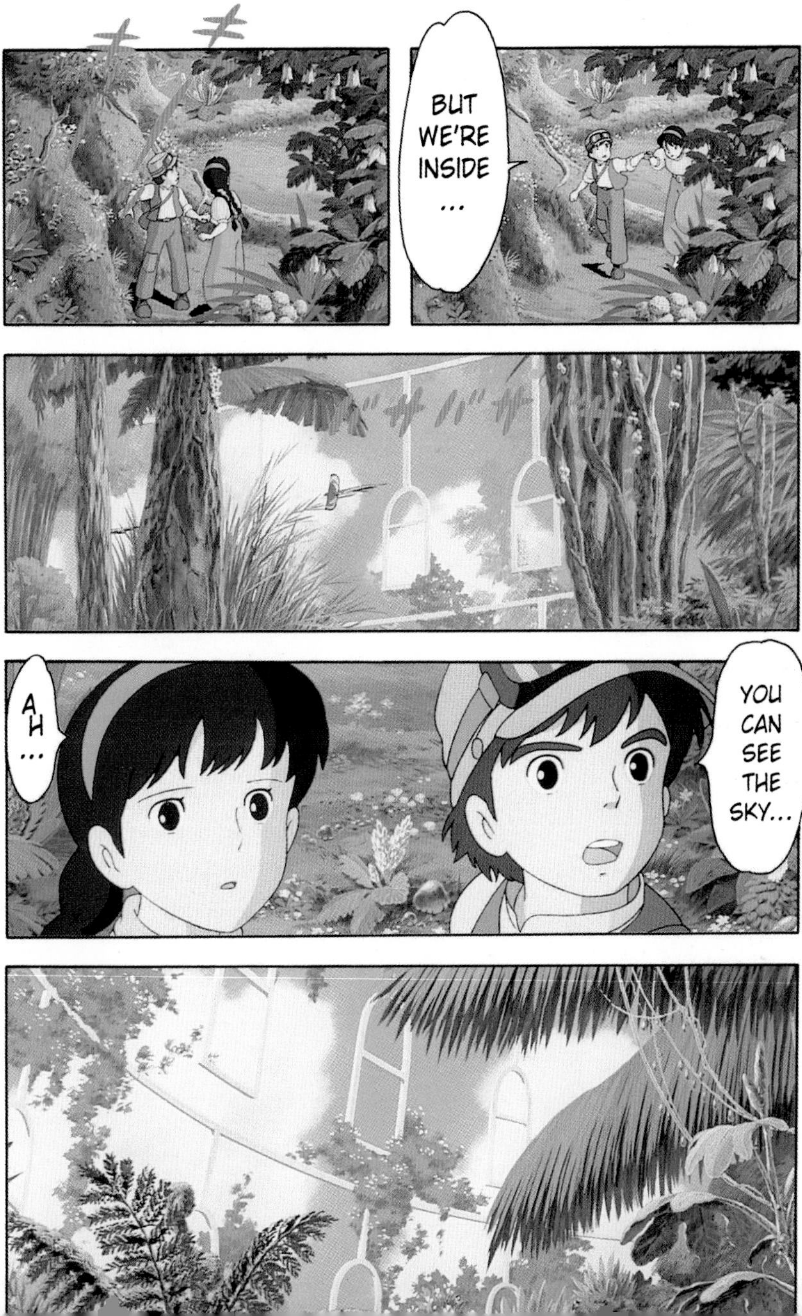
BUT WE'RE INSIDE ...
YOU CAN SEE THE SKY...
AH ...

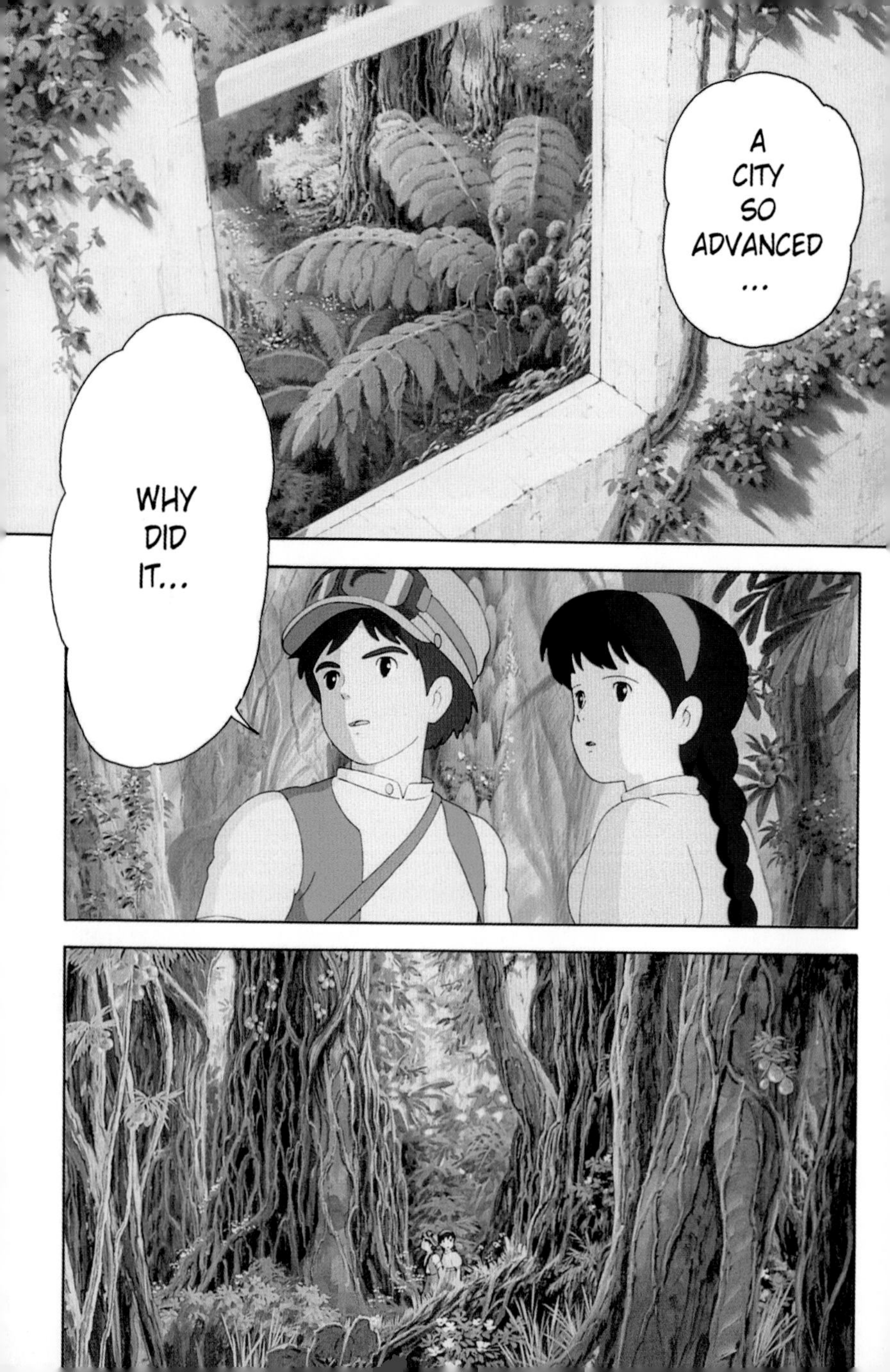
A CITY SO ADVANCED...
WHY DID IT...

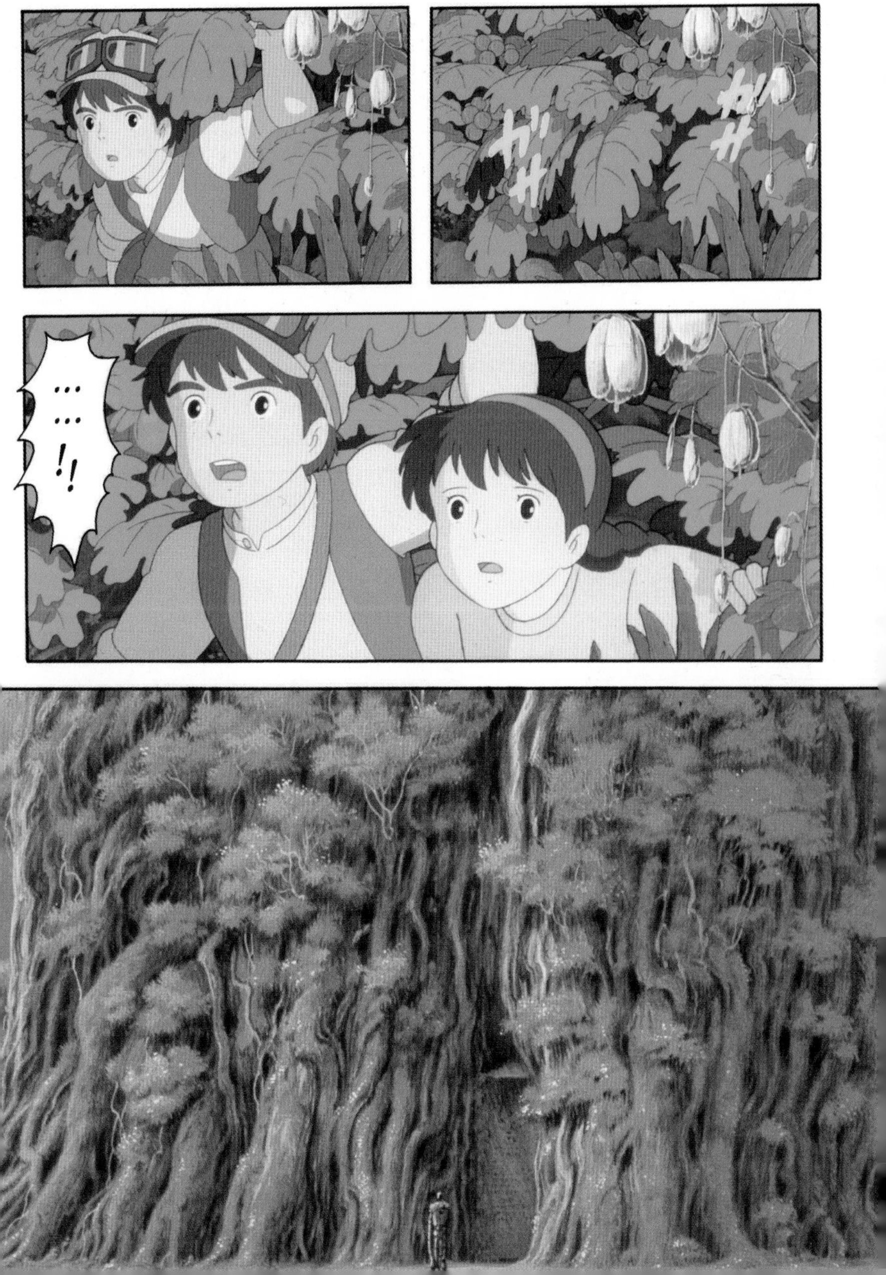
ガサ
ガサ
……!!

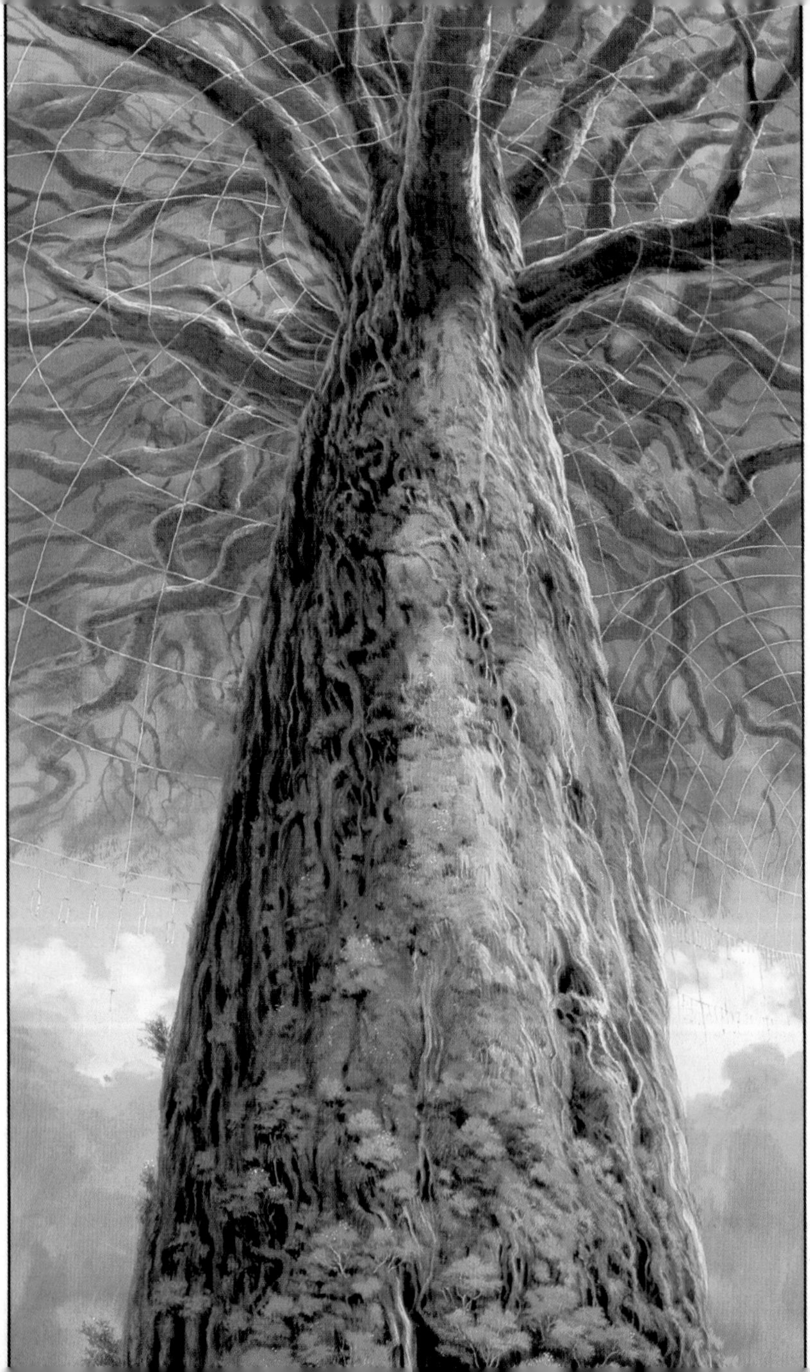

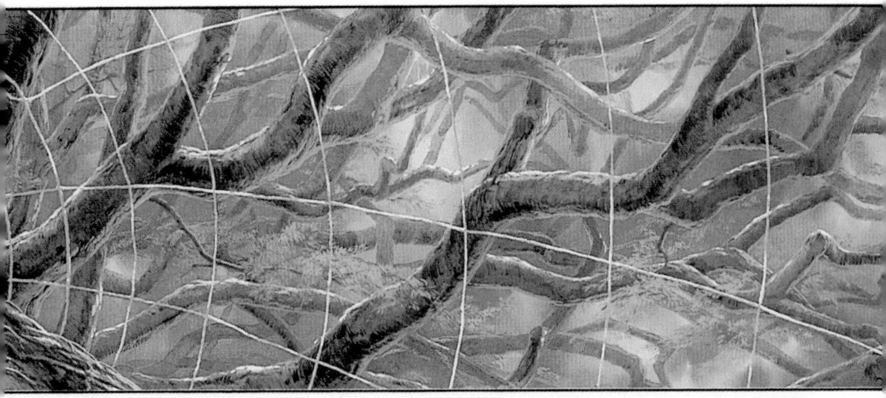

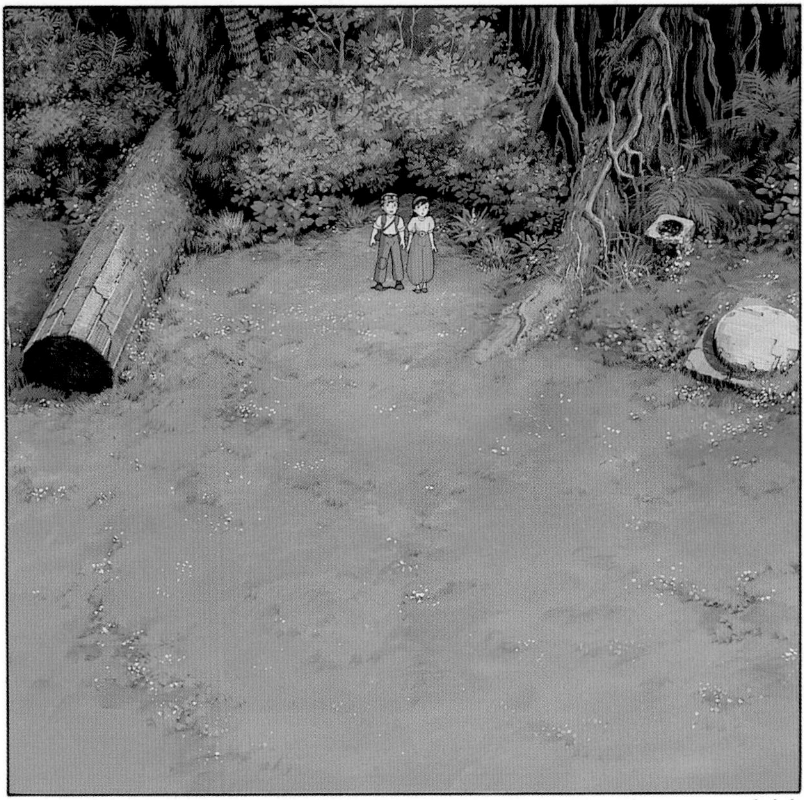

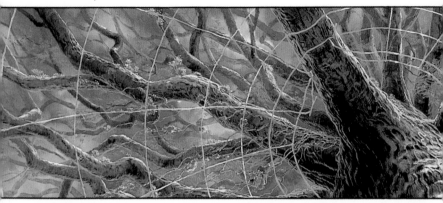

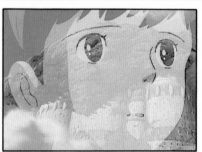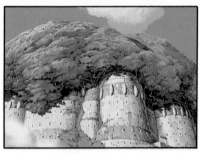

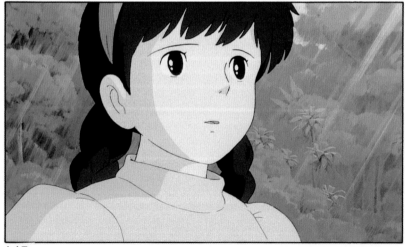

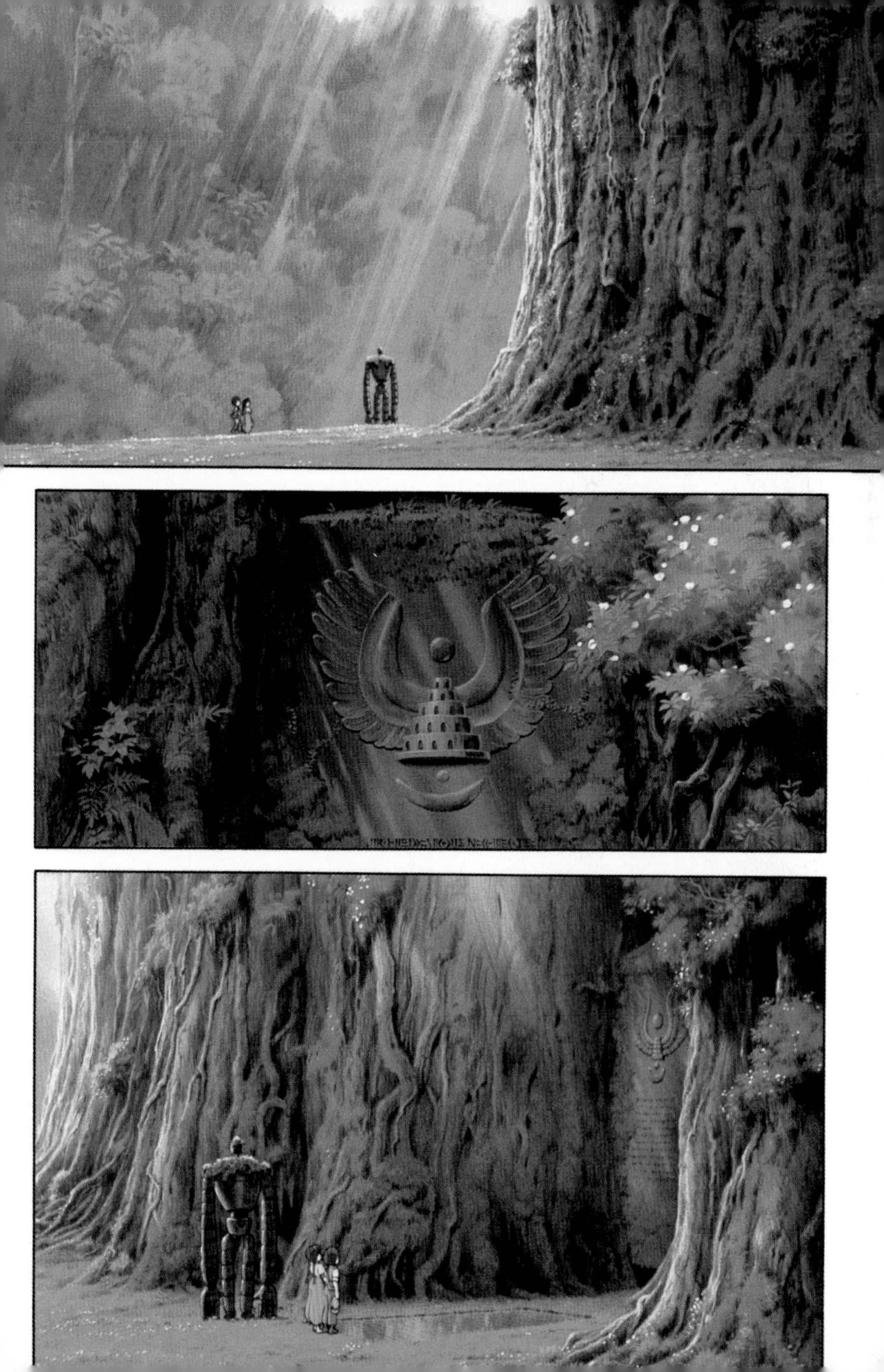

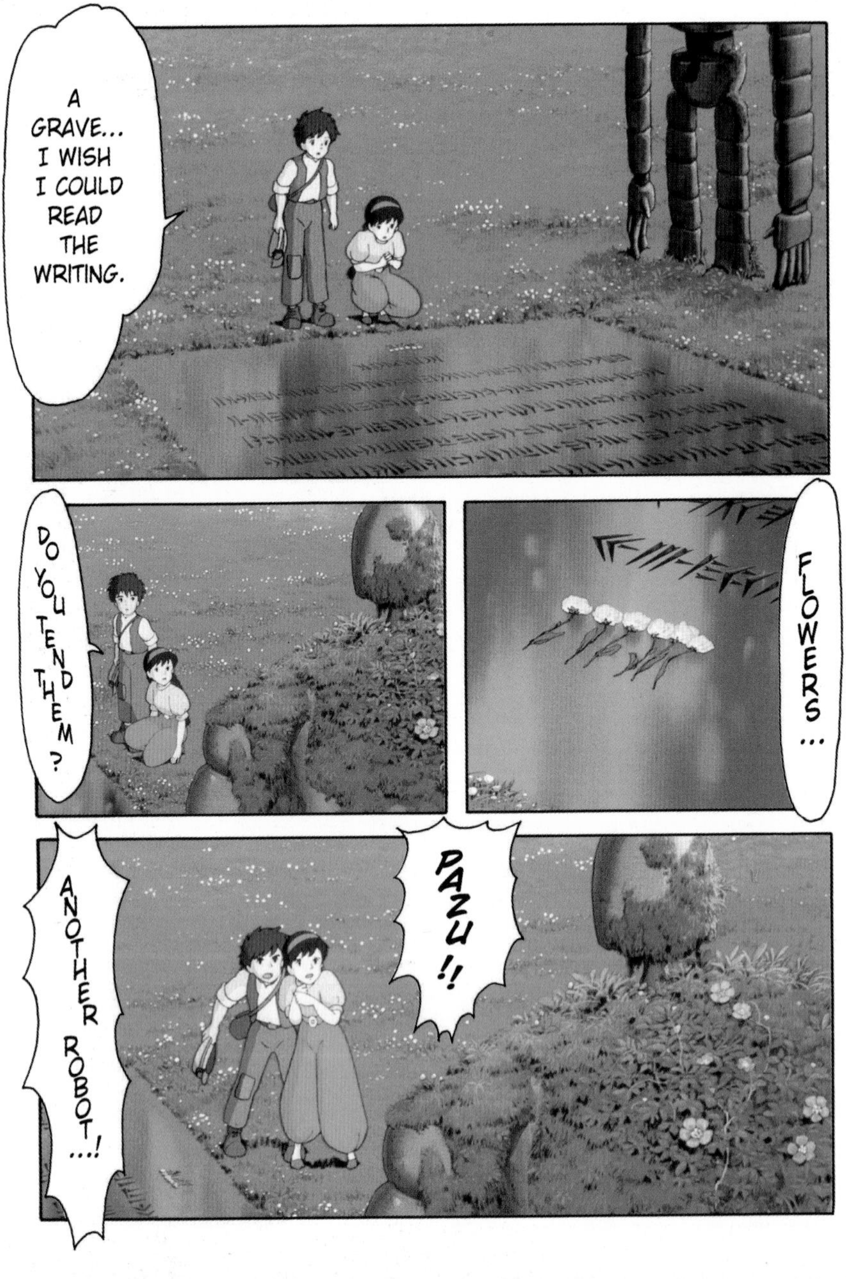
A GRAVE... I WISH I COULD READ THE WRITING.
FLOWERS...
DO YOU TEND THEM?
PAZU!!
ANOTHER ROBOT...!

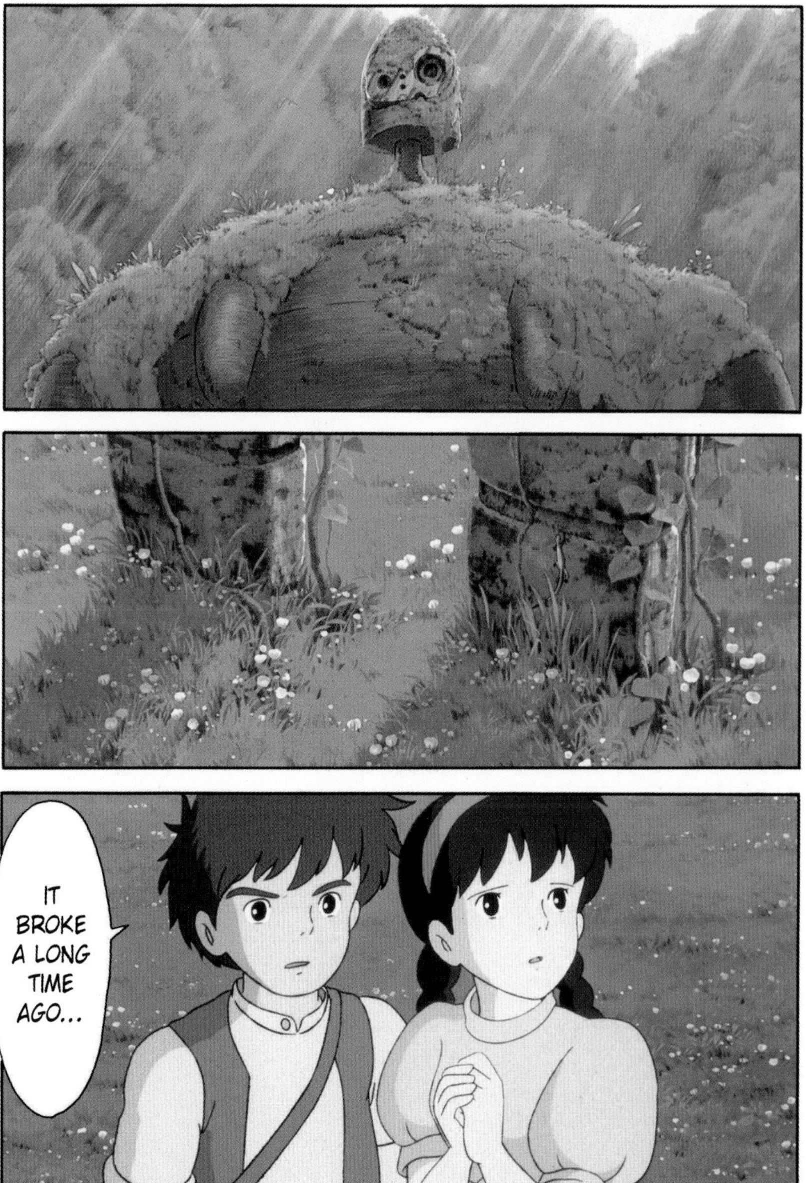
IT BROKE A LONG TIME AGO...

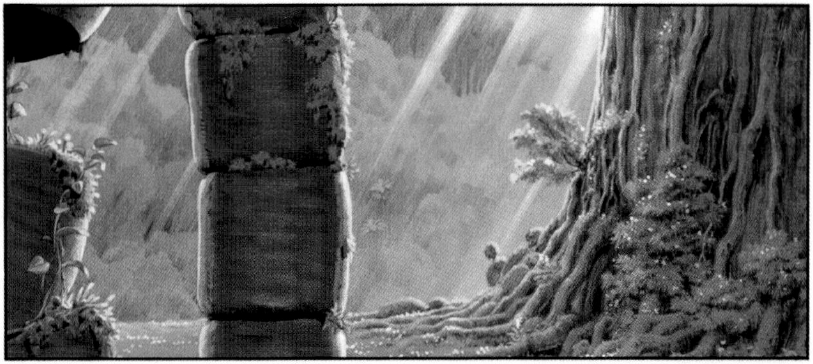
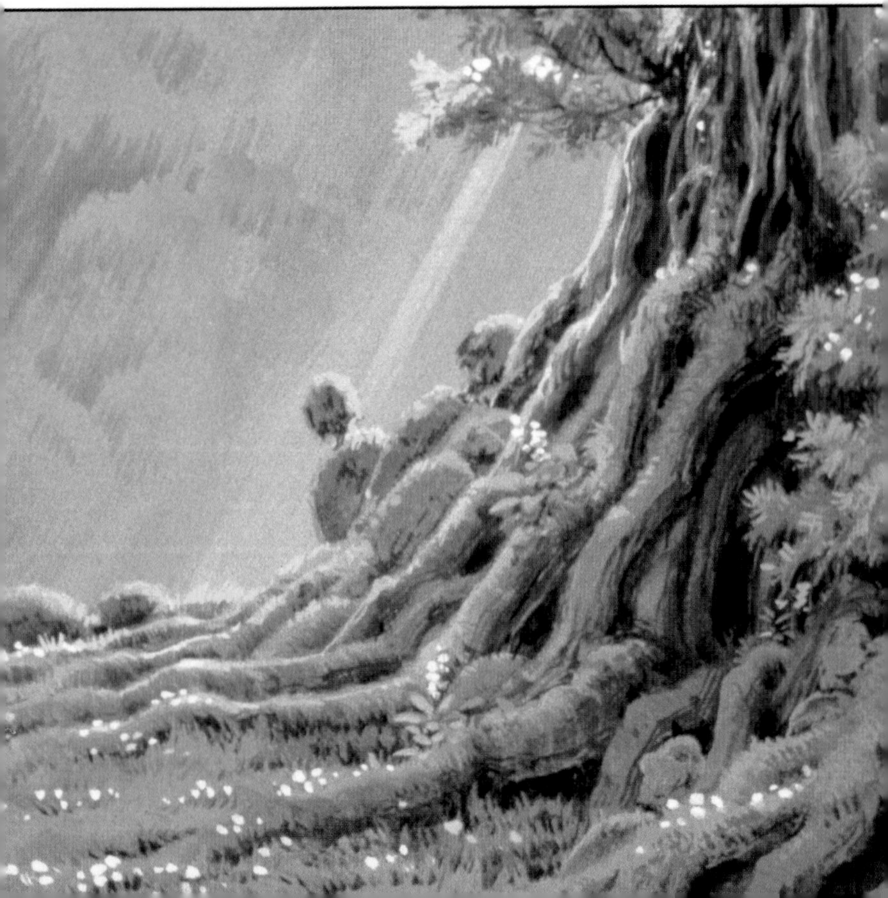

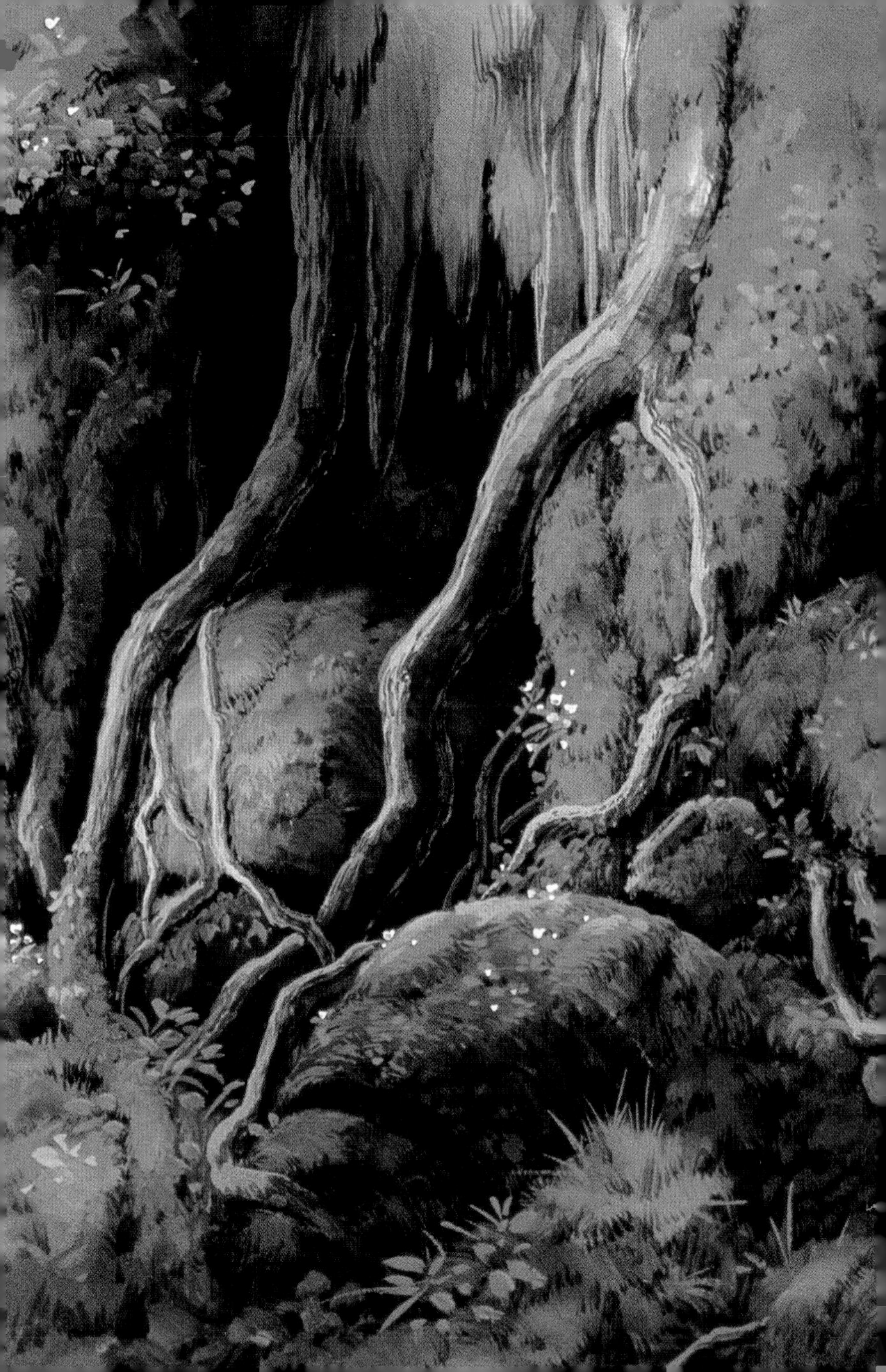

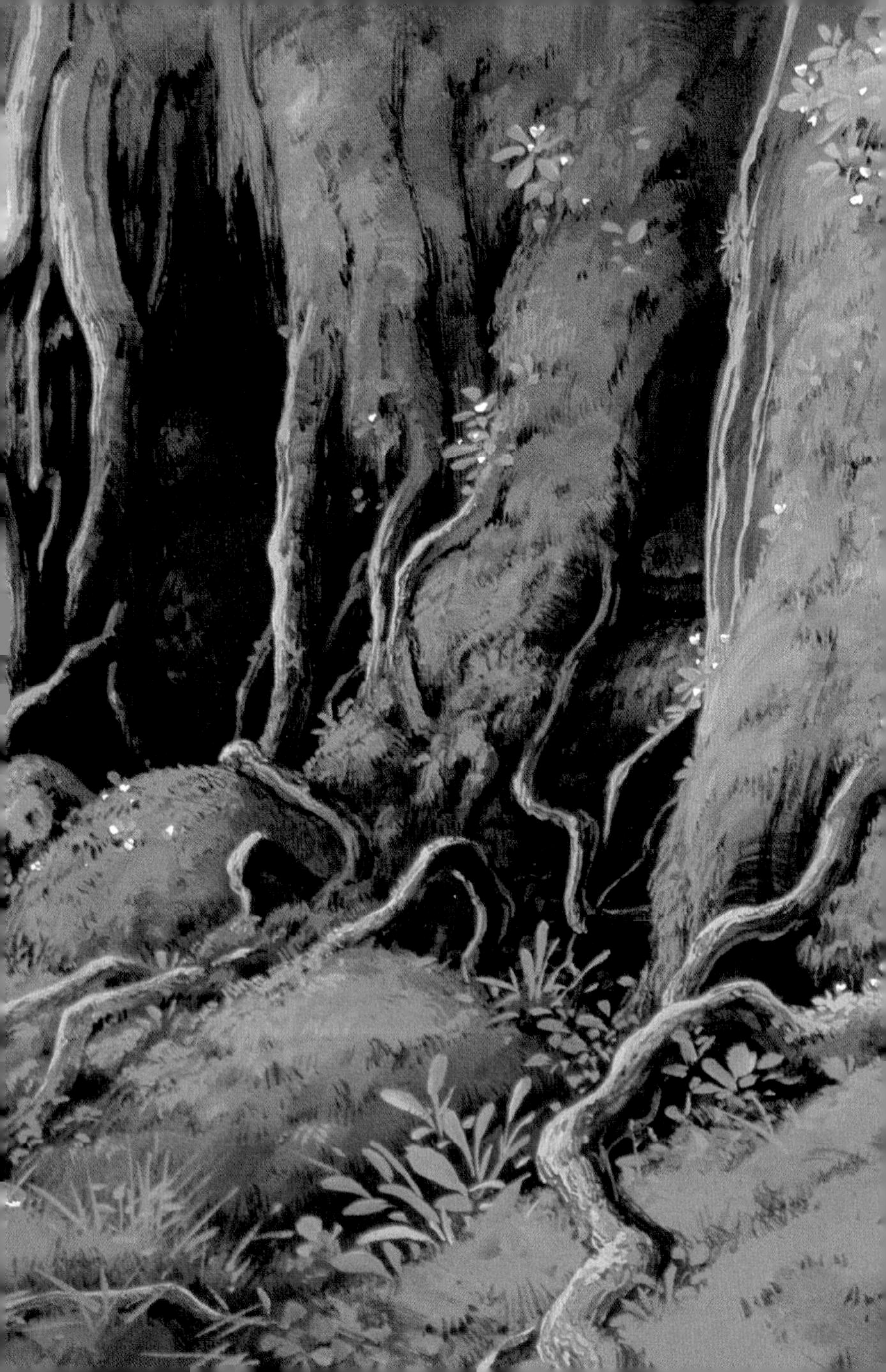

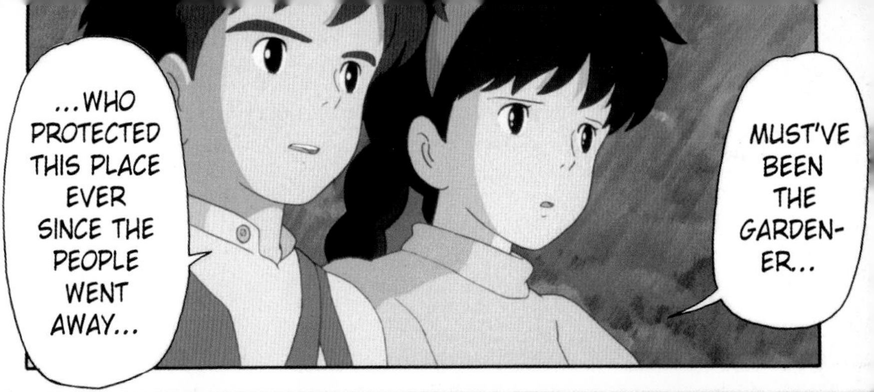
MUST'VE BEEN THE GARDENER...
...WHO PROTECTED THIS PLACE EVER SINCE THE PEOPLE WENT AWAY...
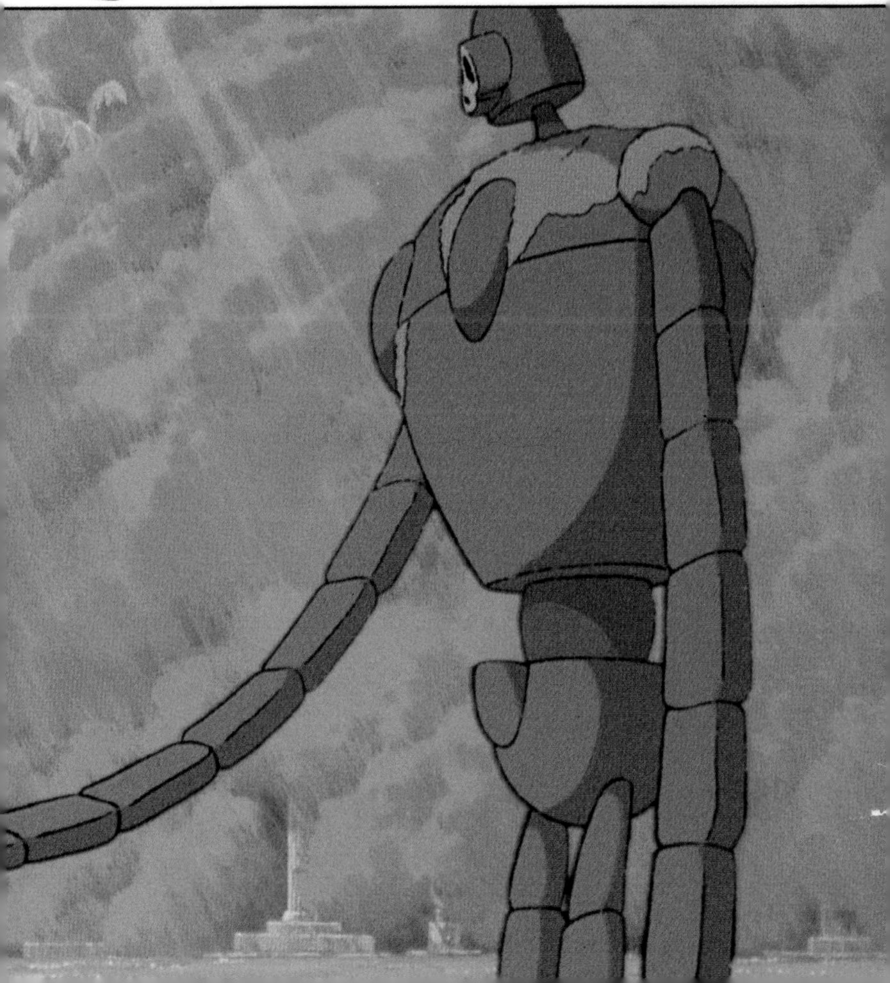

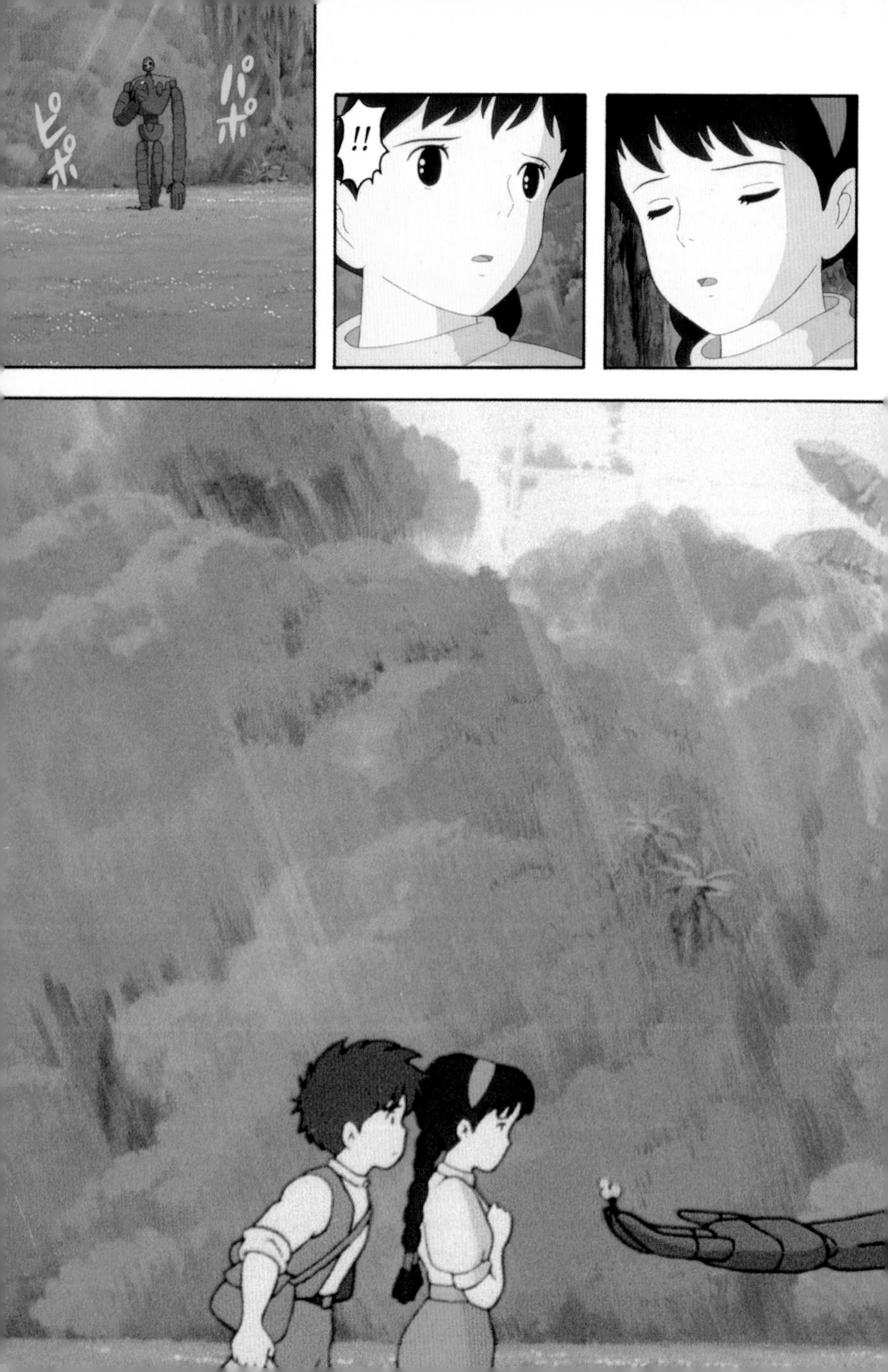
!!
パポ
ピポ

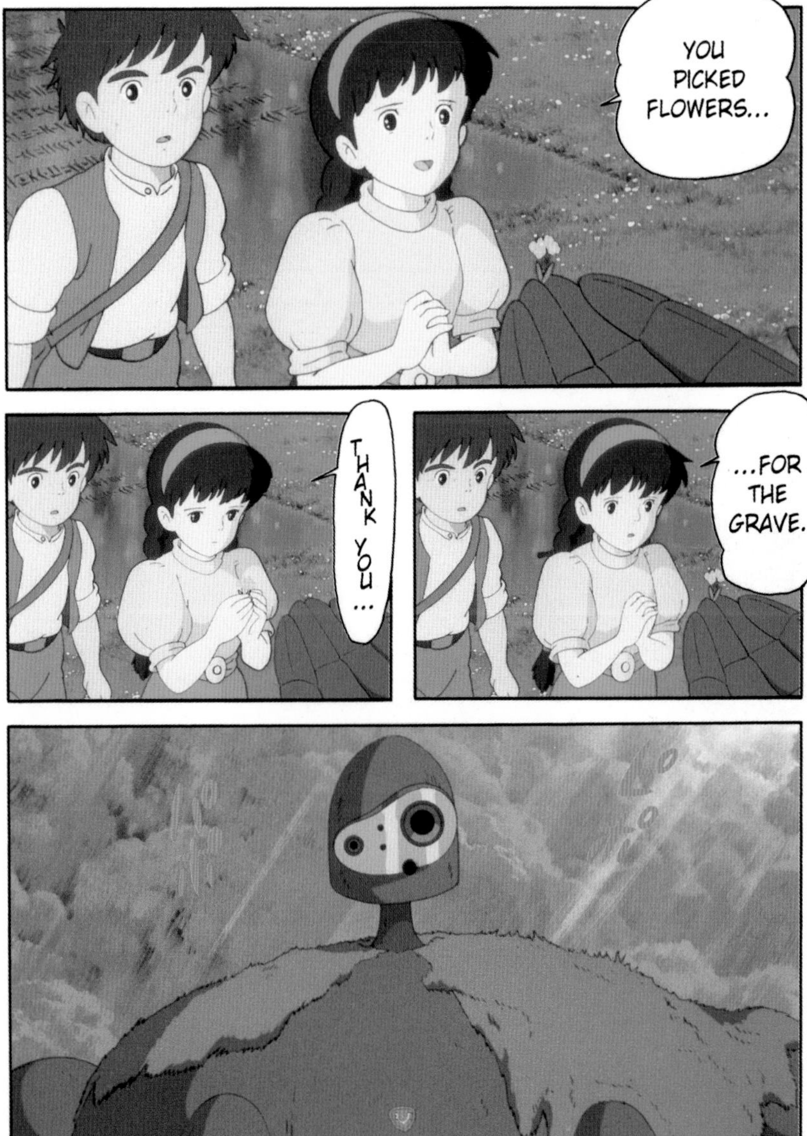
YOU PICKED FLOWERS...
...FOR THE GRAVE.
THANK YOU...

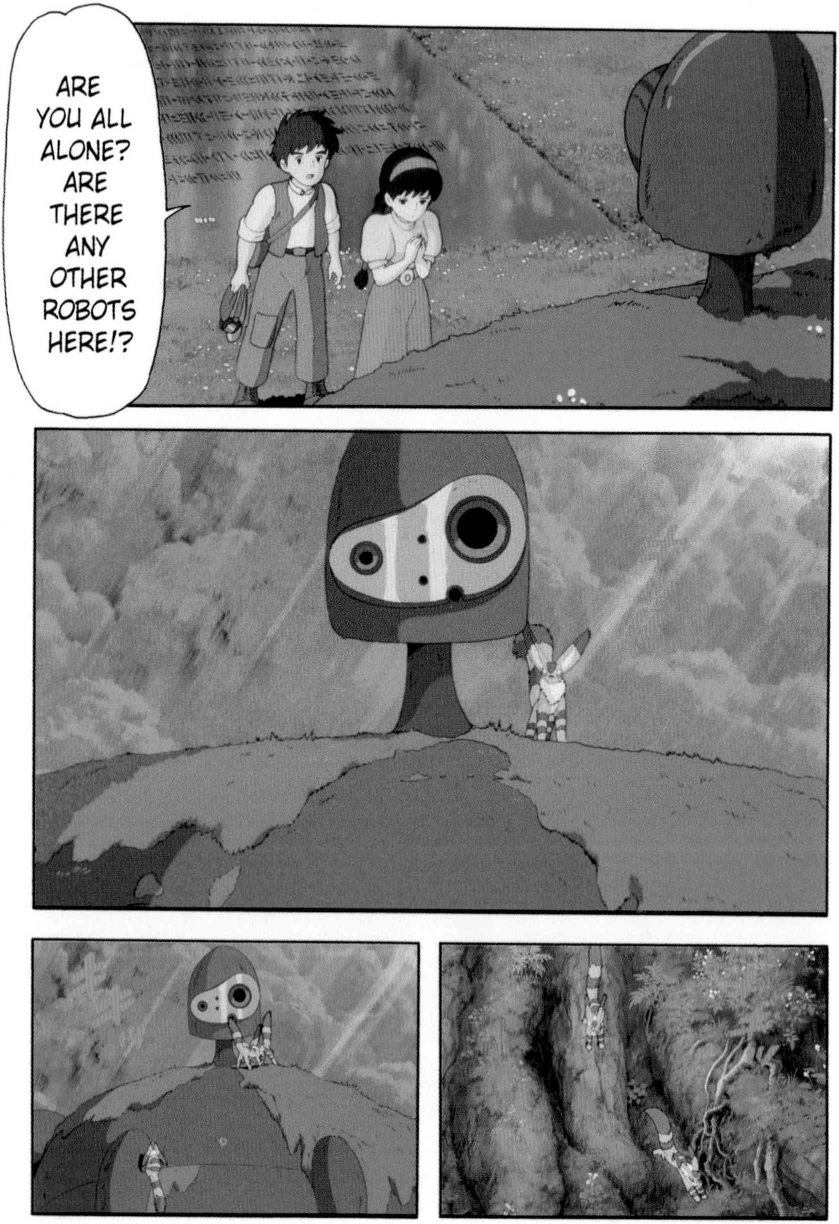
ARE YOU ALL ALONE? ARE THERE ANY OTHER ROBOTS HERE!?

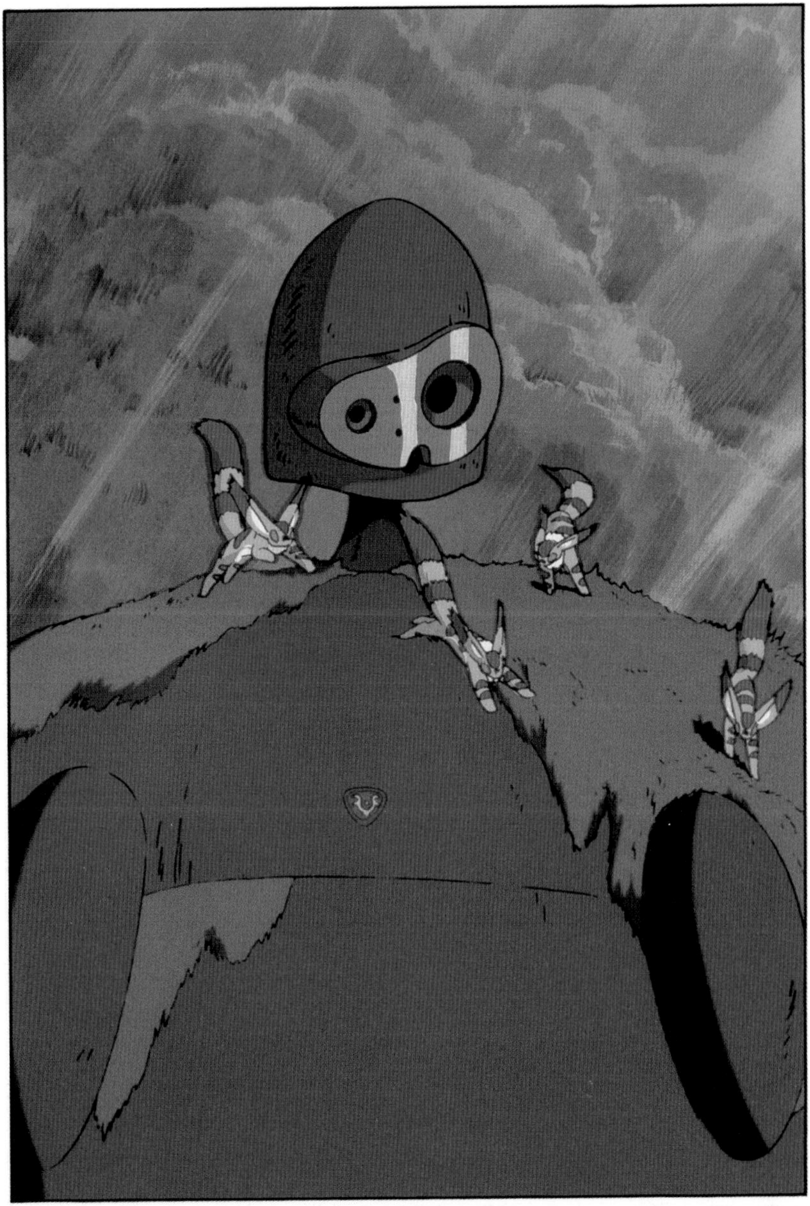

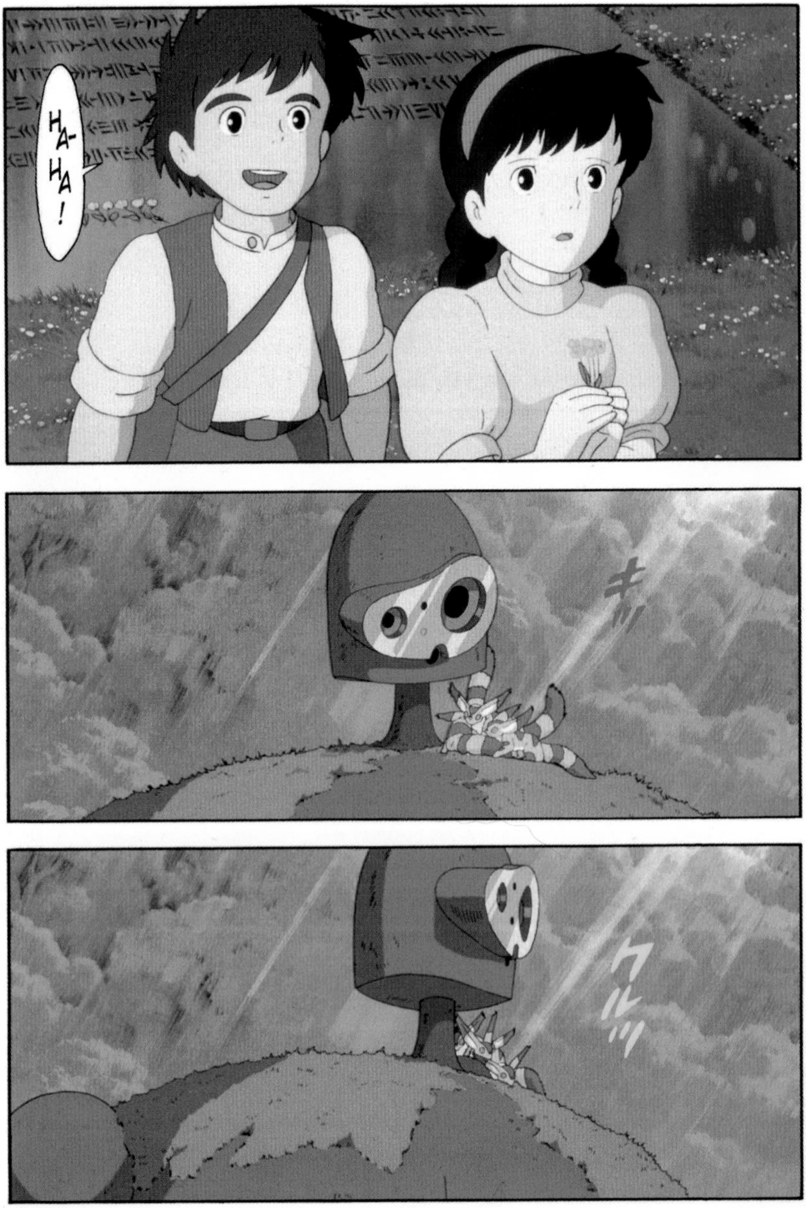
HA-HA-HA!
キリ
クルッ

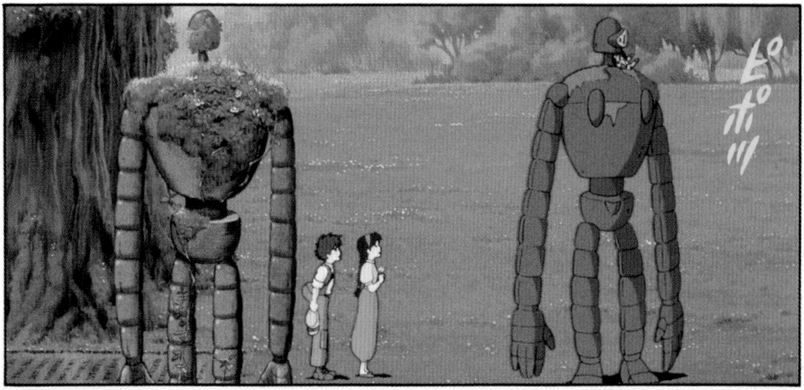
ピポッ

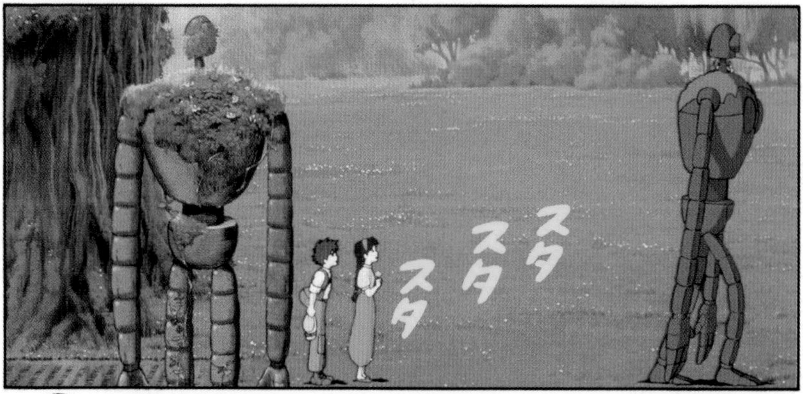
スタ
スタ
スタ

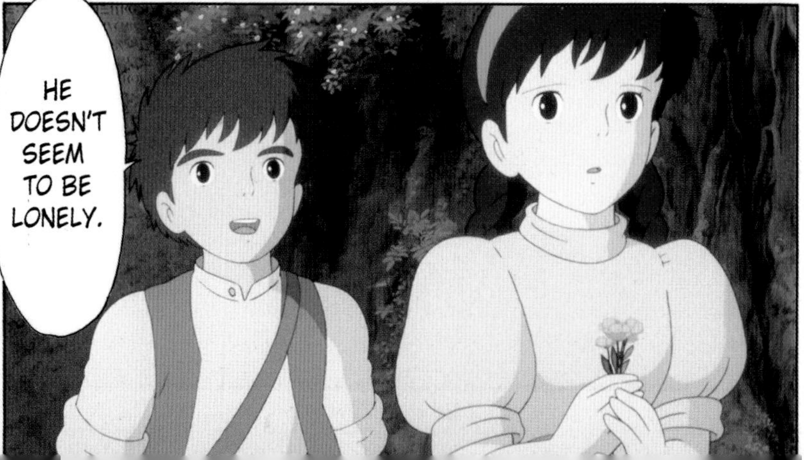
HE DOESN'T SEEM TO BE LONELY.

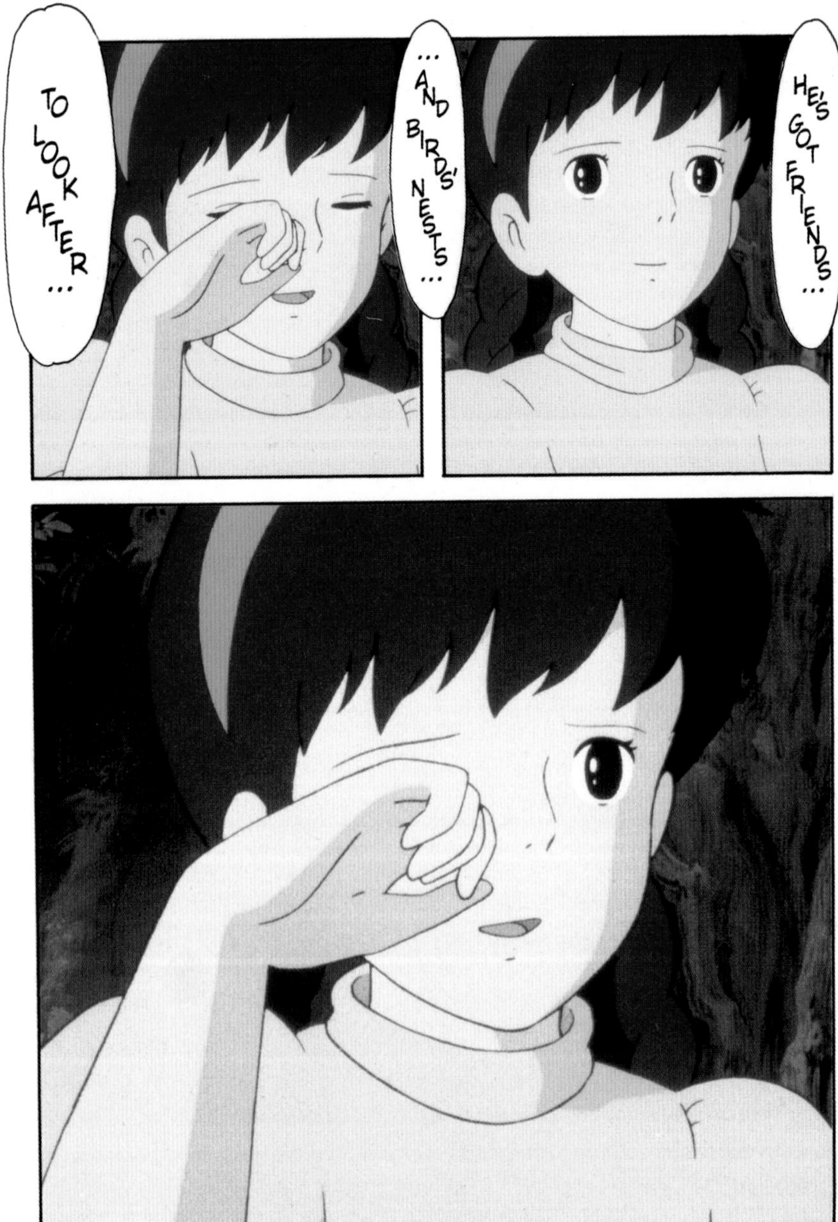
HE'S GOT FRIENDS...
...AND BIRDS' NESTS...
TO LOOK AFTER...

TO BE CONTINUED

Your Guide to *Castle in the Sky* Sound Effects!

To increase your enjoyment of the distinctive Japanese visual style of *Castle in the Sky*, we've included a guide to the sound effects used in this *manga* (comic book) style adaptation of the actual *anime* (animated) movie. These sound effects are usually written in the phonetic characters called *katakana*.

Looking at an example on page 5, you can see how the sound effects are listed: first, by page and panel number (so 5.1 means page 5, panel one); then, the literally-translated sound spelled out by the katakana (so "FX: PARA PARA PARA" is the sound spelled out by パラパラパラ on page 5, panel 1); finally, how this sound effect might have been spelled out, or what it stands for, in English (so [fwip fwip fwip] is how we might spell out this particular sound, the turning propellers of the pirate airship *Tiger Moth*—you'll be interested to see the sometimes different way Japanese describe the sound of things!).

If there are different or multiple sound FX in the same panel, an extra number will be added to the index to show them apart; for an example, see 20.1.1 and 20.1.2. Remember all numbers are given in the original Japanese reading order: right-to-left.

You'll sometime see a small "tsu" at the end of a sound FX, which looks like this: ツ . This isn't part of the sound itself; it's just a way of showing that the sound is the kind that ends suddenly, rather than the kind that fades out: fades tend to be indicated by two or three dots. You'll also see a mark like a long dash: — . This means that the

sound lasts for a while. Sometimes instead of the long dash, extras of the same vowel are used instead; it's the artist's choice. Note that the — and the ツ can be combined!

Very occasionally, a "spoken" sound FX will be given not in katakana, but in *hiragana*, a second, parallel phonetic system written "in cursive," used in Japanese mainly to denote grammar and to spell out native words (that is, as opposed to those words imported from other languages). In *Castle in the Sky* Vol. 3 this happens on four occasions—for 20.1.2 FX: GURU GURU [twirrl twirrl] 29.5.2 FX: GUTSU GUTSU [glug glug] 29.8 FX: SUSU!! [fssh!!] 125.5 FX: YO!! [fup]

Note that two of these four have っ , the small hiragana version of "tsu" on the end, which signifies the same sudden ending of the sound as the katakana "tsu." In order, all four of these FX are spelled out in hiragana as ぐるぐる, ぐつぐつ, すすっ, and よっ ; if these four FX were in the usual katakana, they would be would be グルグル , グツグツ , ススッ , and ヨッ . Why use hiragana for these particular sound effects? For native speakers of Japanese, it sometimes seems like the more "natural" way to render a certain sound in a certain scene, especially if the sound is "spoken" in some way, like a laugh or shout.

One important last note: all these vowels in katakana or hiragana should be pronounced as they are in Japanese. In Japanese, "A" is *ah*, "I" is *eee*, "U" is *ooh*, "E" is *eh*, and "O" is *oh*. Try putting these effects into your style of speaking!

160

5.1 ——FX: PARA PARA PARA [fwip fwip fwip]

5.2 ——FX: GUOOO [rrrrrrr]

5.3 ——FX: GUOOO…[rrrrrrrr…]

5.4 ——FX: BUUUUN [vrrrmmm]

6.1 ——FX: BUUUUN [vrrrmmm]

6.2 ——FX: GUOOON…[rrrrrrrr…]

6.3 ——FX: UIIIIN [vweeen]

6.4 ——FX: BUU… [rrr…]

7.1 ——FX: BUUN [vrrrmmm]

7.2 ——FX: PATAPATAPATA [wip wip wip]

7.3 ——FX: GASSHII!! [ftunk!!]

7.4-5 ——FX: BUUUN [vwoom]

8.1 ——FX: GACHAAN [kaching]

8.3 ——FX: SUTA [fup]

8.4 ——FX: GISHI [fwinch]

9.2 ——FX: GACHAAN [kaching]

10.1 ——FX: BYUU [fwee]

10.2 ——FX: BUWA [fwom]

10.3 ——FX: BYUU [fweee]

11.5 ——FX: GACHA [chak]

11.6 ——FX: GASHU GASHU GASHU [thoom thoom thoom]

12.5 ——FX: SU [fsh]

13.1 ——FX: KUI KUI [fip fip]

17.1 ——FX: PACHI PACHI [tapp tapp]

17.3 ——FX: GUI [tugg]

17.5 ——FX: GOOOO [rrrrrr]

19.4 ——FX: DODODO [tmp tmp tmp]

19.5 ——FX: DODODO

[tmp tmp tmp]

20.1.1 ——FX: UOOOO [whirrrr]

20.1.2 ——FX: GURU GURU [twirrl twirrl]

20.3 ——FX: GUGU [fut fut]

20.5 ——FX: GASHIIN [klaaang]

20.6.1 ——FX: GASHIIN [klaaang]

20.6.2 ——FX: GOGOGOOO [rrrrrrr]

21.1.1 ——FX: BARABARA [fip fip fip]

21.1.2 ——FX: GOOOO [rrrrrrr]

21.3-4 ——FX: GOGOGOO [rrrrrrr]

22.1-2 ——FX: GOGOGOOO [rrrrrrrr]

22.3 ——FX: GOOO [rrrr]

22.4 ——FX: GOOO [rrrr]

22.5 ——FX: GACHA [chak]

23.1 ——FX: ZUZUZU [fsssh]

23.4 ——FX: BA [foosh]

24.3 ——FX: GACHA [chak]

24.4 ——FX: BATAN [chud]

25.5 ——FX: BA [fwoosh]

26.1 ——FX: DOTADOTABATA [fwafwawud]

26.3 ——FX: EHEHEHE [haha]

26.4 ——FX: JITABATA [fwip fwop]

26.5 ——FX: DODODOOO [tmp tmp tmmmp]

27.4 ——FX: GOOOOO [rrrrrrr]

28.1 ——FX: KAAAN KAAAN [klaak klaak]

28.2-3 ——FX: GOOOON [rrrrrrrr]

28.4 ——FX: KAAN KAAN KAAN

[klaak klaak klaak]

28.5 ——FX: GASHAN GASHAN [klang klang]

29.5.1 ——FX: KARI KARI [snip snip]

29.5.2 ——FX: GUTSU GUTSU [glug glug]

29.7 ——FX: CHIRO CHIRO [hm hm]

29.8 ——FX: SUSU!! [fssh!!]

30.1 ——FX: KONKON [tok tok]

30.4 ——FX: KACHA [chak]

36.1.1 ——FX: GATSU GATSU [mnch mnch]

36.1.2 ——FX: MORI MORI [chomp chomp]

36.1.3 ——FX: GATSU GATSU [mnch mnch]

37.1 ——FX: GON GON GON [tunk tunk tunk]

37.2 ——FX: GOOON [rrrrrrr]

38.1 ——FX: GUOOO GUOOO [shnorr shnorr]

38.2 ——FX: SUU SUU [zzzz]

38.3 ——FX: GON [tok]

38.5 ——FX: GOSHI GOSHIO [rubb rubb]

39.1 ——FX: KATAN [chud]

39.3 ——FX: GUUU SUUU [shnorrr]

40.1 ——FX: BYUUUUU [fweeeeee]

40.3 ——FX: PA [fsh]

40.5 ——FX: GACHA [chak]

40.6 ——FX: HYUUUU [fweeee]

41.1 —FX: HYUUUUU [fweeee]

41.3 —FX: BYUUUU [fweeee]

42.1 —FX: PA [fsh]

42.2 —FX: GASHI [tugg]

42.3 —FX: BYUUUUN [fweeee]

42.4 —FX: DOSA [whud]

43.4 —FX: BURU [brrr]

44.3 —FX: FUWAA [fwom]

44.4 —FX: MOZO MOZO [sshf sshf]

44.5 —FX: SUPO [woop]

45.1 —FX: BYUUUUUU [fweeeeee]

49.3 —FX: GOSOGOSO [shp shp]

53.1.1 —FX: GOOOOO!! [rrrrrrr!!]

53.1.2 —FX: GASHI... [tugg...]

53.2 —FX: BA [fsh]

53.3 —FX: BABA [fwoowoosh]

53.4 —FX: PAOU [fwoom]

54.1-3 —FX: ZUZU ZUZU ZUZU [woowoowoom]

55.1 —FX: ZUGOO [rrrrrrr]

55.2 —FX: PITA [zing]

55.3 —FX: DOU [foom]

55.4 —FX: DOU DOU [fwoom fwoom]

56.1 —FX: GOOOOO... [rrrrrrr...]

56.2 —FX: ZUZUZU [fwoofwoosh]

56.3 —FX: DOKA DOKA [blamm blamm]

56.4 —FX: DOU DOU DOU DOU [boomsh boomsh boomsh boomsh]

57.2 —FX: SU [fsh]

57.4 —FX: ZA [fsh]

57.5 —FX: BUOOOO [fwooosh]

59.2 —FX: ZUZUZU... [woowoowoosh...]

60.1 —FX: GUOOOON [whirrrr]

61.4 —FX: GUGU [tugg tugg]

62.1 —FX: GUGU [tugg tugg]

62.4 —FX: BA!! [fwoosh!!]

64.3 —FX: WAHAHAHAHA [ha ha ha ha...]

64.4 —FX: RIIN RIIN [brring brring]

65.2 —FX: HYUUUUU [fweeee]

65.3 —FX: BAN [tunk]

65.4 —FX: KARA KARA KARA [klak klak klak]

66.5 —FX: ZA [fsh]

66.6 —FX: BIIIN [fwiing]

67.3-4 —FX: HYUUUUUUN [fwoooosh]

68.1 —FX: BYUUUUUU [fweeeee]

68.3 —FX: GIGIGI [krinch krinch]

69.1 —FX: GURARI [fwoom]

69.4-6 —FX: GYUUUUN [vweeeeen]

70.1-2 —FX: BYUUU [fweee]

70.3-4 —FX: UUUN [eeeee]

71.1 —FX: GUGU [tugg tugg]

71.4-5 —FX: GIGIGIGIGII [kreeeeech]

73.2 —FX: BYUUUUUN [fweeeeeen]

74.1 —FX: GOOOOO [rrrrrrrr]

74.6-5 —FX: BYUUUU [fweeeeee]

75.1-2 —FX: BYUUUU [fweeeeee]

77.4 —FX: GOOOO [rrrrrr]

78-79 —FX: GUOOOOO... [rrrrrrrrrr...]

80.1 —FX: GOGOGO [rrrrrrr]

81.3-4 —FX: GOOOOOOON [rrrrrrrrr]

81.4 —FX: MISHI MISHI [krinch krinch]

82.1 —FX: BYUUUUUUUU [fweeeeeeeee]

83.2-4 —FX: GOOOOOO [rrrrrrrr]

83.4 —FX: ZAZAAAA [foofooosh]

84.1 —FX: GOGOGOGO... [rrrrrr...]

85.2-5 —FX: HIIIIIIN [fweeeeen]

85.4 —FX: ZA [fsh]

86.4 —FX: KIIIIIN [vweeeen]

87.1.1 —FX: GOOOOOON [rrrrrrrrr]

87.1.2 —FX: ZUZUZUZU [krrrr]

88.1 —FX: GOGOGOGO [rrrrrrrr]

88-89 —FX: ZUGOOOOO [rrrrrrrr]

92.1 —FX: GOON GOON

162

[tunk tunk]

93.1.1—FX: DOGAN [bwam]

93.1.2—FX: DOKA DOKA [twok twok]

93.2—FX: DOU [fsshaa]

93.3—FX: ZUGAN [blamm]

93.4—FX: BABAU [krakoom]

93.5—FX: ZUBA [krakkl]

94.1.1—FX: BAKA [krak]

94.1.2—FX: BEKI [twunk]

94.1.3—FX: BOKA [bwom]

94.2—FX: GIGIGIII [krrrrr]

95.2-4—FX: GAGAAAN [ka-boom]

95.4—FX: DOU [bwam]

96.1—FX: GOOOOO… [rrrrrrrr…]

96.2—FX: ZUBAU [krakoom]

97.1—FX: GIGIGI [krrr]

97.2—FX: BAU [bwam]

97.3—FX: BAKIN [krak]

100.1—FX: DOU [blamm]

102.1-9-FX: GOOOOOO [rrrrrrrr]

103.2-6-FX: GYUUUUUN [fweeeeeeeen]

104.4—FX: ZA [fsh]

104.5-6-FX: ZA ZA ZAAAA [foooooosh]

105.1—FX: KIIIIIIIN [ziiing]

105.4—FX: BARIBARIBARI [krakkkkl]

106.1-2-FX: GOOOOO… [rrrrrrrr…]

106.4—FX: PIKA [zakk]

107.2—FX: BARIBARIBARIIII [krakkkkl]

107.3—FX: BA [zing]

107.4—FX: BASHIIN [zaaak]

109.3—FX: KA [zakl]

109.4-5-FX: BARIBARIBARI [krakkkkl]

112.3—FX: HYUUUUUUU [fweeeeeeee]

113.2-3-FX: FUWAAAAA [fwoooom]

114.1—FX: ZAZA [fssh fssh]

114.2—FX: FUWA [fwoom]

114.3—FX: SHAAAA [fssssh]

114.4—FX: PIIIIN [ziiing]

114.5—FX: FUWARI [fwom]

115.3—FX: ZAN [fwich]

124.3—FX: KYA [AIEE]

125.5—FX: YO!! [fup!!]

125.6—FX: DADAAA!! [tmp tmmmp!!]

127.2—FX: GASHI [thup]

127.3—FX: HAHAHAHA [haha-haha]

127.4—FX: HAHAHAHA… [hahahaha…]

127.7—FX: DOSA [whud]

127.9—FX: WAHAHAHA [hahahaha]

128.1—FX: CHICHICHICHI… [chirp chirrp…]

128.3—FX: PIPO PA… [beep blip bip…]

130.1—FX: GUI [tugg]

130.4—FX: PIPO [beep blip]

131.2—FX: GOTO [tup]

131.3—FX: SU [fsh]

132.3.1-FX: PIPO [beep blip]

132.3.2-FX: CHICHICHICHI… [chirrp chirrp…]

132.4—FX: CHICHICHI… [chirrp chirrp…]

132.5—FX: SUTO [fip]

133.1—FX: PIPO PIPO [beep blip beep blip]

133.3—FX: DA [tmp]

135.2—FX: BASHA BASHA [plish plish]

140.1—FX: KYAAA KYAAA [kaa kaa]

140.2—FX: BASABASABASA [fwip fwip fwip]

142.1—FX: GASA GASA [fich fich]

153.3—FX: PAPO PIPO [bip veep beep blip]

154.4—FX: PIPO PAPO [beep blip bip veep]

155.2—FX: KI!! [eep!!]

155.3—FX: KIKI [eep eep]

155.4—FX: KIKI [eep eep]

157.2—FX: KI [eep]

157.3—FX: KURU [fwip]

158.1—FX: PIPO [beep blip]

158.2—FX: SUTA SUTA SUTA [tup tup tup]

This book is printed and should be read in its original Japanese right-to-left
format. Please turn it around to begin!

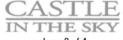

volume 3 of 4

Original Story and Screenplay Written and Directed by HAYAO MIYAZAKI

Translator/Yuji Oniki
Touch-up & Lettering/Susan Daigle-Leach
Design/Izumi Evers
Editors/Carl Gustav Horn and Alvin Lu

Managing Editor/Masumi Washington
Editor in Chief/William Flanagan
Director of Licensing and Acquisitions/Rika Inouye
Sr. V.P. of Sales & Marketing/Rick Bauer
Sr. V.P. of Editorial/Hyoe Narita
Publisher/Seiji Horibuchi

Printed in Hong Kong

Published by VIZ, LLC
P.O. Box 77010
San Francisco, CA 94107
10 9 8 7 6 5 4 3 2 1

First printing, July 2003

www.viz.com